P9-CMY-463

The ETERNAL AUDIENCE OF ONE

The ETERNAL AUDIENCE OF ONE

RÉMY NGAMIJE

SCOUT PRESS

NEW YORK LONDON TORONTO SYDNEY NEW DELHI

Scout Press
An Imprint of Simon & Schuster, Inc.
1230 Avenue of the Americas
New York, NY 10020

This book is a work of fiction. Any references to historical events, real people, or real places are used fictitiously. Other names, characters, places, and events are products of the author's imagination, and any resemblance to actual events or places or persons, living or dead, is entirely coincidental.

Originally published in South Africa in 2019 by BlackBird Books

First Scout Press hardcover edition August 2021

SCOUT PRESS and colophon are registered trademarks of Simon & Schuster, Inc.

For information about special discounts for bulk purchases, please contact Simon & Schuster Special Sales at 1-866-506-1949 or business@simonandschuster.com.

The Simon & Schuster Speakers Bureau can bring authors to your live event. For more information or to book an event, contact the Simon & Schuster Speakers Bureau at 1-866-248-3049 or visit our website at www.simonspeakers.com.

Interior design by Jaime Putorti

Manufactured in the United States of America

10 9 8 7 6 5 4 3 2 1

Library of Congress Cataloging-in-Publication Data is available.

ISBN 978-1-9821-6442-3
ISBN 978-1-9821-6444-7 (ebook)

For my mother, Gemma Akayezu
(17 June 1954–5 November 2016),
who taught me, Amélie, Ange, and Brice how to be strong.

And for my father, Gilbert Habimana,
who continues to show us how.

We are together, always.

Part 1

CROSSROADS OF HELLO AND GOODBYE

Ukize inkuba arayiganira.
To survive the thunder is to tell the tale.

—RWANDAN PROVERB

PROLOGUE

A long-forgotten essay:

The Last Ticket Out of Town
By Séraphin Turihamwe

Windhoek has three temperatures: hot, mosquito, and fucking cold. The city is allowed two or three days of mild spring weather in early September before the unrelenting heat crowds them out until May. The summers are long and sweaty, so much so that job offers can be sweetened by the promise of air-conditioning (and an overseeing committee to adjudicate on room temperature disputes because white people do not know how to share). Summer nights are stifling. Cooling breezes heed their curfews and leave the night air still and warm from the day's lingering heat. The departing sun brings out the mosquitoes. They are organized, they are driven. If they could be employed they would be the city's most reliable workforce. Alas, people do not have my vision. From sunset to sunrise they make enjoying a quiet evening drink on a balcony a buzzing and bloody affair. June, July, and August are bitter and cold. An ill wind clears out the gyms. Running noses are the only exercise anyone gets in the winter.

The city is called a city because the country needs one but, really, "city" is a big word for such a small place. But it would probably be offensive to have a capital town or a capital village so someone called it a city. The title stuck.

Life is not hard in Windhoek, but it is not easy either. The poor are either falling behind or falling pregnant. The rich refuse to send the elevator back down when they reach the top. And since cities require a sturdy foundation of tolerated inequalities, Windhoek is like many other big places in the world. It is a haven for more, but a place of less. If you are not politically connected or from old white money, then the best thing to be is a tourist. The city and the country fawn over tourists. The country's economy does too. That is when it is not digging itself poor.

That is Windhoek. The best thing to do in the city is arrive and leave.

The mistake you want to avoid making is trying to "make the most of it." My parents did that. I have not forgiven them for their sense of optimism. You will notice it in many people. There is a strange national pride I cannot explain, a patriotic denial of reality.

Beware of that optimism. It will creep up on you. It will make you notice how, in the early morning, the streets are hushed and the city's pulse is slowed down to a rhythmic, nearly nonexistent thump-thump. The only people to be seen on the streets are drowsy night shift security guards, the garbage collectors hanging from the backs of dumpster trucks as they do their rounds, and a few stray cats. That is when it is at its best. Windhoek has not yet prostituted itself to neon and skyscrapers, so a horizon is always a short hill climb away and nature still squats on its outer extremities. The views are spectacular.

The same optimism might lead an early riser to be up before the sun to see how the approaching light gently shakes the city awake. Alarm bells ring as children and parents prepare for school; the blue collars make their way to a bus or truck stop and wait to be carried towards places of cheap labor; and the white collars take their time getting to desks and offices. As the day brightens, the cracked tarmac that lines the city's main arteries sighs and stretches, preparing for the new day when the increasing traffic will become a viscous mess of commuters and taxis.

When it is going at full tilt, Windhoek does so at a slow hum. It pays respects to the Gregorian calendar and then some. Mondays and Tuesdays are busy. Wednesdays and Thursdays are reserved for concluding auxiliary matters. On Fridays everything shuts down with the firm understanding that the weekend is in session and nothing and nobody should upset the established order of things. The city has strict boredom and business hours and it keeps them.

The autumn days after the high summer are the best. The sky is afire with an intense passion; it burns with bright orange and red hues which tug at unprepared heartstrings before blushing into cooler pinks that tickle the clouds. The day's fervor cools down into violent violets as evening approaches.

Windhoek has good days and it has bad days. But, ideally, you should not be here long enough to know that. If you have made the mistake of tarrying too long in the city, and forgotten to purchase the last ticket out of town, you might have to do something more challenging: actually live here.

1

Beginnings are tricky because there are no countdowns to the start of a start. There is nobody to point out that *this* moment right here is where it all begins. Life starts in the middle and leaves people trying to piece the plot together as they go along. The only certainty is this: everything that is not the end must be the start of something else.

So disappointment must be curbed when one sits down to this story to find the trailers have been missed and the action is already devolving. It would be rude to walk out in a huff, squeezing past sourly retracted legs while spilling popcorn all over the other patrons.

Nobody ever makes it to the start of a story, not even the people in it. The most one can do is make some sort of start and then work towards some kind of ending. Endings are tricky too. But that is a discussion for another time.

Right now, we are concerned with starts.

It occurred to Séraphin, as he sank lower into the uncomfortable three-seater sofa in the lounge, and not for the first or last time, that family was something that had to be survived. He reckoned the public acknowledgment of such a truth would irrevocably destroy the foundation of human happiness. Stock photography would never be the same again, for one thing.

The day already felt insufferable: twelve or more hours spent cooking, cleaning, and arranging furniture in preparation for the New Year's party with the handful of Rwandan families clinging together for community in Windhoek. He took private comfort in the fact that after tonight, it would be only two weeks before he could return to his university, with its curated diversity, its distance from family, and its perpetual air of youth in the fickle-weathered city of Cape Town. Séraphin wondered whether his desire to be distant from his family marked him as an ungrateful son. Or whether his sentiments were mirrored in other twenty-somethings who flourished in the absence of parents and siblings, whose characters were compressed and restricted by the proximity of dinnertime disagreements about religion, education, or the trajectory of a career. What he knew for certain, though, was how easy he breathed as soon as his family was behind him, when the adventure and uncertainty of Cape Town lay ahead, with Table Mountain's flat top commanding the horizon, a monolith which said, "Here be adventure, kid. Welcome."

In South Africa's Mother City he felt cramped corners of his being relax and stretch as he filled out his skin. Avenues of his mind opened up as he envisioned the people he could meet, the meandering conversations he would have about parties, picnics, and politics. He would be with his friends once more. They would pool their arrogant youth together and cash in on capers that would be the subject of sly jokes and cell phone group chats.

Ah. Cape Town.

Even thinking about Cape Town's smoggy summer air made Séraphin smile, but it also made him anxious about how little joy he found in spending time with his brothers, mother, and father. Home, to him, was a constant source of stress, a place of conformity, foreign family roots trying to burrow into arid Namibian soil that failed to nourish him.

Eish. Windhoek.

His attempts to invent a reasonable absence from home this year had failed.

At five o'clock that morning—the hour most loved by early-bird mothers and despised by night-owl sons—Séraphin's mother, Therése, had come bustling into his bedroom, drawing back curtains and telling him to wake up. "Séra! Up! Now!"

The prone figure on the bed opened an eye.

Therése opened the windows, leaning out to smell the crisp morning air, tasting its coolness. By nine o'clock, sweat patches would bloom under every armpit. "We must get started," she said.

Therése backed away from the window and noticed Séraphin had not moved. She clapped her hands together. A loud crack, which could have spurred on a team of wagon-pulling oxen, rang in the room. Séraphin opened his eyes and said, "Yes, Mamma, just now."

"Now is *now*, Séra!" He heard her walk next door to Yves's bedroom. A few seconds later another gunshot went off. He listened for the third and final explosion that would pull Éric, his youngest brother, out of his slumber. When it came it was even louder than the preceding two. It was followed by the sound of his mother walking back down the corridor. Séraphin shot upright and swung his legs out of bed. Even if he was about to become a graduate for the second time, and even if he believed his mother held a smidge more affection for him than she did for his brothers, he would not risk her ire so early in the morning. Not on a day when she would be operating at her most dictatorial.

Therése came gliding back into the room. "You are up," she said. There was no question in her voice. That was the way it would be for the rest of the day. His mother would be a monstress, and her sons were blood-bound to do her bidding.

"I wasn't given a choice," Séraphin replied.

"You don't need a choice. You need a shower, breakfast, and then you need to arrange the lounge."

"It's always arranged. Nobody sits in it." Séraphin rubbed his eyes. "I think the lounge is fine, Mamma."

"When it is your turn to entertain," she began, "you will learn the difference between good enough for the family and good enough to avoid gossip."

"So, the other families deserve better than we do?" Séraphin attempted to look disappointed.

"You deserve nothing, Séra," she replied. She crossed her arms on her small chest and drew herself up to her full height, which would have been just tall enough to reach Séraphin's chest if he were standing next to her. "What I deserve are sons to help me prepare for today and, would you know it, I have just the ones to do it: the dishwasher, the carpet cleaner, the window wiper, the sweeper, the potato peeler, the fire starter, the meat roaster, and the waiters too."

Séraphin groaned. Again he thought about what he would be doing if he were in Cape Town. What parties would he be gearing up to attend? What crumpling of bedsheets could have ushered in the New Year?

Ah. Cape Town.

Therése, as though pulling an important thought out of the air, said, "And, of course, there is that one son who has to wash the walls, sweep the yard, pull weeds from the interlocks, and make sure the house looks like it was built yesterday, all in forty-degree weather." She added, more quietly, "That'll be the one who gets out of bed last."

Séraphin stood up with false alacrity. "Jeez, Mamma, relax. Your favorite son is on the job!"

Therése walked out of the room in a mock huff. Secretly, she was pleased to have amused her eldest son. Lately she had been feeling distant from him and his brothers. The fierce and fearful closeness of their flight from Rwanda to their eventual settling in Namibia was dissipating. She felt as though her sons did not need her kind Rwandan words and comforting proverbs; they had developed their own English wit, picking up the language so quickly that even a question posed in Kinyarwanda would elicit an English response. Now they spoke using words and phrases that seemed to contradict the meaning of what was said. "Bad" was good, "good" was not so good, and "ill" did not mean "sick." Their Kinyarwanda was used sparingly, for politeness, and to wheedle favors from her.

Séraphin stretched. "Just two more weeks after tonight," he said aloud.

He walked to the bathroom and splashed water on his face. He leaned on the wide sink, his hands resting on opposite edges, and flexed and rolled his shoulders. His reflection looked back at him in the smudged cabinet mirror.

"Survive them," it said.

"And then love them," a second voice replied.

"Thank goodness, it won't be too long now." A third voice.

"Just two weeks and then—" said a fourth.

"—Cape Town," sighed a fifth.

"Well," Séraphin said, straightening, "let's get this day over with."

The morning passed in a blur of cleaning with the occasional berating from Therése about lackluster dusting, inattentive mopping, negligent arranging, distracted potato peeling, wasteful and uneven chip slicing, and shoddy dishwashing that would, according to her, shame the entire family. Exasperated, Séraphin waited until his mother's attention was occupied by Éric's weed pulling. When he heard the Kinyarwanda exclamations and criticisms, he sought the solitude of the lounge.

As a rule Séraphin tried to keep his sojourns to this city to a minimum by spending as much time as he could in Cape Town, but even he could not lie away the December holidays this year. There were no courses to take for unnecessary credits, or student jobs to fill out like in previous years. With his vacation work applications having been denied by all the Cape Town law firms to which he had applied, he was left with no choice but to return home after his last examinations.

The rejections had been uniform in their ardor towards his academic credentials. They were also firm and cool when they stated their reasons for not taking him on. They could not, by law, accept a non–South African or non–permanent resident for the position, trailed by the mandatory best wishes for all that he might do in his future endeavors. Séraphin had tried to make light of the bruising rejections by searching for an email that broke the well-established formula. The best one came from a young, personable director who ran a boutique law firm.

From: mark.kratz@kratzandco.co.za
To: seraphin.turihamwe@remms.ac.za
Subject: RE: Vacation work application
Hi Séraphin,

Hope you are well. No matter what you said in the interview—which was impressive, by the way—I know you applied to other law firms and I know we were not your first choice either. At best, we were a choice, but not the choice. I also know your inbox will be filled with rejection emails because the law is the law and nobody is going to risk their affirmative action rating by taking you on.

You are probably tired of reading blah-blah-blah emails trying to make you feel better, so I will just cut to the chase: you are the right person with the wrong papers. I think you knew that before you even applied. Also, I'm not sure if this is really for you. Don't know why I got that impression but I just did.

Good luck for what comes next, Séraphin. And what does not.

Mark

The parting message had bounced through his head as Séraphin boarded the packed cross-country coach back to Windhoek. Mark was right. His heart was not really in law, but, even so, he could not stop himself from going through the motions. It was expected of him. As the coach pulled out of Cape Town, heading north towards Windhoek, it carried with it the curiosity of first-time travelers, the relief of the homeward bound, and the sulking silence of one. Ordinarily, Séraphin slept through bus rides, fatiguing himself the night before by partying or binge-watching a television series. After checking his luggage in, he would take his seat and sleep, only waking up at the South African border. His traveling patterns ensured he was never awake to see the monotonous, recycled Christian entertainment provided on board. The disappointments of the past weeks, however, had connived to drive sleep away, leaving him tired but awake and obliged to listen to pastors preach against evolution, offer postapocalyptic condolences for man's innumerable follies, and promote limited-edition DVDs which, for a fee, could guarantee citizenship in the everlasting Kingdom of God.

By the time the bus pulled out of Springbok, the last northern stop before a straight run to the South African border, his mood was poisonous enough to constrict his airways. The pastor on the television screen asked the trapped congregation to give their life to Jesus. A hand shot up into the air at the front of the bus and Séraphin heard a voice say, "Praise Lord Jizzos Christs."

A night breeze did little to cool Séraphin's pique when he disembarked to have his passport stamped by a disinterested border official on the South African side. The man flicked Séraphin's passport open, scanned the study permit, and placed a departure stamp on a convenient page with a gap. Back aboard the bus, Séraphin's spirits plummeted whenever he contemplated going through the Namibian border post, a port of entry which was porous for white tourists and semipermeable for black African nationalities. Immigration officers would process the queuing travelers with haste, casting cursory glances at familiar passports and rubber-stamping them in a steady rhythm that permitted the passengers to board the bus and catnap all the way to Windhoek. Every so often a detailed search required by the border police would make a stop longer by twenty or thirty minutes. The duration of such a police stop was dependent on the presence of non-Namibian passport holders from countries of international disrepute. Nigerians, Angolans, Congolese, and Cameroonians. Basically, anyone who said "Lord Jizzos Christs" was immediately flagged for invasive luggage searches. A bored dog would sniff at their bags while the unlucky passport holders were subjected to the indignity of having their neatly packed clothing and underwear deposited on the dusty, interlocked pavement and flicked through by a rude baton or a dirty boot.

On such occasions an uncomfortable silence fell on all the travelers. Some would walk away to smoke or converse in low voices, hoping for the discovery of contraband or undeclared goods to warrant the unfolding scene. Others—including Séraphin on days when his Rwandan passport wasn't the lowest desirable denominator—would simply stand in silent solidarity, bemoaning the accidents of geography that determined fair treatment. To the disappointment of the guards and the relief of the bus driver and the other travelers, the foreigners would soon be released and permitted to go on their way. Suitcases would be squashed back into the bus and the journey would resume. Over six years of traveling the same route to and from university, Séraphin had mastered the humble and polite demeanor of the voyaging black man: "Yes, sir" and "No, sir" and "Thank you, sir, I will repack my suitcase now, sir" and "Rwandan, sir, permanent resident stamp is on page two, sir."

On his latest return to Namibia, his toxic mood made him forget border control etiquette. The passport control officer in the ramshackle office on the Namibian side paged through Séraphin's passport, squinting at stamps, trying to find a discrepancy in his travel documents.

"The permanent residence permit is on the second page," Séraphin began, "the study permit on the fifth, and there is space on the sixth for a stamp. Please don't stamp on a new page unnecessarily. It doesn't look nice."

The official stopped paging through the passport and fixed Séraphin with a baleful stare. Séraphin attempted to return it as his sanity finally pushed to the forefront of his being. The rest of the queue shuffled nervously behind him. Being flippant with a border official was an act as criminal as carrying a kilogram of heroin in a handbag.

Séraphin muttered an apology. "Sorry, boss."

The official let Séraphin stew in his solecism for a few seconds longer. He reached for the reentry stamp, tattooed Séraphin's passport, and limply held it out to him. Séraphin reached for it. The official clung to it.

"Chief," he began, "you don't make jokes like that, you understand? Otherwise, I keep you here all night. The bus will leave you, you understand? You will have to call *your* people to come and get you, you understand?"

Séraphin had the good sense to mutter a quick "Yes, sir," and make his way to the exit. As the official reached for the next passport, Séraphin heard him say, "These foreigners, eh, they think they can just behave any way they want. Not in Namibia."

Séraphin walked to the bus, took his seat, plugged in his earphones, and ignored the rest of the ride until the bus arrived in Windhoek, delivering him into his parents' emphatic hugs, his brothers' bored fist bumps, and a monotony of hot December days spent in frustrated solitude or squabbling with his family.

On the sofa, Séraphin pulled his cell phone out of his pocket and saw there were no messages in any of his group chats. Everyone, it seemed, was too busy with something, somewhere else. He looked around his family's lounge.

Like most lounges in immigrant family homes it was a shrine to diaspora. Every picture that showed some form of triumph against the humbled life most immigrants are forced to live abroad found its way to a frame or a mantelpiece. There was Séraphin's father, Guillome, beaming as he leaned against his new Volkswagen Jetta; Therése, looking attentively at a computer screen in an office; Yves and Éric showing off gap-toothed smiles on their first days of school; and Séraphin, attempting to look regal in his prefect's blazer and tie.

The rest of the room was mostly taken up with furniture. Around the laminate wood coffee table were two black three-seater sofas and two plump armchairs that were never sat in. Most of the family life happened in the kitchen and the television room: food, the English Premier League, and the Sunday blockbuster films were what really brought the household together. Selected from a weekly flyer in a newspaper and paid off in monthly installments, the furniture set was like most others Séraphin had seen: uniform in its gaudy ugliness, weak in the way of structural integrity, and totally deficient when it came to comfort. Its only purpose, as far as Séraphin could tell, was to call attention to a family's upward mobility. House guests lavished attention upon the set and inquired about its cost, only to be shushed by the proud owners—"to talk about the price of a thing is to cheapen it," he had heard his mother say once. The sofas were sat in once or twice by a family member when they were entertaining and then rarely thereafter, lest they be worn out before a new set could be purchased.

Glass-fronted cabinets were positioned in three of the room's four corners. They held ornamental china dogs and the plates that were brought out only on special occasions like the New Year's party planned for this evening. For the rest of the time their shelves were home to misplaced keys and half-read newspapers. A voluminous *Webster's English Dictionary* occupied a whole shelf by itself. It was kept company by a Good News Bible on an adjacent self. The Bible was a curiosity for Séraphin, who had never seen his parents or brothers open it despite their Catholic upbringing. Like many Roman Catholics who practiced their faith on a part-time basis, or when an airplane experienced a violent dip in the middle of turbulence, Séraphin opted to show his piety through waning Mass attendance and, eventually, distance-based faith. "Like distance learning, Mamma. God is everywhere anyway, right?" he had told her the Sunday after he was confirmed. The *Webster's English Dictionary*, unlike the Bible, brought the good words to the family. It delivered swift, cross-referenced justice to anyone who spread falsities of vocabulary.

Carefully spaced out on the walls were pictures from former and present lives. While the average immigrant family will diligently collect the trappings of their surroundings to fit in and impress—the language, a house, a car, a dog—few things matter more than winning the war of memories.

A frame held his father's graduation photograph from university in Brussels. Tall and well built, Séraphin's father had dark skin and his hair was a black halo around his head. His eyes bristled with the kind of intellectual curiosity that was all the rage when Africa sent young men from villages to former colonial capitals to learn about engineering and medicine and commerce and bring their knowledge and polished accents back home to their fellow countrymen. In other frames on the walls were pictures of Séraphin's father and uncles standing in poses that looked like the Jackson Five were touring Rwanda. In each photograph, Séraphin's father could be spotted by his height and his stare, which dared the camera to make him look anything less than handsome.

Next to his father's portrait was a picture of Séraphin's mother. She had the look of a woman who might once have commanded a hefty dowry. In the portrait she stood before a small brick house with a blue door. Her hands were clasped in front of her and she wore a well-cut grey pantsuit. Séraphin had been told that the house in the picture had been her elder brother's; she had lived there after completing her secretarial studies at L'École Parisienne. The portrait had been taken on the day she had secured her first job, as an office administrator at the local United Nations office. In all of her pictures, Séraphin's mother was smiling or laughing genially.

Another frame showed a young girl surrounded by what could only be called a tribe of boys, their numbers and resemblance driving home the point that in the bygone Rwandan days parenthood was a numbers game; the more offspring one fielded, the better the odds were of defeating the child mortality rate. Séraphin's grandmother from his mother's side looked shyly at the camera. Surrounded by her brothers, she stood out only because she wore a yellow pinafore dress. Barring that, she could have disappeared into the mass of round heads, shaven bald to combat lice, mistaken for a boy in an oversized flowery shirt.

Elsewhere, a chubby, one-year-old Yves crawled on a mattress; three boys with too many knees among them stood together in matching soccer uniforms; a small, round face in a blue shirt smiled at the world as though the fourth grade of primary school were the promised utopia; and, further along the wall, a much older version of the boy looked past the camera hesitantly, his graduation robes billowing around him. Séraphin frowned with displeasure at his graduation photograph. In it he could see the fear and uncertainty he had appeased by securing parent-pleasing postgraduate study.

Séraphin, to his disappointment and his parents' relief, had found out that an English degree was a precursor only to law school and not to the fabled life of the traveling intellectual and writer. Pursuing the English degree had been a negotiated and protracted affair. The normal qualifications, which offered a safe and predictable income, had been arrayed before him after secondary school. Something in finance or, better yet, accounting. Anything in engineering, medicine, or law. None of the five had held much appeal to him, though he could already see the pride that would mist his parents' eyes if he chose any one of the careers on offer. He decided law was the least constricting.

Quite by chance, he had won an essay competition that secured a scholarship to study English. A paid undergraduate was a rare thing to come by so he promised his parents he would pursue the law degree after he'd completed the English one. His parents allowed him to enjoy three years of missed lectures and cavorting in the arts before collecting their pound of flesh. There were impending retirements to be thought about, futures to be planned, and roots to be anchored. Now, with graduation awaiting him in the New Year, doubts about practicing law grew within him. Mark was right. Séraphin would need luck for what came next. And what did not.

The lounge had been vacuumed and dusted. Some wooden garden chairs and cushions would be brought in from the backyard when the numbers swelled beyond what the lounge's furniture could accommodate. Séraphin would scuttle to and from the kitchen, bringing drinks. After the fresh fruit juices and water would come the cold Heineken beer, followed by red wine along with unknotted tongues and gossip. He would have to smile, shake hands, accept hugs, and utter polite phrases in broken Kinyarwanda. He would have to accept compliments about how tall he had grown, and then answer some questions about his future as a lawyer.

If the Spanish Inquisition was deemed barbaric, it was only because nobody had ever written about conversations between East African parents and their university-going children. The questions would be detailed. Whatever answers he gave would be noted, filed away, and gossiped about in the event that he failed to deliver on them.

As Séraphin slumped further into the sofa he caught a glimpse of his mother walking out of the kitchen and into the dining room, calling out orders in Kinyarwanda to Éric. She shouted for a batch of chips to be taken out of the pot. "Ni ugu kuramo amafiriti!"

His mother was never still. Séraphin reckoned if she were to die today she would be up tomorrow, bright and early, preparing her own funeral. Her brown forehead was shiny with sweat and her new braids were in a net to protect them from absorbing the oily kitchen air. As soon as the house bell rang she would disappear into the main bedroom and reappear in flowing, flowery kitenges, trailing whiffs of expensive perfume. She would beam and hug each guest, cheeks touching twice, and then usher them into the lounge.

As she walked back to the kitchen she saw Séraphin in the lounge.

"Séra, you cannot come and help Yves with the fire?" she asked. "We need to start with the meat soon." She sounded stern, but Séraphin sensed it was not genuine.

"Did he finish with the garden?" Séraphin asked.

"No," Therése replied, "but we need to do other things now. Éric is busy with the chips. But you could have helped Yves, it would have looked much better."

"Ah, Mamma, you know I am allergic to manual labor," he replied.

"You are lazy, Séra." She walked back into the kitchen. He could hear the sound of glasses being placed on a tray. Séraphin reached for his phone once more. Still no messages.

"I'm not lazy, Mamma," he called after her. "I just don't want my brothers to stand in my shadow so I'm giving them chances to be great."

From the kitchen his mother laughed. "If you are so concerned about your brothers' greatness, then you will help Yves get the fire going."

"Tell him to use the Fire of Christ that burns within him. He was confirmed not too long ago, right? There should be enough left to light the braai."

Blasphemy was always a shortcut to good fun in the household. He could hear glasses clinking as Therése carried a tray into the dining room. "Séra, I do not like those jokes. And you had better not make them later if you don't want to scandalize us," she said. She came into the lounge and fixed him with a look. "Today you will be nice."

"I'm always nice, Mamma," Séraphin said.

"Sometimes," his mother said. "But you will not do that thing where you make people feel dumb around you."

"What thing?"

"Sarcasm," Yves said, walking in, his hands black and sooty from handling charcoal. His light brown skin had taken on the just-burnt dark brown of someone who had been in the sun too long.

"Et tu, Yves?" Séraphin stabbed his midsection with his cell phone.

"Yes. That is the word. Sarcasm. Don't do that," Therése said. She went back into the dining room and started placing the glasses on a small serving table. "And go and help your brothers," she called out.

"I just got the fire going. It will be a while before we can braai the meat. Will you do that?" Yves asked.

"As far as I'm concerned, brother, I'm here to eat. Nothing else," Séraphin replied, loud enough for his mother to hear. "Like most Rwandans."

"If you don't help, you won't eat," his mother retorted. On her way back to the kitchen with her tray she paused in the lounge doorway. "What are you doing in here anyway, Séra?"

"I was talking to my girlfriend," Séraphin lied. He and Yves waited for the anticipated reaction.

"Do not talk about such things around me," Therése said quickly.

"What *things*?" Yves pressed.

"Girlfriends," Séraphin said.

"Girlfriends?" Yves's tongue tasted this new word.

"You know, girls who are friends," Séraphin replied, "and sometimes more than friends." Yves and Séraphin watched their mother inhale sharply.

"They have"—Séraphin made a cupping motion around his chest—"abundant affection—"

"—and no lack of attention." Yves attempted to lift a heavy derrière behind him.

Séraphin cackled and swished an imaginary lock of hair. "They have long hair, the white ones. They let you touch it if you have the right accent."

"And longer hair, the black ones," Yves said. "But they'll only let you touch it if you've paid for it," he added with exaggerated airs.

Séraphin stood up from the couch and came to stand in front of his mother, looking down at her. He hugged her as though giving her comfort. "I'm so sorry, Mamma," he said gently, "that this is where our allowance is going. But, you know, concubines do not maintain themselves."

Over his mother's head, Yves stifled laughter by covering his mouth, forgetting the soot on his hands. When he pulled them away his lips were covered in black smudges.

"Shit," he said.

"Enough!" their mother shouted. Séraphin felt a finger poke him sharply in the ribs. "You boys are sick with girls. It is all I hear about these days. You are going on about these . . . these things—"

"What things?" Séraphin asked, ready to start the carousel again.

"Séra! Yves! Stop it. Go and make yourselves useful." Therése put some steel in her voice. She looked at Yves. "That language is not welcome in this house. You can swear in your own house, not in mine."

"Okay, okay." Yves held up his black hands in apology.

"And you," she said, rounding on Séraphin, "you will not bring up girls in my presence. Not after—" She let the unfinished sentence hang in the air and Séraphin, who knew what was unspoken, smiled in apology. Yves, confused, was about to ask what was going on when a look from Séraphin cut him off. They had had their fun. Now it was time to let their mother be and get back to work.

"I'll go and get some juice," Séraphin said.

"Do you need money?" Therése asked, trying to transition into party preparations.

"I have enough from yesterday's grocery run." Séraphin squeezed his cell phone into his pocket and strolled to the front door, which Yves had left open.

"The nectar of the gods, bro," Yves said. "Don't shame this family with preservatives."

"You boys are fools," Therése said. "You want people to judge our hospitality? You do not know how these things go. If we were back in Rwanda—"

"—we would be dead."

Whenever their mother began heckling them with bygone times in Rwanda they cut it off with the certainty that in days not too far past they would most certainly be dead and no amount of tradition, pure fruit juice, or carefully arranged lounges would save them. Neither of them noticed the pained look that flickered on their mother's face, vanishing as Therése focused on the day's remaining tasks. "Yves," she said, with more authority, "the fire. And get those dirty hands out of the lounge. Séraphin, juice!" She whisked herself into the kitchen.

"Shame," Yves said.

"Considering I was born out of wedlock, you would expect her to be a little more chilled about—"

A metal tray banged down on a kitchen table.

"SÉRAPHIN! YVES!"

The front door slammed as Séraphin departed for the shops. Yves made a determined dash for the bathroom to wash his hands.

In the kitchen, Therése wondered where she had gone wrong in nurturing her sons that they could make terrible jokes with such impunity. She wondered where she had learned the patience to put up with them. She noticed the pot of chips bubbling away on the gas stove. Éric was nowhere to be seen.

"*Merde!*" Therése walked over to the pot and stirred the chips. She shouted for Éric to come to the kitchen and attend to them. This, she thought, is not how things would have gone in Rwanda. There, children had respect. But in Namibia, quite the opposite seemed to be true.

She blamed the high school they had attended, pricey, with its ideas about how children should not be beaten. Therése blamed cell phones, the way they stole her sons' attention. She blamed the Internet and how its content was the sole subject of conversation at dinnertime, a vast wilderness of sound, pictures, and videos she could never keep up with. Therése blamed the friends they hung around with. One of Yves's had even gone as far as calling her by her first name at supper once and she, to defuse the palpable silence that had descended upon the table, laughed and passed the peas anyway. Later that evening she had pulled Yves aside and said, "Don't bring that rude boy to supper again." She felt guilty about it the next day and apologized for being old-fashioned and even just saying that seemed to age her twice as fast.

Mostly, though, she blamed a downed plane, radio broadcasts, the resurrection of long-held ethnic hostilities, Western indifference, nights of fear and days of hate which eroded carefully built futures and devoured connected pasts, forcing families to survive first and learn to live and, hopefully, love later. After all, she told herself, you only love after you have survived.

And her family, thankfully, mercifully, had survived.

II

Windhoek West, in December, is a sprawling mélange of ghost mansions, boxy business enclaves, and desolate streets wilting beneath the sun. Ordinarily, the suburb is astir with residential and minor commercial activity, but at the tail end of the year it becomes still. During the day, the pot-lid-hot temperatures drive whatever is left of Windhoek West's life into cool living rooms and sweaty siestas. At night, red pilot lights perched above garage doors and windows are all that remain to alert potential burglars that an armed response team is a short drive and rough beating away. As the city's life migrates to the tolerated cold waters of the Atlantic Ocean in tourist-swamped seaside towns or crowded and boisterous family gatherings in Namibia's northern and southern regions, Windhoek West becomes a taciturn purlieu.

Besides a few families on Séraphin's street, the only people who remain behind are the dead classical composers and scientists who live a second but anonymous, mispronounced, and misspelt life on street plaques. Brahms, Beethoven, Bach, Mozart, Puccini, Strauss, Schubert, and Verdi; Behring, Best, Curie, Jenner, Pasteur, Roentgen, Watt—their importance is irrelevant to many of the suburb's residents. In days past, though, they were the heated trivia subject inside a grey Volkswagen Jetta carrying Séraphin, Yves, and Éric to their private high school, where intimate knowledge of such personalities impressed teachers but failed to win the affections of teenage girls.

The three brothers tried to outdo each other by stating the streets' namesakes and their achievements. Their knowledge became a source of pride for the car's silent passenger, Guillome, who worked tirelessly to ensure that his sons' home environment was hostile to ignorance. He would deny his growing boys nothing if it was in a book, and permit them to watch television for hours on end provided they watched nature, history, and science programs. Each evening when he came home from work he would ask, "So what have we learned about the world today?" and smile at the competition to impress him.

Of the three, Séraphin continued to consume the world in gulps, through books, television, and radio stations. He watched travel programs with a desperate longing to see the human-saturated streets of New York, Tokyo, and Lagos, and to taste the wriggling delicacies of Asia and South America. Guillome noted, with some trepidation, how vividly Séraphin's conversations about his future life were always in some far-off place, and always in the singular.

"And why would you go to Oslo?" Guillome asked him one night at supper. Therése had managed to get hold of some cassava flour and leaves to cook ugali and isombe, served with a portion of thick, saliva-draining brown beans. The boys were embroiled in their usual feuding and Séraphin had mentioned he would someday travel to Oslo to see the fjords.

"I saw a Ford," Yves contributed. "It was red, with a big spoiler. So you don't have to go all the way there to see it. And I saw it first."

"No, dummy," Séraphin replied, "fjord—like f-*yord*, not the car."

"Don't call your brother a dummy," Therése snapped.

"Where did you learn about fjords, Séra?" Guillome asked.

Séraphin swallowed a big gob of ugali. "*Boy*, a book by Roald Dahl."

"So, Séra, you want to visit the place because Roald Dahl wrote about it?"

"Yes," Séraphin replied. "It sounds nice." He paused to put some food on his fork and then added, "And far."

Therése and Guillome shared a look. These days Séraphin spent more time alone in his bedroom and expressed himself with sharp, cutting comments. Therése noted how distant he seemed, as though he was in some interior world. What kept Guillome and Therése awake in their bedroom, though, were Séraphin's silences. They were brooding, cavernous, palpable—Therése almost felt like apologizing when she spoke to him in this state.

"Of course," Therése prodded, "a holiday in Norway would be fun together?"

"No," Séraphin replied and Therése watched as her son retreated to that inner place she could not understand. "I read somewhere that people are much better in memories. And memories don't take up so much luggage space or need visas."

Therése and Guillome chewed in silence, she with renewed worry about her son, Guillome with mild surprise. They stayed awake late that night, their bedroom air afire with their worried whisperings, concerned about what Séraphin could have meant and lamenting the lack of an extended family or culture to fall back on. "It's just a phase," Guillome said softly to his wife. "I'm sure he will grow out of it."

Séraphin did not. His mind grew fat on images and stories of places far away, and his soul longed to amble in the side ways and byways of places he had only read about in literature or seen on television. His mornings would be Viennese while his afternoons would be Parisian and he would spend his nights dancing in Havana to salsa and merengue. His happiness, he thought, would be found at the end of a pen, in a seat on a plane, with the wheels forever leaving the ground, going—always going. He masked his desire for difference with a boisterous exoskeleton of machismo, locker room talk about girls and their bouncing anatomy. By the time Séraphin reached university, he was determined to be a citizen of the world. His heart was a library of longings, his mind a hive of buzzing trivia.

Arriving at the Portuguese convenience store, he nodded to the bored security guard, crossing into a semicool interior that smelled of bread and oily chips. A queue snaked its way behind the shop's deli counter, where day-old sandwiches, tattered pieces of fried hake, and passionless potato salads stood under the cold light of a bain-marie. In the juice aisle the price tags made him wince. They bore the crossed-out numbers of the previous day's prices and announced, smugly, the new levy on goods one could have bought for less yesterday. Placing juice cartons in his pushcart, he wheeled it into the biscuit aisle, browsing the shelves, feeling peckish. Another cart from the opposite direction approached his and slowed down.

"Séra?"

He looked up. His face heated. "Jasmyn."

She smiled and moved towards him, standing on her toes to throw her arms around his neck. Surprised by the forwardness of her greeting, he still had one hand on his trolley. The other was caught in a furious debate about where to rest on the no-man's-land of skin between her neck and her lower back.

"Upper back," said a voice. "Safe space."

"Only if you want to wind up in the friend zone, nigga," said a second.

"Lower back, then?"

"I say you grab the booty," the other replied. "For control!"

Séraphin settled for an awkward pat-pat in the middle of her back. "Hi."

She wore a light citrusy perfume and even with the hesitant Morse code of his back pat he could feel the warmth of her skin. Jasmyn pulled away and looked up at him. "Long time," she said.

"Yeah, it's been a minute," he replied. "Keeping well?"

"I'm trying to. Work, rent, life—the usual shit." Her shoulders shrugged, the shadows of her collarbones showing themselves underneath the light film of skin. "But I'm still holding out for my best life."

"Isn't everyone?" Séraphin hoped the question would keep the conversation going.

"What've you been up to? I haven't seen you in forever."

"I'm in Cape Town. Final year of law. Then—" He paused, lifting his hand to encompass the vastness beyond graduation. "Life."

"Cool. Gonna move back when you're done? You never liked this place."

"Maybe. We'll see."

A smile hovered on Jasmyn's lips. "Anyway, you're massive now. I don't think you were this tall the last time I saw you." She let her eyes take him in. "You look good." The "good" was stretched out, like a too-small scoop of peanut butter on a too-large slice of bread.

"You look good too." He avoided her direct gaze, casting his eyes to the neatly packed shelves.

"Thanks." Jasmyn flashed him a grin that sent a rivulet of sweat sailing down his back. "When do you leave for Cape Town?"

"Two weeks."

"Soon."

"Is that disappointment I heard?" asked a voice.

"Definitely disappointment," replied another.

"Well, let's get coffee sometime and catch up, yeah?" She dictated her number to him and he called it after he had taken it down. "Cool, got it. Séraphin—with an *é*," she said as she typed.

"And Jasmyn—with a *y*," he responded. They exchanged a look.

"Well," Jasmyn said, "I need to get home. Family party tonight. We ran out of some spices."

"I'm the juice boy. I gotta get home before my mom sends out the search-and-rescue."

At the mention of Séraphin's mother, Jasmyn's smooth cheek turned the slightest shade of pink and her gaze flickered away. The shelves were subjected to an intense gaze, probably the only time the assortment of confectionery had ever been so appraised. Jasmyn made the first move, wheeling her cart away. "So, yeah, enjoy the party," she said. "And happy New Year in advance."

"You too."

They moved apart, slowly, Séraphin's back feeling sensitive with Jasmyn behind him. He walked straight to the pay-point and unloaded the juice cartons, fumbling and handing too many dollar bills to the cashier. After paying he exited the shop, his stride sprightly, his mind preoccupied, his cell phone itching with the number of one Jasmyn—with a *y*.

III

Once upon a private school enrollment charter there were two Jasmines: Jasmine with an *i* and Jasmyn with a *y*. Both were pretty and intelligent in the way of girls whose parents are moneyed. They glowed with the health of children raised without chores, and the poise of privilege dangled heavily from their neat ponytails and wholesome smiles. They were smart, kind, and helpful; they were prized teacher's pets. To avoid being ostracized by their peers they were generous with the treasures of their neatly packed lunch boxes: chocolate bars were fragmented into tiny fractions and shared, while sandwiches with thick slices of pastrami were passed around for delicate nibbles.

Jasmine van Zyl was fair-skinned, with blond pigtails, grey eyes, and a shy smile. She had inherited a robust frame from her deep Afrikaner roots, which stretched all the way back to the settling of Bloemfontein in colonial South Africa. Jasmyn Wolff was cream-colored, with soft hair that frizzed in the weather. Her eyes were light brown and bewitching, ringed by a green halo if one looked closely. She was all bones and curls, the product of an Owambo father in political exile in Moscow and a white mother from West Germany, also in Russia to learn the inner workings of the failing Communist economy.

When Namibia gained independence, airplanes began flying in all the men, women, and children who had lived abroad during the country's armed struggle against South Africa's apartheid embrace. Exiled families returned in droves, from Zambia, Zimbabwe, Angola, Tanzania, Cuba, and Germany—doctors, engineers, architects, political scientists—all coming home to be part of the country's bright and free future. Some came to lead. Some came to serve. Others came to steal. Jasmine's father, who owned a lucrative construction company, met Jasmyn's father at a state dinner in the early days of the Namibian republic.

"Of course," Jasmine's father said, "such a young country cannot hope to get far without roads, hospitals, schools, and other concrete structures to drive the economy and bring in foreign investment." He fronted a proposal to Jasmyn's father: a partner was needed to deal with all of the handshaking and back clapping of the young democracy's new black leadership. Jasmyn's father was reluctant to agree at first. Socialism was still strong in him and capitalism was the enemy that made sister strive against sister, brother enslave brother. Jasmine's father changed tactics. He offered Jasmyn's father more than a title; he backed it up with equity. He sweetened the deal with promises of skills transfers and the integration of black faces into the construction company. It took some time but eventually Jasmyn's father was sold.

Jasmine's father's surname was removed from the company to distance it from the recent past. He maintained the industry contacts and intellectual capital amassed over the years. Jasmyn's father, with his political connections and dark complexion, roped in the government deals that flowed into the freshly liberated economy.

The new construction company quickly became one of the brightest rays in the young republic. Its cranes were a feature of the Namibian skyline as brick by brick, dollar by dollar, Windhoek grew. Their friendship became genuine after the money came in. Their families holidayed together. Their daughters, born three months apart in the late eighties before the men knew each other, progressed through school together, surrounded by the best of the Namibian upper crust. After primary school, St. Luke's Roman Catholic College, with its evergreen soccer field; its blue, grey, and white uniform; and its sterling academic reputation.

It was not long into eighth grade that their fathers' fortunes flagged. The lucrative deals from political connections dwindled. A fresh crop of young, hungry political cadres and comrades culled the elderly businessmen out of boardroom meetings. The two men's once bountiful plates were reduced to begging bowls. They sold their construction firm and took early retirement.

Jasmine's family, when not in Windhoek, retreated to their farm, where they ran a luxury lodge for shooters of big game. Their wealth still ran deep in shares and properties stashed here and there. Jasmyn's family, now thoroughly indoctrinated in the ways of the rich, fell from Icarus heights without a parachute. The luxury cars were repossessed and their heavily mortgaged mansions were sold to defray debts. The fall hit Jasmyn's father hard. Drinking and absenteeism became full-time professions when his fortunes failed. Their family tumbled west across the windy city to a somber house in Brahms Street.

The girls knew they had to move on to new friendships as the world spun and their bodies were possessed by puberty.

Jasmine was the first to blossom. Womanhood added weight to her hips and her breasts ballooned. Her face was peppered with pimples. Her lips were thin, suggestions more than real anatomical features capable of holding a layer of lipstick. Her hair went from spun-gold blond to dull yellow. To make things worse, her left eye became a bit lazy. Children's cruelty christened her Jasmine-with-the-Eye.

While Jasmyn's family slipped across the tracks, adolescence, at least, remained kind to her. It bequeathed her a pair of smooth legs with toned muscles. Her lips were locked in a perpetual pout. Her small ears were adored. Her shapely nose was praised. Her petite waistline provided enough motivation for boys to study and gain promotion with her through the grades. Her breasts bounced with healthy vigor in hockey matches and made netball practice as popular as basketball games against rival schools. Her posterior was the star of many short-lived, sticky rendezvous between sweaty boys' palms and blood-hardened genitalia. She was aware of her sexuality. It confused male teachers and explained away incomplete homework. It threatened female teachers with the possibility of classroom rebellion if it even seemed as though they were picking on her just because she was unable to correctly balance chemical equations.

When Jasmine and Jasmyn passed each other at St. Luke's, Jasmyn nodded politely to Jasmine out of respect for their former friendship. Jasmine did so out of deference paid to preternaturally beautiful girls. The two had little in common except their determination to lose their virginity. Jasmine considered it a rite of passage that would confirm her womanhood. Jasmyn considered it a matter of time.

Jasmyn is the first to misplace her virtue. It happens at the commencement of the eleventh grade. At one of those high school parties common to posh neighborhoods where parents are fond of traveling abroad for business, leaving their teenage children at home with a warning not to throw parties. Jasmyn lets her boyfriend, Keaton—an older, twelfth-grade, boy from a rival high school—press his nagging advantage home. It is all over in under a minute. A swift bite of red pain which fades to an aching itch. There is no romance, no page-turning passion. The soundtrack of the whole cherry-bursting affair is the chorus of Joe Budden's "Fire" from the lounge below, accompanied by the ecstatic shouting of teenagers drunk on cheap beer and vodka.

Jasmyn and Keaton emerge from the master bedroom holding hands, trying to appear casual, failing to fool anyone. News of the deflowering diffuses around the party. Jasmine hears whispered words of Jasmyn's tryst and feels an acute disappointment that even in this she has to yield to Jasmyn.

In the ways of teenage relationships, Keaton and Jasmyn's does not last. It walks and limps, sometimes crawling to its final death throes like a bleeding Bollywood hero. Chat rooms are abuzz with gossip.

JohnNotTheBaptist: This Keaton guy has so many chances with Jasmyn. How does he do it, man?

MadeYouLuke: Bra, he's white. Girls will forgive anything white guys do.

JohnNotTheBaptist: Ja, it's true. Black guys are guilty until proven more guilty.

MadeYouLuke: Not you, John, you're always guilty.

HannaStacia—Selma_Nella: She took him back.

Selma_Nella: Told you she would.

HannaStacia: Shame, she doesn't know her first doesn't have to be her last. Keaton is fine, but he isn't thaaaat fine.

Selma_Nella: You made up with John and he isn't half as fine as Keaton.

HannaStacia: You wouldn't understand.

HannaStacia: By the way Séra says your username is a type of food poisoning and Selma_Fudd would be better. Like the bald dude from Looney Tunes.

Selma_Nella: Send him a big voetsek from me.

TheaElleC—Tri_SeraTops: Gossip! Jasmine-with-the-Eye also lost her virginity.

Tri_SeraTops: Eh?! To what?

TheaElleC: Don't be an ass Séra! Layton Green.

Tri_SeraTops: Basketball Layton?

TheaElleC: Only Layton at school. He says he was drunk and she forced him. But people saw them through Tiff's brother's bedroom window and there was no force there.

Tri_SeraTops: Oh shit!

TheaElleC: Promise me that when you lose your virginity you'll close the curtains.

Tri_SeraTops: Of course!

TheaElleC: And have some nice music. Like some of your playlists.

Tri_SeraTops: Haha! Okay.

TheaElleC: Maybe we should make Jasmyn a breakup playlist.

Tri_SeraTops: That's lame.

TheaElleC: True. I also know you're thinking of a name and you have the songs.

Tri_SeraTops: You know me too well. We shouldn't be friends anymore.

TheaElleC: What'll you call it?

Tri_SeraTops: Soundtrack of the Disconnect.

So it comes to pass that by the middle of the eleventh grade both Jasmine and Jasmyn have lost their virginity. At Tiffany's party, with the writhing mass of pubescence taking cues from Rupee's "Tempted to Touch," Layton stumbles towards the dance floor and pulls Jasmine against him. It is an awkward combination of apologetic waddling on her part and eager hip-thrusting on his. At the song's conclusion Layton leads her through the house, pulling on door handles and finding a utility closet occupied by a boy and girl slobbering kisses on each other, a guest bedroom occupied by another couple in flagrante delicto, and, finally, an empty bedroom at the end of the hall.

They collapse on the bed. In an uncoordinated mess of kissing they hastily unbuckle their trousers. Jasmine remembers to offer Layton the condom she has carried around in hope and it is fumbled onto an erect member. She looks away most of the time, trusting the providence of her shaking hands and whatever past experience Layton has. Then she finds herself pressed underneath him.

The first thrust shoots a pain through her. The second hurts even more. She bites her lip and pulls Layton deeper, determined not to let the tears in her eyes discourage him. Layton is lost to his own rhythms. He hammers himself into a climax before collapsing on top of her. After a breathy minute, Jasmine rolls him off her. Layton has fallen asleep. She stands up slowly, crimson snaking down her leg. She feels nauseous from the punch and Layton's callous performance. She pulls on her clothes and walks out of the room, looking back at Layton, his buttocks exposed above the belt line of his cargo pants.

For the most part, Jasmine and Layton's clunky dancing went unnoticed. Their tryst would also have gone unnoticed but for Paulus "Pontius_Paulus" Amukongo and Jurgen "Jurgen_Naut" Nacht, who, after baptizing an otherwise unobtrusive rose bush with their urine, passed a lit bedroom and the Green_Layton himself pumping away like a piston.

They set chat rooms alight with one-sided hyperbole and a few blurry photographs, a passing mercy for Jasmine. By the time Séraphin catches wind of it, rumors have become bloated with blame. Jasmine is suspected of spiking Layton's drink, putting a hex on him, and, succubus-like, having her way with him. Even Jasmine's friends do little to stop the gossip.

Thankfully, it is not too long before "Die Stem" calls to its Afrikaner seeds to come home and make roots. Her parents pack up their lives in Windhoek and make their way to South Africa. Jasmine sees an escape from hushed conversations and an empty chat room.

AllThatJazz—Green_Layton: Why won't you talk to me? This is fucked up. Why can't you stop all of these rumors?

AllThatJazz: Okay, it's all my fault. I slept with myself. Fine. You'll be happy to know that I'm moving away. All the best with your life.

While Jasmine's life spirals into depression, Jasmyn's is quite different. Her latest breakup with Keaton has held its course for three months. They are not talking, which means, of course, that they are tuned in to each other's activities via third parties. Soon, word spreads that Keaton has moved on. Perhaps, Jasmyn thinks, it is time she did the same.

Boys are renounced. She reclaims her starting positions in netball and hockey. She immerses herself in academic demands. She even joins the school's writing club, the Quill Club, which meets on Friday afternoons to weed out all but the most dedicated aspiring writers.

Jasmyn is late to her first meeting and arrives to find the group's twenty members working in groups of two. Mr. Caffrey, the senior English teacher, casts around the classroom for a group she can join.

"Séraphin, John—I'm entrusting this young lady to your care. Be sure to give our club a bad reputation," he says with a wink. He smiles at Jasmyn to welcome her. She is not like the other Quillians: comic book and video game boffins with intricate knowledge of the arcane, the mythical, the mystical, the fantastical; romantics with overstretched, flowery sentences; or literary aspirants, perspicacious in their wit and voracious in their consumption of words. Still, the club has no membership requirements and Mr. Caffrey is glad to see another student show interest in writing. He has learned to take them however they come and wherever from.

There is a shuffling as Séraphin pulls an empty
to John's frustration.

"Jasmyn, we're writing opening sentences that
hand over their money to us," Mr. Caffrey says. "
that'll make a drug addict buy a book instead of the next high. The scenario is this: teenage superhero or -heroine begins to narrate their autobiography. Get creative. Avoid clichés. And no profanity."

A groan runs through the room. Mr. Caffrey is the only teacher at St. Luke's who does not hand out detention slips when a swear word slips in his classes. He has realized the only way to make ancient texts relevant is to drop a cuss word. So the restriction on expletives in today's writing exercise feels like a betrayal.

Jasmyn's group—note how quickly it becomes Jasmyn's group—turns to her.

"Any ideas?" John asks. His acne-crossed face red with eagerness to please.

"I'd rather add to your ideas if you've already prepared something," Jasmyn says.

"Not much," Séraphin replies. "We started thinking about our character. John suggested we make him—or her—about our age, funny, awkward, and with some sort of struggle. Mr. Caffrey likes a good character struggle."

"Cool." A small frown creases Jasmyn's forehead. "How about this: Being a hero sucks because you never get to do what you want. That's what the bad guy does. All you do is try to stop them. Basically being a hero is parenting, but with powers that can level a city."

"That's funny," Séraphin says, "and kinda true."

"Mos def," John says. "When you think about it, superheroes"—he looks at Jasmyn—"and heroines, are always being interrupted by a bad guy, right? Doc Ock is robbing a bank, so Peter Parker cuts a date with Mary Jane short, and the Joker cuts into Bruce Wayne's wank time. Makes total sense."

"Easy on the Batman jokes," Séraphin says.

"Séraphin here," John says, "is besotted with the Dark Knight."

"He's better than Superman."

"What's wrong with Superman?" Jasmyn asks. "I think he's cool."

John beams.

"Fuck Superman," Séraphin says. "Dude crash-lands on Earth, is adopted by a family just like that, and his biggest worry is a green rock? I have something better: Home Affairs and their queues. Let's see him get through that shit faster than a speeding bullet."

"I've never thought of that, actually." Jasmyn giggles. "You're funny."

Séraphin glows.

"Ready to present your sentences?" Mr. Caffrey calls out.

When the group presents their introductory sentences to the rest of the class, Mr. Caffrey applauds them. "Excellent," he says. "Whose idea was it?" The boys turn to Jasmyn. Mr. Caffrey finds it hard to hide his surprise. "Good, really good," he says as he turns back to the room. "All your opening sentences were quite good, and no, I'm not saying that to make you feel better about your pimple-ridden excuses for faces. I mean it. There were some clever ones, and some that could really explode on a page with some work. Like Jasmyn's group here." He motions for Séraphin, John, and Jasmyn to sit down. "Quillians, writers, readers, fellow knights of the word, remember our call to arms."

As one, the assembled club members say: "Truth first, then fiction."

"Then fame and fast women," a voice calls out from the back.

Mr. Caffrey turns to Jasmyn. "Ms. Wolff, welcome to the club. These are my charges, such as they are. Beware. Here be monsters."

The rest of the club nods to Jasmyn in welcome.

She is one of them.

She is a monster.

And where there are monsters there will always be stories, and regardless of how a story starts—whether it is with "once upon a time" or "in the beginning" or some other way, say, with a long-forgotten essay—it is a general rule that the monsters will make the middle towards some sort of end.

There were two Jasmines.

One with a *y* and one with an *i*; one was pretty, one was not. They used to be friends. One is somewhere in South Africa, her fate unknown. The other is in the Quill Club, with Séraphin, around just long enough for the spark of a start to ignite and catch fire here, once upon a private school enrollment charter.

IV

Everything is funny when you are a virgin and the girl who could save you from your chastity is sitting on your bed making bad jokes. That is why Séraphin—seventeen, virgo intacta, general knowledge aficionado, and junior prefect at St. Luke's—keeps a controlled stream of laughter flowing as Jasmyn talks about her family. Her father drinks enough for three people; her mother is sober for two. Her twin younger brothers, Raphael and Rainart, worship the ground Liverpool Football Club lose upon.

"That's actually funny," Séraphin replies, releasing another parcel of laugher. Her family sounds pedestrian compared to his. But everything is funny when you are about to lose your virginity.

Éric, in total contrast to his brothers, is a steadfast member of St. Luke's Friday detention program. His misdemeanors are legion and legend: wearing the incorrect school uniform even though he was dropped off at school in the correct attire; leaving school premises during school hours; changing a teacher's laptop wallpaper from a skiing holiday snapshot to a spread-eagle spring-breaker. He is the youngest of the trio and by the time he starts high school, a year early, his parents have been worn down. Éric still bears the cherub looks of his youth. His cheeks are round and dimpled when he smiles or blushes, and his skin is lighter than his brothers', something that makes Therése feel proud and guilty at the same time. They are all her sons, all products of her womb. But there is a special unacknowledged pride when she looks at Éric.

Yves, despite a boisterous toddlerhood, has become a quiet, lanky boy. Like a giraffe, he is all legs, eyelashes, and silences. His academic pedigree is unexceptional but he is a diligent student. His interests are in the imaginary world of dragons and knights, witches and wizards, manga, and the comic book multiverses. He is slow to anger and deliberate in speech, which often gives people the impression of slowness. His delayed responses, however, are often the result of boredom.

Therése finds herself outnumbered in the family, a woman trapped between the egos of varying degrees of manhood. As her sons, one by one, successfully wage wars of teenage self-determination and flee her doting care, she has become directionless, uncertain about what to do with her free time. She immerses herself in gardening—Séraphin refers to it as hospice care for flora—completing the arts and crafts projects she finds in women's home and leisure magazines, and burning her way through complex cooking recipes. New meals are approached with care by the rest of her family, each waiting for someone else to take the first forkful and pronounce it safe for consumption.

Guillome is embroiled in the responsibilities of his job's new position. A recent promotion has him working to late hours of the night, a tired mess of grunts when he comes home. His attempts to speak to his sons are met with shrugs and clipped answers.

"Dad, do you mind?" Séraphin says, back to him, books piled on his desk, cell phone not far away. Guillome and Séraphin avoid each other for the most part.

"Er, Papa, I have to do this homework . . ." Yves says. His answers are like the opening moves of novice chess players. "The day was okay. School was fine. I have homework."

"Yo, so, good talk, yeah?" Éric says after a reprimand. Guillome does not know how to handle it. More often than not he is amused by Éric's disregard for rules.

"I'm serious, Éric." He tries to sound stern. "Why would you put flour on the ceiling fans?"

"Ah, you see a ceiling fan, it's a hot day, and you just wonder, you know?"

Guillome rubs his tired face and walks out of Éric's disheveled room.

Despite his constant fatigue, Guillome has discovered a purpose in his labor: providing for his middle-class family. They are the proud owners of a four-bedroom house with an extensive yard; they own a car; there are whispers of owning dogs; they own a large flat-screen television, a shiny silver fridge, and a black gas stove that swallows the light when it is polished and cleaned. His family has climbed up the ladder; they are suburban; they are planting roots; and, in time, he is sure they will flourish. With the right education and encouragement—especially for Éric—they could ascend a level further: they could run a business.

And further than that? Guillome does not allow himself to dream too much. The past is never far from his mind, and so he holds the future at arm's length.

Then there is Séraphin, the pioneer of puberty and the family's first herald of changing dynamics. Still beholden to his brooding silences, still a citizen of a world he has not seen, he is Promethean in his attempts to bring modernity to a household choking under nostalgia. He is the bringer of casual greetings—hi, yo, what's up, what's good—and egalitarian titles which dub everyone a dude, bro, homie, or man. He has even attempted to fist-bump Therése in parting. Whereas Yves is pacific in his fantasy-filled thoughts, Séraphin's temperament is protean. An argument is always fomenting around him, and Guillome and Therése have come to fear every instance in which he directs his terrible attention towards them and asks, "Why?"

Therése and Guillome, raised in a place and time when parental authority was papal, are caught off guard by the word, which places an onus on them to provide reasons for their rules, reasons they have not hitherto considered nor deemed necessary. Therése and Guillome hate the word. It brings clashes of wills to the house, which leave the combatants—and even innocent bystanders—battered, bruised, angry, and sulking. The word swallows happiness whole. It leaves Guillome and Therése wondering whether they will ever secure a reprieve from being too old, too Rwandan, too parental—too *them.*

Maybe if they accepted that the times they were a-changing, they could have seen Séraphin's cultural camouflage, Yves's ill-fitting blackness, and Éric's truancy as the blowbacks of new lives which would not fit old templates.

Who is to know? Who can point at particular instances in these lives and say, "This is where it all starts to go wrong. This is where the past runs out."

Is it here, when the Kenya Airways flight starts boarding, with Therése and Guillome herding their young sons onto the airplane? Or is it here, when a so-called friend borrows heavily from Guillome and Therése, promising to return their favor with interest before vanishing into the Canadian unknown with his family, leaving the two with a difficult choice to make about Yves's university education?

Nobody knows.

But look here, at Séraphin and Jasmyn on his bed. This might be the beginning of something. Not the First Word of the First Chapter of the First Book, but the start of a secret something that will be part of Séraphin, Yves, Éric, Therése, and Guillome's lives for a long time. Here, in this room with this laughing boy and this girl with the hazel eyes, where everything is funny because losing one's virginity is dependent on good humor.

This might be a start of a start.

Maybe.

* * *

At St. Luke's, when grade eleven and twelve students prepare for their year-end examinations they are permitted to study at home. Parents never doubt that their children will use the time to study. It is that unequivocal trust which permits Therése to leave Séraphin in the house today while she goes grocery shopping.

"Séra!" Therése calls out in his room's direction. "I'm off! I'll be back later, okay?"

"Yeah, okay." A muffled reply comes from behind his bedroom door.

"There's some food in the fridge if you want. I won't be long."

Silence.

"I'm waiting for you to say goodbye, Séra."

More silence. And then, eventually, an exasperated "Goodbye, Mamma."

As the sliding gate clicks home, Séraphin emerges from his room and watches Therése's hat cross Vivaldi Street before rounding the corner onto Mozart. He waits for a few minutes and then reaches for his phone.

Sera_Phyne: She's gone.

JazzMyne: I'm on my way.

If the jump from Quill Club seatmates to this moment feels strange, it should not. The one thing this musical decade of decadence did was to make sure teenage romances flourished with ease. Take chronic boredom, the sweet LimeWire and Napster nectars, pour them onto a blank compact disc, and pop it into a Nero oven at twenty times writing speed and one had the pirated score of romance.

Jasmyn had finally shed her Keaton shell and Séraphin had grown taller and leaner. He passed a basketball as well as he wrote a descriptive sentence, and, floating somewhere between jock and nerd, Jasmyn decided it was time to try someone different.

Enter Séraphin from stage left.

"Dude, that CD you made was the shit," says John another Friday at the Quill Club.

"Thanks," Séraphin replies.

"Maybe you should make us some," a voice behind them says. It is Jasmyn, seated next to one of her girlfriends—even her friends are joining the Quill Club.

Séraphin and John turn to each other and Séraphin says: "Sure. What do you like?"

"Everything," she says.

"Nobody likes everything," Séraphin says. "Not even me."

"Okay," Jasmyn says. "Surprise me."

That night, with a broad music collection at his disposal, Séraphin sets to work.

He delivers *High School Mixtape, Vol. 1: Confusing Sadness* to Jasmyn the following week, dropping it on her desk in English before heading over to his seat.

"I like Puddle of Mudd and Staind," she says the day after.

"Me too."

Those two magic words that make teenagers clap their hands like a cymbal-bashing monkey in their heads: "me too." In the future these words will divide, but for now they unite. It only takes two more me-toos—*The Short Version of a Long Story* ("It's been a while since I heard Mel C and Left Eye!") and *Time of Your Lies* ("Nice wordplay")—to go from verbal to digital conversation, all hush-hush, waiting for each other to show up online, and texting each other until one of them falls asleep. Inevitably, their conversation builds towards that crescendo of teenage aspirations:

JazzMyne: You haven't?

Tri_SeraTops: No.

JazzMyne: I thought you would've.

Tri_SeraTops: Still one. With a capital V, like the Vulcan greeting.

JazzMyne: What?

Tri_SeraTops: Live long and prosper.

JazzMyne: You're strange, Séraphin.

Tri_SeraTops: I've been told.

JazzMyne: But I like it.

Tri_SeraTops: Me too.

JazzMyne: You're lame. And your username is lame.

Tri_SeraTops: Apparently I charge too much in basketball.

JazzMyne: You should change it. Some of my friends call you Sera-Fine.

Tri_SeraTops: Really?

JazzMyne: Yeah. But don't get a big head now.

TheaElleC: You changed your username.

Sera_Phyne: Yes, I did.

TheaElleC: John says you've been making Jasmyn mix CDs.

Sera_Phyne: John needs to keep his nose out of other people's business.

TheaElleC: Touchy! What do you guys talk about anyway?

Sera_Phyne: I don't know. Music, I guess. She's funny. I like her.

TheaElleC: . . . okay.

Sera_Phyne: What?

TheaElleC: Nothing.

JazzMyne: You changed it.

Sera_Phyne: I did.

JazzMyne: I like it.

Sera_Phyne: Hehehe. Me too.

JazzMyne: How is the bio study going?

Sera_Phyne: Okay, I guess. Gets boring studying at home the whole time.

JazzMyne: Next time your mom leaves let me know.

About fifteen minutes after Therése departs, Séraphin and Jasmyn are on his bed. He's laughing and trying to appear relaxed. She's totally at ease. They lean against a wall scrapbooked with Séraphin's youth: posters with frayed edges depicting the world's most popular rock-rap fusion band; the Arsenal Holy Trinity of Patrick Vieira, Dennis Bergkamp, and Thierry Henry; a bald-headed black man soaring to a basketball hoop, tongue out. Here and there can be seen rectangles of wanderlust: the Empire State Building, Christ the Redeemer, Victoria Harbour, and brown, undulating sand dunes vanishing into a blue infiniteness of sky.

"What's that one?" Jasmyn asks.

"Sahara Desert."

"Why that?"

"Not sure." Then he adds, "Looks peaceful."

"You know we have a desert too, right?" Jasmyn gets off the bed and crosses over to a long writing desk. Next to the CD player are thin red, orange, purple, blue, and green cases grouped by color. A neat hand has taken the care to name the discs in permanent marker.

"What's this one like?" She holds up a purple case with *Soundtrack of the Disconnect* written on it.

"Sad songs, really depressing stuff. You don't want to listen to that. Trust me."

"And this?"

"More sad songs," Séraphin says as she puts *Crumpled Bedsheets* back down on the desk. "The purple ones are sad ones; red is for all the romantic cheese; orange for the happy ones; blue for gym; and the green ones have study music."

"So much sadness, Séra," she says. The purples outnumber all of the others.

"Yeah, well, high school."

"This one sounds like a good one," she says, looking at *All That Glitters Is Good* in its orange casing.

"Don't play that unless you're prepared to spend the next hour dancing. I nearly failed tests because of that CD."

"And this?" She holds *After the Winter*.

"Lighter, happy stuff. More chilled. But it's good. I like that one."

Her eyes glide over the blues. "*Between Rock and a Loud Place*; *No Guitars for Quitters*; *Shoestrings and Sweat Patches*. How do you come up with these names?"

"They kinda come to me in the moment. One minute I'm busy with chemistry homework and then, bam, *Smells Like Team Spirit*."

She comes back to the bed. "Playlists are clearly your thing." The curves of her body make straight answers a bit hard for Séraphin, whose eyes dart from her eyes to her pronounced chest before finding Patrick Vieira's knowing grin.

He coughs. "Playlists for all moods and times."

"So what do you have for this moment?" Her eyes tease him.

Another cough. "I have something."

Jasmyn kicks off her shoes and pulls her legs onto the bed, crossing them underneath her. "Put it on."

Séraphin goes to the desk, shuffles through the discs, and pulls out a transparent casing.

"No color. Is that a good thing?" Jasmyn asks.

"I didn't know which color to give this." His voice is tightening, dwindling to a whisper. "Maybe I'll know later."

"What's it called?"

"Nostalgia for the Near Future."

On the bed, Jasmyn smiles. "Clever."

A brief whirring emanates from the CD player as it prepares for a momentous performance. A red light flashes. Once, twice, thrice—and then it plays.

"Can you turn it up?"

Séraphin rotates the silver knob to the right and stands sheepishly next to the desk. Jasmyn beckons him to the bed. He sits next to her, hands in his lap. Their bodies observe a short silence before Jasmyn leans towards Séraphin and kisses him, whispering softly as she tugs at his bottom lip. "I've been searching for you . . ."

The kiss is light, airy. And as she pulls away he is tugged in the undertow of the passing sensation. He blinks his eyes open and finds her looking at him. "What?" Séraphin whispers.

"Nothing." She kisses him again, longer this time, with careful deliberation, and then pulls away. "How's that?"

"It's, er, nice," he says, swallowing past the chokepoint that has developed in his throat. She laughs softly again and kneels on the bed. She motions for him to do the same.

When they are facing each other she reaches for the bottom of his T-shirt and lifts it gently. He helps her pull it over his head and arms. Then she tugs at the corners of her own top, pulling it off in one smooth movement to reveal a small concave belly button at sea in light skin. She reaches behind her back to unclip her bra and, just before it slides off, Séraphin involuntarily closes his eyes and then forces them open. Her breasts are round with flat nipples, almost faint upon her skin. Even as his eyes gorge themselves he notices something peculiar.

"They're different sizes," he blurts out.

Jasmyn laughs at his surprise. She wiggles her chest to make them jiggle. "Yes, they are." She looks at him closely. "Feel them." Séraphin raises his left hand and passes a fleeting touch against the right one. Jasmyn laughs again. "They won't fall off, you know," she says. "Here, let me show you."

She takes his hand and presses it against her breast, his fingertips against the hardening light brownness. As she does so she looks at Séraphin's face, attentive. When she releases his hand to its own exploration he pulls away first, looking at her for permission. She nods slightly. His touch is naive, slightly ticklish, but it kindles warmth under her skin. She reaches out to touch his exposed torso—dark, brown, and lithe from athleticism but not yet fully developed. As she leans forward to kiss his neck he can smell the heat of the day on her coupled with a cool, fresh fragrance his nose cannot place. Then she pushes him back on the bed and he feels a hand slip underneath his basketball shorts. He inhales sharply when it arrives at its destination and, again, Jasmyn watches his eyes narrow with the new sensation. She alternates firm and gentle strokes until she sees his eyes close and his breath become heavy. Then she releases him at the elastic of his shorts. He anticipated a two-step undressing—shorts first, then boxer shorts—and nearly sits up in consternation when he feels the entire assemblage being tugged. Jasmyn whisks them off before wriggling out of her jeans and underwear too. From top to bottom her figure is one smooth, unbroken curve, and the patch of womanhood is dark and fine. She picks up her jeans and pulls a crinkly packet out of the pocket before coming to lie down next to Séraphin.

They kiss once more, Séraphin driven by curiosity and Jasmyn by a mounting need. She delicately tears off the top of the packet to produce a translucent sheet, which she expertly slides onto Séraphin before rolling on top of him. She places a palm on his stomach to steady herself and then slowly, with great care, connects the two of them, letting out a small gasp at the turgid pressure inside her.

Séraphin's mind is a thrashing live wire as sensations course through him: the pressed heat which makes their skin sticky, the shortness of breath in the small room, and the enveloping warmth on top of him. His inexperience pins him to the bed and, when Jasmyn finds her balance, he lets her dictate the pace and the rhythm. Eyes wide open, the sight of her atop him is mesmerizing.

Jasmyn pinches her thighs and the pull in Séraphin's loins intensifies, forcing him to sit up. The near future which shall be immortalized in nostalgia is close at hand. He can hear the roar of the Highbury faithful behind Thierry Henry, cheering with mad ecstasy, and Martin Tyler's energetic commentating—"What a glorious strike! Mark this day! This boy is going to be phenomenal!" Patrick Vieira's grin is no longer cheeky but welcoming. He finally understands Bergkamp's ascension. Séraphin feels Jasmyn's hands clawing at his back, as though attempting to release a pair of bound wings, allowing them to fly from his body. As they pull deeper into each other, Jasmyn's teeth on the muscle of his shoulder and his face buried in the sweet smell of her neck, Séraphin's bedroom door swings open and his mother walks in.

"Séra—!"

V

Therése was a beauty, and a smart one. In the old days, when Rwanda was feeling the bite of independence, she had the prudence to secure a scholarship to Paris to study at L'École Parisienne. She surmised that in twenty years on her family's farm in Gisenyi she had seen enough of the green countryside and the brown soil that ran like melted chocolate when it rained. When she was younger, she could walk the five kilometers to school at the village's ramshackle collection of long houses. But after she completed high school her horizons looked bleak: an eternity of planting and harvesting, fetching firewood, drawing water, peeling and cutting potatoes, killing and plucking chickens, marriage, and child-rearing. She did not want to be her mother or the majority of her aunts. So Therése secretly planned an escape.

On a small flyer she picked up on the last day of school, she could see two smiling students, a woman and a man, walking in a paved courtyard. She imagined them discussing something worldly and grand. She looked at the intelligence and freedom in the woman's eyes, how straight her hair was, and the smiling acceptance of the pale-faced man walking next to her. She longed for the intellectual equality promised by education, and desired to be valued beyond the thankless sweat of her labor or the fecund fields of her womb.

Therése hesitated, but only momentarily, when she arrived at the regional government office, a rickety brick-and-mortar house with two rooms full of paperwork, to hand in her application. She bundled her nerves into a rough bale of confidence and then strode past the office door. Sitting behind a wooden desk was a man in large spectacles that magnified his eyes, making him appear shocked at whatever was before him. He was hard at work on a black typewriter, which clacked away with machine-gun speed. The man's attention was so rapt that Therése approached the desk timidly.

"Where do I place the applications for the scholarships for secretaries?" She suffused her query with diffident politeness—men in the area bore little resemblance to the smiling student in the flyer.

With his eyes still on his paper and his fingers playing the typewriter's keys, the man asked in a smooth French accent, "*Marseille, Nice, Bordeaux, ou Paris?*"

"*Paris, monsieur,*" Therése replied.

"*Déposez la demande sur la pile intitulée 'Étudiants' à votre droite,*" he said. Therése placed her application on top of a stack as gently as if it would break upon contact and shatter into a hundred pieces of rejection, a thousand chores, and a million little sighs of regret.

As Therése moved across the room to the door, the clerk—whose name was Alphonse—paused his typing to look admiringly at her figure. It was solid like most of the girls' from the area, but filled with feminine curves. He cursed himself for not engaging her in conversation. These village girls were easy pickings.

"If your application is successful," he said to her retreating figure, "you will receive an answer in a month." She turned to face him. The oval of her face and the curve of her eyebrows made him swallow uncomfortably. Her neck was long and her bosom was laden with all of the fruits of young femininity. "If you are accepted, then you will have to get a passport before you can go to France. You have a passport, no?"

Therése's face flushed. Alphonse saw an opening. "No problem, I can arrange a passport."

"*Non, monsieur*, please do not trouble yourself. I have an aunt in Kigali who can help me with that," Therése replied after blushing for the required length of time. "You would be doing so much already by just helping me submit the application."

Alphonse smiled. All he had to do to slide beneath her skirt was move her application to the top of the pile and write a short motivation to support her candidacy. "You can come back to check on the application in a week," he said.

"*Oui, monsieur*," she said. She even curtsied.

But Therése was no fool. She had heard of Alphonse's deviance. Also, what she wanted was what she had dreamed of, what she had read about, what she had only tasted in carefully constructed sentences with French adjectives, memorized from a weathered poster stuck to a classroom wall.

Une promenade ensoleillée sur les Champs Elysées.

Une tasse de café chaud dans un café. Un pique-nique dans un jardin.

Une danse amusante dans une discothèque.

Alphonse had no hope of providing that.

Therése walked out of the office and called her mother's youngest sister, a woman held in contempt for daring to go to the city, taking up with men as she chose, even wearing pants like a man. Over the phone, they planned a coup: applying for a birth certificate, taking a passport photo, and then submitting her passport application at another village office staffed by a cheerful clerk who was publicly and proudly married.

When Therése finally walked into Alphonse's office a month and a half later, he flourished her successful application and some flight tickets. She waited until she had stowed the paperwork in her battered handbag before she brushed his leathery and lecherous hand off her shoulder.

When she announced her departure to her parents they were greatly displeased. They prophesied her inability to integrate into European life. But Therése could not be talked out of her decision. She tried to appease them with promises of returning with a diploma and the prospect of a job in Kigali which would allow her to buy them the latest trappings of modernity, but they merely sighed and "O-ho"-ed disparagingly at her heightened ambitions.

Boarding her flight from Kigali to Kinshasa with four other girls also bound for Paris, she was wowed by the size of the plane, the luxury of the economy seats, the kindness and beauty of the dark Zairean air hostess who made safety announcements and answered questions about the limited variety of on-board food in fluent French, heavily accented English, and stuttering Swahili. Therése's seatmate, Bernadette, came from a neighboring village and was headed to another secretarial college in Paris. She gripped her chair in fear and cried out when the aircraft made its ascent. She wanted her feet back on the ground, in the rituals she knew and understood.

"Why did you apply for this?" Therése asked her.

"It was my aunt's idea. She said it would be good to study," Bernadette replied. Therése smiled at the prevalence of aunts who encouraged their nieces to revolt against their fathers' wishes and their mothers' acceptance of the way things were.

"Your aunt did the right thing," she told Bernadette. "In a year or so we will be back, and then you will thank her. You will be an educated woman."

The title drew a curse from Bernadette. To be an educated woman was like being deflowered by the devil.

"But a year is a long time," Bernadette said. "And I am not sure whether there are many Rwandans in Paris. How do you expect us to fit in with all of the white people?"

Time, change, no Rwandans, white people—all the things that scared Bernadette thrilled Therése.

"I'm sure it won't be hard," Therése said. "There are many black people in Paris. Congolese, Senegalese, Cameroonians, Ghanaians—I have even heard there are parts of Paris that are just black. And there are Germans, Swiss, Spanish, and Italian people. You don't have to go with what you know."

Therése's mouth tasted the possibilities of diversity, hitherto just words on a vocabulary list. They were becoming people she could meet, hands she could shake, conversations she could have, and handsome, accepting gentlemen she could walk next to on a campus while discussing something worldly and grand.

"But you must be around your own people," Bernadette said. "You need to be around your own people."

Therése smiled at Bernadette and squeezed her hand in assurance. Then she turned her head and gazed out of the cabin window. Not for the last time in her life, she remarked at the strangeness of travelers who try to take home with them.

Therése loved her Parisian life. She hovered in the top five of her class and felt as though her sylvan soul had been remade in the culture and clutter of Paris. She was a tram-taking, café-visiting, book-reading, concert-going *belle noire* who did not gawk at the city's night lights. Her jeans hugged her body and her dark skin stood out in a crowd. Only for the briefest interval of time did she flounder in the bustle of her new life. The abundance of milk, sugar, and bread forced her to observe a period of culinary conservation out of respect for her former life. Electricity was an omniscient god and she became its awestruck follower, but after a few weeks, it was just another passing comfort. Hot and cold water at the turn of a handle was a power she relished and exercised injudiciously. It was not long before she realized there was also an endless supply of croissants and no shortage of discotheques or white boys trying to kiss her on the dance floor. She decided to shed her village virtue and enjoy a life without shortage, routine, or the threat of marriage. She had not managed to find the young gentleman she could walk next to on a campus while discussing something worldly and grand, but she had faith it would happen.

She had, at least, been kissed by a young and curious Parisian boy—she considered all white men to be boys of varying ages. His mouth was light and fleeting on hers, his pink tongue slithering past her lips for an electric instant that tasted like sweet tea. Later on, she would forget the faces of boys who kissed her but remember the flavors of their tongues. Ettiene was sickening strawberry, François was warm bread, and Lucien, the first man she took to bed, always tasted like toothpaste. He insisted on brushing before they kissed. At first she had felt ashamed by the ease with which advances were made at her. Sometimes she felt like a frontier her lovers had to cross, but when she realized she was guilty of the same thing she relinquished her judgment and focused on enjoying the many flavors of masculinity.

Seven months into her studies, at a friend's house party, she met Guillome. His torso occupied every inch of his shirt, and his maroon bell-bottom jeans accentuated a prim pair of buttocks and strong thighs. He had a solid jaw and a corona of jet-black hair. When he was not flashing his perfect white teeth at a clever comment or some particular insight he favored, he had a pensive look. Guillome also had a laugh that sounded mischievous, rather unnatural in a man who otherwise exuded calm and poise. He was studying pharmacy in Brussels. Like Therése, he had been chosen to bring European knowledge back to Rwanda.

Their first meeting was accidental. Therése's friend from secretarial college Madeline had dragged her into the narrow kitchen to introduce her to the other Rwandan at the party.

"*Il étudie à Bruxelles. Est-ce-que tu le connais?*" Madeline asked Therése, who replied that she did not know every Rwandan in Europe. She did, however, cast a raking glance at Guillome, who was leaning against the counter with the most casually cool stance she had ever seen.

"*Mais vous êtes tous deux du même pays. Vous vous entendrez,*" Madeline said, and vanished. *You are from the same country. You will get along.* Therése stood rooted to the spot.

Eventually, he asked, "*C'est ton amie?*"

Therése's being quivered at the sound of his deep voice. She found herself replying with a shy "*Oui.*"

"Her party sucks but at least her friends are good to look at and, hopefully, chat to," Guillome said. Thérese blushed. A polite and curious conversation started between them. They found it strangely comforting to speak about home, their parents, their tribes of siblings, and the food they had grown up with.

"The French complicate their food," Guillome said. "Sometimes I just want something simple. Like boiled potatoes and beans with a little salt. Rwandan food."

"The salt comes from the cook's sweat—there are no spices in our foods."

"Still, you have to admit the French cook like they are trying to make up for lost wars. *Il est trés compliqué.*"

Therése laughed. The party grew, swelled, and dwindled around them. Therése detected Guillome's desire to return home, to build, create, and advance the Rwandan cause; Guillome picked up Therése's distaste for domestic life back home.

"You think the situation should be different?" he asked. He was not challenging her. He seemed genuinely interested.

"The problem with Rwandan women," Therése said, "is Rwandan men. They want tradition and the future at the same time."

"You cannot have the future and the past?" he asked.

"No," she said, fiercely. "If you want to go into the future you must be prepared to lose something. Rwandan men want the here and now of fancy cars and telephones, but they also want to come home and find their supper cooked by a woman who cannot use the telephone or drive the car. What kind of foolishness is that?" She built up momentum and then, fearing she had said too much, ended her treatise with a limp "That's what I think," and sipped her drink.

Guillome took a deep breath and then looked at her levelly and said, "I agree," and flashed a brilliant smile that made Therése's insides fidget. "Who did you come with?" he asked.

"No one," she said. "And you?"

"I was supposed to meet a friend," Guillome said. Therése was crestfallen. Of course he had a friend, some *mademoiselle*, tall and pale, with long skinny legs, who read complex French poetry and smoked cigarettes daintily. "But I am glad he didn't show up," Guillome added.

Therése's face could have thawed a glacier.

Their romance was firm and fast, each only slightly disappointed that they had come all the way to Paris to fall in love with someone from home.

Therése finally walked across L'École Parisienne's campus with a man who looked at her as an equal. That he was a dark-skinned Rwandan man was just fine with her. Their conversations would frolic with ease from the trivial to the complicated, their young minds agile and alert. It was not long before they talked themselves into marriage.

They were in Guillome's apartment in Brussels, listening to jazz records, lying on a bent sofa with cushions rubbed shiny and smooth. Therése always liked how his massive frame encompassed her smaller one when they lay next to each other, as they were doing just then. She would run her hands over his chest and listen to him talk about the future, when a whole generation of intellectuals would call Rwanda home.

"They are all returning," he said, "even the ones who have married abazungu. My mother said there are whole villages of grandmothers trying to teach white women how to pound flour. Imagine."

"And you want to go back too, Gui?" She was the only one he allowed to call him that.

"I don't know, maybe." He stroked the top of her head, his hand pulling the tufts of tough hair. "What will you do when you finish here?"

"Go back home. I have to work off the scholarship. But I am not sure if I can adjust to Rwanda after"—her left hand swept in a wide arc of generality—"all of this."

Guillome followed the sweep of her hand and said playfully, "You came all the way to Europe and all you are going to miss is this apartment? My god, you really are a village girl. If I had known, I would have impressed you with my two-plate stove and a train ticket or something. Now I have wasted all of my time on you. I could have had umzungu too. We would have caramel kids with soft hair that would not make them cry when they have to comb it." He pulled at her hair again. Therése smacked his hand.

"Your white wife would not have to squeeze their heads between her thighs to wrestle the knots in their hair, that is true. But you would be a widower within a year because she would not be able to eat anything in Rwanda. O-ho, you think croissants are being sold by the roadside or what?"

He laughed, a deep laugh that made his chest reverberate and her body vibrate in resonance. "But at least we would miss Europe together."

"Is that what you want?" she asked, raising her head and turning to look at him. "You want someone to miss this with you?" There was no humor in her voice. Some sort of fork in their lives had been reached.

"No," he said, looking at her straight. "I want someone who wants what I want for myself."

She raised her eyebrows. Guillome had a way of drawing out conversations, speaking in segments. "And what is that, Gui?" she asked softly.

"I want to go back to Rwanda, but I don't want to go back to be Rwandan. I don't want to sit on the porch of my farmhouse and drink with all of the other banana farmers and talk about the past like it isn't dead. My children should see the world. I cannot have my boys circumcised by someone high on powders and invented spirits." He looked away from her, into the wide expanse her hand had just encompassed. His right arm reached out and traversed the same arc as he said, "I want an unscripted future."

Therése was moved by his desire for a life unlike the one they had grown up in. He had the pale scars of a hundred little cuts on his back and stomach from a fever bloodletting and since she had known him he seemed to hate sitting around in bars drinking and talking and talking about drinking. He would suggest cafés and cinemas and art galleries instead. He was determined in his studies and outspoken in classes, unlike other foreign black students who were cowed in lectures, yielding to their supposed betters. Even in his skirt-chasing days, he said, he had always pursued women who seemed to be out of his league, smart women. "Because," Guillome said, "if you wanted to fuck their brains out it would take more than one night." She was secretly pleased that after a year of lovemaking she could still excite him, that they could still have debates about politics and literature and films and listen to his jazz records together. She did not want it to end.

"And do you want that future alone or with someone, Gui? If that is what you want, then we can get it together. I am not going back to Rwanda to cook and clean and be beaten and talked about sadly to a mistress who does not know the pain of giving birth to five children. I also want my future. We have fun here, Gui, but we could have this and more"—another wave at the infinite unknown—"and we can get it together. There is more for us, no?"

A short silence alighted between them before Guillome said, "I agree."

He said those two words in the same way when he heard the sound of reason in an argument. It meant he had thought something over, had dedicated time to it, evaluating its shortcomings and its merits, and had come to the conclusion that he could, indeed, add his assent.

Therése looked at him pointedly, like the man from her application flyer, and said, "If you give me my life, I will give you yours."

It was Therése who proposed the marriage, and Guillome who accepted. They lay on the couch for the rest of the evening, planning the rest of their lives.

Therése was the first to graduate. She extended her student visa to keep Guillome company in the final months of his studies. They would return to Rwanda together, announce their intention to marry, circumvent the long-winded traditions of courtship, and defy their ancestors by having a quiet church wedding. On their flight back from Europe, the air hostess lingered by Guillome's seat, offering him the small comforts of a drink. Therése's stare eventually drove her away. As she retreated, Guillome patted Therése's hand gently and whispered, "Don't worry. She would last all of five minutes. But you, you are going to take a lifetime."

Therése blushed. She was returning to Rwanda qualified, traveled, loved, and determined to bring the world home with her.

Guillome and Therése secured work in Kigali immediately, he as a pharmacist at a new hospital and she as an office administrator for the United Nations Development Programme. They decided to postpone their marriage while they made a foothold in the city. Their postponement lasted all the way through Therése's pregnancy, scandalizing their parents. When a fat baby boy with big eyes was pulled from her womb they agreed to call him Séraphin, the angel, for his calmness. And Turihamwe, "we are together," as a sly reprimand for their parents and social circle. When Séraphin turned one, though, they married in a big traditional ceremony—to their displeasure.

With the wedding done, their lives resumed their patterns of coordinated career moves and promotions. Guillome moved on from the state hospital to work in the administrative arm of the nascent pharmaceutical industry, allowing them to move out of their one-bedroom flat to a spacious two-bedroom house. Two years after Séraphin, Yves was born. Both having secured promotions, Guillome and Therése moved to a roomy mansion in Kiyovu, which required a maid and a gardener to maintain it. To Yves they gave the name Mugisha—"another blessing"—for they seemed to be the recipients of unending beneficence.

Perhaps they were tempting fate. Rwanda began changing and tensions around the country grew. The politics of ethnicity were becoming all-consuming, enraging, and dangerous. Therése and Guillome trusted in education, development, the foreign banks which operated in the country, and the healthy community of well-intentioned investors and volunteers to discourage regression and factionalism. Plus, things were not too bad in their lives.

Time passed: Séraphin was four, Yves was two, Guillome was putting ink to paperwork for the country's first independent medicines distributor, and Therése was managing the communications of the entire United Nations mission in Kigali. Their prosperity was praised and envied in equal measure. Their lounge had real china plates, a large cuboid Sony television with color display and a videocassette player. Their fridge was filled with milk, rare custard, cold fruit juices, and imported beer. They entertained generously and offered aid to family, friends, and enemies alike. The passage of time did little to calm the country's seething grudges and grievances. It did, however, bring Guillome and Therése's lastborn into a country living in fear. Éric Uwituze was named as a blind hope for calmness.

"We can wait," Therése whispered in bed late at night. "Things will get better."

"I agree."

It soothed her on nights when the air was hot and pressed, when mosquitoes made the darkness sing. The country seemed ready to spark. Each passing day brought news of tension, and each night their lovemaking was rushed and anxious, fading into whispers of plans that they still wanted to see through. The schools Séraphin and Yves would attend, the need for another house girl to help with Éric, and the money that had to be sent to their parents and delinquent siblings.

The night mortars and gunfire were heard through Kigali, Therése awoke in a panic. Her dreams had been filled with gaping chasms into which she tumbled endlessly. When they heard the first boom she thought surely the house had slipped into such a fissure. Guillome had already leapt out of bed, scrambling to the living room to peek through the curtains, making sure windows and doors were locked. She made a dash for Séraphin, Yves, and Éric's nursery. She imagined opening the door and finding the room destroyed, the debris of their dreams crushed beyond recognition. She could hear Yves and Éric crying. The boys were alive. She rushed to Éric's cot and picked him up before going to Yves's bed. While she murmured soothing phrases to the two crying children, Therése looked around for Séraphin.

"Séraphin! Uri he?"

"Ndi hano, Mamma." The reply came from the adjoining room, which was sometimes used as Therése and Guillome's study.

Guillome came into the room and sat beside her. The bed creaked with their weight. She pressed Yves and Éric to her body and rocked them back and forth. When they were calm, she passed them to Guillome, who took them into his arms. Then she stood up to go and fetch Séraphin. At the door she paused and turned back.

"We have to leave, Gui." Therése's voice was shaking. "For the boys."

In the darkness of the room, with explosions sounding in the distance and history unfolding about them, Guillome breathed deeply, as though he were steeling himself to command the country to peace. Then his shoulders slumped, and he sat, bent and hollowed.

"I agree."

For the first time in her life, Guillome's words did not calm Therése. She felt light on her feet, as though gravity had lost its grip on the earth and she would float into the sky and into endless space. The study door was ajar. Séraphin was at the window, standing on tiptoe, looking out through a gap in the curtains. Wearing only his underwear, he was a beanpole of knees, sharp shoulder bones, and a round stomach. From the doorway Therése could see his face trying to process the sound of distant disaster.

She pushed the door open and entered the room.

"Séra—"

VI

In a country far removed from the closeness of violent nights, where the fear of a bad school report rivals that of a report from a gun, Therése stands in a supermarket bemoaning the cost of avocados, guavas, mangoes, and sweet potatoes. These commodities grew like weeds in her country. Now they are luxuries, circled in newspaper shopping supplements which bear a word she has come to loathe: "sale."

It speaks of cheapness. It is an opportunity for poverty to flaunt itself, chasing down red stickers and asking sales assistants where to find things that could not be afforded yesterday but are now within the ambit of carefully monitored family budgets. She casts her eyes over the heat-smacked produce. Ruefully, she smiles at the thought of buying bananas. On her family's farm such a thing would be unheard of. The apples are green with hints of yellow softness. They make Therése feel cheated of the crunch apples are supposed to make when you bite into them. The ashy-skinned potatoes peer at her cart in pity. The mangoes are stunted, not like the ones back home, which required two hands to eat them. The avocados are green grenades stacked in too-ripe heaps. A last glance at the mangoes persuades her to choose five for her family, a treat they might enjoy.

When she is done, she pushes her cart to a cashier who nods a greeting and begins scanning her groceries. Therése watches each item's price flash on the cash register's periscopic digital display. The cashier weighs the fresh produce on a scale, presses the corresponding number on a keyboard, and sticky price tags roll out of the machine like impudent white tongues. When her bag of mangoes receives its sticker, Therése stops the cashier. "The price, it is wrong," she says.

"Sixty-three dollars and fifty cents," the cashier replies. Her English is bad, and sixty-three comes out as "siggisty-three."

"No, they are on special."

"Meme," the cashier says, "the price is the price—you can see on the display."

"It is not the price in the newspaper." Therése fishes a leaflet out of her shopping bag. It is crowded with reduced prices for mincemeat, fresh milk, cheeses, biscuits, juices, and the mangoes. "You see, the price here, it is fifty-five for five. Not sixty-three." Therése involuntarily places emphasis on the *x*.

The cashier presses a green button under her till, which rings a bell above her counter for the floor manager. "You are from here?" The "here" sounds like "he-yeah."

"No, I am not from here," Therése replies cautiously.

"You are from where?"

"Rwanda."

"Luanda? You are Angolian?"

"No. Rwanda." Therése is used to the response. "It is further away." She makes a mental note to tell Séraphin about Angolians. Maybe he will laugh at that. Therése searches for a geographic marker that will orientate the woman and end the conversation. "It is near Kenya and Uganda."

"O-ho." The cashier's reply does not suggest any knowledge of the whereabouts of these two countries. "You don't speak Oshiwambo? Or Afrikaans?"

Therése always fears this line of inquiry. To be from elsewhere and not have learned to speak any of the local languages seems to be a capital offense.

"No," she says. "Only English."

"My dear, you must learn." The "meme" reserved for grown women has been dropped. Instead she is a young child, to be told about the workings of the world. The "dear" also comes out sounding like "dee-yeah."

"Yes," Therése replies. A queue of shoppers has formed behind her and she is reluctant to hold up service, especially for five incorrectly priced mangoes and an inability to speak Oshiwambo or Afrikaans.

The floor manager arrives and looks inquiringly at the cashier.

"She says the price is wrong."

Therése hands the flyer to the floor manager, who lets out an exasperated breath. Now she must press three buttons, swipe a card with a magnetic strip on it through a slot to void the transaction, then press four more buttons, and enter the bar code of the mangoes so their new price can be reflected on the register's display, which she does with poorly concealed irritation before pulling her elephantine figure away to attend to another ringing bell down the line.

The mangoes, now correctly priced, are pushed to the end of the counter. "Two hundred and seventy-five dollars and eighty cents," the cashier says.

Therése pulls her purse out of her shopping bag. She counts the notes carefully before her breath stops. "*Merde,*" she whispers. "I am sorry," Therése says in a small voice, "I do not have enough money."

"Ewa! First you make me change the price and now you tell me you do not have enough money to pay?" The cashier folds her arms across her chest. The cashiers to either side of her cluck something to themselves.

Therése closes her eyes and wishes herself to another country far, far away where her purse would be lined with crisp Rwandan francs and American dollars, where any item she needed or wanted would be within her reach. She had worth, she was employed, and she had bank accounts in her name. She never had cashiers crossing their arms at her. When Therése opens her eyes she is still standing in front of the irate cashier who does not know where Rwanda is and the queue behind her shuffles awkwardly in annoyance. Therése's chest rises as she takes a deep breath and says, "You will have to remove them."

There is an uncomfortable stare-down between Therése and the cashier before the latter rings the bell for the floor manager again. A person at the back of the queue swears audibly and moves away to find another line. Preferably one without a foreigner short of money. The floor manager returns and asks the cashier what the problem is this time.

"She wants them removed," the cashier replies. "She does not have enough money." The addition is said at volume so that everyone in Therése's vicinity is made aware. The floor manager shoots Therése a venomous look before doing her complex button-and-swipe routine to remove the offending mangoes from the till slip. She hovers by the cashier to make sure there are no other corrections to be made. "Two-twenty and eighty cents," the cashier calls when the new price flashes on the display. Therése hands over her money and cups her hands to accept the change. A few coins slip from the cashier's hands. Therése picks them up off the counter one by one.

Outside the sun is already ferocious despite it being only ten o'clock. The street is crowded with taxi drivers baying for passengers. They run to shoppers with laden trolleys and guide them towards a parked car with one or two passengers already in it, all the while filling the air with promises of immediate departures—"Mamma, we are going right now!"—before bundling shopping bags into the boots of their cars and graciously ushering the new passenger to a back or front seat. The vehicles crawl two or three meters before another potential passenger is spotted, prompting the drivers to switch off their engines and turn to the sweating fare payers with mock apologies. "Just one more, eh? Then we go!"

Therése scans the street for a driver who has managed to wear his waiting passengers' patience thin. The front seat of his battered Toyota Corolla is completely occupied by an obese woman fanning her sweaty forehead with a newspaper, while a younger man in cheap corporate attire makes a show of opening and closing the back door, threatening to leave. The driver opens the back seat for her, forcing the young man to scramble to the other side of the car in a huff. Therése clambers in and clutches her shopping bag to her chest. The driver starts his car and looks for an opening in the traffic, squeezing his vehicle into a gap without permission. The irate hooting which follows the taxi driver's maneuver hurts Therése's ears and embarrasses her vicariously.

The taxi ride out of the city center is not long and she sulks all the way home, nearly forgetting to tell the taxi driver where to stop. He slams on his brakes with exaggerated force and stares at her in the rearview mirror. She hands him his fare and waits for her change, which is handed back with poorly hidden ire. When Thérese alights in front of her house she is angry she could not complete the day's shopping; the notes she meant to take are sure to be lying on the kitchen counter or the lounge table.

Therése's hands rifle through her shopping bags for her house keys. Inside the compound she traverses the paved rectangle in front of the garage where Séraphin and Yves sometimes play basketball, shooting at a mounted hoop above the garage doors. She climbs a flight of stairs to the balcony entrance of the house and finds the sliding door open. Séraphin probably came here for a break between his studies, she thinks. Therése marches to the kitchen and dumps her shopping on the table. She scans the kitchen counters but does not see her money. She goes into the lounge and is disappointed to find the room devoid of all currency. Perhaps, she thinks, it is in her room, in another purse or handbag. She walks down the corridor to her and Guillome's bedroom, but pauses outside Séraphin's door. The music in his room is really loud, which is strange because he usually studies in silence. Therése pushes the door and enters the room.

"Séra—"

VII

"And then," Séraphin says, "while Jasmyn's riding me like the horse she came in on—see what I did there?—my mother walks in. Into my bedroom."

This is a scene from another country, another time, a different year.

Séraphin is much changed from the young boy who found everything funny so that he could lose his virginity during a study break while his mother was at the shops. He is older, for one thing, a law student, and he has a solid group of friends—Bianca, Richard, Godwin, James, Adewale, Andrew, and Yasseen.

Séraphin is conducting the comedic movement of the conversation around him like a maestro. Left hand for rhythm and timing, right hand for the entrances and exits.

Cue shock.

"Shit! Shit! Shit!" James's sip of beer catches in his throat.

"You're fucking joking!" Bianca is short of breath, laughter burning in her belly.

After Bianca's expletive disbelief comes Andrew's more controlled "No way! I can't believe this! There's no way." Next to him, Adewale, the devout and deviant Christian, laughs, cries, and crosses himself.

Richard and Godwin lean on each other for support, thumping their fists on the table and sending a ripple of upset glasses and cutlery tinkling. "Oan, you're fucking lying," Godwin splutters.

Next to the two towers of Pisa is Yasseen. His thin, bony frame remains composed, but he picks up his beer and shakes his head before taking a sip.

At the center of this bubble of delirium sits Séraphin. He looks ruefully at his glass of orange juice and shakes his head as his friends laugh. He takes a long drink and puts the glass back on the table.

"What happened next?" asks Bianca, the first to catch her breath.

"Well," Séraphin says, "one moment we was fuckin' and then"—he pauses, signaling to the percussion to get the cymbals ready—"we wasn't fuckin' no more!"

Cue laughter and chaos.

If a snapshot were to be taken of the moment and presented to a grandmother still mourning the loss of a son or daughter whose bones lay, anonymous but not forgotten, in some unmarked grave, a strong case could be made for history's compromises, contractual clemency, and constitutional amnesia. Look at this picture, grandmother. This is what your husband fought for, this is why he was beaten. This is why your son was taken. Look. Look at all these smiling faces, all these complexions together, all these nationalities. This is your Rainbow Nation. Be still, grandmother. Be still.

In one of Cape Town's leafier suburbs, the surface of a large wooden table is populated by beer mugs being drained of their froth-topped amber fluid; wine and cocktail glasses bleeding red, cerulean, and lime-green liquids down slender, slight, and muscular necks. On two wooden benches, in varying states of fermented merriment, is a congregation of youth. Their religion is the here and now. They have the wisdom of a thousand sages at their fingertips and their heads are swollen with solutions to the world's aches and scrapes. They are heedlessly promiscuous with their ambitions and chaste in their fears of disappointment for they are the offspring of opportunity. They sit along the wooden benches, drinking, nibbling thin chips, complaining about everything, including their sex lives.

"My drought needs to end, guys. If it goes on any longer I'll be a virgin all over again," Bianca says.

"How long's it been?" Séraphin asks.

"Long enough to start shopping for rechargeable batteries," Bianca replies. She wraps her hand around a cocktail of violent colors and daintily raises it to her lips before saying, "I came to university for A-grade D."

"You're lesbian, Bee," Séraphin says.

"I know. But it sounded cool."

Bianca paves the way for a welcome descent to this most persistent of preoccupations. They smirk at the treachery of erections and bemoan the evasiveness of the female orgasm.

"Never put your faith in anything that requires twenty-two minutes to decide what it wants to do in life."

"Honestly, if I hook up with another girl who doesn't know where I can find her orgasm, or at least give me road signs for how to get her there, I'm going to stop, turn on my PlayStation, and play some first-person shooters. Now, those buttons I know how to press."

Boasts are debunked and booed down:

"Seven times in one night, Rich? Really?"

"So, what, friction just stopped working that night? Have you heard of the word 'chafe'? Please stop lying to us, we're all friends here!"

There are confessions that elicit chuckles at self-deprecating performances:

"Bro, the mistake I made was opening my eyes because then I could see the booty. I came so quickly I just had to roll off her and apologize."

"Don't sweat it, man. I've had performances shorter than a Mike Tyson fight."

The subject matter of lost virginities crops up and everyone contributes their share of plucked petals.

Bianca, the first to tell, says she felt pricked by her boyfriend's long, thin member. "I felt like I was visiting the gyno. And it was so brief I felt like a virgin three days after." Seeing eyebrows rise around the table she quickly adds that she only did it to fit in with the other girls. "Sjoe, guys, if you don't want to be exiled to the Lost Land of Lesbians you lose your virginity to a boy fast!"

The male half of the party is rotten with stories of spectacularly reviewed first-time performances. Their thin veneers are easily pierced, though. James failed to maintain his uprightness and had to postpone his partner's exit from the realm of virginity by a few days. Andrew farted during his first orgasm. Yasseen had his virginity clinically excised from him by a pretty and determined high school friend who never brought the matter up again, insisting they remain friends for the rest of their school days. Richard panicked at the sight of blood and ran out of the room, texting his girlfriend two days later to apologize for abandoning her. Their relationship did not survive. Godwin was drunk throughout his, waking up to find his escort into manhood a not-so-distant cousin. Adewale said he was so scared of divine retribution he clenched his eyes shut and quoted Bible verses.

The laughter that follows each story grows in volume until the other patrons of the pub start throwing annoyed glances at the table. They withhold their anger because a confrontation with such diverse youth would be met with allegations of discrimination, something the pub and its pink-faced management are determined to avoid. So the assembled group is allowed to laugh clamorously through each story. Séraphin's is the last.

"I didn't know shit from shit," he began. "If Jasmyn hadn't taken charge of the situation, we'd still be sitting on that bed today. I knew nothing about what needed to be put where. Or, rather, I did, but only in my head. You know, you meet, you kiss, your clothes evaporate from your body, and then sex just happens automatically. But it's never like that in real life. It's awkward. It could've been worse if it wasn't for Jasmyn. She came prepared to snatch me from the clutches of chastity, brothers and sisters." Séraphin elevates and drops his voice like a spiritually inflamed preacher with the collection tray in sight. "She came to do the Lord's work and rescue this unwashed, unworthy, uninitiated urchin from the prisons of purity and deliver him upon the threshold of his future life. I can't remember how she did it but she managed to get the rubber on and then she climbed on top of me. Thank God. If I had to figure out the mechanics and hit the bullseye the first time I would probably have rubbed myself raw on her thigh or something. Why're you laughing? First time is the smallest target and I am no Deadshot, fam. I was just lucky to be present. I don't think you guys understand how hot Jasmyn was. I just let her do whatever she needed to do."

The whole table was beside itself. The new Séraphin was far removed from his fumbling past and this was not what they expected to hear from him.

"Anyway," Séraphin continued, "so it's in and she's on top. I don't know what to do with my hands. Should I touch her boobs? Should I hold her waist? I don't know. So I clench my hands to my chest, praying mantis–style. Stop laughing, this shit is real. So she's going and for a while I'm just enjoying it. Then I get that warm feeling in my toes. I know what it is because puberty is time for practice. Anyway, the show's nearly over. Jissis! I'm putting hands to whatever part of Jasmyn I can get to. Finally, I feel like I'm about to explode but I don't want it to end. I'm thinking of anything that will postpone the inevitable. Dead babies and spiders! Dead babies and spiders! But it's not working! It's about to be that time, man. And then—and then—" Séraphin paused, his audience waiting for the obvious. Instead, after taking a drawn-out sip of juice, he calmly delivered the unfortunate conclusion that sent everyone into shocked laughter and exclamations.

"Then," Séraphin says, after they stop laughing, "I panicked."

"This is going to be bad," Richard says.

"Yes," says Séraphin. "It is. I threw Jasmyn off me, so quickly she hit the wall next to my bed."

Once more the table laughs long and hard. "My mom just stood there for a few seconds and then she walked out and closed the door behind her. Jasmyn and I got dressed so fast. You haven't lived until you're trying to get dressed at speed with an erection. It keeps getting in the way. I convinced Jasmyn that she needed to leave and I would deal with whatever fallout came after that. We walked out of my room and down the corridor and into the lounge and, bam, there's my mother, sitting in the lounge."

"Jirre fok!" says Yasseen.

"This is so bad," says James. "So she just sat there?"

"Yep," says Séraphin. "She just sat there. Jasmyn said, 'Good afternoon, Mrs. Turihamwe.' But it made the whole situation worse because my mom hates it when we're addressed by each other's names, so she looked at Jasmyn and said, 'That is not my name, child.' Now I know my mother is seriously pissed off. I walk Jasmyn to the gate and we stand there awkward as fuck, not sure what to say. Then she says, 'I'm going to go home now' and walks away, and I go back in the house to face my mom. Long story short: She called all the fires of damnation upon me. I was cussed out in English, French, and Kinyarwanda. I didn't even know my mother knew such swear words. Eventually, she ran out of steam because I wasn't putting up any resistance. Then she told me she was so disappointed in me. Like only a mother can express disappointment. I think if she could've pressed the undo button on my life she would have. Yoh! I've never heard my mother so wounded."

"She would be, though," says Yasseen. "You were supposed to be studying for a biology exam and instead you were doing home-based practicals. Did you pass the exam?"

"A-plus, my man."

"Did she tell your dad?"

"No, she didn't. I struck a Faustian deal with her."

"What was the deal?"

"That's between me and my mom, fam," says Séraphin, taking a swig of juice.

"Wow, Séra, that's the most messed-up shit I've ever heard," says Andrew. "Shit should be a film."

"Stick around, kid, my life is based on a true story," says Séraphin.

"I don't even want to imagine that happening with either of my parents," says Bianca.

"You know what was the worst part? I had to wait a year before I actually experienced an orgasm. A whole year—can you imagine? And for a long time whenever I was about to come I panicked and looked towards the door just to see if my mom was there." The freshly kindled fires of laughter take a long time to burn themselves low.

"Fuck. I thought I'd heard stories but that's something else," says Richard after a while.

"Right, I think this calls for some kind of toast," says Yasseen. Everyone reaches for a glass.

"To what?" asks Séraphin.

"To remembering to close bedroom doors," says Richard.

"Fuck you guys," says Séraphin, smiling. "Cheers."

The hubbub of the pub stops as a pause button is pressed somewhere. *Whrrrrrr!* Greyish lines flicker on the screen as the tape is rewound. The play button is pressed just in time to bring a lounge in Windhoek West into focus. The camera zooms in on the two people sitting on opposite sides of the room. Therése glares disdainfully at her son; Séraphin absorbs her stare and deflects its withering power around the room by looking distractedly at carefully collected artifacts of their life in Namibia. His calm visage belies the cold dread roosting in his chest.

"Who was that girl?"

Séraphin sucks at his saliva glands before he says, "That lovely lady was Jasmyn."

Therése's eyes narrow and her head rotates a little so that her ears are better tuned to detect Séraphin's insolence. "Séraphin, you will not speak to me like that."

Therése's tone corrodes the air around her. Séraphin sits still in his seat.

"Jasmyn," Therése says to herself after another minute slinks by with its tail between its legs. "In my house, Séraphin? In my house with a girl who doesn't even know our names. This girl doesn't even know who we are, where we come from. Look at me."

Séraphin faces his mother.

"I will say what I have to say and you will listen, Séraphin. For once you will listen. You will not bring your bad manners to this house anymore. Not in my house where I have given up my life to raise you and your brothers. You constantly tell me I am old-fashioned. You can say that about an old dress. But you will never say that to me or your father as long as you live in this house. We are old and our rules and ways mean nothing to you. That is why you carry on with these sneak-thief activities with this Jasmyn person the day before a serious exam. No! I will not allow this. I can understand you are growing and changing. But I am telling you that you need to think about how you grow and how you change. If it is not good for the household, leave it outside. Séraphin, look at me. In my house there is only one man. If you think you are a man, then you must make your own home and be a man there. But you know you are a child, Séraphin. The purpose of children is to be raised. You have a year left in this house before you go to university. In that year you will be raised. I do not want to hear arguments between you and your father. I do not want to see you fighting with Yves or Éric. You can complain in your bed. You can complain outside. But you will not complain where anyone in this house can hear you. You have tried to be a man in my house, Séraphin, and you have failed. So you will be a child. My child. Turihamwe?"

It is not every day when the power imbued in Rwandan names makes itself felt. It is, however, quite clear to Séraphin that his mother is doing more than just calling out his name.

Turihamwe?

Are we together, Séraphin?

Séraphin feels his being summoned to the fore, stretching out before him like a lake. Hitherto he was convinced he would wade into its waters with graceful certainty. But now, seeing its vastness, he is scared. He looks at his mother. In her he sees a similar vastness, tamed by a power he did not realize she had. Séraphin bows his head.

"*Turihamwe*," he says.

His mother sighs.

It is a start, a small one, but a start nonetheless.

VIII

For the most part, the past is right where it belongs: in the past. It is where choices make sense, where mistakes are sometimes forgiven. The past is certain and settled, even if human beings are not. They constantly sift through words, deeds, and bones to try to explain today or predict tomorrow, all the while forgetting the universe's secret joke: there is no tomorrow, for it has already come.

The pull of the past is to be avoided for the present, where Séraphin, after returning from the shops with boxes of fruit juice, is conscripted by Therése to complete a cornucopia of chores. Coated with the sweat of industry, Séraphin retreats internally to his Department of Dealing with Shit, a chaotic, cavernous hall filled with the chatter of a hundred thousand Séraphins.

There are five of them huddled around one Séraphin, who has the rest nodding along to his argument that they must engineer a situation in which they can meet with Jasmyn now that they have her number.

"I say," says pro-Jasmyn Séraphin, "we call it. That's why she gave it to us, right? She expects us to call."

Another Séraphin interjects. "Shouldn't we wait a little? Three-day rule and all that."

The other Séraphins look at him in disbelief.

"You're wasting your time playing it cool with hot girls."

"This is the call-up, Séra. Like when the apprentice leaves the monastery and comes back years later to face the master."

"Ey, yo, Séra, I figured out what we should do after graduation. I say we take a year off and just figure shit out, you know?"

"Yo, this new playlist is fire on flames. It's called *Hi-fidelity Infidelity*, get it? It's all R&B shit. Then there's this one: *The Golden Age of Worry*. It's all angsty and confusion, but with a positive undertone. Really made for the times, you know."

Séraphin pushes through the crowd of thoughts, pausing to sign off on playlist ideas and promising to think about taking time off after graduation. The Call Jasmyn Action Group surrounds him and peppers him with their interests, drowning out everything else.

"Okay, fine," Séraphin says. "I'll call her." The room erupts in applause and cheers. "But not tonight," he adds quickly before the ideas start getting ahead of themselves.

After Éric finished frying the chips, he was told to start grating carrots for a soup; Yves sweated as he banked down coals and prepared to roast meat on the braai outside; Séraphin sliced cucumbers, tomatoes, and onions, and shredded lettuce leaves for a salad that would be pillaged for its olives and feta. When Therése began pulling out the ingredients for a mountainous potato salad, Séraphin was forced to peel and cut potatoes. Eventually, he found a reasonable excuse to go and help Yves. His brother stood next to the brick-and-concrete fireplace built into the back wall, spearing and turning meat with a pair of tongs, trying to stay out of the smoke.

"Did you bring juice?" Yves asked.

"Nah, sorry. But I can get you something if you want."

"It's fine. I'm nearly done anyway."

"What's left?"

"The chicken." Yves tossed his head towards oven trays stacked with the roasted and basted goodness of his labor. The beefsteaks and lamb cutlets looked dark brown and one or two were a bit burnt. The pork chops were bronzed to perfection. Séraphin walked over and scanned them for the smallest, pulling it out.

"God bless swine," said Séraphin. He took a bite from the chop before handing it to Yves. "Pass me the tongs, I'll do the chicken."

Yves gratefully stepped out of the smoke and took the proffered chop. "Gonna be a long night," he said, picking his way around the bone.

"I swear the older these people get, the harder they party," Séraphin said. The tongs darted into the fireplace, picking and flipping chicken at speed.

Yves finished cleaning the meat off the bone and sucked on it out of boredom. "So, Séraphin, there will be questions tonight."

Séraphin turned to face Yves. "Bro, tonight all of the Agent Smiths in the world could fire their questions at me and they wouldn't hit me. What do you plan on doing after you graduate—I'm thinking of a master's degree. Whoosh. Oh? In what—commercial law, maybe, it's a big field. Whoosh. And then you will become a lawyer, no? Lawyers make big money in Namibia—Yes, uncle, they make a lot of money. Whoosh. Oh, we will be so proud and your parents too—Yes, I'm certain they will be. Whoosh."

"Good luck with that." Yves looked at his brother in silence for a while. "Seriously, though, what do you plan on doing after you graduate?"

"I don't know, man. All of my applications for work in Cape Town law firms were rejected."

"And here?"

"I haven't tried for anything here."

"Why?"

"Well, the purpose of home is to be left."

"Hmm," Yves said.

Too late Séraphin realized what he had said and began to apologize. "You know I didn't mean it like that, Yves."

"I know, Séra. You often don't mean things the way you say them."

Séraphin turned back to the chicken. In his first few years away he would return home full of stories for his younger brothers—cafés that catered to epicurean whims; attractive women who did not let skin color stand in the way of a good romance; parties that left the body depleted and the mind scrambled. He would enjoy being the center of attention, the caveman bringing home fire. But what began as storytelling strayed too close to bragging, and soon Yves and Éric stopped looking forward to hearing about what they were missing out on.

"Anyway," Yves said, breaking the somber pall, "the only real justice in the world is that you'll get nailed by at least one of the questions you'll have to answer tonight. You aren't that slick, Séra."

"You're probably right." Séraphin started tossing the cooked chicken pieces into a serving bowl. He pulled off the last drumstick and took a bite. The sweet, tangy, and herby flavors brought a satisfied moan out of him. "God, I'm good," he said. He passed the drumstick to Yves.

"How many people do you think will come?" Yves asked.

"Honestly, I don't know. Let's take this shit inside. The mosquitoes are already out."

"Which playlist are we going with?"

"I'm thinking about premiering *The Department of Native Affairs*."

"Sounds promising."

"All the African jams we grew up with, man. Jeff Maluleke, Brenda Fassie, Wes, Salif Keita, and Papa Wemba."

"Lucky Dube?"

"But of course, brother."

"The old folks'll love that. They're going to dance hard. If they aren't too drunk."

"Like that'll stop them," Séraphin said.

IX

A gathering of Rwandans in exile—also known as a sigh of Rwandans—always winds up being more than the reason for the meeting in the first place. Be it a Sunday lunch after church, the graduation party of a daughter, or a New Year's fête, nothing stops the recent buds of exiled life from calling to forgotten roots in a faraway land. Food and drink allow the shared language of struggle to find voice in roundtable discussions. At such events, the animated voices of those who have lived and lost paint the night with tales of woe, injustice, stolen land, missing relatives, and lucky escapes, then trail into silence as the narrator is lost to suppressed memories of terror; fearful crouching next to small black Sanyo radios, listening to scrambled news reports, hoping for aid, and praying for foreign intervention.

But first come the greetings—hugs, cheeks kissing each other once on each side—and then the complaints. The heat is cursed as newspapers are used to fan sweaty foreheads; the sporadic rainfall is bemoaned; and the price of food is a mortal wound felt by all. Last come the problems of child-rearing in the city.

"But these children are growing wild in this country. Just last week Fabrice was watching a video on television with nothing in it but buttocks! When I turned it off he was angry with me. These things would not happen in Rwanda, I'm telling you!" a mother's voice will say.

"You must be firm and vigilant," says another voice. "These Namibian children drink and smoke from an early age, you know. I have seen them. God must help me if my children pick up these habits."

The irony of their Namibian-born children learning, speaking, and dreaming in English while surrounded by the trappings and aspirations of Namibian life totally eludes them. They are convinced they are still Rwandan and that if they but exercise moral fortitude—restricting television-watching hours to two or three a day—they will stem the tide of cultural change. They pray and fast so as to gain understanding about the most recent phenomenon they have encountered in their teenage children's lives: the sleepover.

"I have heard that they go to someone's house and watch movies, and eat, and dance, and then they sleep over."

"But if that is all that they do, why do they need to go outside to do it?"

"It sounds like an opportunity for smoking and drinking. And that is not even the worst, I hear. They could even be engaging in sex."

The other assembled voices gasp.

"It is not easy to have children in Namibia, I am telling you," says the first voice. All of the other voices nod their agreement. The simultaneous sigh of the mothers registers a solid four on the Richter scale.

These people are not extraordinary. They are not strange. They are immigrants. They change the channel when a Hollywood lens attempts to capture what they have lost. Naught but their collective recollections can comprehend what photographs of mass graves and long lines of fleeing families desperately try to articulate. They are kings and queens without their kingdoms, stripped of their former finery; promising academics, businessmen, farmers, and budding politicians brought low, grateful to serve in any way they can in their new country of refuge as teachers, lecturers, entry-level and underpaid administrators who are preternaturally punctual at work, never take leave, and accept extra duties and the prejudices of their colleagues without complaints. Their determined labor has been purchased at the low price of distant disaster and their futures have been auctioned to the wind.

These are refugees.

Guillome and Therése's lounge is full of politicking, goading laughter, and the resurrection of oft-told stories. In the dining room are bowls of isombe soup, which will evaporate as soon as the call for supper is made; trays of samosas, which have already had their numbers reduced by marauding hands; and mandazi, brown and golden, fried to perfection. There are salads of varying chlorophyll concentrations and oven trays holding sponge cakes. When each guest arrives, they ring the front doorbell, prompting Séraphin to go and open it for them. He observes the code of greeting—right hand, clasped by his left for the parents—and allows himself to be pulled into bosom-squashing hugs by the women.

"Séraphin, you have grown so big! Bite? Amakuru ki?"

He replies in hesitant Kinyarwanda that all is well. His responses draw laughter from the guests, who remark that his Kinyarwanda is good.

"Please, come in," he says after a few seconds of polite smiling.

Some guests have children, most of them in their late teens or early twenties, dressed in fashions straight from the television. Snapback caps, tight jeans, and luminescent sneakers with garish colors for the boys and simple jeans accompanied by T-shirts or blouses for the girls, betraying the interference of mothers. They greet Séraphin in a complex code of fist bumps, clasped hands, and finger snapping.

"What up, Séra? All good?" Angelo asks, strolling with bowlegs to prevent his jeans from falling off. His younger sister Beata stares at her cell phone, throwing Séraphin a disinterested greeting.

"All good, man," Séraphin replies. "But, Angelo, your pants are a problem. This place is too old for the new school. Best to pull them up."

Angelo shrugs. "Nah, I ain't going to be forced to be here in the way they want, you feel me?"

"For sure," Séraphin replies, "but it's only for a couple of hours. You know how these folks are."

"Ait, I feel you, fam."

Angelo's family is followed by Credence, Clement, and Valentin's. The three boys are a year apart and bristle with deviousness. Credence, at twenty-three, is a year younger than Séraphin, the eldest child in the Rwandan community.

"What up, Creed?" Séraphin says.

"Yo," Credence says, "you still ballin'?"

"When I can."

"Yeah? A couple of us jam over at the university on Sundays. You should come through."

"When you start playing real basketball I might show up."

"Smart guy, huh?"

Credence, Clement, Valentin, and Séraphin share a laugh before Séraphin ushers them into the house along with their parents, Olivier and Marie Chantal.

Next to knock is Uwimana, a dainty and shy girl flanked by her serious and frowning parents; then a family that pulls up to the house in a gigantic four-wheel drive, new and glossy and destined to never see a dirt road in its life. The impressive hulk of horsepower is diminished by the short family who step out of it: a bald man with owlish glasses, a kindly woman whose hair is flecked with so much grey she has lost the desire to keep fighting it.

A long black Mercedes-Benz pulls up to the gate, a little late. The family that climbs out of it is impressive, even if Séraphin would never admit as much under congressional interrogation. The father, Espoir, is even taller than Séraphin, Yves, and Guillome, and his shoulders are strong. His face is smooth and clean-shaven and his hair is regally streaked with grey. His wife, Claudine, is slim and endowed with feminine features that press into Séraphin's psyche. Their son, Thierry, is just a little bit taller than Séraphin, a tad more muscular, and at least five shades lighter, as though his sensitive skin professed an allergy to melanin at his birth. When Séraphin opens the gate for them, Espoir shakes his hand firmly.

"It has been a long time, Séra, no?" Espoir says.

"Yes, it has," Séraphin replies softly.

"How is the family?" Claudine asks. Séraphin notices the glances she throws at their house and front yard, taking in the thirsty plants and the corners where the paint has chipped.

"They're well," he replies.

"That is good to hear," Claudine says. "You know Thierry? The last time you would have seen him the two of you would have been small."

"Yes," Séraphin says, squaring to face the lighter version of himself. "I do."

The two young men shake hands, squeezing in strength instead of friendship. Séraphin notes the expensive white Jordans matched against his own generic swooshed sneakers and feels his footwear being dunked on. The squeezing hands separate.

"Well, Séra, will you show us in?" Espoir asks in a voice that irritates Séraphin because of its power to make him jump to attend to its request.

"Of course. Everyone's inside except Papa. He had to do something at work, but he'll be home soon," Séraphin says.

"Working? On New Year's Eve?" Claudine asks. Her penciled eyebrows do a poor job of masking her pity.

"Yes," Séraphin continues, "if there's work to be done, he does it."

Quickly, to dilute this profusion of privilege, Séraphin leads them into the parliament of the past which has convened in the lounge.

"*Mais*, but they do not want to learn, these children," said Angelo's father, Adrien. He used to work in a bank in Kigali. His wife, Sonia, was a nurse. Had life but plodded along in the way they'd expected it to, they would have raised a comfortable middle-class family that wanted for nothing. Instead, history hiccupped, a presidential plane was shot down just outside Kigali, killing the presidents of two neighboring countries, and their slow and steady ascension through the strata of Rwandan life was permanently derailed. Adrien and Sonia found themselves fleeing the capital city with nothing but their infant son and a briefcase containing Adrien's financial management degrees, some of Sonia's nursing certificates, and a handful of Rwandan francs, just enough to allow them to cross into Mobutu's Zaïre and then, through crafty means, to board a flight from Kinshasa to Dar es Salaam in Tanzania. For three years, Adrien worked as a freelance bookkeeper to pay the rent while Sonia kept the lights on and the table set by working as an unregistered midwife. When Sonia fell pregnant with Beata, she swelled with more than just the child; she felt as though she was carrying the seed of providence, growing heavy and expectant for circumstances beyond the constrained life they lived in Dar es Salaam.

Guillome had written to Adrien and told him of a place with a slow pace, good schools, decent pay for anyone who had a college degree, and a sympathetic attitude towards foreigners if they could contribute. Adrien and Sonia had packed their home into four suitcases and migrated to the freshly liberated country in southwestern Africa. Adrien found work as an accounting lecturer and Sonia contented herself with volunteering at Roman Catholic orphanages. Adrien's once industrious and ambitious life slowed down; it became a metronomic routine of marking and grading papers. He would shake his head sadly at the students who failed his subject, the vanguard of an incompetent and poorly qualified generation that would be responsible for the country's overhyped economic future. "I do not understand why they do not study," he would say to his wife after a few hours of scratching angry red crosses on poorly answered scripts. "They take everything for granted, these students. But maybe real peace allows mediocrity to prosper."

In the lounge, Séraphin had commenced his precarious dance with prodding questions.

"So what is next, Séraphin? You are finishing next year, no?" Adrien asked.

"Yes, I am," he replied. One out of two, a decent rebuttal.

"That is good. Your parents will be so happy."

"Yes, I am sure they will," Séraphin said cheerily, pouring beer for Adrien.

"And then you will come back to do your articles here?" Adrien asked. A direct question, but not sharp enough to pin Séraphin.

"That is one of the options."

Adrien nodded as he reached for his beer. "What else would you like to do? You have always been a bright boy, not like Angelo. You know what he wants to become? A music producer."

Sonia threw Adrien a vicious look and as Adrien began to mollify his wife for his impropriety Séraphin knew he had dodged the first of many probing inquiries.

As each family had arrived in the jumble of hugging and cheek-butting, children had nimbly taken shelter in the television room, where they could engage in topics more to their tastes. Olivier and Marie Chantal watched their three boys flee the lounge and follow in Angelo and Beata's wake. They sat across from Adrien and Sonia.

Séraphin excused himself and went to the kitchen to prepare a fresh tray of drinks.

But for the accident of history, Olivier and Marie Chantal would probably have owned their own house with a big yard. Olivier had studied chemistry in Paris, returning to Rwanda to take part in the empire-building days of his country. Marie Chantal had worked as a legal secretary. In the present day, Olivier's life was as stable as the noble gases his university students could not identify. Marie Chantal, occasionally, would work as temporary office administrator for the Namibian branch of the United Nations Development Programme. When her family had first arrived in the country she had been called regularly to fill in for younger receptionists who vanished from their posts without notice. Marie Chantal expended the entirety of her expertise answering telephone calls, taking down meeting minutes in neat and extinct shorthand, and typing documents at a speed that awed her colleagues. Despite her attempts to make herself an asset to the office, it became clear there was no forthcoming permanent appointment. Eventually the work dried up.

"The last email from the director said: 'Unfortunately, we cannot continue to engage you on a temporary basis. We have to give preference to local candidates. Otherwise, we could wind up in trouble for hiring foreigners. I hope you can understand our delicate situation,'" Marie Chantal quoted. "I am told I am old, but then I read newspapers and people complain about young people not being dedicated to their jobs or having the skills. What is that?"

"It is how it is here," Therése said. "The jobs are there, but these young Namibians are too proud to do them. They want to jump from the classroom to the chief executive's desk. But if people like us work, then we are stealing jobs."

"But then what must happen? We can work, we want to work. So we must sit and do what?"

"You must wait," Therése said. "It is what we do. We are The Waiting."

Some of them were waiting for their children's acceptance to universities in South Africa. Some were waiting for contract extensions or renewals. Some were waiting for their refugee status to be reaffirmed. Others yet were waiting for news from Rwanda, where uncles, aunts, brothers, sisters, and cousins were still missing.

Everyone sighed.

"But what of the teaching, Olivier? Akazi karagenda?" Therése asked, pushing back the silence for a minute.

"Ah," Olivier began, wiping a froth moustache from his face after a satisfied sip of beer, "teaching here is a tragedy. The students do not work at all and the teachers are blamed. I do not know why these students fail so badly. They have everything here. Running water, electricity, transport."

"We had to wake up and get water and wood before we could even go to school. But here, they wake up to tea and cereal. With sugar, even," said Sonia.

"Things were different then," said Adrien. "We knew the consequences of failure. We knew we had to leave the village."

"This is true," said Olivier. "We knew we had to stand on our own."

"Namibia is a young country," said Therése. "Things are still going right. Most people are eating, so most people are not hungry. And because most people are not hungry, they are not angry. The country lives in South Africa's shadow and in its favor. Have you seen Independence Avenue? Crowded with South African businesses. Do you think there are Namibian businesses in South Africa? If things go bad in South Africa, then maybe we will see how the country responds."

"*C'est ça*," said Olivier. "But there are too few Namibians to grow this country. And what do they do? Scare away the foreigners."

"They say we are taking all of their jobs. But the Namibians are leaving for South Africa or not coming back from university," said Sonia. Everyone nodded. "Have you seen the newspapers? They want to stop foreigners buying land now."

"When they say 'foreigners' they mean black Africans," said Adrien. "But black Africans don't own land here in Namibia. All of the land is owned by South African whites. We barely own our own homes in poor suburbs."

"Always blame the black foreigners," said Therése. "That is how it is in Africa. If you are German or British or French or Portuguese, you are an expat. Blacks are foreigners, or refugees, or aliens."

"We should have moved to America," said Sonia. "Everyone who fled there is a citizen now. But even getting the permanent residence papers is hard here."

The doorbell rang, taking Séraphin to the front door. A minute later, he ushered Uwimana's family into the lounge. Her parents,

Eugene and Immaculée, took seats in the two remaining armchairs and Uwimana made a beeline for the television room. Séraphin went back to the kitchen to prepare yet another tray of drinks.

Eugene and Immaculée could have become minor land barons in Rwanda. Their families had vast tracts of farmland in the south of the country near the Burundi border. But one cannot take land across the border into Tanzania under cover of darkness, paying bribes here and there in Rwandan francs and U.S. dollars, praying the convoy is not ambushed by gangs of ethnically motivated ill-doers. Eugene and Immaculée went from landowners in Rwanda to lessees in Tanzania and, eventually, Namibia. Their matchbox apartment never ceased to elicit painful pangs at the memory of their airy house with endless banana plantations surrounding it. Eugene held a minor post as a technician in the Ministry of Information and Broadcasting while Immaculée, like many Rwandan wives, was forced into housewifery.

César and Solange were the next to arrive, the subjects of numerous jokes about owning a four-by-four that had never seen a dirt track in its life. They had been abroad when the bloodletting started in their country and had considered it imprudent to go home. Luckily for them, Namibia was hungry for engineers and César's services secured him a work permit. In the lounge César and Solange were accommodated on the first round of garden chairs. Solange was reserved while César was animated, full of stories of road-building irregularities and angry contractors as Chinese companies chewed into profit margins in the construction industry.

"*Mais*, these Chinese have everyone running scared," he said. "The cost of a project will be, what, forty million? The Chinese will say they can do it for twenty. Who does the client go for? The Chinese work every day, only pausing for their new year. Nobody is talking about all of the local firms that are suffering. It is a massacre."

"We all know how it goes," said Olivier. "First you have colonialism, which comes with slavery. Then you have liberation and independence. After that comes forgiveness and then development money.

With that comes the race to the top. Then you have two types of citizens: the Havefricans and those who are not. Then what happens? We all know here."

The doorbell chimed again. On his way to open the gate, Séraphin ran through the guest list in his head. Everyone was here, weren't they? Adrien, Sonia, Angelo, and Beata—remind Angelo to act proper; Olivier and Marie Chantal with Credence, Clement, and Valentin; Eugene and Immaculée—make sure Uwimana is not feeling lonely; César and Solange—the family without children and, therefore, the most secretly pitied. So who could this be?

Espoir, Claudine, and Thierry. Séraphin took a deep breath.

The television room is a large rectangular room with a light brown carpet that spreads out and splashes from corner to corner. It has waist-high shelves containing tightly packed Disney cassettes that have all been watched into photographic memory, and an assortment of TDK tapes containing western, thriller, science fiction, and action films, or WrestleMania and Royal Rumble matches.

It was the most neutral place for a group of Rwandan children too young to engage in the scab-picking of history. Angelo, Beata, Credence, Clement, Valentin, Uwimana, Yves, and Éric squeezed into the couches. Their conversations sparked and sputtered as they struggled to find common ground. Despite their parents' closeness, it was hard for the assembled children to be united by the same bonds of trauma and loss. Yves and Éric did their best to drive conversation but, eventually, fingertips would blaze away at cell phones. Besides the age differences, there were issues of class to contend with. Séraphin, Yves, and Éric were private-school royalty; the rest attended public schools. Though unspoken, the difference made itself felt in cagey conversations about immediate futures.

"How is school, Uwi?" Yves asked. The youngest in the group, at fifteen, Uwimana was also the quietest.

"It's okay," she replied.

"What grade are you in now?"

"Ten."

"I hated grade nine. The maths was hard. I spent too much time playing basketball to take it seriously, though," Yves said, hoping an academic weakness would provide for some sort of conversation.

"Of course," said Credence. "Man, St. Luke's kids always came to play in the newest kicks and we would still wash them when the whistle blew." A small laugh rippled through the group. St. Luke's was known for many things, but athletics was not one of them.

On the television screen, sports highlights from the past year were playing. Rows of Pakistani cricket fans waved their hard hats in a stadium. Panting cyclists labored up the Alpe d'Huez. A muscular black woman smacked a tennis ball, which blurred with speed as it bounced past the reach of a hapless pale-skinned woman. The woman turned to the crowd, biceps curled, veins popping against her dark skin as the victory unleashed a primal roar into the manicured Wimbledon grounds.

"She looks like a man," Éric said aloud.

"Really? Then why don't you look like her?" said Uwimana.

There was an intake of breath. Faces looked up from flickering screens.

"That was cold," said Credence, clutching his throat.

"Éric, you're going to leave it like that?" asked Angelo. "Ek sal nie los nie! Clap back. And fast."

"Screw you guys," he said in a huff.

"Man, Éric, you're being had, bro!" said Valentin.

Just then the doorbell rang. The group got to their feet, shuffled out of the television room, passing through the dining room and into the lounge, where they greeted each other's parents. When the greetings were concluded, they all trooped back to the television room, this time with Thierry and Séraphin added to their number. Not finding seats, Séraphin grabbed two chairs from the dining room, passing one to Thierry, who placed it on the opposite side of the room so that he and Séraphin sat facing each other. Thierry asked for still water.

"Err, yeah, we have tap water. Would you like ice with it?" said Séraphin.

"I don't drink tap water." Curious eye contact ping-ponged among the rest of the company.

"Well, we don't buy water, so unless you want juice or something, I don't have anything else to offer you," said Séraphin.

"Is it organic?"

"Say what?" said Credence under his breath.

Séraphin ran a hand over his short hair and said, "I don't know. It's juice, man. It comes in a box. The box is recyclable. That's good enough for most of us."

"Grape, then."

"Cool. Be right back." Séraphin walked out of the television room. It took him a while to load a couple of trays with drinks and snacks in plastic bowls that could be passed around. Still water, he thought to himself. When he walked back into the television room he set the trays down on the coffee table and let everyone help themselves.

"This is a blend, yeah?" asked Thierry.

"What?" said Séraphin.

"I mean, this isn't just grape, right? Like, it's mixed with something else?"

"It said grape on the box."

As Séraphin sat down, Yves raised his eyebrows and let his eyes flick at Thierry. Séraphin raised his in response.

"So," Séraphin said, beaming, "what's new, Angelo?"

"The usual," Angelo replied. "School, sweat, and stress."

"How's the music thing going?"

"It ain't easy, man. But I have some new mixes I hope will sell."

"Hopefully not the house nonsense you made last time," said his sister Beata.

"There was a song that was eight minutes long," added Valentin. "And the beat only kicked in after five minutes."

"That mix was fire," said Angelo with a trace of hurt in his voice.

"It was," said Beata. "It burned my eardrums."

"Ouch," said Clement.

"Let's lay off the music thing," Séraphin said. "How're your studies, Creed?"

"Okay. Just hope I can get a scholarship next year so I can study in South Africa."

"Sweet," said Séraphin. "Where're you thinking of applying?"

"Pretoria, Rhodes, Johannesburg, Cape Town—wherever I can get in."

"You're doing chemistry, right?" asked Angelo.

"Yeah," replied Credence. "Third year. It would be cool to do my honors somewhere else, though."

"Pretty sure if your marks are good you'll be able to get something," said Séraphin. "Those places are always looking to make up their diversity quotas. Get the marks and you're in."

"Getting in is okay. It's the fees that kill us."

A series of nods bobbed up and down the room. All of them were studying at the local university so they saw each other on a regular basis, even though they did not hang out or share social circles. Séraphin was the only one who was studying abroad. After Credence's comment he had the good grace to avoid the subject.

"What are you studying, Thierry?" asked Valentin.

"I'm not studying right now."

There was a creasing of foreheads as everyone tried to figure out the real meaning of the answer. Did Thierry mean that he had completed his studies or that he was not studying at all? The former seemed more likely, the latter an impossibility.

"Have you finished, then?" asked Credence.

"No, I started but I stopped. I was doing medicine. I didn't dig it, you know?"

They did not know.

"So what're you doing now?" asked Valentin.

"Taking a gap year," said Thierry. "Actually, more than one. To figure things out, you know? I want to study, but I ain't gonna do it just because people say I should do it. You know?"

"So what d'you do now that you're not studying?" Beata asked. Her phone was lightly clutched in her hand, in danger of being dropped. The majority of her body's resources were dedicated to sifting through Thierry's seemingly impossible answers.

"Travel," Thierry replied. "Did most of Southeast Asia last year, year before that South America, and before that Europe. Did Egypt, Morocco, Uganda, Mozambique, and South Africa. Last place I visited was Cape Town last year."

"Yeah, Séraphin's studying in Cape Town," said Angelo.

"Massively overrated," said Thierry. "I still don't get the hype."

Yves silenced Séraphin with a slight shake of his head.

"You're Rwandan, right?" asked Beata.

"Yes," said Thierry. "But now I am Canadian."

Espoir and Claudine's freshly minted Canadian citizenship distanced them from everyone else in the lounge by several years of declined asylum and refugee immigration programs. Their Canadian passports brought more than easy travel. They brought security in a country where the worst thing that could happen was losing a pop star to America's bright lights. They put genuine maple syrup on nearly everything, supported the Toronto Raptors faithfully, and even took the time to learn the rules of ice hockey so they could cheer for the Maple Leafs. Autumn was fall, jam was jelly, the boot of a car was a trunk, and Espoir called New Year's "a wonderful gig."

Therése had temporarily blanched when she saw them. She forced herself to be hospitable. She embraced Claudine and moved to embrace Espoir, exchanging clipped greetings with him before leading everyone back to the lounge while Séraphin hurried outside to bring two extra chairs in from the yard. Therése felt a sliver of sweet malice as she watched Claudine and Espoir try to settle in the oldest garden chairs in the house. She also felt a bit embarrassed as she watched Claudine's eyes travel around the room, assessing everything before their gazes clanged together.

"It has been so long since we saw each other," Claudine said.

"Ten years," Therése stated flatly.

"How is Guillome? Séraphin told me he was still at work."

"Yes, he is," said Therése, wincing at Séraphin's inability to master the Rwandan art of discretion in the face of family enemies. He had given away their station in life: Guillome was working on New Year's Eve as though he were some underpaid security guard. "He had a few matters to tie up, but he will be home soon."

Séraphin asked Espoir and Claudine what they would have to drink. Both of them asked for juice.

"We don't drink anymore, you know," said Claudine. The rest of the party looked at their drinks without shame, taking sincere sips out of solidarity. "And how are the boys?" she asked Therése.

"*Comme ci, comme ça.* Séraphin will graduate next year whiles Yves completes his honours. Éric will be in his fourth year."

"And where are they studying?" Espoir asked.

"Séraphin is in Cape Town, Yves and Éric are here." Therése's bosom felt hollowed and heavy when she talked about Yves and Éric.

"Soon you will have a house full of graduates."

"We are thankful," said Therése. "Imana yaradufashije." There was a murmuring of agreement at every fortunate part God had played in their present lives. All questions about the capriciousness of his Divine Plan would be kept for later when they were alone. "And what about you?"

Claudine gushed about the Canadian social welfare system and the generous paternity leave that made white men such good fathers. The quaint French settlements in Quebec, she said, were her favorite places to visit and in the holidays she enjoyed skiing. Therése, Sonia, Solange, and Marie Chantal noted the subtle emphasis placed on the plural: *the holidays*. Unlike them, she did not speak of *a* holiday, an event which happened once every so often. No, Claudine had traveled to so many places, checked into so many four- and five-star hotels in so many countries, she had forgotten each individual place she had visited. She spoke in geographic swathes: "Northern Europe was exquisite, much better than Eastern Europe. Still, it is worth seeing. Latin America is a place you *must* visit."

Out of foreign world to travel, Claudine and Espoir had even visited Africa. It was a novel experience for present company to hear of their continent spoken of in such detached terms. "West and East Africa were too loud," Claudine said, "too busy and too dirty." Southern Africa, the couple agreed, was just hot and dirty. "But Namibia is clean," added Claudine.

"Yes." Therése said it with a bite in her voice. "It is always good to travel to places near and far to find them clean. What could be more important for an adventure?" Therése was glad Séraphin was out of the room or her hypocrisy would have been held against her for a month at least. She tried to make up for it by asking how Thierry was doing.

"He is fine," said Espoir. "He is taking a bit of a break from his studies at the moment."

"He is not studying?" Therése asked. A single eyebrow rose, just slightly. The thrust in her question could not be hidden from the rest of the party, who held their breath at this unimaginable shortcoming in the otherwise unblemished life of Canadian Rwandans. At least all of their children were studying. Even Angelo.

"Not at the moment," said Claudine. "He was doing medicine but he stopped it."

"Temporarily," added Espoir.

Therése and the rest of the party sipped their drinks to cover their small smiles. So the son had found medicine too hard. "What is he doing now?"

"He is traveling, trying to see as much of the world as he can," said Claudine. Then, turning to her husband, "How long has he been abroad now, Espoir?"

"Three years," Espoir replied.

"Yes, he has such wonderful and funny stories about his travels," said Claudine. "We keep telling him he should write about them."

Therése felt her attack being parried. That Thierry could have a respite from responsibility for so long spoke of a level of privilege that existed only in films. Her throat closed with emotion as she thought of Thierry traveling and writing without a care in the world. What would her children do with those kinds of opportunities?

Séraphin came back into the lounge to see if anyone's drinks needed replenishing. Claudine asked him how his studies were progressing.

"They're fine," he said. "Next year will be my final year."

"And then what will you do, Séra?"

Séraphin was about to throw a distraction their way before he noticed how attentively everyone was watching him. Adrien and Sonia, Olivier and Marie Chantal, Eugene and Immaculée, and César and Solange: they all gazed at him with expectation. He looked at Therése, whose eyes also shone with some sort of eagerness. He was being penned in.

"Um—" he began before Adrien cut him off.

"Master's degree, no? And then articles here in Windhoek."

"That is good," said César. "Very good. Lawyers are valued here."

"At least we can sleep knowing that we will have one of our own representing us if the need arises," said Marie Chantal.

"Of course. The salaries these lawyers have here in Namibia are ridiculous," said Eugene. "Séraphin, that is what you must look at. Commercial law. Avoid human rights work—human rights do not pay the bills."

"Séraphin will be brilliant at that," said Sonia. "We will come to court to see you in action, eh?"

"Tuzaba turihamwe," Adrien said. "We shall be together." Séraphin felt the core of his being vibrate. They all looked towards him in optimism. He looked at his mother, whose eyes beseeched him to accede to the future being mapped in front of him.

Turihamwe, no?

He felt his stomach tighten in bitterness before he marched a smile onto his face and said, "Of course."

Everyone sat back in their seats and smiled, happy to know that at least one aspect of the future was decided. The first generation of their community's graduates would come into the world soon. And who better to lead it than Séraphin Turihamwe, all-conquering hero of studies home and abroad.

Who better indeed?

X

Foreigners have no business being underqualified or underperforming, so Guillome diligently collected certificates or diplomas in business administration or international drug procurement and distribution each year. He did this so that every two years, when his contract was up for review with the Ministry of Health and Social Services, he filed a thick dossier of recent qualifications which, coupled with his years of service in the department of drug procurement, distanced him from any clauses in national employment policies which stated that a local was to be preferred in the event similar qualifications were held by a foreign applicant. The reviewing committee would open his reapplication, flip through each degree and leaf through the neatly typed curriculum vitae before signing his reappointment, giving Guillome another two years of stability to work more than he should for less than he was worth.

Not once had he ever been late for work. His leave days accumulated like forgotten pennies in a glass jar. He smiled at everyone, at every task shirked by his colleagues which wound up, inevitably, and with deadlines looming, on his organized desk. At first his tireless work ethic was viewed with suspicion, forcing the rest of the department to pedal faster just to keep up. Eventually, though, they became conscious that the race was rigged and they allowed the pace to slacken. Guillome became the workhorse of a sluggish peloton.

He rarely participated in meetings, choosing to remain mute and observant. After such meetings, he would walk back to his desk and wait for an email from the top brass stating what needed to be done. He would then find some way to complete the tasks while attributing all glory to his immediate superiors, who would present his work to their bosses.

Once, one of his superiors blundered into one of Guillome's reports without bothering to acquaint himself with the territory of the subject matter. Without any trace of shame, he said, "Pause for effect here." The rest of the conference room looked at their notes in embarrassment. Everyone knew Guillome's work was being peddled under false authorship. What made everyone sheepish was the violation of their agreement to appear as though they knew what they were talking about in front of their superiors. A few minutes after the presentation an angry email plopped into Guillome's inbox:

Next time don't embarrass me like that. I want reports two days early so I can read over them. And I want you there for them too.

Guillome's past ambitions were well behind him. He rose each morning prepared to spend a day with his two mistresses: duty and deference.

It was duty that required him to spend New Year's Eve in his cubicle, typing a ministerial review of the national antiretroviral rollout program at speed. Deference made him use a template cover page, which attributed authorship to someone who had not woken up early to compile it. The report, in a meritocratic world, would have been submitted to his superiors a week ago. However, the approaching year's end presaged office talk of farming projects, holidays by the seaside, or shopping trips to Cape Town. Such was the urgency and importance of their holiday plans that the colleagues to whom the report had been tasked had not even bothered to compile a basic abstract for the submission. It thus fell to Guillome, the only person who owned no farm to work, who seemingly had no family to go home to or had any desire to take a break of some sort, to come to the office and spend the last day of the year writing the report and then personally delivering the finished manuscript to the minister's house.

Guillome's broad shoulders slumped as he hunkered down to his keyboard. He ploughed ahead, paragraph by paragraph, until half past nine. Guillome printed the manuscript and then bound it before driving through Windhoek's ghostly city center to the minister's house.

Guillome approached the dumpy hut outside the property's iron gates, where the guard sitting inside slowly eased his bulk off a plastic chair and cast him a disinterested look. He asked Guillome if he was a guest.

"No, I am here to deliver a report for the minister," said Guillome.

"The minister is busy inside. Just wait, I will call. Someone will come," said the guard. He reached for his walkie-talkie and pressed a button, summoning noisy static. Guillome waited while the man spoke into the receiver in Oshiwambo; he caught a few words: "O-minister" and "deliver o-report-a." After some more static the guard said to Guillome, "Just wait here, neh," and slumped back down in his seat. Guillome took a couple of paces then stood facing the street, the report tucked under one arm. A little further away was a black Mitsubishi Pajero. He admired its angular frame, its unassuming presence, and thanked the Japanese for making cars that did not break down when you had to evacuate your family from a capital city on fire.

"You are from which tribe?"

"Sorry?" Guillome's mind had wandered far from the smooth tarred road to a rutted one, both sides viscous with worried faces lugging wooden carts carrying children and scant possessions, straight necks and stiff heads balancing bundles of clothes or basins of whatever worldly goods were deemed essential for survival. The long, anxious drive in the Pajero, Therése clutching his left hand as he carefully navigated the pitted roads. In the back seat, asleep next to each other,

Yves and Éric were totally oblivious to what was unfolding around them. Séraphin sat quietly, looking out of the windows in curiosity. He made eye contact with two boys about his age as Guillome squeezed past. The boys were in a wheelbarrow pushed by a determined man with a frown on his face. They looked at each other, their fates separated by the car window before Guillome angled further away from the creeping terror behind.

"You are which tribe?" the guard repeated.

"I am Rwandan," Guillome said.

"Near Kenya?"

"Yes," replied Guillome, impressed that a country smaller than many of Namibia's regions could make it into this security guard's general knowledge.

"That is far," the guard said. Guillome nodded. "You are which tribe? Hutu or Tutsi?"

Guillome hesitated. Then he said, "Hutu."

"O-ho. You are the ones who did the killing. Or you are the ones who did the dying?"

Guillome looked at the guard balefully, an intake of breath swelling his chest and audibly issuing from his nostrils. "Everyone," he said, "did a bit of both."

The guard sucked his teeth and gazed out at the quiet street. Guillome looked at his watch.

"You are refugee," the guard said. It came out as a statement of fact.

Guillome breathed in deeply. "No," he said. "I am a permanent resident here in Namibia."

"But you are from Rwanda?"

"Yes."

"Then you are refugee."

The guard took his silence as an invitation. "All of us, we are refugee." He chuckled. "If you are not white, you are refugee. If you are white, then you are not refugee. You know how I know we are all refugee?" Guillome raised his eyebrows in inquiry. "Because we are not home. Everyone that is not home is refugee. Even me, I am refugee. I am not home. I am here." He waved his hand at the warm night air. "This is not home. So I am refugee."

Guillome decided to be taciturn. He never engaged in political discussions with locals. As far as he was concerned, politics was for people who could, in some way, control the fate of their lives. People who could take things, own things, and pass things on. Everyone else, those who lacked the will or the means to do so, just had to keep quiet and work.

"Do you know how to not be refugee?" The guard was undeterred. The man seemed determined to expound some long-held thesis about displaced identities. Guillome raised his eyebrows but made no comment. "Make home. Small home. Big home. But home. I try to make home here." The guard knitted his hands together over the bulk of his belly. "Here, I try."

"Where are you from?" Guillome finally asked.

"The north. I come here for work. Because home is no work. And if home is no work, then you cannot make home. So I come here. Like you. Refugee. I try to make home." The guard inclined his head toward the house. "You are working with the minister?" he asked.

"For," Guillome corrected. "For the minister."

"They live well, these ministers," he said, a sly look passing over the offensive taste in the yard. "They make home."

Just then the wooden door of the mansion opened and a lady in a tight-fitting blue pencil skirt and a white blouse came out. She made her way towards the street, her stilettos clicking on the driveway, a stumble and a sprain a lapse in concentration away.

"You have the report ready?" the woman asked, coming to a precarious halt.

"Yes, madam," said Guillome, handing her his day's work. Although twice her age, he deferred to her position.

"It's late," she said.

"I am sorry. It took some time to put in all of the necessary details and then to edit it. I have also emailed a soft copy to you and cc'd the department head."

"It's late," she said again. "You said you emailed it as well? Then why bother bringing this?"

"I was instructed to bring a copy personally, madam."

"Is there anything else?" she asked stiffly.

"No, madam," he said.

"Then I shall hand this to him tomorrow. I hope he is not angry. It is very late."

The walk back to the house was more labored and Guillome stayed to watch in case there was a fall, some small justice for the aide's rudeness. But there was none. When the last wonky step had vanished inside and the big wooden door had closed, Guillome and the guard exchanged a look.

Guillome shrugged and began to walk to his car.

"Happy New Year," the guard called after him.

Guillome paused. He turned back. "Happy New Year," he said.

By the time Guillome arrived home, all of the assembled guests were eating, the adults in the lounge and the children in the television room.

In the television room everyone was glad for a respite from the freshly revealed smallness of Windhoek life, as confirmed for them by Thierry. They had no tales to offer of travel in faraway places like Bali or waking up on a beach in Ibiza—"Telling you, man, that shit was dope. Ibiza was crazy!" Thierry said "crazy" so that it stretched over four syllables as opposed to its usual two.

Séraphin longed for midnight, which would bring with it the countdown to Cape Town. He planned on having a cra-a-a-azy year—with *five* syllables.

In the lounge, talk of Canadian life came to a halt when Guillome arrived. After putting his head into the television room, greeting the room at large, he took a plate and served himself. Having noted that all of the available seats in the lounge were taken, he toted one of the dining room chairs with him when he went back through. He placed it next to Espoir's garden chair. He smiled politely at Claudine in hers. How many years had it been? Therése would know exactly, but Therése wasn't looking at him.

Espoir's email, which had popped into Guillome's inbox, with its affectations of friendship, had taken him by surprise.

From: espoir.tuhuze@writemail.com
To: rwibonera-nzira.guillome@writemail.com
Subject: Longtemps

Mon ami, it has been too long. My family will be in Namibia in December. Maybe Christmas or New Year's would be a good time, no?

Espoir

Therése had snorted with disgust. "They have no shame. No shame, I tell you. Gui, are you going to invite them here?"

"You know we have to," he had replied. "It wouldn't look good if we turned them away. There would be talk."

"About us not having them over but not about their sneak-thief ways?"

"We must invite them, Therése. Which one will it be? Christmas or New Year's?"

Therése had chosen to storm away, gusting around the house like an avenging, cleaning wind, blowing the boys out of the television room with a look, and sulking herself into a fury that not even the best cooking or gardening shows could soothe. Later, in the brooding darkness of their bedroom, she had given her terse pronouncement.

"New Year's. There will be other people around." Then she had rolled over, turned her back to him, and pretended to be asleep for the rest of the night.

"You had to work tonight? On New Year's Eve even." The sympathy in Claudine's voice would have bedeviled a hungry crocodile.

"Work is work," replied Guillome. "If it has to be done, it has to be done."

"*Mais, c'est la vie ici, non?*" said Adrien. "We work and then work some more."

"It is so hot," said César, passing a hand across his forehead. The night had not cooled with the setting of the sun. The heat lurked around the house like an uninvited guest.

"It would be cold in Canada now, no?" asked Guillome, turning to Espoir. Despite the man's more impressive physique, he seemed diminished beside Guillome, whose personality added bulk to his being. Although quiet and reserved, Guillome commanded respect. The only people who did not fall under his spell, it appeared, were his work colleagues—to them he deliberately cowed—and Séraphin, who seemed immune to most authority.

"Back home it would be freezing," said Espoir.

"Yes," Guillome said. "Back home."

The statement seemed innocent enough but it caused Therése's eyebrows to rise, just a fraction. Was her husband, the diplomat, being sarcastic?

"How is home?" Guillome asked, this time looking straight at Therése, grinning slightly.

"It is busy," said Espoir.

"Are you still working as a pharmacist?"

Espoir wriggled in his chair. "No," he said. "I stopped doing that a while ago."

"Espoir *owns* a pharmacy now," said Claudine proudly. Espoir gave his wife a fleeting smile before turning back to Guillome.

"This is good news," said Guillome, leaning back. "This is what we must strive to do, to start businesses."

"But it is tough here," said César. "Here you need money and some miracles to get started. Then you need to pray you are not sabotaged by envious people."

"It is true," said Marie Chantal. "Namibians do not like working for foreigners."

"You cannot hire foreigners because then people will be angry at you," said Olivier, "and you cannot hire locals because they do not work. And even then," he added ruefully, "you will be the wrong tribe."

Guillome chuckled at the last statement, remembering the guard from the minister's house. "But," he said, "we must try. We must make home here."

Murmurs of agreement went around the circle, followed by a few slow sips of juice and beer.

"How did you get started, Espoir?" asked Eugene. "Even in Canada it cannot have been easy."

Espoir fidgeted, putting his glass of juice down and picking it up again. Everyone was looking at him. "One day I saw an opening at the pharmacy I was working at and I went for it."

"The money was not hard to find?" asked Marie Chantal. "Over here, even if you have a good idea, finance is not easy."

"Espoir worked and saved every day to get the pharmacy," said Claudine. "He never went to bars or spent his money on useless things." She barely noticed the chagrin her comment aroused in the room. "And then God did the rest."

God's generosity was acknowledged by a focused effort on everyone's part to find something interesting to look at. Most turned their attention to their drinks. Guillome and Therése looked at each other and smiled.

"We have been so lucky," Claudine continued. "It is why we wanted to come back and visit. To see if we could help in some way."

Espoir looked at the palms of his hands as though they bore testimony to hardships the others could not see. "*C'est très difficile, ici,*" he said. "But now that we are in Canada we hope that we can help out. I have some contacts now, and if there is something I can do to help, I will." He stopped. No one seemed inclined to fill the silence. "We could even start a Little Rwanda neighborhood like the Chinese with their Chinatowns," Espoir finished.

Guillome and Therése forced the cold engines of politeness to hum into life, permitting a smattering of laughter before the fuel of good humor was exhausted.

"In no time we could all be Canadians, no?"

This time, there was no polite laughter. Everyone remained silent. The pall was broken by Séraphin coming in to see if anyone needed something to drink.

"No, no. I think we are fine, Séra," said Guillome.

"You used to play basketball, Séraphin, no?" asked Espoir. "What position?" The questions came at Séraphin like a fast-break pass. Everyone in the room was glad for a change of topic.

"Yes," Séraphin said. "Shooting guard."

"That is good. Thierry plays basketball too. He is the point guard on his team."

"Cool," said Séraphin. He forced himself to tarry in the lounge a bit longer. It was obvious he was required to be an outlet for tension in the room.

"The point guard is the person who controls the speed of the play," Espoir explained to the rest of the party. "Thierry was quite good in high school too. Do you still play, Séra?"

"I played a lot in high school," Séraphin told him, "but studying takes most of my time these days."

"Of course," said Espoir, nodding. "Was your team good?"

"We made it to three consecutive finals." Séraphin crossed his arms. Everyone looked from father to son and back again, smiling at the resemblance. "We lost all of them, though."

"All of them?" Espoir's forehead creased.

"Yes. To the same school too. The other team had Angolans who didn't understand what age groups were." A rustle of laughter. "We were under-fifteen, -seventeen, and -nineteen. The other team was under-thirty."

The room lit up with good humor. Guillome appreciated how Séraphin could lighten a mood, and cursed how he could darken it at a whim.

"Thierry's high school team was also really good," said Claudine. "They won *their* finals. And his school voted him as the most valuable player."

"Cool," said Séraphin.

"What other sports do you enjoy?" Espoir asked him.

"I only play basketball," Séraphin replied.

"You know your father used to play soccer?" said Adrien. "He was really good."

"Yeah, everyone says that," Séraphin said. His brow rolled itself into puzzlement. "But I am not so sure, you know. Some soccer genes would have been passed on to us. Yves tried for St. Luke's team once."

"And?" prompted Adrien.

"Offensive bench wasn't a real position," said Séraphin.

More laughter.

"And what about the studies?" asked Espoir, changing the subject. "If you ever decide to do your master's abroad, Séra, you must come to Canada. Have you heard of McGill?"

"Yes," replied Séraphin. "Very good university."

"Yes. Thierry was studying there," said Claudine. "It would be lovely if the two of you were there. You could even room together."

"Yeah, sure," said Séraphin.

Séraphin and Thierry's corpses would probably kill each other again if they were forced to share a coffin. He smiled politely and excused himself to set up the sound system outside. When Séraphin cued up Senegalese funk, Cameroonian blues, Congolese rock, Kenyan jazz, South African kwaito, and Nigerian soul to compile *The Depart-*

ment of Native Affairs, he hoped that it would do the trick when it was time to dance. It did not disappoint.

Anyone watching the alcohol-loosened twirling of Rwandan parents with children too cool to dance with them would have remarked upon the nuance of the music and how at the signal of a drumbeat a foot would stamp and at the command of a guitar string a hip would sway. As the New Year's countdown began, glasses were filled with beer, juice, and champagne that had been left to chill in the freezer, and as the year came to an end there was emphatic hugging and back clapping.

"Happy New Year!"

"Bonne Année!"

"Umwaka mwiza!"

The hope and the promise rang out into the air.

Guillome and Therése kissed and hugged. As their bodies pulled close, Therése whispered into Guillome's ear, "I do not want those people to come to this house ever again."

Her husband pulled back from her and said, "I agree."

Thierry's family was the first to depart, just ten or so minutes into the New Year. When Espoir shook hands with Guillome he said, "We should have that talk about what we spoke about a long time ago, eh?"

Guillome said, "I will think about it." He looked around at the dancers, the enthusiastic and the reluctant. "You know, it is not so bad here. We have done well. Better than we could have hoped for. We should learn to let go of things." He turned back to Espoir and said, "Especially the past—it is an unhealthy place to revisit. Those things will poison you."

Espoir looked long at Guillome as the two men stood apart. Eventually, he said, "It is not always like that."

"Maybe," said Guillome. "But sometimes it is like that. And when it is like that it is better to make a new way." He smiled at Espoir. "But we shall speak soon. Mutware neza." The two men shook hands a final time and then Espoir looked for Claudine and Thierry. They were talking to Therése. The two men made their way over.

"Murakoze cyane," Claudine said. "We shall see each other soon."

"Yes," Therése said, "we shall. Maybe here again, maybe somewhere else."

The two couples exchanged hugs once more and then Guillome flagged Séraphin to open the door for them. At the gate, Séraphin shook hands with Espoir and Claudine politely. He offered the hand to Thierry, who held a closed fist instead. Séraphin bumped it with his.

"Good night, Séraphin," Espoir said. "All the best with the studies. We need more lawyers, you know."

"Fewer lawyers," Séraphin said. "Just more people following the law."

"That is also true. Please keep in touch. You never know where there can be opportunities. Well, we must go."

"Yes," Séraphin said, "you must go."

Espoir and Séraphin looked at each other for a while before the elder man walked to his car. Séraphin harrumphed and locked the gate. He went to his bedroom, where he sat on the bed with his cell phone.

Sans_Seraph—HiLos_Of_E: Fools, lords, and lady! Happy New Year! May your unfortunate souls continue to plague this poor world in your own special ways.

JustSayYaz: Mabruk! Have a good one, guys.

AddyWale: God bless! Happy New Year!

RichDick: Happy New Year! No fucking power on this end so this phone is going to die soon!

GodForTheWin: Oan, this Zim life is tough. Power's been out for a span. Anyway, Happy New Year, gents.

BeeEffGee: Happy New Year, friends. Missing all of you morons.

KentTouchThis: Happy New Year from Zanzibar! Cool vibe here.

KimJohnUn: Enjoy @KentTouchThis, that place is dope. We East Africans know how to jam. All the best for the year everyone. See you all soon.

Before Séraphin put his phone away a brand-new message flicked onto the screen.

Wolff_Jazz: Happy New Year!

Sans_Seraph: Happy New Year to you too, Jasmyn. Catch up soon.

Wolff_Jazz: Tomorrow, if you aren't doing anything.

"Whoa!" a Séraphin said.

"Dude," said another.

"It is so on!" said a third.

Séraphin put his cell phone away and went back outside, his spirits bobbing up and down like a buoy at sea. Swept up in the brilliance of his own playlist, he even joined his parents on the dance floor and welcomed whatever uncertainty might be coming his way.

Before this chapter closes something has to be said about the generosity of God. It is often said that the Lord works in mysterious ways, but the wary spiritual auditor will find otherwise. Unbeknownst to Claudine, who believes her husband's acquisition of the pharmacy was down to his sober habits and a favorable interest rate, is a series of emails between Guillome and Espoir from six years ago.

Guillome is contacted by Espoir, who is already living in Canada, asking for financing to start a pharmaceutical company there, which would then acquire medicines and stock the Namibian market. Guillome has the expertise and Espoir has, since his arrival in Canada, been rustling up the necessary contacts to get the venture off the ground. If Guillome can get his family to Canada, Espoir says, the formal registration and incorporation of the company would be hastened and they could work jointly to get the venture going. "Send me your family's particulars and we can start working on your paperwork," Espoir says over a scratchy phone call.

There is, of course, a fee and not a small one. Séraphin will be off to university soon, and while the scholarship their eldest son has been awarded will cover all of his undergraduate tuition, the rest of their savings have been put aside for Yves and, eventually, Éric. It is a risk, but a risk worth taking, they decide.

Canada!

The first world is calling.

So, ten Western Union money transfers make their way across the Atlantic Ocean to Toronto. Espoir sends them emails letting them know the money has been received and that the agents are already hard at work lodging their applications. All that is needed is time.

The months pass.

The emails, once regular, dwindle.

From: rwibonera-nzira.guillome@writemail.com
To: espoir.tuhuze@writemail.com
Subject: Visa Application

Is something wrong?

From: espoir.tuhuze@writemail.com
To: rwibonera-nzira.guillome@writemail.com
Subject: RE: Visa Application

Everything is fine. These things take time. C'est la vie, n'est-pas?

From: rwibonera-nzira.guillome@writemail.com

It has been a while. How is the process going? Is there any other documentation you need?

From: espoir.tuhuze@writemail.com

I have bad news. I went to the Immigration Office to see how far along the application was and they said that nothing was filed in the beginning. I have been contacting the agents and they are not replying. I will send you another email tomorrow.

From: rwibonera-nzira.guillome@writemail.com

This is bad news. I am hoping that something can be done to correct the situation.

From: espoir.tuhuze@writemail.com

My friend, I have tried as much as possible to get in touch with the agents but they are nowhere to be found. I will restart the application process for you.

From: rwibonera-nzira.guillome@writemail.com

The application is not so important anymore. Any news with the money?

From: espoir.tuhuze@writemail.com

I have no news, my friend. I have tried my best but there is nothing.

From: rwibonera-nzira.guillome@writemail.com

I see.

What is unknown to Guillome and Therése is that only seven of the ten payments are given to the agents, who, after receiving their take, vanish. The other three payments remain in Espoir's bank account.

Guillome and Therése smell a swindle but have no way to prove it. For a while they are crestfallen, but then they pull themselves out of their malaise. It was too good to be true. From the Rwandan grapevine they hear that Espoir has acquired a small but lucrative pharmacy in Toronto. But how he did it remains a mystery to most people. God's generosity then grants Espoir's family citizenship. Guillome's family acquires yet another lesson in trust and blind faith.

But only immigrants will understand the ability of a community to treat enemies like friends and cling together even with the possible threat of drowning. Disappointments are swallowed because no disappointment can be as large as leaving or losing home.

Everyone has to stick together. Even the sneaky. Even the sly.

Everyone is part of the family.

And everyone has to be survived.

XI

The earth spun across the finish line of one year in third place, an eternal bronze medalist. Séraphin woke up on the first day of the New Year earlier than he had the entire time he had been in Windhoek. He cleaned up the debris of the previous night's party with verve and energy. *The Ambler* put on its pop-laced shoes and walked through his earphones as he stacked dirty cutlery, crockery, and glassware in the kitchen, running hot water into the sink and attacking the grease. While the rest of the household slept Séraphin scrubbed, rinsed, dried, wiped, and put away the dishes. He rearranged the furniture in the lounge and the television room. He left the unpleasant tasks such as sweeping and mopping the large house for Yves and Éric, who woke up later. The two brothers found Séraphin in the television room. They took seats on the remaining couches.

"Morning," said Séraphin cheerily. His brothers answered with grunts. "I just wanted to let you know that I did the dishes."

"We can see that," said Éric.

"You know what that means, don't you?" said Séraphin.

"Fuck off, Séra." Yves rubbed his eyes and yawned.

"That means I'm off the hook for the rest of the day. You know how Mamma gets after New Year's." Séraphin raised his voice a couple of octaves. "Boys, how can we go into a new year with a dirty house?"

"Early bird gets the worm, huh," said Éric resignedly.

"Fuck the worm, bro, I ate the bird."

After a few minutes of watching replays of explosive firework displays from around the world, Yves asked Séraphin what he planned on doing for the rest of the day.

"Hopefully," Séraphin said, "I'll start the year with a bang."

Wolff_Jazz: Hey.

Séraphin let a minute pass before he replied.

Sans_Seraph: Yo!

About thirty seconds passed before Jasmyn replied.

Wolff_Jazz: What's up?

Sans_Seraph: Not much. A bit tired from last night. You?

Wolff_Jazz: Same. Family party. Always a dramatic affair.

Sans_Seraph: Family is a synonym for drama.

Wolff_Jazz: Funny.

Ding-ding!

The bell for the first round sounded. No committed punches were thrown; the two retreated to their own corners, coaches shouting instructions, cutmen scrutinizing faces for anything that needed patching up, and hype men offering encouragement.

"Let her control the next round," said a Séraphin. "All you gotta do is dance. In the third, you drop her."

Ding-ding!

Wolff_Jazz: So I might've been a bit tipsy last night when I wrote you that second message.

Sans_Seraph: Okay.

Wolff_Jazz: It was actually quite awkward bumping into you, but I am glad I did.

Sans_Seraph: Yeah?

Wolff_Jazz: Yes. Been wondering when I would see you again. You know, with how things ended.

Sans_Seraph: Things didn't end, they just stopped.

Wolff_Jazz: Yeah . . . about that . . . there's a story for that.

"Bob, duck, weave! Don't commit! Move!" screamed another Séraphin.

Wolff_Jazz: Anyway, I wanted to know if you wanted to meet up or something . . .

Sans_Seraph: Is "or something" more interesting than meeting up?

Wolff_Jazz: No.

Sans_Seraph: Meet up then.

Ding-ding!

"Good round! She's going to go for the opening in the third round. She'll swing hard for it. That's when you drop her, y'hear?" said another Séraphin.

Ding-ding!

Wolff_Jazz: Cool. No grand plans for the day?

Sans_Seraph: Pretending to get started on resolutions.

Wolff_Jazz: Wanna hang out?

"Now! Hit her with the old pun-two!"

Sans_Seraph: Like hangman I do.

Wolff_Jazz: Wow. That was bad.

Sans_Seraph: Can't start a year without a bad pun.

Wolff_Jazz: Going to have to take your word for it.

"Nice! Now, counter!"

Wolff_Jazz: Is my place okay?

Sans_Seraph: Sure. Do you still stay with your folks?

Wolff_Jazz: Nope. Small place in Eros.

Sans_Seraph: What time should I come through?

Wolff_Jazz: Whenever you get bored.

Sans_Seraph: That would be now-ish.

Wolff_Jazz: Works for me.

Sans_Seraph: Text me your address and I'll make my way over then.

Wolff_Jazz: Cool. See you soon.

Ding-ding! Ding-ding!

The Super Text-Weight Champion of the World rose from the couch and stretched in victory. He passed Therése in the corridor. She asked him where he was going.

"Just to see a friend. I'm taking the car. And I did the dishes." The bargain had been struck.

"Okay. Be safe."

"But of course," said Séraphin, walking out of the house, a spring in his step, a gleam in his eyes, a jangle of keys twirling around his finger, and a familiar crinkle in his pocket.

St. Luke's Roman Catholic College nestles in the valley of Klein Windhoek, cradled between two small hills which make the setting sun ooze through the school grounds. High-ranking politicians and government officials pay their fees early and contribute generously so their vacuous offspring can attend despite slipping grades. It is where the hardworking immigrant class strives to send promising children to see the trappings of privilege and be motivated to desire and pursue them. This is the school Therése and Guillome decide their boys will attend, even if they must starve themselves to pay the fees.

In the year of Our Lord Jizzos Christs 2006, when we flick back to Séraphin's final months at St. Luke's, the year is nearly at an end. The Great Sulk, as this passage of time will later be known, could not give up its ghost any sooner. An acceptance letter to the finest university in Africa, in the city of Cape Town, is the only thing that brightens a period of self-imposed exile from family life. The pressure of the twelfth grade is a welcome excuse for being scarce around the house. As the seasons change, the mystery of Séraphin's continued silence gnaws at Guillome, Yves, and Éric.

The roots of his silence and his much-changed character are unknown to many except Therése and, as luck would have it, Mr. Caffrey, who managed to pry the answer out of Séraphin one Friday afternoon in October after the Quill Club had disbanded for the week.

"Séraphin, a word, if I may?" he said. He sat on the desk in front of Séraphin, placing his feet on the seat of a chair.

"So?" said Séraphin.

"Er, right." Mr. Caffrey looked for a way to elicit something from Séraphin other than the usual silences. "Right," he said again. "I just wanted to have a chat about your writing, Séra."

"Is something wrong, sir?"

Mr. Caffrey allowed the Quillians to address him by whatever title they deemed fit. Among writers, Mr. Caffrey liked to say, there were no ranks; only those who chose to write and those who did not. The use of "sir" spoke of a guardedness he had noticed in Séraphin throughout the year.

"Nothing at all. I just wanted to have a talk about writing and, er, whatever else came to mind."

"Okay."

Feeling the void opening before him, Mr. Caffrey resisted the urge to fill it as quickly as possible. He gazed around the room before attempting to reengage with Séraphin. "Let me get to it. I have noticed your silences. Everything okay with you?"

"Yes."

"Right." Mr. Caffrey gazed around the classroom. "So what're you going for? The tall, dark, mysterious stranger?"

Séraphin let out a laugh, which helped to defrost the frigidness of their talk. "That sounds like something Éric would try."

"I swear, if he could channel his energy into the right things he would be unstoppable."

"Isn't that what they say about all wasted potential? Look, Mr. Caff, what did you want to talk to me about?"

The use of the more familiar title signified some willingness to engage. "Just the silence, Séra. It shows in your writing too. It's become detached. Like you're studying the world in a petri dish as opposed to being down in the gunk and the ooze of everyday life."

"I, er, hadn't noticed."

"Your last essay submission"—Mr. Caffrey sprang off the desk and walked to his table, opening a drawer and leafing through papers to find the one he was looking for—"was a clear example of what I'm talking about. Here it is. 'The Last Ticket Out of Town.' May I ask why you called it that, Séra?"

Séraphin shuffled in his seat before saying, "It's the name of a playlist, sir."

"Care to elaborate?"

"I make them." Mr. Caffrey's face seemed to demand a better answer. "I make themed playlists. And when you set last week's topic I didn't have any ideas so I named it after that playlist."

"Okay," Mr. Caffrey said. There were stranger ways to find titles for writing submissions. "And this is about leaving Windhoek?"

"Just leaving, I guess," Séraphin replied.

"And going where?"

"Anywhere." Séraphin looked around the classroom and then back at Mr. Caffrey. "Anywhere that isn't here, you know."

"And when you say 'here,' do you mean Windhoek? Or are you speaking about whatever life space you're in at the moment?"

"Is there a difference, sir?"

"A huge one." Mr. Caffrey walked back towards Séraphin's desk. "If it's Windhoek, the situation can be solved quickly. Just leave. If it's a life situation, then leaving isn't the answer. It just provides new coordinates for dealing with the past." Mr. Caffrey took up his seat on the desk once more and scrolled through Séraphin's essay. "I liked reading this. It was funny. At first I figured that it was just youth being bored. I get the feeling there is a larger underlying disappointment here. Am I near the money?"

"Close," said Séraphin.

"Do you want to tell me what motivated this piece, Séra?"

"I just don't feel like I belong here, you know. I don't mean to be arrogant or anything, Mr. Caff. Like, I don't think I'm a big fish in a small pond. I just think I'm in the wrong pond, if that makes sense."

"I can understand that. This isn't the easiest place to be young. Not with everything you're reading or watching telling you and showing you how awesome the rest of the world is. I also felt that way when I was growing up in Nairobi. And that's Nairobi, a big place."

"I thought you were British."

"I am. And I am not. My accent has changed so much over the years, but I'm from Kenya. I only have the one passport too. Not that dual-British-citizen shit everyone else has. Have you ever been to Kenya?"

"My family lived in Nairobi, in Parklands, for a while."

"Ah." Mr. Caffrey seemed to lose himself in thought, then pulled himself into the present. "Anyway, at some point everyone feels at odds with wherever it is they're living. It rains too much. Or the trains are slow. Or the coffee they want isn't available. Or their village is getting the shit bombed out of it. Sooner or later everyone feels like home is a haven for less and they start looking for places of more. When they find it they like it for a while, and then they get bored with it too. Tolerance applies to more than just drugs, you know. So the cycle starts again. That's what I get from this piece, Séra. But that's only one part of it." Séraphin shuffled in his seat but offered no reply. "The other part is either family or a girl." Mr. Caffrey caught Séraphin's gaze for an instant before he looked away. "So which one is it, Séra?"

"Both," said Séraphin in what he hoped was an offhand manner.

"How so?"

"It's weird," Séraphin said.

"Really?" Mr. Caffrey looked at Séraphin in disappointment. "The best you can tell me is that something is weird?"

"Trust me, Mr. Caff," he said.

Mr. Caffrey ran a hand through his hair and then, in a world-weary voice, said, "Nothing is weird, Séraphin. Nothing is bad. Nothing is good either. Everything is just different. Take me, for example. I'm teaching high school English, Séraphin. This isn't what I thought I'd be doing by this time. Sketchy career trajectory; no property; a divorce under my belt; and, still, a long list of things to do before I turn whatever age I must turn in order for things to click together. I thought I would be further than this. Better off too. But I just think of it as different. Whatever weirdness you're going through," Mr. Caffrey continued, "has got nothing on mine. High school English is like serving on the front lines of ignorance. You see some weird shit."

When he stopped talking a hush settled between them, incubating their thoughts. Séraphin's hatched first, poking at the air hesitantly. "Well, er, my mom walked in on me losing my virginity. And she, er, used the incident to blackmail me into silence at home. And, er, the girl I was losing it to stopped talking to me."

Mr. Caffrey snapped out of his musings and fixed Séraphin with an incredulous look. "Are you serious?" When Séraphin nodded, he let out a laugh that exploded across the room and nearly threw him off the desk. Eventually he straightened up. "That's the funniest thing I've ever heard—but you need to learn to tell a story like that with more flair, my friend." Mr. Caffrey dabbed at his eyes with his tie. "I thought walking in on my wife was bad, but, shit." He laughed a little more, then collected himself. "Now it makes sense why you'd want to leave. After that I would want to be as far away from home as possible."

"Yeah," said Séraphin. "It's just awkward at home."

Mr. Caffrey could not help but laugh again. "And the girl?"

"She just stopped talking to me," Séraphin said. "And then she left St. Luke's."

Mr. Caffrey frowned. Only two people had left St Luke's in the last year. One was Jasmyn; the other was a timid Spanish boy called Joaquin. Mr. Caffrey let out an impressed whistle.

"I know," said Séraphin.

"And was it love or hormones?"

Séraphin cocked his head to the side. "I don't know, Mr. Caff. Maybe."

"Hmm."

"It's just weird, you know. It"—Séraphin looked at Mr. Caffrey as though hoping the answer would be self-evident—"hurts, you know?"

Mr. Caffrey looked away. "And it'll hurt for as long as it has to. You hurt until one day you don't. You just have to be around for it all. I won't lie to you about that."

"Nothing helps, huh?"

"I've heard of some things that are rumored to help. But they're the kinds of things I cannot in good conscience tell you about as a teacher. And I wouldn't even tell you about them as a friend. They don't work. What I can say is this: You need to be the lead actor in your life. Don't be a costar to your excuses. I believe in the parlance of your generation the proper term is 'Own your shit.' I know too many people in my life who're too scared to do that. Don't be one of them." The two looked at each other for a while before a small nod bobbed from Séraphin's head. "So where to next year, Remms?"

"If I can get the fees, yes."

"What do you plan on studying?"

"Not sure, sir."

"The best thing to be at university. Have you ever considered English?"

"That's not a real degree, Mr. Caff." Séraphin quickly added, "You know, with Rwandan parents."

"Don't worry, I understand. Tell you what, there's an English scholarship for East African students at Remms you'd be eligible for—I know because I got the same one. If you write me a kickass essay I'll send it in and write a strong recommendation letter for you. If you get it, you can spend three years messing about before you have to get a real degree." Mr. Caffrey smiled to himself. "You still have your Rwandan papers?"

"Yes."

"Good. Let's see if they can't get you something positive for once. Remms—Séraphin, I tell you, a man can get into glorious mischief there. Best years of my life. You'll enjoy it. Just don't invest too much in it. You'll have good days and bad days. But it'll feel like a dream, where everyone is always young, always excited about the next thing.

Just don't get sold the dream. University ends. You need to be ready for wherever it is you'll wind up, here or somewhere else."

Séraphin nodded as he chewed on his bottom lip. Mr. Caffrey looked at the young man in front of him, knowing full well the gravity of his message would make sense only much later, when it had been relegated to the past. "It's getting late," he said. "Help me close up. I'm sure we have other places to be."

Mr. Caffrey smiled encouragingly at Séraphin and then climbed off the chair. Together they closed the windows and drew the curtains. As they walked out of the room, Mr. Caffrey switched off the lights and the whirring ceiling fans. Séraphin turned to Mr. Caffrey. "Walked in on your wife?"

"I should've known. Or I knew but I didn't want to know. I can never tell which."

"I'm sorry."

"For what? Don't apologize for things you don't plan on making better, Séraphin. Never offer empty platitudes. Silence is better."

Mr. Caffrey offered his hand to Séraphin, who shook it. They walked towards the parking lot where Mr. Caffrey's battered Beetle waited for him. "Enjoy the weekend," Mr. Caffrey said as he wrestled with the door. "And, Séraphin, take it easy. Life has stranger things in store for you. Stick around and I'll tell you, kid. My life is based on a true story." Mr. Caffrey rapped a salute to Séraphin as he sat down in his car. "That's all it is in the end anyway."

"What?"

"This life, Séraphin, it's just a story. But only a story when you make it through, that's the real trick."

Parked outside Jasmyn's house, Séraphin watched the black gate slide open. He inched the car up a steep driveway that leveled onto a wide courtyard paved with reddish-brown interlocks. The courtyard yawned onto a wide view of the city skyline. On the right, a mansion sat atop three garages. A series of stairs led to a balcony that protruded over them and led into the house. On it he could see three plump women lounging in deck chairs. Smoke emanated from somewhere out of sight and the smell of roasting meat wafted down to him. From behind the three women came a man whose great weight and gait made Séraphin think of a walrus bull coming out to meet a challenger. The man wore nothing but blue shorts, which would have been skimpy on everyone else. The round, bald head gleamed in the sunlight. He scratched his pale belly and then asked, "Jasmyn?"

"Yeah," replied Séraphin.

"She's coming," he said, before walking away to attend to his braai.

Jasmyn appeared from the side of the house. She was wearing a pair of red running shorts and a white top that seemed painted on her.

"Yo," he said.

"Hello." She lifted one foot off the hot ground like a heron. "Let's get inside quickly."

They walked towards the house, Séraphin turning in the direction of the stairs that led to the balcony. But Jasmyn led him around the left side of the house on a tapered walkway. A sloping garden on his left encircled the house and he could see into the neighbor's yard, where a blue swimming pool stood unmolested in the midday heat. When they rounded the house they arrived in a backyard shaded by a tall willow. Jasmyn led Séraphin across the yard to what she introduced as her flat.

"It's as big as a house!" he exclaimed.

The interior of the lounge was cool. The walls were an off-white and the floor had clean, light-brown carpeting. The room was divided into two, one half occupied by a coffee table with three armchairs gossiping together, and the other dominated by a large chesterfield sofa facing a wide-screen television on a low table. One lounge window looked out into the backyard while another faced the blueness of the sky overlooking the neighboring house. The lounge was separated from the open-plan kitchen on the right by a long counter and two bar stools. Jasmyn asked Séraphin if he wanted something to drink.

"Juice," he said.

Séraphin made his way to the kitchen counter and perched on a bar stool. Jasmyn poured juice into two glasses and passed one to him. "What do you do to live in a place like this?"

"Advertising," said Jasmyn.

"Must be doing well, then." He took a sip of the cold juice.

"Not really. Otto lets me stay here as a favor."

"The walrus?"

"That's mean," Jasmyn said. Séraphin could detect amusement in her voice. "He's my uncle and he's sweet. He lets me stay here rent-free."

"What pitiful job do you do in the big bad world of advertising?"

"Social media—trying to humanize brands one click at a time."

"Sounds riveting."

"It is," Jasmyn replied, "to someone without brain cells—and I have at least three."

"How're your parents?"

"Mom's okay. She's living in Germany. Dad passed on."

"Sorry to hear that."

"Don't be. If he'd loved his liver a little more, he could've lived a little longer and left us with fewer problems." Séraphin knew a line of inquiry was closed. He asked after her brothers. "All grown up. They're studying at Wits at the moment."

"So when do they plan on attending a real university?"

"Funny. And your family, how're they doing?"

"The usual: Mom's at home, Dad's always at work, Yves is finishing his computer science honours next year, and Éric's in his fourth year. Both of them are here."

"Cool."

They sipped their juice for a couple of seconds before Séraphin said, "So, Jasmyn, the last time we were in the same place things were hella awkward. Then, poof, you vanished after the exams." Jasmyn avoided making eye contact, hiding behind another sip from her glass and then walking around the counter to sit on the chesterfield. Séraphin strolled over and joined her. "You've no idea how many free drinks that story has gotten me over the years. People love a good virginity story. Which makes me think Mary must have killed it back in the day."

Jasmyn laughed. "Look, Séra, bumping into you yesterday was totally unexpected. But I'm glad I did. I've wanted to apologize for a while but didn't know how."

"It's fine. It was a long time ago."

"Still."

They looked at each other, then sipped their drinks once more.

"So what happened?" Séraphin asked.

"Dark times. My dad loved the horses a bit too much, but they didn't love him back. The school fees were the first thing to go. They let me write my exams and I transferred out. Anyway, soon after, Keaton showed up again. So we dated again and then we ended it again. Twice. Don't look at me like that. Then I just focused on studying and getting the heck out of Namibia. Then you went off to Cape Town and I went to study in Germany and I decided it was all in the past."

"It doesn't matter now," Séraphin said. "I only hurt for like a year or so. I made some killer playlists, though. Shit like *Broken Mood Swings* and *The Half-Life of Love*."

"Sounds depressing."

"You have no idea." Séraphin smiled. "It's a little funny now since it's so far away."

"I'm glad you can have a laugh about it."

"Don't you?"

"Sometimes, and other times I still feel like that was just the worst thing that could've happened."

"Nah. I've seen worse." She looked at him curiously. "Varsity will do things to you," he said by way of answer.

"I'm sure." They were quiet for a while longer. Then Jasmyn said, "You seem different somehow. I don't know, more chilled. And you're more filled out. You must have turned into a heartbreaker."

"Can't break what's not there," Séraphin replied with a chuckle.

"Don't be an ass, Séra."

The room felt heavy with expectation and it grew dim as a cloud drifted past, high above. Jasmyn asked if Séraphin had any new playlists.

"Just naughty ones," he said.

"I'm glad. Because I could do with some right about now."

In the cavernous hall in Séraphin's mind, the Séraphins paused in the middle of whatever they were doing, mouths agape. Quickly, the chain of command was shifted to a five-star general experienced in negotiating girls out of their clothes. Séraphin connected his cell phone to the television's auxiliary port, navigating to his music library, pressing play when he located the playlist he wanted. A hollow ringing bounced across the surround speakers before a rattling bass line announced the confident intentions of a Philadelphia-based rap group.

"I like this song," Jasmyn said. "But it's very boastful."

"The Roots and Musiq Soulchild have never said anything I can't back up."

"Look at you, so sure of yourself."

"I am."

Instead of going back to sit on the couch, Séraphin went and stood next to Jasmyn, pulling her to her feet and kissing her, softly. She relented to his pressing lips, which traced a fine line from her mouth to her neck, her head rolling around, attempting to catch the string of kisses. With practiced execution, Séraphin peeled her out of her top and reached around her back, pinching and unhooking her bra strap in one smooth movement. Her eyebrows arched in surprise and she instinctively brought her hands to cover her breasts before Séraphin gently pried them apart. She pulled away from Séraphin for a moment and said, "Seriously, that was too slick."

He stepped closer to her and pulled off his shirt, throwing it on the chesterfield.

"What have those Capetonian girls been teaching you?"

"Let me show you."

XII

Rwanda is a big name in a small country. It is a memory commencing with two loud booms that wake Séraphin up. Curiosity drives him to the next room, whose windows face the street. He hears his mother calling to him. He answers, but stays by the window, trying to find the source of the crackling. His mother comes into the room, desperately calling his name. Then he is bundled into her arms and carried into the corridor. His questions about what is happening are not answered. His parents shush him and his brothers gently as they drag mattresses into the corridor in case bullets come through the windows of the rooms facing the street. Yves and Éric fall asleep quickly near their mother but Séraphin is eager to know what is happening. In the darkness, he hears his father rotating the knob of his world receiver, getting static in return. Séraphin's earliest memory of that faraway country is falling asleep on a mattress in a corridor, with his parents' hushed voices whispering urgently to each other.

The next day seems to go on forever. It starts with his father and mother waking him and his brothers in the early morning for a hasty breakfast of bread and tea. Then his father whispers to his mother, who clutches his arm fiercely. An argument ensues in muted tones.

Séraphin sees his mother sigh and then let go of his father's arm. His father vanishes from the house and his mother locks the doors behind him. Séraphin and Yves are prohibited from entering any of the other rooms in the house. They can play any games they want as long as they are quiet. Sometimes Guillome comes home carrying a loaf of bread, sometimes a chocolate bar, which is carefully shared between the boys. At night when his father and mother think he is asleep, Séraphin hears them talk about curfews, shops being looted, the neighborhood emptying. His father says they are going home and his mother scrambles around the house packing suitcases with clothes and what remains of the food.

"Turi mu rugo," Séraphin says. We are home.

"No, Séraphin, to our family home. In Gisenyi."

The Rwandan countryside is a blur of green as they drive west towards the family farm in his father's sturdy Pajero. On the side of the road there are long lines of people walking, carrying bundles on their heads. He thinks they look like ants carrying leaves.

The family farm is another out-of-focus vignette of rain in the afternoon, which pours on the land in earnest. Wrinkled women hug him and his brothers. At night, in the long house, stories are told under the light of a paraffin lamp. When he, his brothers, and his young cousins start to doze, the stories become somber. The monthlong stay on the farm is peaceful for the most part but the westward sweep of disaster is inevitable.

Accompanying the women to the nearby river to do their laundry, Séraphin and some younger boys are allowed to splash in the shallows where they can be monitored. One day, while the boys are playing, pushing each other into the water, a scream pierces the air upstream. The boys scramble out of the river and run to their mothers, who stop their washing. A bloated mass of black and blue, dressed in tattered clothing, rounds a bend in the river. Everyone scrambles up the riverbank, abandoning their laundry. A woman carrying an infant screams, "Bya tugeze ho! Bya tugeze ho!" as she runs. Only Séraphin stands on the riverbank and watches the ghastly floater pass by. When the corpse vanishes from sight he runs home, telling his parents about what he has seen in excited bursts. The news does not seem to impress his parents or the rest of the extended family. Their wails are a sound of pure, unadulterated distress that fills his eardrums and nightmares for days to come.

It has reached us! It has reached us!

Bya tugeze ho!

"What has reached us, Mamma?" An answer is never received.

That same day the Pajero is loaded again. There are quarrels about staying or fleeing. For Guillome and Therése, the decision is simple. They must leave.

The partings are sore, the promises to make contact and see each other soon are rushed.

Tuzabonana.

The Pajero is angled towards the Zaïrean border. The three kilometers to the border are clogged by hooting cars and desperate human traffic. The wait to cross over is so long Séraphin falls asleep in the late afternoon and wakes up on the floor of a dark living room in Goma.

"Mamma?" he calls out.

"Shh, Séraphin!" His mother materializes out of the darkness and sits next to him, pulling him close to her and rubbing his head gently. "Sinzira, Séraphin," she says quietly.

A cough alerts Séraphin to the presence of other life-forms in the dark. As his eyes adjust he sees other prone figures lying on the floor. The whole room is full of sleeping people.

"Why can't we go back home?" he asks his mother. In the low light he does not see her tear up as she tries to coo him into sleep. Before he succumbs, his father appears from the blackness and squats next to his mother.

"Birakomeye cyane, Therése. Nago dushobora gusubira inyuma."

"I agree," she says.

This is how diaspora happens.

Things are hard.

We cannot go back.

It has been agreed.

In the bright morning of a nameless day in June Séraphin has his first airplane ride aboard Air Zaïre. "Tugiye hehe, Mamma?" Séraphin asks. Where are we going?

"Kure, Séraphin," his mother replies.

Far away.

Going away is something of a pastime with Séraphin, whose bus tickets are booked for the middle of January. The days sense his enthusiasm to leave and kick themselves into a time lapse of clouds, congregating like smokers catching a drag at work and scattering. Guillome wakes up and dresses in stop-motion, eating his breakfast and kissing his wife before he exits the door; Yves and Éric wake up and rifle through kitchen cupboards, pouring cereal into bowls, chewing at chipmunk speed before they spread around the house. The last to wake is Séraphin, who crawls out of bed around ten or eleven o'clock and spends the day reading, scrolling through cell phone messages, occasionally being berated by Therése for some task he has forgotten. In the afternoon, Yves and Éric return from their university campus complaining about long registration queues, timetabling issues, and bookstores low on textbooks before the academic year has begun. They whisk themselves off to their rooms and then, later, Guillome returns home. Therése makes supper and arranges it carefully on the table. Hands pick at the food quickly so that dishes are halved in seconds. Plates are stacked and cleaned and then, like clockwork, Séraphin changes his clothes and says he is leaving the house. Questions are asked and evasive answers are given. Séraphin takes taxis past winking traffic lights, impeding or accelerating his progress to Jasmyn's house. The cell phone message, opening gate, swift walk to her flat, juice poured in a glass or tea in a cup, television turned on, and channels flicked through before the program is discarded for twining and untwining as the night passes on. Around four in the morning, Séraphin wakes up, dresses, heads back across town, and passes out in the softness of his pillow. The next day the sun rises and the scenes repeat themselves, until the evening before Séraphin's departure for Cape Town. Lying in the afterglow of their exertion, Jasmyn and Séraphin look up at the rotating ceiling fan.

"How was work?" Séraphin asks.

"Do you really want to know or are you just asking?" Jasmyn rolls onto her side and runs a digit down Séraphin's left arm.

"Just asking."

"Then it doesn't really matter, does it?"

"Right."

"If you really wanted to know, that'd mean we'd be in a relationship."

"What?"

"That's how it works, isn't it? If you hang out with a girl when she's on her period, talk about how the day was, and watch a whole film with her, then you're in a relationship with her." Jasmyn inches closer and rests her head on his chest.

"Right."

Her fingers trace an arc around his belly button. "I'm going to miss this," she says.

"Me too."

"Looking forward to Cape Town?"

"Yeah. I hope it all works out in the end."

"Things don't work out, you know. Only the things you work on do."

Séraphin digested the words in his mind before droning out a "Hmm."

"Like your useless sex game way back when."

"What?"

"You were useless. But now"—Jasmyn's hand makes its way down to a place that responds to her gentle touch—"you can make someone confuse technique with love." The movement of her hand causes his breathing pattern to quicken. She looks at him with a grin on her face.

"I"—his words stall as Jasmyn presses an ignition switch—"might've had some, er, instruction."

Jasmyn laughs. "Instruction, huh? Is that what we're going to call hoeing around at university?"

"It's only hoeing if people get hurt."

"And you haven't hurt anyone with this?" She squeezes a little, making Séraphin shift a bit. Jasmyn giggles, watching him take pleasure in her stroking. Then, without warning, she stops.

"Tease," says Séraphin, opening his eyes and sitting up.

Jasmyn gets up and sits on his lap. "It's been fun while it lasted," she says.

"It has."

"But you're leaving and we both know we can't pretend like there aren't other people in the world. It's better we leave it like this when everything's still fun. Before we're bored and asking each other what we're thinking all the time."

"Who says I would get bored?"

"I can tell you get bored with things. With people. When they hold your interest they're the best things in the world. But when they don't anymore you put them down, without warning, and they're confused." Séraphin and Jasmyn look at each other for a while.

"That was the most piercing pillow talk in the history of the world," he says. "How much do you charge for your services?"

She reaches over to a bedside drawer, opening it and pulling out a condom. She slips it on him and then lowers herself onto him.

"I charge by the hour," she says softly as she wraps an arm around his neck, working her navel from side to side and then back to front.

"You won't make a living, then," said Séraphin. "Because I won't last that long."

"I know. You're useless like that."

"Is that so?"

He reaches around her with his right arm and pulls her close. Then he grabs a fistful of hair, pulling on it so that she arches her back. His left hand steadies him as he synchronizes with her rhythm.

"Okay," she says, breath coming quickly. "Not so useless."

"Thought so."

The bus ride from Windhoek to Cape Town is infinitely more optimistic than the reverse, despite the weak air-conditioning and the Christian program on TV. Séraphin has mastered all of the nuances of boarding, so his suitcase will probably be the fifth to be removed from the luggage trailer, allowing him to hail a taxi at the Cape Town bus station quickly. He has also saved the goodbyes for last, choosing instead to go straight to the stewardess to find his seat number and climbing aboard the double-decker coach, happy to discover he has an east-facing window seat. East-facing seats are not roasted by the sun on the southward journey. Only then does he alight from the coach to bid farewell to his parents and brothers.

Therése is standing next to Guillome, her right arm looped through his left. "You must study hard. No distractions this year, okay?" she says.

"What distractions?" Séraphin asks innocently.

"Drinking, drugs—" Therése begins.

"—dames, damsels, and demoiselles," Yves interrupts.

"Chicks, birds, lasses, concubines, maidens—" Séraphin continues.

"Enough!" Therése's voice signals that the limit of acceptable family conversation has been reached. "Gui, these boys are trouble." Guillome smiles into the distance.

Éric says, "Ladies."

Séraphin and Yves turn to him and look at each other.

"Always late, bro," says Séraphin, shaking his head.

Guillome moves to embrace his son and a cumbrous hug transpires between the two, the father squeezing firmly, and the son tapping gently on his father's shoulder. Therése pulls him towards her fiercely. She clings on to him for a few seconds before letting go with one last admonition to study hard and focus. Séraphin and Yves's hands clap together as they pull each other closer so that their shoulders bump together. "Check you, bro," says Yves.

"Check you," says Séraphin. As they move apart their hands remain clasped and each raises an index finger to point at the other. "And, remember—it's all you!"

Séraphin turns to Éric and offers his hand. Éric takes it and, smiling wanly at his older brother, shakes it. Séraphin wishes him all the best for the year, then breaks the contact, closing the departure ceremony. "Let me go and get my seat," he says.

"*Bone chance*," says Guillome.

"Thanks."

"*En français, Séraphin*," Therése says. Her voice trembles with an emotion that always made Séraphin a little heartsore.

"*Oui, Maman*," he replies.

"Your French sucks," says Yves.

"Yours swallows," Séraphin retorts.

"Okay! Go, Séraphin," says Guillome.

Séraphin smiles at his family, walks to the bus, and boards. In the aisle seat in his row he finds a dainty girl. She has a sun-freckled face and sandy hair tied in a loose ponytail. She tries to make herself thin so he can squeeze into his seat. He pulls his iPod out of his pocket and unwinds the earphones wrapped around it, plugging them into his ears.

"Wow, you don't see those anymore," says the freckled girl, gesturing at his music player.

"Guess that's why they call it a classic." He scrolls through his music library and settles on his usual aural companion for the Cape Town trip: *The Last Ticket Out of Town.* Dexter Freebish's "Leaving Town" starts with its familiar chords.

"I'm Annika."

Séraphin shakes the proffered hand. "Séraphin," he says.

They fall silent as the last of the passengers take their seats and the bus hums into life. Séraphin cranes his neck to see if his family is still perched on the pavement but he can't make them out. As the bus approaches a red traffic light, a throaty honk demands his attention. His father's Jetta pulls up next to the bus and his mother leans across his father, waving energetically. His father tosses him a wave. Yves, in the seat behind his father, shakes his head. Séraphin flashes him a grin. Then the bus strains forward and the Jetta angles off to the left towards home.

"Where're you going?" Annika rolls her ponytail through her hands.

"Remms. You?"

"UCT."

"Then you'll transfer to a real university after that, of course." The look of distress clouding Annika's face quickly makes him say, "Just joking. You must be a first-year."

"How d'you know?"

"You haven't learned the art of the comeback."

"Okay. What year are you in?"

"Postgrad law. What're you studying?

"Psych and sociology."

"Cool."

Before he can resume his playlist, Annika asks what high school he attended. "St. Luke's," says Séraphin.

"Really? Me too."

"Maybe you know my brother. He'd be about your age. Éric."

Annika says, "Éric Uwituze?"

"Ah, you know him, then."

"He's my ex-boyfriend."

Séraphin turns to Annika and pulls the other earphone out of his ear. "He is your what?" Annika laughs. "Of course you dated him under duress."

"He was a nice guy. A troublemaker, but a nice guy."

"Damn. I didn't think he had it in him. You need some sort of medal for dating Éric. Like a Purple Heart."

"He isn't so bad."

"Clearly."

The conversation peters out as the bus escapes the city proper and picks up speed steering south. The landscape, green from the recent rains, stretches to the left and to the right. Séraphin plugs his earphones back into his ears and presses play.

When the stewardess announced their impending arrival at the Noordoewer Border Post, Séraphin pulled his cell phone from his pocket and sent Yves a message.

Sans_Seraph: Nearly at the border post.

YvesSaint: Hope the admin goes well.

Sans_Seraph: It's usually quicker when you're leaving the country. By the way, dude, Éric had a girlfriend. I'm sitting next to her.

YvesSaint: Annika. She seemed nice enough when I met her.

Sans_Seraph: How did I not know this?

YvesSaint: You're never here, dude. And you don't talk to Éric.

Sans_Seraph: Dude's just weird.

YvesSaint: Dude's also your brother.

Sans_Seraph: Verdict's still out on that.

YvesSaint: Goodnight, Séraphin.

He was about to put away his cell phone but then decided to compose another message.

Sans_Seraph: Are you up?

Wolff_Jazz: Don't send me booty call messages if you aren't going to follow through.

Sans_Seraph: Hahaha. Sorry, not sorry.

Wolff_Jazz: Asshole. Where're you?

Sans_Seraph: Nearing the border.

Wolff_Jazz: Cool. What're you listening to?

Sans_Seraph: New playlist I made recently.

Wolff_Jazz: Don't be coy now. What is its name?

Sans_Seraph: Crossroads of Hello and Goodbye.

Wolff_Jazz: Sounds deep.

Sans_Seraph: It is.

Wolff_Jazz: Don't drown in it.

Sans_Seraph: Too late.

Wolff_Jazz: Well, safe trip. Work in the morning. First full night's sleep in a long time.

Sans_Seraph: Yeah. Gonna miss that taxi ride of shame.

Wolff_Jazz: Goodnight, boy.

Séraphin closed the chat.

"You seem happy," Annika said.

"I am. I like this part of the trip," Séraphin said. "We're heading off to Cape Town."

"The land of MILFs and honeys," said a Séraphin leaning over the back of the seat in front of them.

"The start of a start." A second Séraphin next to the first.

"Or the end of an end," said a third in the opposite row.

"So excited for what comes next," said the second.

"And what might not," replied the third.

"I hope I like it," Annika said.

"You will. Trust me," said Séraphin.

Part 2

THE HIGH LORDS OF EMPIRELAND

Utazi nyakatsi ayinnya ho.
He who does not know the good grass will shit on it.

—RWANDAN PROVERB

XIII

Séraphin had a *walk*: languid but accentuated with purpose by his broad shoulders and chest, eyes cast forward, a slight frown on his forehead on some days, and a distracted smile on his lips on others. People made way for him as though he were a swaggering sage with some secret nirvana reached inside.

The walk did not just happen by itself. It commenced on a tiled kitchen floor in Kigali. Séraphin was an awkward bundle of clambering hands and dragged knees fueled by a biological need to move, exploring the giant, incomprehensible world of Guillome and Therése's young marriage. Affection and attention were abundant in the profuse quantities only firstborns can know and the curriculum of life was thin. Eat, sleep, and be adorable. He excelled at those.

And silence. He excelled at silence too.

Séraphin was quiet for a baby. Guillome and Therése panicked often in his infancy, checking on him when he went hours without crying, waking up afraid to see if he was still alive. Sometimes he would be awake and regard them with inquisitive eyes. The same eyes would orientate him around the house, perpetually amazed by what lay just a bit ahead. In his early attempts at walking, he stood like a tottering totem pole, ready to fall from the exertion of becoming a biped. Then, after a few seconds of savoring the new mobility, he would fall backwards onto his bottom.

With each step, the world became more complicated. Soon, Yves and Éric would form a cartel of cuteness and alienate the elder brother. At some point, Séraphin learned how to run, and the world became a treadmill beneath his feet. He would dash around the house to avoid beatings, become a blur in the primary school yard. In high school his speed helped him on the basketball court and the athletics track.

It all happened so fast, as things do in retrospect. One moment he was crawling, the next he was walking. Then he was running. And then the world was running away with him. Séraphin's first steps in Cape Town were hesitant ones. They were taken in the dingy, crowded, and noisy air of Cape Town station, where trains, buses, and taxis converged in a rare mixture of race, class, and privilege, as the city gobbled up its daily supply of labor. And again in the evening when it belched it back towards the surrounding suburbs.

Séraphin hadn't anticipated such a mixture in the station precinct. The rickety tables displaying counterfeit designer sunglasses, jackets, and perfumes were unexpected. Here were Congolese—Brazzaville and Kinshasa—belting out the prices of their goods. "Gucci belts for two hundred rands! Prada sunglasses for one hundred!" Coloured women and men with teeth missing selling bunches of grapes and downcast sunflowers. West African pidgin could be heard nearby from a stall that sold cell phone covers. A Pakistani-looking man was peddling pirated CDs and DVDs. A Somali with a high, smooth forehead sat near a table laden with sweets, packets of crisps, and a cooler box stuffed with ice and cans of fizzy drinks.

The dirtiness of the station was disappointing. Was this actually Cape Town? It was.

This was Cape Town station before the World Cup. Before the national need to stand on international ceremony smeared a veneer of cream-colored, polished tiles across its floor. Before the heathen food and sweets vendors were pushed out and the existing fast food chains were proselytized to newer, higher health standards. Before the new religion of customer service was pressed upon the station. It was practiced by rote, its tenets never really taken to heart. Beneath the propriety lurked the pestilence of indifference which would flare out in station cashiers who were tired of being asked questions about late trains or shrugging security guards who huddled together and watched crowds of commuters suck in their tummies to squeeze past malfunctioning turnstiles.

"It isn't working, sissie. Use the next one. No, the next one! Thank you!"

But when Séraphin first arrived in Cape Town, the station was lit by a dirty secondhand light. He had expected glitzy stores, restaurants, and cafés, or at least clear signs that might point him to a taxi rank where he could catch a ride to Remms. He found none of these things. The disappointment was stomached. The city would surely have other opportunities to impress. He dragged his suitcase behind him towards a security guard sitting next to a shoe repair shop. He asked where he could catch a taxi to his university.

"Which one? UCT, Cape Tech, or Western Cape?" The guard was annoyed that his bored staring at the crowd had been disturbed by a lost university student.

"Remms, sir," Séraphin said. "Can you tell me where I can find a taxi, please?"

The politeness in Séraphin's voice softened the guard a little. He pointed Séraphin to a wide exit. "It should be eighty rands to Remms. If they charge you more, they're cheating you." An extra, unsolicited kindness.

"Thank you, sir."

Séraphin wheeled his suitcase towards the exit and the line of taxis outside. The drivers were huddled together, talking and laughing. When they saw him approaching, they called out to him.

"Where to, boss?"

"Remms? This way, boetie!"

"Brother, come to this one."

Séraphin asked what the fare was and they all shrank away. One said, "We'll discuss it on the way there."

"Eighty rands," said Séraphin.

"Hayibo! At least one hundred rands!" said one. Séraphin stood for a while, uncertain whether he should pay the price they wanted. Just then, a driver at the end of the line waved a hand.

Séraphin walked towards him.

"Where are you going?" The accent was definitely francophone.

"Remms."

"How much?"

Séraphin hesitated and then said, firmly, "Eighty."

The driver winced visibly and took a deep breath. "Okay, let's go."

The driver was from Benin and his name was Idriss. He was chatty, telling Séraphin about how new students in Cape Town loved to party and drink too much. "Sometimes they cannot even walk. Can you imagine?" He looked in the rearview mirror at Séraphin for confirmation of shock. Séraphin shrugged. He knew nothing of drinking into stupors. "You look like a sensible boy. No crazy partying for you, eh? You must study hard. Namibia? I have driven some Namibians. Some students. To UCT, to UWC. And Remms. They all look smart when they arrive. I say to them, 'You must study hard.' And then they say to me they are studying hard when I drop them off at the clubs. Sometimes three clubs in one night? Three! When I pick them up they are drunk. You know what they say to me? They say, 'We work hard and we play hard.' What is this nonsense? There is only work." Séraphin offered tidbits of agreement here and there.

Idriss reached into the glove compartment and pulled out a battered business card without a name, just a number. "If you ever need a taxi anywhere, you call me. Give my number to your friends too. I will drive you anywhere you need to go for cheap-cheap." Séraphin said he would be sure to give him a call. "Good. My brother, Cape Town is not scary. There are many Namibians here. You will see." He let out a little laugh.

"I'm actually from Rwanda. I live in Namibia."

"O-ho! Rwandan? Also many Rwandans here. You will see. Namibia, eh? That is a nice place, no? I have heard it is a good place. Maybe good for a little business, no?"

Séraphin debated whether to engage in a full-blown debate about his reluctant hometown. He said it was nice.

"Nice? My friend, for people like us, anywhere but home is heaven."

Séraphin smiled at the "us." Idriss dropped him off at Remms, and Séraphin handed over a crisp hundred-rand note, telling him to keep the change, though Idriss made no effort to offer any. "You are clearly not from here, my brother. *Mais, merci beaucoup*. And, remember, you call me whenever you need a taxi."

Idriss drove away, leaving Séraphin with his suitcase at the front of his university residence. The next time he took a taxi—from Remms to the Waterfront—he was charged what he later found out was the standard fare for tourists and other foreigners who did not know any better. When Séraphin told Idriss about the incident a while later, he laughed and said, "It is in the way you walk, maybe. Or the way you ask for a taxi. You must tell, you must never ask. I am not supposed to tell you these things, but we are from the same place, so I must help." Séraphin resolved from then on that when he needed a ride, he would call Idriss. He also resolved not to look like an out-of-towner. He would fix the walk.

The completed Séraphinic March of Progress was the strut he had now, the one where faces and bodies moved out of his way as he walked the streets of Cape Town, that bittersweet Mother City. Now, in his final year of study, for Séraphin it was bittersweet indeed. Sweet that he had experienced this city, bitter that he might eventually leave it all behind.

The bus had arrived at the station in the early afternoon, unprecedentedly ahead of schedule. Séraphin helped Annika find a taxi that would drop her off at her UCT residence, telling her not to pay more than a hundred rand. Idriss hadn't been available to fetch him from the station today as he had done for the past six years, but he'd sent a younger driver in his place. Jean drove out of the city center and up through Vredehoek, with the bulk of Table Mountain looming up in front of them, and pulled up outside the Remms postgraduate residence. Séraphin paid his fare and added a generous tip.

Séraphin made his way to his room on the top floor, enjoying the commanding view of the Cape Town city center spread below him: the blueness of the water, the cranes lining the shore, the ships floating in the harbor, and the antlike cars scurrying on the streets and highways. Unpacking his suitcase and arranging his room was quick work, done in a few minutes, leaving him with enough time to walk down to the cluster of grocery stores that supplied the campus.

In the aisles, he browsed for food and toiletries. As a last-minute thought, he got condoms. As he pulled the packet of twelve off the shelf he could not help smiling at a memory of a particular day in his first year when, after the initial shock and pleasure of arriving in Cape Town had lowered his financial inhibitions, he found himself choosing between buying baked beans and condoms.

He had gone for the condoms.

"You can fuck on an empty stomach, trust me, but you can't go to war without a helmet."

The wisdom was pronounced much later, of course, and to his core audience, who, at the time, were squashed around a table in a crowded café. Séraphin now tossed the packet of condoms into his trolley and wheeled it to the till. The cashier scanned the milk, sugar, tea, pasta, bread, and canned goods, but refused to touch the condoms, shuffling them across the bar code scanner using the shower gel bottle.

"They don't bite," Séraphin said. The cashier ignored him and rang up the total. Séraphin handed her his card. At the last minute, he realized he had not asked for a plastic bag.

In Cape Town you had to pay for a plastic bag; in Windhoek the cashiers started packing automatically. It usually took about a week for the familiar routines to return.

Séraphin asked for a plastic bag and drew a disgusted look from the cashier. Now she had to ring up thirty cents. Séraphin reached into his pockets and handed her a fifty-cent coin. He packed his own groceries—it was much too early in the year to become irked about trivial things. The Mother City would present numerous opportunities in the coming days.

As he walked back to his residence he pulled his cell phone from his pocket and wrote a message.

Sans_Seraph: Are we getting ourselves into some sort of mischief tonight?

GodForTheWin: Are we the High Lords or not? Of course.

BeeEffGee: Count me in.

KimJohnUn: Glad you're back, Séra. I'm in.

AddyWale: Me too.

KentTouchThis: Can I bring a friend?

RichDick: You have friends?

Sans_Seraph: Are they real?

KentTouchThis: Very real. Her name is Silmary.

BeeEffGee: Please tell me this one is of consenting age.

KentTouchThis: Fuck you guys! Bianca, you won't be able to keep your hands off her.

BeeEffGee: Hope she will be able to keep her hands off me. Remember what happened with the last girl, Drew.

Sans_Seraph: Nobody's to make any moves on Andrew's friend. Are we agreed, m'lords? And lady?

AddyWale: Agreed.

KimJohnUn: Agreed.

AddyWale: Copacetic.

Sans_Seraph: Nigerians and their big words, though . . .

GodForTheWin: We'll let Andrew prosper for once.

JustSayYaz: Hahaha.

Sans_Seraph: Bianca?

BeeEffGee: Meh.

Sans_Seraph: Then we're in concurrence. Meeting at the usual place?

XIV

Remms University is named after Estienne Lazarre Remms, a French Huguenot farmer turned industrialist and politician who donated stolen land from his own estate just beneath Table Mountain for the university's creation. Imbued with the paranoia of men who fear they will be forgotten as times change, he decided that his name needed to make a leap towards immortality.

The dreams, ambitions, and fears of the man were helped along by the realities of the day: Remms had acquired much through the country's laws of exclusion and eviction and the migration of blackness allowed Remms's university to be built in half the time that it took to dream it.

In summer, the campus wore a lush green mantle as pristine as a fresh haircut. When the winter chill crept up on Cape Town, the campus changed to couture of ochre, amber, and magenta. While the rest of the city looked drab as a dripping nose, Remms remained an amalgam of impressive colonnades, faculty buildings, and private enclaves.

Upon Remms's death, which came a few years after the inception of the university, a mausoleum was erected on the slopes behind the campus to allow his spirit to look over the institution he had helped to bring into issue, and to gaze at the ocean that had brought his ancestors fleeing persecution from France to the Cape Colony. Later, a statue of the man—caught in an energetic midstep as though it were about to stride off its plinth and walk down to the campus below—was added to the memorial. Carved into the plinth were the words of a poem found in one of his journals:

In the cool of night and heat of day,
With toil and trouble, and God's favor too,
In this land I made and dreamed of empire.

Remms Memorial was, at first, deemed sacrosanct. A wrought iron fence was placed around the perimeter to keep the hoi polloi out. But the memorial's vantage proved too alluring to the university's student population and it became common sport to sneak up there in the middle of the night and become uproariously drunk. After an intoxicated student nearly impaled himself to death on the spikes of the fence it was decided that access would put an end to stupidity and the iron ring was removed, allowing the commanding views to become common property. It was rumored that Remms's ghost could not decline a finely rolled blunt. He would step off his granite block and share a few puffs, offering a wise word to a wayward student, or providing a revelation to master's or doctoral candidates. It became especially common for literature professors to scribble "Go and see the ghost" on the submissions of uninspired students.

Remms University grew and flourished as its research gained recognition, staking claims on the country's intellectual terrain. In its early days the student body was bleached white. Everything in South Africa that could be used as a foothold to a better life was. Through the law of the land and, subtly, the law of God and His Son Jesus Christ, the natives were legislated into alienation and dispossession. Remms, like many institutions of its ilk, had blackness on its campus only if it served whiteness. The situation held sway over the country, with protests and riots and speeches about the injustices of discrimination being put down by force. The elements of protest that could escape were exiled to neighboring countries. Sometimes they were pursued by the righteous state there too, and anonymous black graves sprang up all over Southern Africa. Throughout this dark period of history when white was right and might and life and everything else was death, Remms University carried on.

But the situation called apartheid could work only as long as three conditions held out. Firstly, the natives had to remain pacified. They were not. Secondly, the white minority had to remain united. Already, there were many calling for the system to change its ways. Thirdly, the money had to hold out.

While prisoners were carted off to Robben Island en masse, blackness learned how to consolidate its human tragedy into a love song for freedom that wooed peace seekers. The world fell in love with a man who could forgive despite years of imprisonment. The protests grew in intensity at home and abroad. Whiteness became angry and then it became afraid. Then it balked.

Finally, the money started running out.

As soon as the African National Congress was unbanned, Remms University went on a full-scale baptism of blackness. The Cape governors, administrators, prime ministers, and state presidents whose names littered Remms's campus were plucked from plaques and replaced with names from the struggle and, later on, the freshly transformed country. Names like Sisulu, Tambo, Biko, Mbeki, and Sobukwe would make their way onto faculty buildings and campus residences.

By the time Séraphin arrived at Remms University, the institution had completed a Lazarus act of such aplomb that the universities of Cape Town and Stellenbosch could only look on like angry exes who wished they could tell the world the truth about Remms without sounding bitter. Because Remms was well aware it was built on a shaky past, it was industrious in its efforts to maintain a veneer of diversity and inclusion. Its alumni, trustees, and landed legacy holders showered it with scholarships and donations. Its rankings, enviable press coverage, and the total absence of controversy seemed to be the work of sorcery rather than careful planning, meticulous talent acquisition, and an impeccable nose for staying ahead of and out of trouble.

Amongst Remms's most hated qualities was its penchant to lure academics from rival institutions. Few lecturers or professors could resist Remms's advances when they were made: future chair of this, director of research in that, fiefdoms in freshly created research fields in medicine, law, African studies, and contemporary literature.

Undergraduates too could gain admission to the university through a combination of academic, artistic, or athletic abilities. But the university's determination to ensure its student body remained motley-crewed was pursued with the meticulous zeal of a bonsai artist. The student body grew branches in race and culture pools that produced a diversity divorced from reality.

In the summer of Séraphin's first year at Remms, the campus was in bloom, the riot of flowers along the walkways spilling their colors into the fragrant air. Students walked between buildings or milled around on campus, sitting on the lawns and talking, some hugging each other after enforced absences during the holidays. Séraphin felt the pall of the previous year lift from his shoulders. His attention was drawn to a group of female students walking by. The curves of their bodies were as confusing as the black-and-white stripes on a herd of zebra, lost in a swaying prismatic parade. The effect was dizzying and after a few moments his senses were overpowered. Male students walked past with their bags slung casually over their shoulders, deep in conversation. Their eyes burned with knowing that would not permit them back into the Eden of former lives. Séraphin wanted that knowledge for himself. The Cape Town skyline nibbled at the periphery of his vision. It teased, like a lover whispering words that intoxicated and inspired: "Who will have me? Who shall rule me?"

Estienne Lazarre Remms and Séraphin Turihamwe, in their own ways and in their own times, looked down at the land laid out in front of them and said, "Me."

XV

Robert Sobukwe House stood apart from the other Remms student residences huddled closer to the main campus. It was a long white Dutch-style house with three stories, offering the residents on the top floor a slim but prized view of the sea. Carefully kept lawns colored the premises; here and there, trees offered inviting and poetic shade under which a book could be read. Home to fifty male students, it was one of the smaller residences. In addition it had the unenviable reputation of being classified as "bookish." When Séraphin alighted from his taxi outside the main door that first year, he was taken to his room by Tendai, a senior student who also served as the residence's assistant warden.

Tendai tried to sell him on the appeals of Sobukwe: "It's quiet, so you can actually study here. People complain about the walk to campus in the winter but it isn't that bad. The rooms are larger too." Tendai chuckled. "It used to be called the White House. And it wasn't because of the walls. Here we are." Tendai selected a key from the bunch he was holding and unlocked the door. "Room fifty-one."

A writing desk with knots and scars colonized a corner, some of the shelves of the short bookshelf next to it had sagged from past burdens, and a washbasin with once-white enamel stood near the door. In the middle of the room was a narrow bed that looked so single it could have applied to a dating site. Tendai noticed Séraphin taking in the furniture.

"Cheer up," he said. "The bed isn't that small considering you might not get laid. Once you open the curtains the view's okay in the summer, and in winter when the room gets cold you don't have to walk all the way to the bathroom to take a leak." He looked at the washbasin pointedly.

"Are you serious?" Séraphin asked.

"Just run some hot water with some dishwashing liquid and it should be fine." Séraphin could not decide whether he was joking.

"Anyway, dinner starts at six." He separated Séraphin's room key from his bunch and tested it in the door once more before leaving it in the lock. "Room's all yours. By the way, since you're on the ground floor I wouldn't advise leaving your window open. Not unless you want your gear to be affirmatively repositioned."

Séraphin raised an eyebrow. "Stolen."

"Right."

When Tendai left, Séraphin appraised his situation: the quietest residence on campus, a room with old furniture and a washbasin that had served as the piss pot for innumerable male students before him, and the possibility of being the victim of theft on the off-chance he forgot to close his bedroom windows. His first impressions of Remms were falling short.

Sans_Seraph—YvesSaint: I think I'm in a frat house.

YvesSaint: Hahaha. How bad is it?

Sans_Seraph: Mofos pee in sinks here.

YvesSaint: You're going to do some white boy frat shit. I can feel it.

Sans_Seraph: Tell Mamma and Papa I'm okay.

YvesSaint: Will do.

Sans_Seraph: Time to go and see what university food's like.

YvesSaint: Hopefully nobody pees in it.

The legend of the Séraphin Smackdown has been told many times and each retelling changes the story. But here, on paper made from the lungs of the earth, the truth can finally be told.

When Séraphin walked into the Sobukwe dining hall it was crowded. The older students collected their trays, plates, and cutlery, and moaned a little when the servers dished out rice, butternut, peas and carrots, and a pasty chicken breast. The first-year students accepted whatever was put on their plates. In days to come they would learn how to flirt with the staff for extra helpings. The really sly ones would get second helpings by sleeping with the kitchen staff.

This was not known to Séraphin when he picked up his tray that first evening and joined the queue of students waiting for food. The serving woman flashed him a smile as she spooned some rice onto his plate and he smiled back courteously before moving on to the next stop, where another woman, her braids in a hair net, said, "This one looks quiet." She scooped vegetables onto his plate. The last woman at the counter skewered a piece of chicken and said, "They're all quiet at first. But later when you get them alone, eish!"

Her comment brought laughter from the rest of the serving line and raised eyebrows from Séraphin, who did not understand the joke. Holding his tray steady, he surveyed the hall, looking for a place to sit. He spotted Tendai sitting at a table with some other students and walked towards him. They exchanged a brief greeting as Séraphin sat down. There was little for the two to say to each other so they both tucked in to their supper. The other students at the table were older and familiar to Tendai, judging by their easy conversation.

"These freshers don't know what's waiting for them," said a thick-shouldered boy with sandy-colored hair sitting across from Séraphin. The boy tossed Séraphin a nod. "First comes O-week, then comes whore weeks, and then no weeks." Tendai and the rest of the table laughed.

"The cycle at Remms for first-years," Tendai explained. "They party too much. Then, when it's too late, they realize they're here to study. Most fail."

"Don't worry about it, fresher," said another boy. He was stringy and dark. "We've all been there. Just ask yourself this: If my mother walked into my life right now, what would she say? The answer to that will always keep you focused."

"And Jesus," said another dark-skinned boy with an untraceable accent. He was immediately peppered with crumpled napkins.

"What you don't want to do," Tendai said, "is be fodder for the FAFY crew."

"What's that?" Séraphin asked.

"Fuck a First Year!" said three boys around the table simultaneously.

"You're new," Tendai said. "Maybe it's your first time away from your parents. There will be girls around you. Or boys. You never know. Remms accepts all kinds. Like Michael here, whose sexuality is determined by geography—straight at home, not so much in Cape Town." Michael threw a middle finger at Tendai. "Anyway, what I'm saying is that temptation shall besiege you on all sides and from time to time you can indulge." Tendai placed his hand on his chest reverently. "But from the tree in the middle of the garden you are forbidden to eat. 'Tis the Tree of Failure, fresher. What you want to do is survive long enough to enjoy everything it has to offer."

"Only one way to survive, man," said Michael. "Work harder than you play."

"Work hard, pray hard," said the boy on the other side of the table. Fortunately for him, the diners had run out of napkins to throw.

"That's Jean-Paul, by the way," Tendai said. "Our resident moral compass. He shall speak kindly for the rest of us at the End of Days. But don't take him too seriously. He only spouts that Christian bullshit to get into girls' pants."

The other sinners at the table laughed. They introduced themselves. Like Tendai, Michael was Zimbabwean. Jean-Paul hailed from Cameroon. Preston was the one who had initiated the conversation about first-year students. He was South African. "And definitely getting it on with someone behind the counter," said Michael as he looked at Preston's heaped plate.

The merry gathering was disturbed by the arrival of Dale.

He was a big boy, thickset, wearing scandalously short shorts which showed off his muscular thighs. Dale pulled an empty seat from a nearby table and squeezed in between Michael and Preston. He nodded to the table as a whole and picked up his cutlery. After the first forkful, he turned to Preston and said, "Th-this shit gets worse every y-year, hey? I can't believe th-they serve th-this to us."

The voice that came from Dale's body made Séraphin choke on a mouthful of rice and butternut. If the voice had shown up at the end of a Technicolor cartoon and said "Th-that's all, f-folks!" Séraphin would have sat and waited for the next episode of *Merrie Melodies* to begin. He tried to stifle his guffaws. The others hid theirs in poorly contrived sneezes or coughs. Michael made a show of ducking under the table to retrieve one of the fortuitously dropped serviettes. Only Preston's face remained impassive. His eyes, though, betrayed his otherwise stoic demeanor.

Dale's eyes were pools of anger as he focused on Séraphin.

"S-something f-funny, f-fresher?"

"No." Séraphin cough-laughed. "Nothing at all." He put his fork down and tried to keep his shoulders from heaving.

"S-sure?"

"Very," said Séraphin. He made eye contact with Tendai and laughter bulldozed past his restraint. Dale's eyes narrowed some more. "I'm sorry. It's nothing."

"I-if it's n-nothing th-then maybe y-you can sh-shut the f-fuck up." The joke was over. Séraphin marshaled his humor and tried to return to eating again. "W-w-what are y-y-you doing h-h-here any-way? Th-this is a s-senior table. Leave."

Séraphin had been on the verge of offering Dale a second apology, but the commanding tone that crept into Dale's voice stopped him. Making a show of lifting his tray and looking at the wood beneath it, he said, "You're right. This is an old table. What would you like me to do with that bit of information?"

Tendai, Michael, Jean-Paul, and Preston looked from Dale to Séraphin. But then Preston said, "Yoh! Dale, ek sal nie los nie."

Séraphin smiled.

"No. F-fresher—" Dale began before Séraphin cut him off.

"My name is Séraphin."

"R-right. Y-you need t-t-to move t-t-to another t-table. W-w-what about th-that one?" Everyone looked at the table behind Séraphin, not too far from where he was sitting. It was populated by first-year students. "I-i-it's the r-r-right p-p-place for y-y-you, S-s-sarafina."

Tendai, Michael, Jean-Paul, and Preston looked at their plates. Séraphin nodded politely at Dale and said, "Sure. No problem." He picked up his tray and greeted the boys at the table Dale had designated. "Gents," he said. "Please watch this for me." Then he strolled back to Dale's table and tapped the sitting hulk on the shoulder. Dale turned around and looked up at him. Séraphin said, "Yeah, you're going to have to apologize for that."

"F-for w-w-what?" Dale asked. He stood up, his mass a natural attention-grabber.

"What you said, it was quite unsavory." Séraphin sucked at his mouth to emphasize the sour taste.

"S-so?"

"So, you'll have to apologize."

"I-it doesn't w-w-w-work like th-that h-h-here."

"It does where I come from," Séraphin said calmly.

"And w-w-w-where is th-th-that, f-f-f-fresher?"

"Windhoek," said Séraphin.

Pause.

Now, Windhoek does not mean much to a rugby jock from Pietermaritzburg, where the high school fees cost more than a university degree. Windhoek, at best, is a place on a map in a country that was nearly a province of South Africa. What people forget, oftentimes, is that Namibians never negotiated a peace. They picked up arms and fought. The spirit of struggle lingers in the soil and can infect patriots and immigrants alike.

In Windhoek, there are only two types of blacks: Nesquik blacks and Milo blacks. Nesquik, with its yellow branding and its smiling and happy rabbit, costs twenty Namibian dollars and fifty cents. Milo costs fifteen Namibian dollars and fifty cents. The five-dollar difference means that only a certain type of black person can buy Nesquik.

The thing to bear in mind, though, is not the hot chocolate. It is where the Nesquik and Milo blacks live. Five years after Guillome and Therése moved to Windhoek, they lived in lower Windhoek West, where boys play soccer in worn-out Converse sneakers or barefoot in the absence of suitable hand-me-downs. The soccer balls they play with are made from plastic shopping bags wrapped into tight, reinforced knots. One has to jump down several rungs of privilege to comprehend the hardness of heels that can sprint on tarred streets without bleeding. Milo blacks are tough and wiry. They take offense easily and to insult one, even by doing something as accidental as mispronouncing a name, means only one thing: fight.

Ek sal nie los nie!

The taunt to let some offended party know there is only one way to reclaim their honor.

Ek sal nie los nie!

Bloody noses, scratched cheeks, and choke marks on necks.

Ek sal nie los nie!

Even though his family ascended into the realms of Nesquik blackness with Guillome's promotion, Séraphin is of Milo black stock. And with a fight imminent, only one thing is important: strike first and fast.

Séraphin slapped Dale.

Hard.

Quick.

Open palm.

The rap was loud and unexpected. As Dale's head swung back around to face his tormenter, Séraphin slapped him again.

Harder. And in the same spot. Then, instinctively, he stepped backwards.

After the second thunderclap reverberated through the room, Michael, Jean-Paul, and Preston jumped up to restrain Dale, who tried to swing a fist at Séraphin but found him just out of reach. He could not even swear; his stutter had become too severe. Tendai laid hands on Séraphin, who allowed himself to be dragged backwards. As Dale was wrestled from the dining room in a bundle of angry and defeated grunts, Tendai told Séraphin not to leave. The warden would have to be notified of the incident.

The warden, a diminutive man with Coke-bottle glasses and a bald head, was a mask of concentration, busy scribbling a note when Séraphin walked into his tidy study. Tendai nodded Séraphin into a chair at a coffee table in front of the warden's desk before taking a seat as well. When the warden had completed his writing he came to sit in a chair across from Séraphin. Séraphin's calm demeanor belied his embarrassment.

"So, you're Séraphin," said the warden. "From Windhoek. I hear that's an important fact." The warden's voice sounded like a duck whistle buoyed with a thick Zambian accent. Séraphin's eyebrows shot up again. He saw Tendai shake his head slightly. "What's this business of slapping students whose parents have the caprice to annoy me and the capacity to make your life here a living hell?"

"I'm sorry, sir." It was all Séraphin could think of saying.

The warden's eyes searched Séraphin's face. "No, I can see you are not."

Séraphin remained quiet.

"Tendai has given me a thorough briefing on the matter. He tells me your conduct was incited by a certain slur."

"He called me Sarafina." The warden looked at Séraphin without blinking. Séraphin looked down at his feet. And then he said, "Sir."

"I see." The warden looked past Séraphin for a while and then said, "Tell me, were you offended by this?"

Séraphin and the warden locked eyes. "No, not really, sir. But it was the principle."

"The principle," said the warden, tasting the word. "I'm sure you will be given ample time to consider which principles are worthy of action and which are not." The warden paused. Then he said, "It says on your admission record you're a Remms Undergraduate Scholar—one of the essay writers. That means you have something inside that head of yours. Something that warranted saving your parents the costs of sending you here. Tell me, did you think about what you'd tell them if you were expelled, Séraphin?"

"No, sir," Séraphin said. He looked at the carpet beneath his sneakers to avoid the warden's questioning eyes.

"And yet you had time to think of principles worthy of expulsion. The criteria used to choose Remms Scholars must have become lax." The warden was silent a while longer and then he clapped his hands together. "A disciplinary hearing would be a poor start to the year, for me as the warden of this house and for you. I am certain that after speaking with Dale I can talk him out of causing a fuss over his abuse. But I still have a decision to make. And it is that you, Mr. Turihamwe, should move."

"So I must leave and he gets to stay?" Séraphin's retort was suddenly ablaze.

The warden turned to Tendai and said, "Our Mr. Turihamwe is not good at listening, is he? I said he should move instead of leave the university altogether, a generosity which is not commensurate with his recklessness." The warden turned back to Séraphin. "Yes. You'll move to another residence. I've already phoned the warden of Biko House. You'll pack right away. Tendai will use my car to help you move your things." He sighed. "Let's hope Biko House is a better fit for you. A word of advice, though, Séraphin." He leaned forward in his chair as though offering the most intimate counsel. "You'd do well to learn when to hold your peace."

"I'm sorry, sir. But this is one black who won't keep quiet." The quip surprised both him and the warden.

The warden smiled without any humor. "In time you will," he said. "You'll want friends, you'll want to be invited to dinners, you'll want to fit in, and you'll learn to keep quiet." He sat back in his chair. "Do you know that they call Cape Town the Mother City, Séraphin?"

"Yes, sir."

"Whose mother is it? Not ours. We are its unwanted children. You'll learn to keep quiet and hope for its affections. Soon and very soon. Good night." The warden stood up and went back to his writing.

Tendai and Séraphin walked without speaking until they reached Séraphin's room. While he packed up his room Tendai stood jangling his keys.

"You might like Biko House," Tendai said.

"Why?"

"There are a lot of overly proud idiots there."

XVI

Of the many afflictions that can ail the young and beautiful, the worst one has to be boredom. Between boredom, which is the abode of teenagers, and ennui, which is the natural habitat of anyone earning a salary, lies an equally dreaded middle kingdom: the land of those who have missed out. It breeds a special kind of fear, spread from one youth to another through exclusion rather than contact. FOMO, the acronym of doom.

Walking down from Remms to the Cape Town city bowl, Séraphin could feel the itch to know what the rest of the world was up to. The cars in the evening traffic were so close they nosed each other's rears like curious dogs. Where were all these people headed? What were they going to do when they got there? What was everyone else in Cape Town doing? What did the night hold? So many people, so many possibilities. He felt much better thinking about meeting his friends.

Séraphin always looked forward to the company on such nights. Tonight, after his long absence from Cape Town, he was certain to hear some unbelievable stories. For her sake, Séraphin hoped Andrew's friend was not conservative.

He made his way into Long Street as dusk was falling. Later on, the detritus of the city's club scene would be strewn all over it. Now, though, it was quaint. The curio shops were closed. Boutique fashion stores placed their signature pieces upon gaunt, eyeless mannequins. The Royale Eatery at the top of Long Street was filling up. Marvel, across the street, blared jangling reggaeton to an empty dance floor. Next door, the steeple of St. Martini's Evangelical Lutheran Church peered down the street in pious recrimination.

Long Street Café was buzzing with activity. Séraphin's strut pulled a handful of stares and delicate sips as he passed by.

"Did you scope the woman checking you out?"

The many Séraphins had joined his march. This evening there were six of them.

"Yes, I did," said Séraphin.

"We should holler," said the first Séraphin. He winked at her. She did not return his lascivious nictation.

"No!" Séraphin resumed his walking.

The Séraphins proceeded down Long Street, past the Dubliner, which had already started pumping its signature rock ballads. The first Séraphin hummed along to Chumbawamba's "Tubthumping" as they passed the Green Street intersection towards their destination. The crowd thickened so that they were forced to separate and weave between oncoming foot traffic. In the sudden swell, a woman in a gold, flower-laced bodice and minuscule black skirt approached them. Her hair was dark and long. The toffee-colored skin above her cleavage pulled all eyes toward it. Her high heels ended in sharp, dangerous points and only the finely tuned muscles in her ankles and legs stopped her from snapping a tendon. Séraphin and the woman shared a look and as his strides took him past her he willed his neck not to swing his head around.

The first and second Séraphins stopped, slack-jawed, and watched the woman walk past. They had to skip-jog to catch up to the other four, who were managing to keep pace with Séraphin.

"So you're not gon' look?" asked the first.

"Nope," said Séraphin. "Contrary to popular belief, I don't chase everything in a skirt."

"That gotta be jelly 'cause jam don't shake like that!"

The second Séraphin craned his neck to catch a last glimpse of the posterior.

The third Séraphin spoke up. "Do you two ever hear yourselves?"

"Yes," replied the second. "We hear ourselves quite fine. We just don't care if you hear us, that's all."

"Unfortunately," said the third.

"So what happened back there?" asked the fourth Séraphin quietly.

"I think he was too chickenshit," said a knowing voice.

"You know what?" said the second, winking at the first. "I think you're right. Homeboy here is hung up on Jasmyn."

"On Jasmyn he is not hung," said a fifth Séraphin. "And afraid he is not either. At least, not of that of which you speak."

"What?" asked the second.

The fifth looked at Séraphin, who kept his eyes looking forward. "Time," he said. "Going on without pause it is."

"Huh?" The first looked at the others for a clearer answer.

The sixth Séraphin, trailing behind, breathed exasperatedly. "Fucking morons," he said under his breath.

The fourth said, "It's starting to sink in."

"What?" asked the second. Annoyance nibbled at the edges of his voice.

"This could be the last time we get to do this."

"There would always be a next year," said the sixth. "This one, though, could actually be the last one."

"Where a start there is, an end there must be too," said the fifth.

"And he's scared," the sixth said.

The other five Séraphins turned to look at him. So rarely did the sixth speak that when he did it was an event, oftentimes of great cruelty.

"Here we are," said Séraphin.

The stairs leading up to the Good Night were sandwiched between two street-level fashion boutiques. At the foot of the stairs sat a bouncer on a bar stool. Séraphin and the bouncer knew each other in the way that the frequenters of a pub or club and the bartenders, waiters, and cleaners will come to be acquainted.

"Long time," said the bouncer, whose name was Tashinga.

"Yeah, Tash," said Séraphin, "long time." Hands clapped, shoulders touched, hands patted backs. Séraphin spread his arms, preparing to be frisked.

"Nah," said Tashinga, sitting back on his stool. "You're cool."

"Well, that's a huge disappointment," said the first Séraphin.

"What is?" asked Séraphin.

"There're actually going to let you go gently into the Good Night," said the second.

XVII

The Good Night was one of Long Street's most popular cafés, leading hipsterism through Cape Town's restaurant scene. The burgers were named after famous poems. Courage was needed to tackle the voluminous Invictus, while the Desiderata drowned in meats, cheeses, gherkins, tomatoes, and all manner of desired things. The Road Not Taken was a particular challenge to carnivores who doubted vegetarian burgers were every bit as delicious as their meat variants, and the Still I Rise anchored anyone who attempted to finish it in one sitting to their chair.

The restaurant's burgers were handmade, a method the clientele deemed to be a novel way of making burgers. The chips were so skinny they would not be out of place on a Parisian runway. The menu design was filled with generous white space and slender sans serif fonts. The male baristas grew their moustaches into thick handlebars. Their waitresses' waifish fashion was oxymoronically bespoke and when they brought tables their bills they would slip the paper into a tin can along with the sliver of poetry or prose of the day. The Good Night's deep red, dark green, and brown walls were decorated with rotating exhibitions of local art, some of which was for sale, and booths provided a warm ambience. A passing waitress carrying a tray of empty glasses and crumb-strewn plates saw Séraphin standing in the entrance. "Hello. Would you like a table?"

"Yes, please. For eight. What about that one?" His chosen booth was near the middle of the room.

She nodded. "You can have a seat. I'll come by."

Sans_Seraph—HiLos_Of_E: I'm here. Got us a table. How far are you guys?

There was no immediate response. Séraphin put his phone on the table and spread his arms across the chair's backrest.

The waitress returned. She had dark hair tied in a tight bun, dark brown lipstick, tortoise-shell glasses, and a soft demeanor. Her face, neck, and upper shoulders had freckles, which reduced in their brownish concentration along the length of her arms. The rest of her was hidden in a black top and high-waisted black jeans. Her name was Fallon. "Would you like anything to drink while you wait for your friends?" she asked.

"Just water for now," said Séraphin.

She returned with a glass of bracing cold water. As she put it down, she bit her lower lip while her mind accessed her archived memory. "Have we met before?"

"Maybe," said Séraphin. "I come here often with my friends." He did not recall ever meeting her. The Good Night seemed to have an endless supply of bookish beauties.

"Possibly," Fallon said. "Cape Town's a small place."

Séraphin snorted. "Not that small."

"When you live here it can be." Fallon tucked a rogue wisp of hair behind an ear.

The transience of Séraphin's stay in Cape Town never really permitted him to defy any sentiment from someone who had been there longer. Residence and citizenship always trumped tourism. "Seems large enough to me," he said.

"I know," Fallon said suddenly. "The Circle Jerk of Joseph Conrad Lecturers—second-year English seminar."

"You were in that class?"

"I was," said Fallon. "You really went off."

"I feel a bit embarrassed now, actually."

"You had it in for that guy."

"I actually didn't and don't," said Séraphin. "*Heart of Darkness* is okay. Things just fell apart in that seminar when they tried to shove Conrad and Naipaul down our throats. They sounded like they had group orgasms to their literature. I wasn't buying it."

"V. S. Naai-poes, you called him. That last bit was what really got me."

"You have to believe my vocabulary became better after that incident."

"It seemed just fine to me." Séraphin and Fallon smiled at each other for a while. Then Séraphin asked her what she was up to. The question seemed careless to him immediately. Remms graduates were notoriously sensitive about their post-university exploits. Séraphin felt as though he had put her on the spot by forcing her to tell him how she had wound up in her current employment. "I didn't finish," Fallon said. "Remms got too expensive."

"Sorry to hear that," said Séraphin. It seemed like a factory-line condolence. It also felt strange to have the roles of privilege reversed. It was commonplace for black students to disappear from the Remms rosters each year due to fee increases.

"It happens," she said. "Money is the one thing one should never be ashamed to be without."

"Who said that?" Séraphin asked.

"I did. Don't tell anyone, but I put some of my own writings onto the slips we hand out with the bills."

"Sneaky," said Séraphin, taking a sip from his glass.

"Nobody reads them, or nobody bothers to check if the authors actually existed."

Fallon was flagged by someone at another table and excused herself. Séraphin waited for a few moments, hoping she would return, but she became preoccupied with her tables. He turned back to his phone.

Sans_Seraph—HiLos_Of_E: Do you mofos plan on getting here in this lifetime?

RichDick: Coming with Addy. Be there in five-ish minutes.

BeeEffGee: Also be there in a bit.

JustSayYaz: Same.

KimJohnUn: Still on campus, work suddenly got intense. Going to be a bit late.

Richard and Adewale's arrival brought a welcome end to the tedium that had followed Fallon's departure. "So despite the odds you survived the desert," said Richard. His ruddy complexion glowed and his hair was closely cropped. He wore a faded Tusker Lager T-shirt, a memento from a bygone trip to Kenya, and slim-fit blue jeans tucked into dusty-colored chukka boots. Adewale wore a fitted light grey lounge shirt with the sleeves rolled up. His shirt was tucked into a stylish pair of dark blue jeans with the legs neatly rolled up to expose chiseled ankles in white plimsolls. The label at the back of his jeans was as discreet as a vanity plate on a new sports car. Adewale's adoration of famous brands was eclipsed only by his adulation for his Christian faith.

"It wasn't easy, I'll tell you that," Séraphin replied. "How've you been?"

"All good, man," said Richard. He had spent two weeks in Harare in the December holidays before returning to Cape Town just after New Year's. "It was cool being there. But, eish, the place is struggling."

Richard was busy with his master's degree in electrical engineering. After graduating at the end of the year, he planned to return to

Zimbabwe, forgoing the lucrative prospects of working in a country not crippled by sanctions. "I thought about staying in SA," Richard said, "but I know I'd feel bad. The country's a mess right now. But some professionals are actually trying to keep enough of the country together for when Mugabe eventually goes. Zimbos love Zim. When it's all over they'll return."

Adewale shook his head. "If I went back to Lagos I wouldn't survive," he said. "You know how you can never really reintroduce an animal back into the wild? That's me. It'd be like if you went back to Rwanda now, Séra. You leave and then you're changed, and when you come back the place has changed too."

Adewale had spent that December working on the initial stages of his doctorate in microbiology, and posting pictures of his African dandy life—at a picnic, on a boat cruise, at a seaside restaurant. His captions encouraged the reader to place their faith in God. The group called him Pastor Addy when his reverend streak surfaced, usually when matters of sex cropped up. Adewale would listen to the group's stories and then plead for celibacy, steadfastness, and adherence to the teachings of the Word, even though he was as promiscuous as everyone else.

Adewale and Séraphin had met in the queue at the international students' registration office just after Séraphin had been moved from Sobukwe House. Seeing the younger student shuffling his papers around, Adewale had kindly told Séraphin to arrange them in the necessary order.

The registration officer who attended to Séraphin was a squat woman with short brown hair streaked with auburn highlights. Her lipstick was a thin red line and her hands were fat and stubby. The rings on her hands looked like they constricted the blood flow to her fingers. "You're Rwandan?" she asked. "But your application says you live in Namibia." She turned to the officer next to her. "He says he's from Rwanda, but he lives in Suidwes. What should we do with him?"

"I live in Namibia, ma'am," said Séraphin. The woman turned back to him. "It hasn't been South West Africa for a while now." Séraphin's shoulders had rolled up and then down. "Northern Rhodesia is Zambia, Southern Rhodesia is Zimbabwe, and Bechuanaland is Botswana."

They stared at each other for a few seconds. Then her colleague hurriedly said, "Permanent residency means he will go through the SADC procedures." The registration officer stamped through all of his forms at speed. As Séraphin was leaving, Adewale stopped him at the door and said, "Man, you're really new here." He extended his hand.

"Yes, I am," said Séraphin, taking it. First Dale, then the registration officer. The year was not even a week old and he was finding himself playing the protagonist in altercations.

After discovering that they were in the same residence, Adewale and Séraphin walked home for lunch together. They had been friends in foreignness since.

Back in the Good Night, Adewale was still talking about Lagos. "I would die in the traffic," he said. He paused, as if visualizing the mile-long jams, then shook his head violently. "Worse, the hustle would kill me. Everyone in Lagos is on a hustle. If I told people I was working on a PhD project that would change the world, the first thing I'd be asked would be if that was my only hustle. Nothing is ever enough in Lagos."

When Fallon came by the table Richard and Adewale ordered beer. Séraphin and Fallon smiled at each other without exchanging words. The next person to arrive was Yasseen. His Liverpool shirt drew jeers from the table.

"Yaz," said Séraphin, "we're at a restaurant with respectable people. How d'you wear that shit outside your house?"

Yasseen was the most reserved of the group, rarely contradictory and always a willing participant in whatever adventures the more boisterous personalities proposed. Yasseen and Séraphin sat next to each other in law lectures. It was Yasseen's duty to shake Séraphin awake when criminal and civil procedure lectures came to an end. Only someone who could endure Ramadan could remain alert throughout the forty-five-minute segments of boredom. Bianca had joined the two when the students of her underrepresented color had, one by one, dropped out of law school. Yasseen and Séraphin welcomed her gladly. She was pretty, foulmouthed, and feisty in lectures that threatened to become whitewashed with ignorance.

"So what's been happening?" Séraphin asked.

"Just chilling," Yasseen said.

"No Muslim girls falling off the righteous bandwagon for you?" Yasseen's toffee complexion warmed and he muttered that he might have met a girl.

"Good man," said Séraphin. "You need to tell us all about it later. In great detail. You know how much Bianca likes details."

"And if you speak of the devil," said Richard, "she shall appear."

Bianca walked to their booth. Olive-skinned and sultry with black hair that fell down her back and eyebrows threaded into expressive arches, she commanded a few sly looks from nearby tables, especially in her white dress, which strained to keep her curves in check. She hugged them one by one as they slid out of the booth to greet her. Séraphin hugged her the hardest. "Gotta get a real hug, with the titties mashed in," he said.

Bianca took a seat in the middle, with Yasseen and Séraphin on her left and Richard and Adewale on her right. "So you're telling me only Yasseen got Sauced in the holidays? Really? Rich, I can understand for now. Just trying to stay alive in Zim is a mission. Addy too. I was chasing someone, but she decided she was still into guys. Séra genuinely lives in a desert. But, damn, Yaz is the only one carrying the team."

Séraphin let out a pardon-the-interruption cough. Bianca raised an eyebrow. "I, er," Séraphin began, "may have stumbled across an oasis in the desert."

"Spill! Who is she?"

"Jasmyn," he said.

Bianca's other eyebrow joined its companion. Richard put down his beer. Adewale coughed. Yasseen smirked into his glass of juice. "No fucking way," said Bianca.

Séraphin filled them in on the encounter at the shop, the exchange of numbers—"Damn, she was really after you!" said Bianca—and then everything else that came after, to hoots of laughter.

"So, eight years later you got to expend the nut that got you into trouble. Shit, man, your life is unreal," said Bianca.

When Godwin arrived a few moments later and squeezed in beside Adewale, he demanded a retelling.

"Man," he said, "at least you closed that chapter."

"How was Zim?" Séraphin asked him.

"Bulawayo wasn't that interesting." Godwin described the empty supermarkets, the intermittent power, and the censored newspapers. The exodus of people leaving the country continued but his countrymen were running out of places to go.

"And yet you're planning on going back when you finish your master's," said Séraphin. "In finance, even. You want to work in a country without money."

"Yes," said Godwin. "It'll get better. It has to." Richard nodded agreement. Séraphin and Adewale shared a look across the table. Theirs was not the way of hopeful patriotism.

Fallon materialized with a notepad and a pen. "Are you ready to order?"

"Without Andrew or James?" asked Richard.

"Yes," said Godwin. "I'm hungry."

Ordering was quick.

Séraphin asked for Paradise Lost. "Is that a new one?"

Fallon said it was. It contained a chicken and pork patty drowning in three cheeses, with red onion, gherkins, and Japanese mayonnaise to top it off. "If I didn't want to see you try to finish it I would say *non serviam*," she said to Séraphin.

"Better to reign in Hell than serve in Heaven," he shot back.

"Clever." Fallon clicked her pen, attached it to her notebook, and left.

"What was that about?" asked Bianca.

"Nothing," said Séraphin.

While they waited for their food they spoke about the coming year. For all of them except Adewale it would be their final year. Bianca wanted to do her articles in Johannesburg. Cape Town, she said, was becoming frustrating. "I swear, my parents are ready to auction my ovaries to the highest bidder. They don't understand that even if I was straight I wouldn't necessarily like Coloured guys. But they say it's easier when you have similar backgrounds."

"They wouldn't complain if you brought a white guy home," said Séraphin.

"Of course not," said Bianca. "Super-light-skinned babies with hair that doesn't hate the weather—the Cape Coloured dream."

Surprisingly, Yasseen was also considering a move to Johannesburg. He had lived his entire life in Cape Town and wanted to live somewhere else. "If I stay I can't move out because it isn't the done thing, you know. They'll think I'm looking for an excuse to engage in haram activities."

Richard and Godwin were determined to go back to Zimbabwe. Séraphin was the only one without a clear direction. "I'll just take it a day at a time, see what happens," he said, trying to sound calm.

James's arrival was greeted warmly. He sat next to Séraphin. He had come straight from the Remms Law Faculty, where he was working as a research assistant while completing his master's degree in property law. The soft-spoken Kenyan hadn't flown home to Nairobi to visit his family over the holidays because he had too much work to do before the new academic year began. He'd met with Adewale occasionally but without the rest of the group around it often felt strained. Both of them received grant money, but while Adewale's would wriggle out of his bank account, James's would be saved and sent home to his family.

Fallon and another waitress passed around the meals. Séraphin offered to share with James and asked Fallon to fetch them an extra plate. As they tucked in to their food the chatter continued. James was looking forward to completing his assistantship at the end of the year and also to handing in his thesis. Then he was moving back home to Kenya. "In Nairobi a black man can be a black man."

"You can be a black man anywhere you want, my friend," said Godwin between bites. "All that changes is whether you can be a black man all of the time."

"This place'll make you choose, though," said James. "Trust me, I see it all the time in the law faculty. Either I remain docile or risk being branded a radical."

"Radicals don't get funded," said Adewale. "Don't even play those games. Not while the university is paying your fees."

Race seemed to be a constant concern in Cape Town. It would appear in jokes to summarize the punch line, and in insults to sharpen the bite. At first, Séraphin had taken it as a Capetonian quirk, a habit of geography. Like how Namibians complained about the heat in summer and the cold in winter. Race talk in Cape Town, though, was quite the opposite. It painted lines and built fences; huffy intakes of breath signaled people retreating to safe corners of ideology.

A few minutes later, Andrew arrived. He looked around, spotted them, and then turned his attention to someone still coming up the stairs.

"Howzit, gents?" he said as he approached. Andrew was the oldest of the crew, completing his political science honors degree, and a serial traveler. He was a stalwart T-shirt-and-shorts kind of person. Tonight, though, he had made a determined effort to appear anything but. The results were, as Bianca and Séraphin would discuss later, actually impressive. He wore a sky-blue shirt with a Chinese collar. Charcoal skinny jeans with the ends folded neatly above white nubuck high-tops. The precise word that popped into Séraphin's mind was "dashing."

"Thanks," Andrew said. He turned to his companion, who had just walked up to their booth. "This is Silmary."

Everyone not seated at either end of the booth cursed their punctuality; they wouldn't get to sit next to her. Silmary waved a slender wrist and said, "Hi."

She was dressed simply. Blue jeans and a tight white blouse showed off exquisite collarbones. Her hair was the color of freshly brewed coffee. It ran, unbound, all the way to the middle of her lower back, in semistraight tresses. Her eyes were green and flecked with brown. Her smile looked game for something reckless. Séraphin guessed that she would come up to his chest. If she had to kiss him she would need to stand on the tips of her toes. What Séraphin could not figure out, and what everyone else was thinking too, was what to call her skin color. Séraphin was certain that if she identified with blackness it would welcome her beauty with open arms. Whiteness was never miffed. It already possessed everything that counted. It let the other races feast on scraps.

Andrew decided to sit next to James, which meant Silmary would sit next to Godwin. Godwin shuffled so close to Adewale it looked like he was afraid to touch Silmary.

"You're late, man," said Richard. "We've already eaten."

"It's okay," Andrew replied. "I ate at Silmary's place already." He dropped the information with calculated nonchalance.

I ate at Silmary's place already.

He had been invited to her place. Séraphin imagined an apartment in Green Point or Sea Point. They had probably cooked together, with wine and jazz music. Séraphin hoped they had burned the food. But if they'd burned it then that would have hastened the march towards making out. While Séraphin was making his way to the Good Night, Andrew and Silmary had probably been kissing. And while he had been sitting there on his own, waiting for the rest of the group to arrive, hands had probably slipped under shirts.

I ate at Silmary's place already.

Séraphin took a deep breath and sighed. His phone vibrated in his pocket and he reached for it, looking at the message under the table.

BeeEffGee—Sans_Seraph: Séra!

Sans_Seraph: I know!

BeeEffGee: This girl!

Sans_Seraph: I KNOW!

BeeEffGee: WHERE DID HE FIND HER?

Sans_Seraph: I. DON'T. FUCKING. KNOW!

"Bianca, Yasseen, Séraphin, Richard, Godwin, Adewale, and this is James. Most of them are in law school, which, generally, would make them insufferable, but they're actually cool," said Andrew. Séraphin looked up from his phone in time to smile at her. "These are the guys," said Andrew. When he saw Silmary look at Bianca with a raised eyebrow, he said, "She's lesbian. So she's a dude for all intents and purposes."

"Except I'm not," said Bianca crisply.

"Well," said Andrew with a little laugh, "sometimes I can't be sure."

Richard let out a deep chuckle. "Andrew, you've been missed."

"By someone," Bianca retorted, "somewhere."

"Shots fired!" piped up Yasseen.

"Really, guys," said James. "In new company?"

"So you're the High Lords of Empireland," Silmary said. She looked amused.

Everyone turned to Andrew. He raised his hands placatingly and said, "We were just talking, man."

"I don't know what he told you," Séraphin began, "but believe me, it's better if someone else tells the story."

"What story?" asked Silmary.

"Yes," said Bianca, "what story?"

"There's no story here," said Richard. "None, nada, zilch, zero."

"Nothing to see here, move along, move along," coughed Godwin. After the laughter had settled down he asked Silmary where she was from.

"I guess," she said, "all over. Angola, Zambia, Kenya, Uganda, Ghana, Sierra Leone, Morocco, Tunisia, and Switzerland. My parents moved around a lot." Her father was a development consultant. "I just moved to Cape Town about three months ago for a master's at UCT. English, by the way."

"And how, for all that is good and holy on this earth, do you know Andrew?" Séraphin asked.

"You've got jokes," Andrew said.

Everyone, though, was wondering the same thing.

"My father and his father worked together on a housing project a while ago. Figured one friendly face in Cape Town would be nice."

"She said he has a face," Godwin said.

"A friendly one," Yasseen added.

"Assholes," Andrew said.

"I'm sorry," Bianca said, "but *what* are you? I have to know just so I don't spend the next couple of days on hair and skin care products trying to look like you."

Silmary laughed a little. "My mom is half-Angolan, half-Portuguese and my dad is Swiss."

"Sorry, Bee," said Séraphin. "You're still going to have to check the weather forecast before you decide to straighten your hair."

"Fuck you, Séra."

"Where're you guys from?" Silmary looked around the table.

Adewale did the explaining. "Bianca and Yasseen are from Cape Town, fortunately for them; James is Kenyan, nostalgically; Rich and Godwin are Zimbo, and deludedly; I'm Nigerian, reluctantly; you know all about our South African Andrew, I'm sure. But if you don't, he's an asshole." Everyone thumped the table in agreement. "Which leaves Séraphin, who's Rwandan but lives in Namibia and, generally, would like to be from elsewhere."

Fallon came by again to ask if Andrew and Silmary wanted to order anything. They declined. Her gaze lingered on Silmary.

"I think it's time for wise words," said Richard. It was the signal to get the bill.

"You had help with your burger," Fallon said to Séraphin. "I'm a bit disappointed."

"I'm sure I could've finished it by myself if I was in the mood."

Fallon snorted. "Of course you could. You'd have had to pack it for breakfast."

"Hey, hey," said Séraphin, "if it's doggy it ain't in a bag." Jeers swept the table. Fallon blushed and left to fetch their bill. When she returned she placed the little tin can with the bill in the middle of the table.

"I can never get used to this thing of splitting bills," Adewale said. "This one's on me."

"The scholarship money has come through, has it?" asked Andrew.

"Maybe," said Adewale. He counted out the rands, folding them in next to the bill. The table murmured their thanks. "Right," he said, "let's go."

As they made their way out of the Good Night, Fallon finished cleaning up another table and came back to clear their plates. The tin can had a generous tip in it. It also contained her latest composition. He hadn't read it. She began stacking the plates on top of each other and was about to heft them to the kitchen when she felt a presence behind her.

"Sorry," Séraphin said. "You owe me words."

Fallon blushed, which made her freckles flare up a little more. "This one isn't that good," she said hastily as he reached for the piece of paper still lodged in the can. "Your friends are waiting for you."

"Yeah." He tucked the paper into his pocket. "I'll see you around, Fallon." He turned and walked back to the entrance and down the stairs. Outside the streetlights punctuated Long Street like neatly spaced orange-yellow commas. The others were waiting a few paces up the street in a little huddle.

"Ready?" asked Bianca.

"Ready," said Séraphin.

The High Lords of Empireland, now reunited, strolled to the evening's final destination. Séraphin strode more confidently than the rest, leading the way. In his pocket, Fallon's composition was destined to be forgotten, becoming wet, pulped into a mess as Séraphin's jeans tumbled around a washing machine drum in a couple of days. He would pull the dried remnant out of the pocket when he was ironing his jeans and assume it was a grocery receipt.

If he had been more alert, Séraphin would have heeded Fallon's words, which, like so many pieces of wisdom, did not make themselves known in grand or loud ways. Sometimes, as Therése was fond of saying to Séraphin when he railed against her advice, her rules, or her old-fashioned ways, the most important things were just everyday things. Like family and not constantly looking down at them; like his brothers' company, steadfast and close; like his father's counsel, which told him to take things slowly, that what was not inside could not be found outside.

"Ni ibintu bitoya, Séraphin," his mother would say, "bigira akamaro."

"Yeah, yeah. Small things, big differences," Séraphin would reply, bored.

But Rwandans have this saying because it is true: utazi nyakatsi ayinnya ho. Because when you do not know the good grass from the bad you will shit on both just the same.

Ni ibintu bitoya bigira akamaro. Small things make the biggest differences.

Had Séraphin but noted Fallon's careful composition, some things could have been avoided.

Alas.

Utazi nyakatsi ayinnya ho.

And nyakatsi ya Fallon utazi nyakatsi:

"Time, in its infiniteness, is the most powerful force in the universe. It cannot be escaped. But it is also the most uncreative. It spits out the same shit, but on different days."

XVIII

Facts, once they are so confirmed, do not need human faith to sustain them. They simply are. The only decision left to a person is whether to live in deliberate ignorance of them.

Here is the first fact.

Outside Avec there is a line of club-goers waiting to enter. Some shiver from the excitement. Others are regulars. When the bass line of a song reverberates through the walls, the pulses of those outside thump with desperation. There is a wiggling of hips and tap-tap-tapping of feet on the pavement. Since it is late and the club's hottest hours are approaching, the line snakes from the door and around the corner into Long Street. Shapely legs in figure-hugging skirts step forward inch by inch. Ill-fitting loafers, unpolished brogues, and high-tops scuff the sidewalk. At the front of the line people trickle past the red rope controlled by three pale bouncers in black. One is seated by the door on a high bar stool; the other two have planted themselves on either side of the entrance. The one sitting down is Romeo. A shark smile serrates his face when a trio of women in stilt-high heels approach. He lifts the rope. They hug him and exchange words before making the short climb to the hostess's desk.

The next group approaches for judgment. They are five male twenty-somethings, fashionably dressed in the way of people with enough money to purchase everything the mannequin is wearing. They are dismissed with a flick of the head. The group moves off, shouting, "Fuck you, Romeo! Racist faggot!"

The process of rejection and acceptance goes on. Arbitrary as it seems, it is a fact.

Here is the second fact.

The High Lords and Silmary finally arrive at the front of the queue while Bianca talks to another friend further back in line. Romeo looks over their party and says, "Gents, not dressed like that." Séraphin, Godwin, Yasseen, and James step aside. Adewale, Andrew, Silmary, and Richard are just behind them. Romeo nods to them. "You, you, you, and you are fine." They stand hesitantly for a moment.

"Don't worry, guys," Séraphin says. "Go on ahead." He waves them away and they ascend into Avec.

Romeo turns his attention to the latest quarry, a group of four boys in their late teens. They have made a special effort to dress up and they look handsome. Collared shirts, bow ties, smart jeans, and polished oxfords. He refuses them entry. The boys look shocked. This is their first night out in Cape Town and they were told Avec was the place to be. They decide to go somewhere else.

The next group approaches. The first man's jeans appear to have been savaged by something with claws and vengeful teeth. The second one wears a Tottenham Hotspurs shirt. The third could induce an epileptic fit if he moved quickly enough. Despite their fashion faux pas, they are allowed to enter Avec.

Séraphin, Yasseen, James, and Godwin remain silent. The obvious fact is not voiced. It does not have to be. All of those who have been turned away, regardless of dress code, have been black. Séraphin and his company have one choice: to slink away or go to another club.

Here is the third fact, which will explain the second.

Last year, Avec came under new management. The club's old black walls were lined with mirrors; the blue and green lights that made teeth and shoelaces glow were substituted with rows of red and amber lamps. VIP couches on raised daises in corners permitted those with enough money to lord over the plebeians.

A strange oddity was added to the men's bathrooms. A bronze-skinned man stood in the corner. He was dressed in a constricting waistcoat and bow tie. It was his task to listen to sounds of release and then hand out soap and towels to those who remembered to wash their hands. He would suggestively push a ceramic bowl towards a hastily departing party animal. Some coins would bounce into it. Drunk white guys paid more. But black people would shit the longest, the loudest, leave the foulest stench, and then depart without dropping any coins to soothe his olfactory chambers. As a rule he never greeted them, reluctantly handed them soap, and made them get their own drying towels from the rack. He believed that the back of a black man's ass was his best part and so he was always glad when they turned around and walked out of the bathroom.

Avec's cover charge was also raised. The jump from thirty rands to fifty functioned as a class moat. Finally, a dress code was enforced and a bouncer began weeding the undesirables from the suitably dressed. Bit by bit, week by week, club-goers were confronted by a litany of transgressions that barred them from entering the club. One day it was incorrect shoes, the next it was the absence of a collared shirt; thereafter it was not dressing to a particular theme. Then the management found Romeo and his shadows and gave him the brief: let some in, keep most out; black women, yes; black men, not so much; white people, yes, for that is where the money is. Indians were unhindered. Coloured people were forced to try their luck.

And now for the fourth fact, which brings us to the present day. Séraphin, James, Yasseen, and Godwin are quite aware that the winds in Avec and the rest of the clubs in downtown Cape Town do not blow in their favor. There was a time when they could gain admittance into all but the poshest clubs. Not anymore.

"Maybe it was always like this and we just weren't paying attention," said Séraphin the first night Romeo stopped them. That had been the previous year, just after the club had undergone its transformation. Richard and Andrew had already been let in. Once inside, they'd received a message from Séraphin letting them know they'd been bounced. Richard left Avec in solidarity. Andrew chose to remain inside. To expect conscientious objection from Andrew might have been too much. When they all regrouped at the end of the night, driving home with Idriss, the ride was filled with small talk and barbed wire.

"How was it, Drew?" asked Séraphin.

Andrew volunteered information with gusto. "Crazy," he said. "You guys missed out. Where'd you go?"

"Marvel," replied Séraphin. "It was cool too. Good music, pretty girls. And black people." James, Adewale, Richard, and Yasseen kept mum.

"Come on, man," said Andrew. "You heard Romeo, you guys weren't dressed properly."

"And you were?" said Godwin.

"People like Andrew are always suitably dressed for things in Cape Town." Séraphin rubbed the top of his forearm with a finger.

The bitterness of "people like Andrew" was felt by the whole group and Richard's exemption soured the simile. It was not fair of them. Andrew did not make the rules. Still, the anger had to be directed somewhere and Andrew was a nail in a taxi full of hammers.

"What are you saying, Séra?" asked Andrew.

"I ain't saying anything, bro. Just that all the black guys got bounced."

"That doesn't prove anything," said Andrew. He looked around the taxi for some support. "Seriously, there were many black people in the club."

"That's why five more would have upset the balance," said Séraphin. "Open your eyes, Drew. Lately when we go out only some of us get frisked. Romeo doesn't mess with you. Or Rich. Even Addy, who dresses like there's a runway waiting for him, gets harassed. If haircuts could fix it we'd be sorted because we're fresh as fuck. If it was the dress code then half of the people in Avec shouldn't be there. But you know it isn't, man. You know it."

"So what the fuck am I supposed to do with that information, Séra?"

"*Know* it," said Séraphin. "Just fucking know it."

"Well, thank you, Séraphin. Now I know."

The clicking of the indicator as Idriss turned up to Remms was the only sound for a few minutes. Then Andrew said, "If you know this shit about places in Cape Town, Séra, then why the fuck are you going to them in the first place?"

"Because," said Séraphin, "we can't just let it go. Avoid places just because we're black? Fuck that back-of-the-bus bullshit. In Cape Town? In Africa? Fuck that. If we get bounced, fine. I just want everyone else who gets in to know that shit is fucked up."

"Okay, Séraphin," said Andrew, "the next time we're out I'll be sure to feel guilty about all the places where you've been frisked. I'll pass on the message to every white person I know, yeah? Then everyone'll feel shit and that will resolve the problem."

"Fuck you, Drew."

"Fuck you too, Séra."

"You can't blame Andrew for not seeing things as they are," Bianca said the next day in class when Séraphin told her the story. "He's not really white because he has black friends. Avec isn't racist because they let in some black people. He's never been good at seeing things for what they are. Nobody in South Africa is." She looked around the rest of the law class and shook her head. "Can you imagine if anyone did? It would be chaos."

"Why?" asked Séraphin.

"Because then people would have to pick up their blame and actually try to fix it," said Bianca.

The group avoided Avec for a few weeks but Séraphin and Andrew had not apologized to each other, choosing instead to let time and continued proximity do the work.

Tonight Avec's quota of blackness has been filled. The four compatriots could take their ebony skins to places where they would be welcome, but they wait for Bianca. When she arrives, she doesn't bother standing in the queue. She walks straight to Romeo and gives him one of those boob-grinding hugs that Séraphin is so fond of. As she pulls away she lets her arm linger over his shoulder and they exchange pleasantries like intimate lovers. Then she points to her friends standing beyond the red rope and whispers something in his ear. Romeo pulls the rope aside for them. Bianca gives him another hug. Séraphin pays her cover charge. It is a cheap compromise and when Séraphin brings it up on their way home, all she will say is "The things I do for you guys."

"I don't know why we keep coming to this place," says Séraphin as they walk down a corridor towards the dance floor.

"You know why, Séra," says Bianca. "There's nowhere else for you to go. Not with your tastes."

There is no time for Séraphin to shoot back a response because all of the preceding facts are swept away by the noise which coordinates the pulsating, fist-pumping crowd. In the grips of the DJ's spell, color frontiers have been eroded.

Bianca leads the foray onto the packed floor, looking for Richard, Andrew, Adewale, and Silmary. When she finds them they hug like they have been parted for a long time and arms wave in the air like the tentacles of sea anemones in an ocean current. The next song makes Séraphin's eyes roll so he shouts to the rest of the group that he will see them in two songs' time.

He moves to the bar, using his frame to shoulder people aside. He orders water and, disentangling himself from the jostling bar crowd, steps aside to sip it.

Champagne bottles with sparklers float above the dancers' heads, balanced precariously on swaying trays as they travel toward the VIP tables. Séraphin's eyes seek out his friends on the dance floor. Bianca is in the middle, hands in the air, carefree, snaking her waist to the left and right. Godwin and Adewale are the only ones brave enough to dance with her. James and Yasseen shuffle by themselves and Richard's and Andrew's heads press close as they shout something at each other. Séraphin sees someone approaching him out of the corner of his eye.

"Can you get me a bottle of water too?" Silmary asks. She has to speak at volume to be heard. She reaches into her purse to pull out some money but Séraphin waves her away.

"Still or sparkling?"

"Sparkling."

Séraphin pushes back to the counter and returns with her bottle of water.

"Thanks," she shouts.

"No worries."

"What happened back there?"

"Where?"

Séraphin finds it hard to hear Silmary above the club's frenzy when the DJ slides the next song—a scorpion-stinging track from Eve and Drag-On—so she has to sidle a bit closer to Séraphin, who bends down just a little to hear her.

"At the door. How come you weren't let in?"

"That's just Cape Town. Can't be exclusive when all the black people are getting in, can you?"

"Is it like that all of the time?"

"Depends where you go. This place used to be cool until they decided to become upper."

"So why'd you still come here?"

"Honestly," says Séraphin, looking at the dancing crowd, "I don't know. I guess it's tradition."

When Silmary speaks again she is inaudible. She pulls in closer to Séraphin and puts her hand around his waist to steady herself against the rush of people making their way from the bar to the dance floor. "What tradition?" she asks.

The hand on his waist is not there for long, but when it pulls away it is missed like the familiar comfort of a back rub. "High Lord tradition," he says.

"You should explain this High Lord business sometime."

"Sometime." Séraphin takes a drink from his bottle. "Master's in English. That's going to make you the most underpaid punctuationalist in the world."

Silmary's laugh is lost in the chorus of a new song.

"Probably," she says when she can be heard again. "It's in comparative literature."

"Well, that won't put food on the table for our children," the first Séraphin says aloud before Séraphin wrests control of the conversation back.

"That's why you've got to become a serious lawyer. Keep a roof over our head, food on the table, paper beneath my pen," says Silmary.

"Sounds like a tough ask," says Séraphin, glaring at the first, who shrugs his shoulders, "considering that I might not actually practice law."

"What're you going to do, then?"

"I don't know, maybe use the law degree to fight drug racketeering charges for selling contraband to parents when I become an English teacher," said the first Séraphin, elbowing in again. Silmary laughed a little.

"A drug-dealing, literature-peddling, comma-pushing English teacher," Silmary said. "Has a ring to it."

"Fifty for a metaphor-tamine, hundred for a high-perbole—plus all the marking. We'd never see each other."

"It'll all be worth it. You'll get dedications and acknowledgments, maybe a chapter or two."

"Chapter? I'm worth a book at least," says the second Séraphin.

"Maybe," says Silmary. "But I can't write without source material."

"You got a plan for acquiring this material?" asks the first.

"I might," she says as Andrew appears.

"You guys not dancing?" he asks.

"Not feeling it tonight, Drew," says Séraphin as Andrew places his arm around Silmary, drawing her closer.

"Let's go," he says.

Silmary smiles at Séraphin as she and Andrew move away, leaving him alone near the bar. His phone vibrates.

BeeEffGee—Sans_Seraph: Stop hitting on that girl and come and dance with me!

By the time the electro house begins to take over, Séraphin and his friends are tired of dancing. Outside, Romeo continues to wield his devastating power over the waiting line.

"Remember when we could do this until four in the morning?" says Godwin.

"We're getting old, man," says Richard.

"Not old," Bianca says, "bored."

Adewale calls Idriss but he is too far away to come and fetch them so they have to flag another taxi. "Remms," Adewale says. He turns to Silmary to ask where she stays but Andrew says he will take her home.

"Yes, boss," says the driver. "Let's go."

Andrew exchanges handshakes with everyone while Silmary hugs them. When she embraces Séraphin he says, "Don't forget that chapter."

"I thought it was a book," she replies with a laugh. "Where would I even start?"

"Truth first, friction later." The second Séraphin winked behind her.

"What?"

"Fiction. I meant fiction," Séraphin says quickly. "It's something my English teacher used to say about writing."

"You write?"

"I save all of my Pulitzer Prize–winning compositions for chat messages these days."

"I'll be sure to text you when I get started on that book, then."

"What book?" asks Andrew.

"Nothing," says Séraphin as he gets in the taxi.

Bianca waits until the taxi has rounded the corner and Andrew and Silmary are out of sight before she says, "Well, I'm going to have some seriously age-restricted dreams about that girl."

"Where did Andrew find her?" asks Godwin.

"And why him?" asks Séraphin with his head in his hands.

"Remember the agreement, guys," Richard says. "No moves."

Everyone turns to look at Bianca and Séraphin on the back seat. "What?" they say together.

"No moves," repeats Godwin firmly.

BeeEffGee—Sans_Seraph: You were hitting on her!

Sans_Seraph: Just talking to her.

BeeEffGee: Wordplay is foreplay.

Sans_Seraph: Haha. Don't use my own words against me, woman! Anyway, nothing's going to happen. Promise.

BeeEffGee: Ha! We shall see.

XIX

David Evans Caffrey believed that in writing, as in life, truth came first and fiction trotted afterwards. He did not come to this wisdom benignly.

When growing up in his sprawling Nairobi home, the help's daughter—a wispy girl called Njeri—was, according to the euphemisms of the time, his playmate. It was commonplace for the domestic needs of a rich British family to be taken care of by a black family. Mr. and Mrs. Caffrey were hesitant about taking on Njeri's family because Mrs. Caffrey did not want another child on the property, least of all a girl. She had recently said goodbye to a stillborn bundle that made her womb ache. But Njeri's mother assured the Caffreys that the skinny girl with the tough hair would not be a nuisance. "She dust quick-quick and also peel and slice too," her mother said.

Mr. Caffrey managed to bring his wife around to the idea and Njeri's family moved into the two-roomed house tucked beyond the back garden. The house was not much but Njeri's family considered it palatial.

They kept the property regal. Her father's skill with the rosebushes had them burgeoning with blooms. His rough hands could fix anything. He also knew how to work the electricity, which was temperamental in the old colonial house. His wife cooked and baked, although everything she did somehow fell short of Mrs. Caffrey's standards. The windows were never clear enough, the bookshelves were packed incorrectly, there was too much dust in the lounge. If the Caffreys were entertaining his colleagues from the British embassy or her wives' club, Njeri's mother would labor long in the house. The Caffreys and their demands dominated her days. Her husband would complain about her coming to bed late.

Njeri helped her mother prepare meals and dusted the Caffrey family portraits. Her favorite part of the day was when David came home from school, bursting with all he had learned.

"*A* is for Andy Apple, *B* is for bat . . . *H* for Hairy Hat Man, and *Y* for Yo-Yo Man," David would read aloud.

The letters meant nothing to Njeri. But from the way David spoke they seemed terribly important. She also liked looking at his nature study book, filled with illustrations of cows that looked like crocodiles.

From an early age David knew an artistic career was not for him. What he excelled at was telling stories. He would regale Njeri with tales of the Three Little Pigs and Hansel and Gretel and she would listen attentively, her breath coming fast when the Big Bad Wolf huffed and puffed or when the old crone tried to place the lost siblings in her oven. David enjoyed the power that came from withholding climaxes and giving conclusions.

David and Njeri became easy friends in the way that children do when left to their own devices. Once, even, when Njeri's mother was not watching and Mrs. Caffrey was away, they sat at the same lunch table and partook of the same meal.

The two families lived side by side for many years, with David progressing through his primary school years, helping Njeri pick up her letters.

When a maternal bump appeared in her mother's kitenge, Njeri's father was proud. Njeri would surely have a brother, he said. Mrs. Caffrey feigned happiness; Mr. Caffrey maintained indifference. Njeri's mother continued her domestic duties until her water broke. David could remember the day. His father had just arrived home and his mother had some friends over in the lounge. Njeri's mother waddled to the veranda, calling to her husband, telling him that it was time. Mr. Caffrey came running from the lounge and revved up his olive-green Mercedes-Benz, shouting at Njeri's father to open the gate. Mrs. Caffrey came out of the lounge to find her husband packing Njeri's mother into the back seat of the car and telling her father to climb in the front. He would drive them to the hospital and return later, he said. If Njeri's mother was going to inconvenience them when there were guests to entertain, Mrs. Caffrey said, then the daughter would have to take her place. The silver trays of biscuits and drinks would not carry themselves. Mrs. Caffrey's party went on late. So did the birthing. Mr. Caffrey returned home to find his son and Njeri sleeping next to each other on the sofa in the lounge, David's arm draped protectively over the girl. He teared up as he carefully lifted David and carried him to his bedroom before going back down to the lounge to shake Njeri awake and send her off to her own house. Then he went to give his wife the news.

The day after Njeri's mother gave birth, David woke up to find his breakfast unprepared. Puzzled, he sought Njeri in their house and found her father packing their scant belongings into two suitcases. His arms bulged as he carried them out of the compound, calling to Njeri to follow him. David did not know why his friend was leaving. Nobody would tell him. All his father would say was that it was hard to explain. His mother spent the day in tears.

The truth was this: David had a half sister, a half-Caffrey, half-Kenyan hybrid he would never know. Everything else that came after Njeri and her family left was the fiction which made his reality carry on. His mother distanced herself from his father. The pound of flesh that came out of Njeri's mother was used to purchase Mr. Caffrey's unending compliance. There would be no scandal; there would be no pursuing Njeri's family. There would be David, total, alone. Njeri and her family were never seen again. Where poor people go when they carry the shame of the rich remains a mystery.

The truth that he had a sibling came to David by accident. He assumed Njeri's family had been dismissed for theft. It was left to the next houseboy, a loquacious teenager called Odinga, to help David put two and two together when he was approaching his teens. The news stunned him. His parents refused to entertain the subject whenever he tried to inquire about his unknown sister.

The house seemed to take revenge. The roses died. The cracks in the property multiplied. Odinga departed without warning six months later, leaving the Caffreys without reliable help for weeks. And in that special way that signs become symbols, the old house's electric wiring would, every so often, plunge the property into a blackness which could not be dismissed by telling it to pack and leave.

The half sister was, at first, a curiosity. Then she became a longing. A hurt, burning itself into bile and bitterness when David, growing up in a city overflowing with blackness, found his friendships curtailed by his mother. His friends were black, his Swahili crackled with idioms, Kuti was his cult, and black girls were nirvana.

When it was time to attend university, David's requirements were simple: far, far away from his family. His parents hoped for Cambridge or Oxford or Edinburgh. David chose Remms.

At Remms, David was confronted by the myth of the Rainbow Nation. It allowed him to date a pretty South African girl, Dineo. She was studying politics and history; he pursued English and the classics. David found himself spending a lot of time explaining to his friends that Dineo was a person just like him. She did not kiss differently. She did not make love using any mystical devilry. Little by little, and stare by stare, he learned which places he could frequent with her until, eventually, he grew tired of loving under scrutiny.

The truth was this: he was in love with Dineo but he lacked the courage and the determination to fight for the relationship. The fiction which helped him to disengage from Dineo was this: he wrote her hurtful letters, chronicling how little he had felt for her during the subsistence of their relationship. The ease with which the lies sprang to the tip of his pen surprised him.

At his graduation David decided he would find meaning in a classroom. There was a whole world of Njeris who needed to be taught how to read and write. He worked his way through South African, Lesotho, and Swaziland high schools. His arrivals were defined by energetic, theatrical classes; his departures were marked by a trail of forlorn children sitting at scratched classroom desks while their new English teachers bored them.

After years of amorous exile he fell in love with another black woman. Her name was Selma. His parents, still living in Nairobi, had hoped he would tire of teaching and return home. The house was old, they were old, they needed him around the place. David told them he did not plan to return to Kenya. His posting in Windhoek was in Katutura, the place where nobody wanted to live and, it seemed to him, where nobody wanted to teach either. There were untold numbers of Njeris waiting for him. The government school, with its faded green and blue paint, its windows trapped in perpetual winks of broken panes, and its sun-beaten playground, was where he decided to conduct the magnum opus of his teaching career. Here, he believed, he would make a difference.

The inexplicable love of the land also made him elevate his girlfriend to fiancée. When they flew to Nairobi to meet his parents, his mother looked at Selma as they sat in the lounge and said, "Another one." She swept herself off to her bedroom and excused herself from his wedding, but his father gave David his blessing. The Namibian wedding was a joyous affair. The start of the marriage was happy; the middle and the ending were not.

What David deemed to be true, when he could finally reflect on his marriage without feeling hurt, was this: what attracted people to each other was quite different from what kept them together. The hard part lay in finding the fiction to keep the attraction and the trust going. When he and Selma met, she was attracted to his zeal for teaching. She liked how he talked about his lesson plans, strewn with references to current music, television, and schoolyard slang. She admired his dedication. The profession, though, did not return his ardor. Too many students and too many assignments to grade stole time from their marriage. In addition to this, David's job did not pay well. Neither did Selma's nursing job. Passion for his work made up for the absence of zeroes in David's payslip, something Selma could not comprehend. Why was a white man content with so little? While it flattered their neighbors to know a white person could live among them, Selma wanted more.

There was a string of infidelities. The sincerity of her apologies was lessened by their frequency. David's pardons grew shallower each time. If it hadn't been for Tracy Chapman's "Fast Car," David was certain they would have remained chained to each other, rolling the boulder of their dead love uphill, only to see it roll back down. The night the Sisyphean rock rolled downhill for the last time, David was marking in their lounge and Selma was typing on her phone.

The marking and typing stopped. David remembered that all lives have been lived before, all sadnesses experienced, and all joys looked upon as though they were the only ones in the world. He was not special. Selma was not special. They were not special. There was some comfort in that. They looked at each other as the melody died away, both agreeing to tear asunder what God had put together. A storm of blame ensured neither left the marriage feeling as though they had failed. When the divorce came it was the kindest thing they had done for each other in a long time.

David's mother was secretly pleased.

Perhaps her son would return home in the wake of the divorce. Her first email was a technological marvel that shrank time too rudely, asking if he would return to Nairobi for a while. David said he would not. Her second email came soon after.

David,

Our family has dirty laundry, but dirty laundry is best washed at home. Please come home.

He stared at the message for a while before responding.

Mother,

I don't know whether we have a machine big enough. Remember, we have to separate the laundry, the whites from the blacks.

His mother did not write again.

Spurred by spite at his ex-wife's admonitions about his lack of ambition, he applied for a vacant post at St. Luke's and was immediately appointed. The pay was substantially better. The classes were smaller. He was heartened, however, to find that laziness remained the biggest impediment even at such an elite school.

An evening came when he had a fresh sheaf of papers to grade. It was derailed by the deliberate discovery of a bottle of red wine and John Coltrane. The truth, David thought as he slouched in his chair, was this: Njeri was gone. His Nairobi life was gone. Selma was gone. It was all gone-ness in his life. An empty feeling hollowed out his chest.

But that was not all of the truth, he thought to himself, sitting up straight again. There was his teaching. He performed for a sold-out crowd every day. A conscripted one, sure, but a good actor played for whoever showed up.

David sighed and put his papers aside, reaching for the essay Séraphin had written for the Remms Undergraduate Scholarship program. It would need some work, but Lord knows he had gotten into Remms with less. He read it again. Maybe, he thought, this was the fiction of his life: that his efforts would become immortal through his inspiration. He smiled at the thought. That was not so bad.

All the World's a Stage
By Séraphin Turihamwe

Beginnings are tricky because there are no countdowns to the start of a start. There is nobody to point out that *this* moment right here is where it all begins. Life starts in the middle and leaves people trying to piece the plot together as they go along. It is better that way. If everyone knew where the beginning was, nothing would ever get done because everyone would stand around waiting for things to begin. What my mother says about starts is this: "Everything that is not the end must be the start of something else."

But how do you know an ending from The End? Who tells you? And would you believe them if they said so?

Would you even want to know?

Maybe it is just something my mother believes to motivate herself through her days. After all, she might think, if a flopped cake is not The End then maybe it is the start of many jokes after supper when she serves it. Or maybe the idea is what allowed her to survive leaving Rwanda in 1994 and settle in Namibia and raise me and my brothers. If it is the latter, then I owe her an apology for doubting her. If not, I am skipping dessert.

I guess when you look at things the way my mother does it makes sense that you have to curb your disappointment when you enter the cinema and realize that the trailers have already played, that the title sequence has faded from the screen, and you have missed the first five minutes of the film. You just have to make sense of the bullets and flying cars as best you can. Everyone else is doing the same.

But if nobody ever makes it to the start of a story, and if everyone is in the same boat just bailing and steering as best they can, then I guess the whole point of life is to make some sort of start and then work towards some kind of ending, whenever and wherever it might be. Part plagiarism will permit me to agree with Shakespeare:

"All the world's a stage . . ." upon which we perform for the eternal audience of one.

Only the person who makes it to the end knows what everything was all about. He who survives the thunder gets to tell the tale. Life will only make sense right at the end, when the person who has been living it can look back and realize that the tragic nature of life is actually a comedy.

I guess, then, that the whole point of life is to dive in, hold on, and hope that a flopped cake is worth the laugh at the very end.

XX

"What is the sauce?" asked Silmary. There was a joke afoot and she was not in on it. She looked around for answers.

"You aren't saying it right," said Adewale.

"You have to say it with feeling," Bianca said. "Which only comes from experience."

It was March and the air was warm. The long table they had commandeered at the Old Biscuit Mill was littered with craft beers, plastic cups of fresh juices, and paper plates of thin-crust pizza. The woman selling the pizza was enthusiastic about thin crust. She was also pretty, which was why Richard, Adewale, James, Godwin, and Andrew had handed their money to her. Séraphin, Silmary, Yasseen, and Bianca, unimpressed, hunted down the Turkish family who operated the only stall that valued quantity and quality. They returned with pita bread stuffed with peppers, onions, red cabbage, hummus, and three kinds of dead animal dripping with tzatziki. Seating was scarce in the sea of Wayfarer sunglasses, summer dresses, and sleeveless shirts. Séraphin spied a space at the end of a table that looked like it could accommodate them all and steered the group towards it.

"I can't believe you guys bought that shit pizza," Bianca said. "If you hadn't been so Sauced by that woman you'd have spent your money better." Séraphin, Bianca, and Yasseen refused to share their food. Silmary let Andrew have a bite of her stuffed pita bread. "You chose The Sauce. Now you must swim in it."

"So what is it?" Silmary asked.

Séraphin, who was occupied with his food, looked up to find everyone staring at him. "Why me? I don't like parading my pain as a joke, guys," said Séraphin. The injured look on his face would have been more effective if he did not have tzatziki smeared across his lips.

"You have to hear this story," Richard told Silmary. "It's too funny."

"And so sad," Yasseen said.

"Guys," said Séraphin as he bit into his pita bread and chewed, "I'm not your plaything." He ruffled himself in the way his mother did when he had been young enough to be entertained by her. She would wait for Séraphin and his brothers to work themselves into frustration at supper, asking their father if they were old enough to hear the story, then resign herself to their begging and leave them giddy with laughter. "Please," Séraphin said, "respect my privacy."

"What privacy?" Bianca asked. "Everyone knows this story."

"Not everyone," said Silmary. "It'd better be good."

"It's good," Bianca replied.

"Then let's hear it," said Silmary. Séraphin held out. "Tell you what," Silmary added, "if this story is as good as you're all making it out to be, I promise to share one of my own." She turned to Séraphin. "A story for a story."

"Deal," said Séraphin. He wiped his mouth and took a pull of juice. "Are you listening closely? Because if you aren't listening to this tale of woe and heartbreak you're going to find yourself swimming, nay, drowning in Sauce!" He dropped his voice to a conspiratorial whisper, just as his mother would have done: "The Sauce is a force as old as time. It was there when the primeval atom exploded to create matter as we know it. If you're not into that line of thinking, then The

Sauce was there before God summoned the light into creation. The Sauce was, The Sauce is, and The Sauce will forever be."

The High Lords laughed and cried out a hearty "Amen."

"What's this thing we call The Sauce?" He looked around, a teacher searching for an eager hand. "It's the 'Hey, stranger' just as your life gets back on track, when the memories of past hurts are about to scab and scar and then, bam, 'I miss you.' It's the exes. We're all bound to it. One Sauce to rule them all," continued Séraphin sagely. "How do I know this?" He drained his cup and clanked it down on the table. "I've been baptized and reforged in The Sauce. It can't touch me." He paused. "At least, not in the way it did in the past; it has to switch up its game. The Sauce'll do that. Evolve, come at you in two-point-oh mode while you're still in beta."

"I see where this is going," Silmary said.

"Is that so? If you know where this is going," said Séraphin, "then you must know a bitch named Angie."

It is Séraphin's first year, and on a crowded dance floor at Marvel, Akon and Snoop Dogg are crooning obscenities into the air humidified by perspiration. The economy of movement bestows contact upon any and every person whether they want it or not. Dancers pair up. In the morning more than one person will wake up to find one of their trouser legs faded lighter than the other. That is how fierce the grinds are.

In this quagmire of desire are familiar faces. Tall Richard is bent nearly double to accommodate the girl with her arms wrapped around his neck. Godwin has his dancer pressed up against the wall. She is caught between a rock and a very hard place. Adewale is his own personal Jesus. It seems fitting that one of his disciples is speaking tongues into his mouth. Yasseen, the shyest of the lot, stands apart from the others, avoiding the direct gaze of the woman who moves her hips suggestively whenever he looks at her. She pushes through the crowd to him and envelops his coyness in her curvaceous frame.

And then there is Séraphin, the just-arrived-in-Cape-Town, half-virgin, pent-up storm cloud of the Great Sulk. He does not know what to do with the Coloured girl whose anatomy creases against him. For the second time in his life he will be indebted—and then indentured—to a girl who knows what to do with boys who do not know what to do with their hands. She places his hands on her waist as she dances. "Mo fayaah! Mo fayaah!" the DJ bellows into the microphone.

There are three notable absences here. James has chosen to remain in his room watching reruns of *The Wire*. Andrew is still a ways off from meeting his future friends. Bianca, who currently has a boyfriend and all of the doubts that will soon become certainties, also remains a distant point of connection.

The smoking laws that prohibit chimneying indoors have yet to be passed, so the dance floor is smoky; marijuana wafts from a corner of the club but nobody is perturbed by it. The rest of the evening is a haze of grinding and nibbled necks which ends when the club turns on the bright lights around three o'clock in the morning. Adewale manages to extricate himself from his tongue-twister, haul Richard away from the girl whose hands have found that crucial crease in his pants, and pry Yasseen out of the woman's embrace. Godwin is easier to inveigle away from his charmer because he has reached a pliable stage of drunkenness. Saving Séraphin is a bit harder. The tangle of arms and legs squeezed into Marvel's farthest corner is of Gordian intricacy and barely contained indecency. Richard and Yasseen succeed in separating Séraphin from the entanglement. Outside the club, the friends take deep gulps of semifresh air.

"Ja, no," says Richard after a while. "What happened in there?"

"Cape Town happened," says Adewale.

Séraphin phones Idriss, who arrives just as Séraphin's enchantress exits the club, trailed by some of her friends. "My name's Angelique, by the way," she says. "Maybe we can do something sometime."

With the numbers exchanged Séraphin shoehorns himself into a seat. Idriss shakes his head. "Your parents are working hard and all you do is come to chase women." They laugh and give Idriss a generous tip when he drops them off at Biko House.

"Man, I love Cape Town," says Séraphin as they trudge towards their rooms.

The next morning, only Séraphin manages to wake up for breakfast. His phone vibrates as he sits down in the dining hall.

An_G_Liq: Hey. I had a good time last night.

Sans_Seraph: I had fun too.

An_G_Liq: How're you this morning?

Sans_Seraph: Having breakfast now. My orientation program starts later.

An_G_Liq: Are you a student?

Sans_Seraph: Yes. Remms.

An_G_Liq: Rich boy.

Sans_Seraph: Just lucky when it mattered most.

An_G_Liq: And blessed where it counts too.

Sans_Seraph: What?

An_G_Liq: Never mind. When does this orientation program start?

Sans_Seraph: Just before lunch.

An_G_Liq: What're you up to until then?

Sans_Seraph: Not much.

An_G_Liq: Change that to "You, maybe" and see what happens.

Séraphin involuntarily hides his phone under the table for fear everyone in the dining hall will see it.

"It's a trick," says a Séraphin, sitting down next to him and reaching for his bowl of oats.

"It has to be," says another, sipping on Séraphin's glass of orange juice.

"What if it isn't?" asks a third.

"Does anyone remember what she looked like?" asks the first.

"Long hair with curls," says Séraphin. "Average height, lot of curves."

"She must have liked *something*," says the third. He reaches for Séraphin's yogurt. "I say play along. You've got nothing to lose."

Sans_Seraph: You . . . Maybe?

"Good on you, Séraphin," says the first. "Many years from now we'll look back on this moment and realize this is where it all went south."

An_G_Liq: Definitely. Where d'you stay?

"Is this chick serious?" asks the first.

"Seems pretty serious to me," says the third. "Answer her."

"This isn't weird at all, is it?" asks Séraphin.

"It's weird as heck, bro," says the third. "But this is too good to pass up."

Sans_Seraph: I'm in Biko House, at Remms.

An_G_Liq: See you in twenty-ish minutes.

"No fucking way," says the first.

"Damn," says the second.

"Atta boy," says the third.

"What happens now?" asks Séraphin.

"Well," says the third, "I'd start with a shower and then fix up the room."

The quickest shower in the history of the world is followed by an even faster room cleanup. There is little in the way of decor. Séraphin's Silver Surfer poster is on one wall. Galactus's herald has cosmic rays blasting every which way from his eyes, his abs framed in intergalactic perfection.

"This room screams virgin," says the first Séraphin.

"Don't worry about it," says the third, looking at the room. "Neatness is the best kind of decoration." He walks to Séraphin and puts his hands on his shoulders. "Now, what're we doing for protection? Are we using the cheap government shit in the bathrooms or do you have better stock?"

"Fuck," exclaims Séraphin.

"You just might," says the third. "But you aren't doing it without protection."

"I don't have any others."

"Séraphin in room seven, you have a guest at reception! Séraphin in room seven, please come and fetch your guest at reception!"

It is imperative for all guests in Biko House to be announced over the intercom. This system is designed for security measures but also serves as an early-warning system for cheating boyfriends.

Séraphin's appearance, the hug Angie gives him, the cool way she slides her hand into his almost warrants the back-scalding look of envy Séraphin can feel on his shoulders as they walk away.

A fumble of keys later they are in Séraphin's room. Angie kicks off her Havaianas, shakes out her hair, and goes to lie on the bed. She turns to Séraphin and says, "This room needs decorations."

Séraphin winces. "I'm working on it."

"Don't stress about it," Angie replies. "You have me now."

The laugh that squirrels out of Séraphin is a private quirk which will be heard on rarer and rarer occasions in the future.

"You're nervous," Angie says. "Come and lie down."

The smart thing for Séraphin to do is obey, which he does. They look as uncomfortable as two chicken pieces squeezed into a small takeaway box.

"You need to relax," says Angie. She props herself on her elbow and looks at him. Then she places her hand on his chest. "Unless, of course, you don't want to be doing this," she says, and kisses him.

Séraphin can smell the club's cigarette smoke in her hair. The shift towards nudity is an individual affair but the final run-in to intercourse is a collaborative effort. After they pause so Séraphin can slip on a condom—inevitability does not mean irresponsibility—they are so tightly pressed it looks like they will blur at the margins of contact. Then comes the familiar tingle in the toes and breathless clutching and clawing, and with gentle mastery, Angie finishes what Jasmyn started a year ago.

The pull of history is strong, and Séraphin throws a hasty look at the door.

"It was all going well until I decided to blow on her vagina," said Séraphin.

"Why on earth did you do that?" Silmary asked. "Wait. Don't say it." She cupped her face in her hands.

"Blowjob," Séraphin confirmed.

There were some tee-hees from the table's other occupants. The dramatic retelling was loud enough to make it impolite not to listen.

"She just laughed at me," Séraphin replied. "Then she asked me if I'd actually like to know how to do it. She taught me so many, many things."

"We didn't see him for three days," said Adewale.

"We knocked on his door but we'd never get a reply," Godwin said. "On the second day we heard a moan, so we knew at least one person was alive in the room."

"I was being orientated, guys," said Séraphin.

"Anyway," Richard said, "this girl would come over every Friday and leave late on Sunday. Dude would show up at breakfast on Monday drained of life."

"So that's The Sauce," said Silmary.

Godwin shook his head. "No, that's just the physical part of it all. The emotional part is worse."

"Yep. I was her slave," Séraphin replied, shaking his head slightly.

"So, it's all fun and games, right," Godwin said, "until Angie decided she would be faithful to her boyfriend."

"What?" Silmary looked at the High Lords, who were enjoying her reactions.

"She had a boyfriend the entire time," Séraphin said.

"And you knew?"

"I remember hearing her say it but not really hearing it," Séraphin said.

"That was The Sauce," said Adewale.

"I did hear her tell me about how long they were together and blah blah blah and how they were going through a rough patch and blah blah blah. It was like I was hearing her underwater."

"Guys'll block out the strangest things for pretty girls," Bianca said.

"Anyway, shit started getting fucked up. She'd ghost for a week, and then poof, reappear the next and we'd vanish into my room for days. Then she'd evaporate again. Give me some shit about working things through with her boyfriend and blah blah blah and I still like you Séraphin but blah blah blah."

"He's giving you the short version of a really long story," Richard said. "Dude was a mess."

"Snapping at us all the time," Yasseen said. "We nearly stopped being friends."

"Every time she'd come over," Séraphin said, "I'd have a whole speech prepared about how she had to choose between me and her boyfriend. But she'd say some shit about needing time so sincerely I'd believe I'd be chosen."

"With a capital *C*," said James.

"A capital *C*, fam!" Séraphin said ruefully. "Gold-star kind of shit. Before I knew it, she'd be kissing me and that'd be my resolve shot to shit. Whenever she came over I felt bad, and when she left I felt worse."

"The worst days were when she'd say she was going to come over and then she'd cancel," Yasseen said.

"He was the worst human being then," Godwin said.

"Then I started skipping school because I was depressed," Séraphin said. "I was writing love letters. Making her playlists and shit."

"We're talking Lifehouse, the Calling, LeAnn Rimes, Westlife kind of playlists," James said. "The man was hurting."

"I was in deep," Séraphin said. "I could see Darth Fucking Boyfriend—that's what we called him—dying in painful ways, Angie mourning for a while, then moving on with me. I've never wished for anyone's death, but DFB could've died and I'd have brought a marching band to his funeral. Get this, one time we're lying in bed. I've just given this girl the work of life. And she starts talking about DFB. How cool he is, how her mother likes him, all of the little light-skinned babies they would have, with straight hair and shit—"

"He was white?" asked Silmary.

"Indeed," said James. "When he told us what she'd said we told him it was time to get out. I've never heard someone be that creative with swear words before."

"Then one day," Godwin said, "we all met DFB."

Silmary palmed her face once more.

"So we're in Canal Walk, right," said Séraphin. "We're going to watch *Transformers*. Shit was a massive part of my childhood, so I have my Bumblebee T-shirt on. Tickets have been prebooked. I turn around and Angie and DFB are in the line behind us. And we can't avoid them because this moron"—he pointed to Godwin—"decided to greet them."

"I couldn't resist," Godwin said. "And let me tell you, guys, DFB looked like a *GQ* model. He had those bluer-than-blue eyes that have seen adventure."

"We technically haven't met Angie at this point," Yasseen said. "We've only seen her entering and leaving res. We kinda hate her because of what her Sauce is doing to our friend, but at the same time we know Séraphin's poisoning himself. We introduce ourselves. Séraphin chokes when it's his turn. And I don't know why, but Angie points at his T-shirt and turns to DFB, who's wearing an Optimus Prime tee, and says: *Look, it's Mumblebitch.*"

"BRUH!"

The High Lords and Silmary looked for the source of the exclamation. It came from farther down the communal table. Everyone at the table was invested in the story.

"We fucking laughed at him," Richard said.

"Imagine," Adewale said, "treating us like shit for a girl who'd say that about him to her boyfriend in front of his friends."

"Yoh! It was so cold," said Richard. "Anyway, the cinema isn't ready for the screening so we have to wait a bit longer. We speak to DFB, also known as Chad, and he's pretty cool. He's been to every damn country. Chad's been to Chad. Chad's been to Zim, Nigeria, and Kenya. And he doesn't talk about them like a tourist either. He knows all the places to get good food. Places even we don't know about and we come from there! Imagine."

"Chad's even been to Rwanda," James said. "Talking about how nice the people are after the horror, how clean it is, the gorillas, everything. He asks Séraphin if he's been back and all our boy can do is say he hasn't. Chad's sounding like a better Rwandan than Séraphin at this point. We're quite ready to trade. We don't even know why Angie's messing around with Séraphin in the first place when she has Chad."

"Then we go into the movie," Godwin said. "And we're a fucking mess whenever Bumblebee croaks on-screen."

"So Angie cold-shoulders him for two weeks," Richard said. "We're sure our boy's losing it. But we're all hoping it's part of the healing process."

"He hooked up with her again, didn't he?" asked a voice farther down the table.

"Like Peter fucking Pan," said Godwin.

"In my defense, it was the last time," Séraphin said. "So she comes over again. This time I can't even put in the work because all I can think about is DFB. I ask her what she sees in him. Stupid question, I know. I didn't know about answers that could derail your entire fucking year. She says Chad is a future and I'm not. I ask what that means. Yeah, I know, second mistake. She says she likes me but there's no room for another black man in her life besides the one who made her."

"That," said Silmary, "is super fucked up."

"Okay, so I realize this girl needs to go. But then I get an erection. Why're you looking at me like that? What was I going to do with it? I decide to get a last one for slavery and Nelson Mandela. But after that I was done with her. Swear to god. I played Al Pacino's 'Inches' speech at least once a day to keep sane. I finally became a Remms student, climbed Table Mountain, went to the seaside, even did tourist shit like Mzoli's."

"Why do I have a feeling you went and did something stupid?" Silmary asked.

"I texted her," Séraphin replied. "Don't roll your eyes like that. Who at this table hasn't done dumb shit? Thought so. Anyway, I tell her I think we had a good thing and we should let each other be. I try to end things on a poetic note. She used to feel like she wasn't doing enough with her life. So I told her:

> **Sans_Seraph—An_G_Liq:** You stack up. You measure up. And whatever happens, you changed my world.

"And what did she say?"

> **An_G_Liq—Sans_Seraph:** Your world is small.

Even the High Lords sucked in their breath.

"She broke something inside him with that line," Yasseen said.

"Why didn't you just quit her sooner?" Andrew, sidelined by his absence from the episode, spoke up. "That's what I've never been able to understand."

"I mean, you're a pretty good-looking guy," Silmary said. "You could've gotten with someone else."

In a phone chat later, Bianca and Séraphin would dissect the statement, discussing just what "pretty good-looking guy" means. But at the time they moved on with the conversation.

"You don't quit The Sauce, The Sauce quits you," Bianca said.

"You don't understand how low my self-esteem was then," Séraphin said.

"Don't forget the black-guy hierarchy either," said Godwin. "Black guys got levels for shit they'll put up with." He staggered the levels in the air: "White at the top, because bonus pussy points. Then Coloured girls, because light skin. Black at the bottom, because, well, life. Of the three, black guys don't know how to give up Coloured girls. They're best of both worlds: ass like a black girl, hair like a white girl."

"Coloured girls are not for the faint of heart or weak of soul," Séraphin said. "After that I became a monk. Meditated on the grand mysteries of life."

Yasseen snorted. "He's giving you the abridged version."

"He returned to normal life for a while," Godwin said.

"It didn't last long, did it?" Silmary asked.

Séraphin nodded his head dejectedly. "When you're hurt you have two choices: to hurt or to do the homework." Séraphin picked some crumbs off a napkin.

"It was Sera-Fix or Sera-Fire," said Yasseen with a grin.

"And I chose the fire," said Séraphin.

XXI

The ashes in Séraphin's wake are an arsonist's lullaby. Fire is a callous thing and what it consumes is sometimes not known until it is too late to replace what has been lost. So it was with Séraphin who refused to do the homework, choosing, instead, to pursue the hurt.

When Séraphin finally survived the Angelicapocalypse, he took a sabbatical from all things reproductive for what seemed like a respectful duration. The monthlong midyear holiday in Windhoek was freezing and Séraphin spent the days nursing his perceived slights. He returned to Cape Town in the cold, rainy winter of that year, with Ini Kamoze's "Here Comes the Hotstepper" narrating his lex talionis.

The strut was perfected. Never again would he pay more than the standard fare for taxis. A dedicated gym routine succeeded in recasting his physique. Cape Town quivered and quaked with each step he took as he descended from his bus.

"Fire and flames," said the first Séraphin.

"Forward and march," said the second.

Burn, baby, burn.

First came Nicole, pretty and fleeting, at the Remms East African Society's annual party. Its billing as the hunting grounds of white girls looking for an African adventure was not found wanting. It was a one-shot-one-kill kind of night.

A few days later was Monique, who was stripped out of her clothes almost as quickly as their time together pulled itself off the calendar. Eleanor followed soon after and was gone in sixty seconds, probably less. There was no need for their bathroom rendezvous at a house party to be called anything other than what it was, a happening. Shyann was a senior, prepossessing and open-minded as far as race was concerned. Maybe she and Séraphin could have been a thing had Tasneem, who was equally open of mind and other things, not come along and displaced her.

Raeesa, Robyn, Taytum, and Nadine proved to be a tough balancing act. They all lived in the surrounding female residences and one weekend their menstrual cycles synchronized. Poor Séraphin was forced to watch terrible dramas with each of them as he made his rounds. After two and a half weeks of fooling around with Séraphin, Raeesa found a boyfriend, Robyn got bored, and Taytum caught a bad case of the conscience for not telling Nadine she was in on her best friend's act. Not long after, Nadine asked the twenty-mark question: "What is this?"

"Fun," said Séraphin, and Nadine refused to return his text messages or calls.

Mia worked in the emerging social media arm of a local news company, which was as cool and cutting edge a profession as anyone could hope to have. She was considerably older than Séraphin. Her figure spoke of early-morning runs, juicing and detox fads, the supremacy of salads, and a religious approach to yoga. They met at a rooftop party downtown. Godwin had secured tickets through a friend who worked for the fashion brand being launched.

Séraphin was standing with Richard and Yasseen, looking for a floating tray of finger foods and flutes of champagne. Mia was doing the same. When one passed they teamed up to arrest its passage. Mia found their boyish energy infectious. It soon became clear she had zeroed in on Séraphin. The others left them to converse about the bland music.

"You can't dance to this drum and bass shit," he said. "It sounds like computers sending out mating calls to each other."

"People who come to these kinds of parties don't usually dance," she said. "They come to see and be seen. For once, though, I can tell my girlfriends I saw something nice." Her eyebrows seesawed at him.

"Game recognizes game." Séraphin served a smooth backhand into her court.

"How old are you?"

"Old enough to do whatever you want." No nervous laughter. Séraphin had changed.

What Mia wanted to do was drive across Cape Town to Bloubergstrand, undress Séraphin, and put a squeeze on him tighter than a drought water restriction. When she whispered this to him he swallowed audibly and said, "Well, okay then."

Richard, Yasseen, and Godwin did not bother looking for Séraphin at the end of the night. The squeezing lasted until ten o'clock the next morning, when, after breakfast, Mia asked Séraphin where he wanted to be dropped off. The drive back across Cape Town was sunny and buoyant, both of them looking for an excuse to broach the subject of a possible second meeting. She blanched when Séraphin directed her to Biko House.

"My son is in this residence!"

The screech of the fleeing tires negated the possibility of a reunion.

Séraphin never found out who Mia's son was.

Zainab was Cape Malay and Muslim. She was also infected with apostasy but still refused to eat bacon. When Ramadan came, Séraphin assumed that she would not observe the fast but she did, albeit with some modifications. No liquid or food would pass her mouth from sunrise to sunset. But as soon as evening came, parts of Séraphin would be served up for iftar.

Rachel called in sick for a week when Séraphin walked into her apartment. On the day she was nearly fired Séraphin lay in her bed. She accidentally said, on the phone, "Something's just come up and I gotta sit on it." She decided Séraphin was not good for her career prospects.

One of Biko House's receptionists, Derrick, refused to announce Séraphin's visitors. That was the day the Ashlynn drama happened. The previous night Derrick had shared a supper table with Séraphin's friends. The two groups gelled until Derrick asked Séraphin why he was never with black women. "Dude, you've got more *W*s on your sheet than Barcelona this season," Derrick said.

"It just happens that way," Séraphin said. "Is that a problem?"

"I was just asking."

Godwin said, "White girls are less work. Date, movie, dinner, maybe a little bit of smooth talking to put her mind at ease, and then you're in. You can't pull that shit with black girls. You have to run circles and sacrifice a small goat, and if she is light-skinned you need to call in favors from the Big J. Even if it goes well, you have to pray that Richard doesn't show up and steal her."

"It was just that one time," said Richard.

"You hooked up with a black girl?" asked Derrick.

Godwin shook his head. "Plural."

"How was it?"

"Hooking up with a black girl?"

"Wait, wait," said Séraphin, "you expect there to be a difference? Like her lady parts have a different anatomical structure? Or do you think black girls do some devil dance before coitus?"

"I was just asking," said Derrick.

"Your questions are fucking stupid, bro."

Derrick was on reception duty when Ashlynn came to visit. Derrick told her she could just make her way to Séraphin's room. The screaming went on for a while, with Ashlynn trying to attack Noëmie as she tried to squeeze past Séraphin and out the door. The story seeped across the Biko House fraternity, spilling into the neighboring female residences, where Séraphin became persona non grata. June, July, and August saw him in a sexual exile as bleak as the Karoo wilderness.

There must have been other women, unknown and unnamed, because unloved women are poor markers of time's passage. But in late September of that year Séraphin's sentence was finally reduced and he was permitted to interact with civil society once more.

That was when he met Soraya. She was Indian, which was strange because Indian girls, according to Godwin's extensive research, never dated black guys.

Soraya was the exception to the Godwin Principle.

"She actually likes black people," Séraphin said. "And it isn't because she's traveled a lot. Slavers traveled too and look where that got us."

Soraya and Séraphin had plenty to talk about. He gobbled up all of her travel stories—Canada, Spain, Peru, Chile, Senegal, Cape Verde—and she liked that he liked her stories. The first time they had sex the *reiatsu* of their connection could be felt a floor away. The second time, Soraya nearly confessed love.

If anyone paid attention, and some did, they would have noticed how Séraphin and Soraya began to spend more time together.

"So she's not your girlfriend?" asked Richard one day.

"No," replied Séraphin.

"But you hang out with her when she's on her period," said Godwin.

"Yes."

"Then she's your wife," said Adewale.

If anyone had been present at the start of their end, then they would have been in Séraphin's room the night they binge-watched episodes of *Bleach*, arguing about which captain was stronger and staking claims on specific squad numbers. Anyone in the room would have noted, with their hands covering their eyes, the frenzied kissing that resulted in the emotional shift from lust to the *L*-thing. If they had been tuned to the mishap frequencies, they would also have heard the slow, rhythmic sound of latex on flesh and the tiny tear that permitted love to bloom into life.

XXII

The Great Council of the Séraphins has been convened four times to respond to clear and present danger. The first time was when Séraphin was around ten. He would have been in the fourth grade. The Council convened in April of that year to meet a pressing need: Ralph.

Ralph was the kind of boy who spent his childhood trapping grasshoppers in an old jam jar. When he caught a good number he would break their hind legs and stuff them, one by one, into red ant nests. Ralph watched the hungry hordes swarm over his offerings, pincers clamping down on antennae and soft, segmented abdomens and dragging the meal beneath the cracks in the pavement.

By the seventh grade, Ralph progressed to picking on children. Everyone looked forward to his departure for high school at the end of that year. Even the sisters at Séraphin's convent school prayed twice as hard for deliverance from what was surely the devil's own issue.

One week, Ralph and his minions stumbled across Yves, then in the second grade, sitting with his friends. They were sharing a Cadbury chocolate bar Yves had received, a rare and prized treat in their household. Yves, in his generosity, let everyone take delicate nibbles to extend its life. The brown bar was snatched in transit as it made its way back to Yves. Nobody had seen Ralph walking up to them. It vanished into his mouth and he permitted his underlings to lick the wrapper. Yves watched the disappearance of his chocolate bar and filled its absence with tears. His friends scattered to avoid further confrontations with Ralph and one of them, on the run, came across Séraphin. "Ralph took your brother's chocolate," Yves's friend called out to him.

The Great Council was summoned.

Back then there were only six Séraphins. Each was color-coded according to Séraphin's favorite Power Rangers. Blue, red, black, green, white, and pink. The blue one karate-chopped the air as he spoke. "We must find Ralph."

Together they marched Séraphin around the schoolyard in search of Ralph. Boys and girls followed him like a prophet to see if he would deliver some promised miracle. Séraphin found Ralph and his crew on the dusty soccer field.

"You took my brother's chocolate," said Séraphin when he came up to Ralph.

"So?" Ralph said. His question hushed the entire field.

Séraphin bent down and heaped a pile of sand at his feet. It was time to kick grandmothers.

It was commonly accepted by the male population of the school, and some of the tomboyish girls, that the dispute resolution methods available to the average primary school student were boring and lengthy. Diplomacy involved too many words and compromise was for the sniveling, sickly children who could never throw a decent punch. To circumvent all of these higher-level methods of conflict resolution, grandmothers were invented. Two boys who talked themselves into cross-purposes created a pile of sand or stones at their feet and invested within them the love and respect only grandmothers can command. Each of the aggrieved parties declared they were right and the other one wrong. The piled grandmothers bore witness to the veracity of each claim—if either party was convinced the law was on their side they were invited to kick the other's grandmother. Having one's grandmother kicked demanded immediate retaliation. The other grandmother was subjected to an angry punt. With both grandmothers scattered, the necessary levels of disrespect communicated, and a crowd of bloodthirsty primary-schoolers goading the high-strung fellows, "Ek sal nie los nie! He kicked your grandmother! You must defend your grandmother, eksê!" it would be time for the fists to settle what words could not.

Because trial by grandmother could have only one outcome, it was not taken lightly. When Séraphin finished mounding his granny, Ralph was shocked. The rest of the playground watched the big boy bend down and heap his sand. "This is my grandmother," he said. "What're you going to do about it, refugee?"

The many Séraphins were debating the wisdom of their decision and division was about to make them recant their challenge. But something about the word "refugee" made them all stop.

The word was common in Séraphin's household. His mother inhaled deeply when she changed the channel to CNN and saw lines of people marching from home to hope in faraway African countries. His father uttered the word sourly at supper when he complained about some menial problem he was required to solve at work. Then, he turned to his boys and said, "It is not bad to be a refugee. Einstein was a refugee. But it is bad to be a black refugee. If someone calls you a refugee, they are not being kind. They are calling you homeless and useless and cheap. We are not refugees, Séraphin, you understand? We have a home here, and another one in Rwanda. Maybe someday you will see it, eh?"

Refugee!

Coming from Ralph's chocolate-stealing mouth, the word was as evil and grotesque as the monsters that threatened to destroy a town unless the Power Rangers united to form the all-powerful Zord. The pink Séraphin looked at the others and said, "He's gotta go."

As Ralph stood up, his grandmother just completed, Séraphin delivered the sweetest and truest kick to it. Her ruin covered Ralph's socks and shoes. Before Ralph could react, he was hit in the stomach by Séraphin's tight, white-knuckled fist, which would have bent him in half had Séraphin not launched himself at the taller boy and toppled him. They landed on the ground, Séraphin pummeling any inch of Ralph he could find while screaming, "Don't call me a refugee!"

Chants of "Fight! Fight! Fight!" drew the attention of the teacher on playground duty, who rushed to the field and separated the boys. She struggled to hold Séraphin, who remained a kicking and screaming bundle of righteous anger. Ralph rolled over and spat out a mouthful of chocolate-colored blood and a bit of tongue. He was rushed to the nearby hospital, where the doctor told his weeping mother he would be all right. Only a bit of the tip had been bitten off.

Guillome and Therése were summoned. In the principal's office Séraphin was asked to speak his piece. The anger still burned through him and choked his words. All they heard as he cried was "He shouldn't have called me a refugee!"

Ralph's mother wanted Séraphin expelled. She would have been granted her wish had her son's reputation not turned everyone against him. The school's Sister Mother was moved to dubious mercy. It also helped that Guillome and Therése were stalwart members of the same Roman Catholic parish and their tithes were up to date. When Guillome asked the parish priest to put in a good word for Séraphin he agreed to do so. Ralph's mother, outraged by the injustice of Séraphin's continued presence at the school, moved her boy out. After a period of homeschooling, he was released back into society with a healthy fear of foreigners and a dislike for chocolate.

The second time the Great Council was called to a sitting was when Dale was on the receiving end of two ringing slaps. By then, the Council had upgraded its cool. As soon as the insult dropped from Dale's mouth, every single lightsaber—green, blue, red, and purple—had been drawn in misplaced but united fury.

The third time occurred later that same year, when Soraya fell pregnant. Three separate pregnancy tests and six blue lines confirmed a clear fate. Fatherhood before graduation, the thing Therése had warned Séraphin about before he left home, had come to pass.

"But how?" asked Séraphin.

They had been careful.

They had followed the rules.

"I think the condom tore," Soraya said. They were in her Sea Point apartment. Outside, the Promenade was full of early-evening joggers and couples walking hand in hand. As Séraphin gazed out of the window the number of baby strollers seemed to double and quadruple. Soraya was sitting on the couch, knees pulled to her chin. "What're we going to do?" she asked.

The question echoed throughout the Great Chamber of the Séraphins. The tiered, circular room stretched all the way up to an unseen ceiling. On each tier, rows of Séraphins sat looking down at the central stage, which was bathed with light. There were great and powerful Séraphins from recent times, and older ones from days gone by. Most were products of daydreams, popping into existence from the ingestion of pop culture, niche reading, the imagination and anxieties of a boy not yet a man. The bottommost rows of the Great Chamber were reserved for the Lord Séraphins, who embodied the most constant strains of thought, while the rows higher up were occupied by the youngest Séraphins, often forgotten but still floating around.

The first of the Lord Séraphins walked to the stage to address the Great Chamber. His Afro was round and black, his brow furrowed with concern. He wore emerald-green armor. Before he spoke he produced the three pregnancy tests from some secret pocket. The tests hovered in the air above his gloved hand. All of the assembled Séraphins looked at the floating plastic wands of doom. When the Afro Séraphin spoke it was slowly and deliberately. "We have to tell Mamma and Papa," he said.

"And what do you think they'll say?" asked another of the Lord Séraphins. This one's hair was braided into neat rows and beads jangled at the ends. His basketball jersey was a deep red, accented with black and white. The Ballin' Séraphin's determination on the court was respected by all and his tendency to use a few dirty tricks to change the outcome of a Sunday pickup game was frowned upon until it delivered victory. "Congratulations, Séraphin, this is exactly what we were looking for. Who'd want degrees when you could have children?" He looked around the Chamber.

"Then what do you suggest we do?" another Lord Séraphin asked. He was shorter and wore a black T-shirt with Bruce Lee in midstrike. He pulled off his spectacles and pinched the bridge of his nose. His was the heavy task of reading under self-imposed pressure, ensuring assignment deadlines were met. The Late Night Séraphin was perpetually overworked.

"We do the right thing." The oldest of the Lord Séraphins left his seat to stand next to the Afro Séraphin. His white staff struck the ground with an echoing boom. The White Séraphin's skin was an even brownness and his armor was white and filigreed with gold. His cape was golden. His jeweled belt held a longsword of fine craftsmanship. His counsel was binding but his pronouncements were few and far between. He preferred to let the others manage their own affairs. "Deliberate or not these consequences may be, the outcome remains the same. We have to accept whatever fate comes our way."

"Nigga, please!" said the Ballin' Séraphin.

"What would you suggest we do, then?" asked the Afro Séraphin.

"We have to ask Soraya to have an—" The Ballin' Séraphin hesitated. He felt the consequences of what he was about to say thumping in his chest.

"You have not the courage to use the word," said the White Séraphin. "We must keep it." His words silenced the Great Chamber.

"No."

The word drifted from the highest tier in the room, falling like a wounded bird and landing with a thud on the center stage where the Afro and White Séraphins stood. The Great Council looked up as one. The top of the chamber was obscured by something that launched itself from the highest tier and spread its black wings, gliding down to land on the stage in a whoosh.

"No," said the Black Séraphin again. The feathers of his wings were raven. His chain mail was black as obsidian and had the unnerving quality of not looking entirely real. He turned to look around the Great Chamber: "This right thing, what is it? The White Séraphin says it with such conviction but who knows what it means? Where has his counsel been this past year when all of you have been taking us from one bed to another? If we keep this thing, who will look after it? Will it be you?" He pointed at the Late Night Séraphin, who cowered in his seat. "Or will it be you?" The Ballin' Séraphin crossed his arms and looked at a stray thread on his jersey.

"It will be all of us," said the White Séraphin.

"It shall be none of us," said the Black Séraphin.

The Afro Séraphin looked around the ruffling Great Chamber and sensed opinion sway from their persuasive power. He looked at the White Séraphin, who also sensed it. "Then let us put it to a vote," said the Afro Séraphin.

"There'll be no vote," said the Black Séraphin. "All that'll happen is what needs to be done."

"And what is this thing that shall be done? Give this evil a name," commanded the White Séraphin.

The Black Séraphin reached out his hand towards the floating pregnancy tests. They caught fire and were consumed until there was nothing left, not even ash. Then he looked at the White and Afro Séraphins and said, "Abortion."

All the other Séraphins flinched.

"No," said the White Séraphin. He grabbed his staff tightly in one hand and unsheathed his sword with the other. At the same time, the Afro Séraphin conjured up his blade. "We cannot allow this."

The Black Séraphin laughed. "Foolishness," he said. In his right hand a blade materialized, its edge eager for something to cut.

The three came together in a clash of swords, staff, and sparks. The other Séraphins scrambled to escape the arcs of lightning that lanced through the room. Some of the younger Séraphins, too weak to withstand the forces of power on display, vanished.

Back and forth the three fought. The White shot balls of fire at the Black, and he, in return, threw devastating tendrils of magic that broke the masonry of the Great Chamber when they were deflected. The Afro Séraphin, a skilled swordsman, unleashed a flurry of blurring cuts and thrusts but could not land a blow on the Black Séraphin. The fight shook the Great Chamber. Chunks of stone were blasted from the walls and used as projectiles by each of the fighting Séraphins, levitated and hurled at frightening speeds.

It seemed as though the Black Séraphin would finally be overwhelmed and defeated. The two bearing down upon him sensed a victory and summoned all of their strength. Then the Black Séraphin smiled and winked out of existence.

Behind him, the Afro Séraphin felt a presence. The Black blade bit into him with an intense hunger and chewed from his left shoulder to his navel. The White roared with anger, conjuring an almighty bolt of lightning. He was about to erase the Black from present and future existence when a bloody hand protruded from his chest. The Ballin' Séraphin retracted his hand and said, "Sorry, Whitey, but I'm with Blackie."

"He will remember," said the White Séraphin as he fell to his knees, clutching at his wound.

"You underestimate the power of forgetfulness," said the Black Séraphin. He brought forth a memory of a boy on a riverside, watching a body float by. "Forgotten," he said. The memory changed to another of a boy looking out of a Mitsubishi Pajero window at the fading hills of home. "Forgotten." He flipped through Séraphin's conquests. "All forgotten." The last memory was of Soraya sitting on the couch of her apartment waiting for Séraphin to reply. "Soon to be forgotten."

"Then you know how this ends," said the White.

"Yes," said the Black. He twirled his sword and severed the White Séraphin's head from his shoulders.

Soraya teared up when Séraphin turned his gaze away from the window, the setting sun throwing half of his face into shadow.

"We can't keep it," he said.

Soraya's womb was promptly evacuated.

In the immediate aftermath they tried to return to normal life, sitting at cafés. watching people, and being watched in return. "Let's go," Soraya said when the sideways glances at them became unbearable. The stares they were accustomed to, the ones that showed shock and disapproval of the union between the black and the Indian, now seemed more condemnatory than before.

The two stopped going out altogether. They decided the couch was a better place anyway. It was their place. But it was also the place where the *decision* had been made. So they stopped spending time on the couch. They did not speak of The Thing They Never Spoke About. The thing that made Soraya shiver whenever Séraphin undressed her.

"Are you okay?"

"I'm okay," she said.

The Thing They Never Spoke About made her push away a prying finger she would have welcomed in days past, arching her back to direct its attentions.

The Thing They Never Spoke About made her hold her breath and say, "Stop." Then she would roll over, back turned away from him, crying.

In the first weeks after The Thing They Never Spoke About, when the certainty of avoided disaster was still fresh and the company of friends provided distraction, she said she was okay. She said things would return to the way they were. But when he went to her place he found Soraya sitting on the couch, looking out of the window or at him absentmindedly. At picnics in Llandudno, burrowing her toes into the sand and pulling her knees up to her chest, she would look out towards things that could have been, should have been. And later when he would say, "You know we couldn't keep it, right?" as they lay on his bed, she would only sigh and roll over.

The Thing They Never Spoke About also brought great confusion to the many Séraphins. In the ruined Great Chamber the Black Séraphin held sway with unshakable conviction. None dared to question his lead.

"What is done is done," he said. His voice echoed throughout the room, up and up, but it offered no comfort. The surviving Séraphins kept to themselves, avoiding contact with each other and the multiplication and amplification of the guilt each carried. The Black Séraphin was left to rant by himself, proclaiming his truths to his shadow.

"What I did," he said, "do they not see that it helped us? The thing would have changed everything. The *thing* would have made us like Guillome and Therése. Surely they must regret us, how bound they are to us, to Yves, to Éric. The thing had to be done."

"What *thing*?" asked the Ballin' Séraphin. His performance on the court had waned. He was not alert to sly passes. A draining bucket easily relegated him to the bench, where he found too much time to think about the *thing* and his role in it.

"The *thing*," said the Black Séraphin. He refused to use its name.

"What must we do now?" asked the Ballin' Séraphin.

"Carry on."

"With Soraya?"

The two turned to look at the sleeping figure.

"No. She will move on," said the Black Séraphin. "She'll blame us."

"She already does."

When Soraya broke up with Séraphin, the two Séraphins watched her walk away crying. In the headlong rush to the end of the year she appeared on campus every now and then, shyly waving at him, eyes darting away, walking away from a possible greeting which might lead to talk of The Thing They Never Spoke About. Instead, she vanished into the press of bodies at Remms, another ending, another missed start.

Four times the Great Council of the Séraphins met and three of these meetings have been told. The fourth lies in the future, where all things must go before they are put in the past, like this afternoon at the Old Biscuit Mill, where everyone laughs at Séraphin talking about the foolhardiness of his first year at Remms, about a bitch named Angie, about the hard work of doing homework, the harder work of healing the hurts, and unloved women who are poor markers of time because they melt into each other so that it is unclear where one story ends and another starts. Only Soraya is finite, a moment in time framed by love and love lost, and The Thing They Never Spoke About, which Séraphin does not speak about now either. When he finally comes to the end of his story, with everyone shaking their heads, he turns to Silmary and says, "Right, your turn."

She holds up her hands in apology. "No way I'm following that."

"I'm owed a story and I plan on collecting on it."

"Some other time," says Silmary.

It is March and the year ripens, the days grow fatter and fuller. The young have their pick of the bunch and the calendar is so full of days that the unpicked are allowed to fall to the ground to rot and fertilize the future. There is no rush, there is no haste.

And because there is no haste, time speeds up to make itself felt.

XXIII

Baby gazelles learn how to stand and walk quickly, raising themselves onto spindly legs like amateur stilt walkers. They know they are food for something else as soon as they come into the world. They did not write the rules, but they are bound by them.

The same cannot be said for black students at Remms Law School, where the dark-skinned brethren neither wrote the rules nor learned how to play by them. They come to the faculty as postgraduates, already alumni of the country's top university. They believe everything, including the law, can be conquered with hard work, determination, and dedication. All of these are vital ingredients for success, the dean announces each year in the welcoming hall. The first-year class—on the first day and the first day only—is black and white, Coloured and caramel, Indian and indigenous. These are the brightest, the cream of the crop, the greatest among equals.

The faculty is inundated with applications each year and the dean recites rejection statistics with glee, for nothing burnishes pride like exclusion. All of the faces in the hall nod along to words of encouragement and fluff their feathers when they are saluted as future jurists. The lecture hall is pregnant with promise and prophecy.

All hail the Remms law undergraduates who shall be advocates, attorneys, high court judges, supreme and constitutional court justices hereafter.

All hail!

The hail storm begins almost immediately.

The foundations of South African law are labyrinthine, the jurisprudential principles behind them as fine as the mist which slinks up from the Cape Town harbor, and just as hard to bottle. Everyone struggles. But not everyone struggles the same way, or for the same duration.

The lecturer's speed forces some students to band together. The first test encourages the formation of a study group. Competing cliques try to enlist the friendships of top-performing students. They pass the next test, then they improve, trotting towards the dean's list.

While the herd moves on, stragglers scraping pass marks limp to keep up. The one thing they all have in common is that they are black. They have yet to figure out what Séraphin, Yasseen, and Bianca discovered after a year of floundering, cursing, and crying themselves to sleep.

"You can't make it through law school without Benevolent White Girls," said Bianca. She lifted her glass of red wine and toasted Séraphin and Yasseen. "Gotta thank you for introducing them to our lives."

They were at a sushi restaurant in Claremont. The plan was to have supper before heading to Stadium on Main for some bowling and arcade games to unwind from Remms's academic pressures, which put a squeeze on their leisure time. The excuse to escape the campus was welcomed by all.

Bianca had told Andrew to bring Silmary. She said it felt nice to not be the only girl around. Silmary asked how their studies were going. Richard and Godwin grunted. Adewale said his tests were providing results; not the desired results, but results nonetheless. Andrew said his lecturers were boring, but, in general, he was coping. He just wanted to write his honors thesis and be done with the degree. James complained that his research was stalling. Yasseen asked him if he knew any Benevolent White Girls in his master's program to help him.

"You need BWGs," Séraphin said, "because they know things."

"So many things," Bianca said.

"If it wasn't for Kim, Kelly, and Megan, I don't think Bianca, Yasseen, and I would be sitting here today. We'd have dropped out of law school a long time ago."

Kim, Kelly, and Megan sat at the front of every class and at the top of every marks list. Their fingers typed with speed and understanding, bullet points capturing complex Roman-Dutch law principles succinctly, footnotes annotating difficult cases simply.

Séraphin and Yasseen met them at the commencement of their second year, after clawing their way through their first. If the coming year went anything like the previous one, they were not so sure they would make it to the middle of the term with their minds intact. They sat in the law faculty's cafeteria to formulate a survival strategy or, at the very least, a coordinated panic plan. That was when Kim, Kelly, and Megan walked in looking for a place to sit. The rest of the tables were fully occupied. Only Séraphin and Yasseen's had space. "We can share if you want," Séraphin said.

The girls looked at each other and sat down. While they ate low-fat yogurt and grapes, Séraphin and Yasseen shared a plate of greasy chips. Séraphin looked at the way the girls flicked their hair, the confidence and ease with which they talked and joked. They were assured a space on the ark when the year-end floods came. Séraphin and Yasseen would have to pray they were given the memo.

Kim had auburn hair that begged to be stroked. Kelly's was straight and black. Megan's tended to change color depending on the season. It was blond in this year of new starts. Séraphin and Yasseen tried not to listen to the conversation about holidays spent in homes in Plettenberg, Knysna, and Wilderness, which is to say that they listened attentively, comparing it to their miserable time spent with their families.

Séraphin's first year in law school had chipped at his ego. He was not accustomed to scraping by. His undergraduate scholarship had lapsed with his graduation, prompting a frenzied search for postgraduate funding. He had managed to ferret out an international scholarship for students studying law. Its requirements were easily met.

Rwandan: check.

Financial need: check.

Studying at a reputable South African university: check.

Displaying a keen interest in human rights, international law, and social justice: not really, but why turn down money because of such trivial concerns? Check.

The Séra-Fire had faded long ago, leaving circumspection in its stead. The Thing They Never Spoke About became The Thing He Thought About for a Long Time. Here and there, but not in the gluttonous quantities of the tumultuous first year, there were amorous connections. The memory of Soraya would hurt on some days like a lost limb, trying to connect to what once was. His second and third years at Remms had been comparatively tranquil, absent of hurt and filled with literature lectures and critical academic essays. The first year of law had impounded his flirtatious nature and, looking at Kim, Kelly, and Megan, he felt inferior.

"You guys are in our class, right?" Megan asked.

"Yes," Séraphin said. "I'm Séraphin, this is Yasseen."

"I'm Megan, that's Kim, and that's Kelly."

"We know who you are," Séraphin said. "I'm lying. We just know you're the names next to all of the high marks. You have to scroll down many lines to find us." The KKM trinity laughed politely.

"It's not that bad," said Kelly.

"It's worse," said Séraphin. "We just collected our course readers. The number of readings is fucking ridiculous. I don't know how we're going to get through them."

"You don't have the notes already?" asked Megan.

"Already?" asked Séraphin. "Term's just started. How the hell d'you make notes for everything already?"

"No, we don't make notes. We get them," said Kim. "You know, the magic notes. They have case and article summaries. Well, most of them."

"Wait," said Kelly, "you haven't been reading and summarizing everything for the past year, have you?"

The girls looked at Séraphin and Yasseen like family friends who have just exposed the truth about the Tooth Fairy or Santa Claus to a table of seven-year-olds.

"Damn," said Kelly.

"You read *everything*?" asked Megan.

"We tried," said Yasseen.

"And failed," said Séraphin.

"I thought everyone knew."

"What does one have to do to get these notes?" asked Séraphin.

"Have an email address," said Megan.

When the zip file containing the notes for that year's subjects popped into their emails later that night, Séraphin's and Yasseen's stomachs churned acid in the library. Yasseen looked over Séraphin's shoulder as they scrolled through the case summaries and said: "We're sitting next to those girls tomorrow."

"Those notes nearly made me cry," said Séraphin as he and Yasseen sat down.

"They're pretty cool, right?" said Kelly.

Séraphin turned in his seat to look at the rest of the hall, wondering just how many students were in the dark.

He frowned.

He had never noticed it before from the back of the class, where people were raised hands, ponytails, and side partings. The faces looking back were almost all white.

"So the notes helped?" asked Megan at the end of class.

At lunch they sat together again. This time Séraphin and Yasseen offered to share their plate of chips with the girls. They declined, eating grains and apple slices.

"You're from Windhoek?" said Kim to Séraphin. "It's a nice place."

"Hmm."

"You don't like it?"

"Have you guys seen *The Little Mermaid*?"

"What?"

"*The Little Mermaid.*"

"Of course," said Kelly.

"You know the part where she's in the cave looking at her thingamabobs and gizmos?"

"Yeah?"

"That was me growing up in Windhoek. I wanted to be where the people were."

"That's the funniest thing I've heard," Kelly said.

Back in the lecture theatre, Kelly asked Yasseen and Séraphin why they were doing law.

"Reading English books isn't a real job, apparently. So I came to get a serious degree," said Séraphin.

"Parents," Yasseen said.

"My dad's a lawyer so I guess I was always going to do it," Kelly said.

"Mine's a judge," said Kim. "Megan's is an advocate."

"Really?" asked Séraphin.

"Yeah, but I don't think I'm going to practice."

"What're you going to do, then?"

"See what shows up."

He looked at her as though she had said she could perform miracles. Perhaps she could, this girl who could have the luxury not to know where everything was headed, who could live without a plan. He envied all of them and the way the law ran in their families, how easily it bestowed marks upon them, and how they could address their professors on a first-name basis. Their paths were clear. All they had to do was walk them.

It was Yasseen who called them the Benevolent White Girls, and each term they came bearing gifts of notes. Séraphin could never find the star which made them steer their kindness towards him and Yasseen.

"They've never hung out with us outside of class," Yasseen said. His chopsticks dipped a piece of sushi in soy and popped it into his mouth.

"That's because it would be weird," said Séraphin. "But the BWGs deserve to have our children named after them. I call dibs on Megan. Sounds like a girl from Fresnaye who likes being cheated on by her boyfriend."

"Idiot," said Silmary. "But why don't you hang out with them?"

"It isn't like we do it on purpose," said Séraphin. "Class is like, what do they call it these days, a safe space. We don't have to talk about anything other than law. Outside is something else. Too many differences would come out. Imagine if we had to talk to them about Avec and the fucked-up racial profiling? It wouldn't work. Mostly because they'd say we were imagining it."

"Bigfoot is real," said Godwin, "but racism, not so much."

"If you don't see it, or if it doesn't happen to you, then it didn't happen," said Adewale.

"But how d'you know they wouldn't be cool?" Andrew asked.

"We just *know*," said Godwin. "Black people just know when a white guy's cool or not. Something they say, something they do. Like Richard. When we met he was just some random white guy. Could've gone either way. Then he opened his mouth and I heard that thick-ass Zimbo accent and I was, like, ah, this one's cool."

"The best way to know whether you're going to get along with white people is with the KZN. Never fails."

"If they pronounce it Kinya, Zimbabwee, or Nigeeria, we aren't hanging out."

"It's K-eh-nya," Richard articulated. "Zimbabw-*eh* and Nig-*eh*-ria, like you're surprised."

"It's something you notice," said Adewale. "If you really hang out with black people you stop pronouncing their things wrong because you're around them long enough to hear the correct thing."

Bianca said, "I've sat next to these girls. They're sweet. But you also get the sense that you can't say something in class that might offend their sensitivities and compromise the supply of magic notes, man. I, for one, plan on graduating this year."

Séraphin and Yasseen learned to skirt controversy. Thanks to the notes and the occasional lunchtime tutoring from the Benevolent White Girls, they passed their second year with ease. In their third year Bianca joined them. Her addition to the group was not easy. Bianca considered Kim, Kelly, and Megan to be vacuous. She called them the Ponytail Brigade and for the first couple of days sitting with them she had made it her mission to call out every infraction they made in speech or action. It took an intervention from Séraphin and Yasseen to get her to curb her enthusiasm. It was notes or nothing.

Nothing, as always, was a steep price to pay. Bianca backed down.

"That's how it is," added Séraphin with a sigh.

They left the restaurant and walked down to Stadium on Main. No one said anything when a passing car of students slowed down and someone shouted to Silmary and Bianca, "Can you handle all of those black guys?" They ignored them and carried on walking.

Nobody said anything about the crowded bowling lanes full of Coloured families who threw Bianca questioning looks, trying to figure out which of the party she was dating. Hopefully, if she had sense, it would be one of the white ones.

When the spirit of competition took over and everyone became engrossed by Richard's strikes, obliterating Adewale and James in their final game, the manager walked over and requested they keep the volume down. "Just leave it, Séra," Bianca said when he attempted to protest.

He left it because that is how it is.

At the end of the night, when the High Lords and Silmary left Claremont, Main Road was full of high-heeled girls walking into or out of clubs with the grace of a just-dropped springbok walking over a minefield. Fair-haired rugby jocks with arms as thick as thighs and thieves bumped into people without apologizing because, well, that is how it is.

Andrew drove Silmary home. Everyone else piled into Idriss's taxi. With nothing for company but a stack of administrative law notes waiting for a ruler and a highlighter, Séraphin put on *Aftermath Before the Event*, a moody compilation that seemed to suit the times. It was already April and the fiction was that this was the best time of his life. The truth was that this was also the worst. And so he started reading and highlighting and working towards graduation and then—

And then?

XXIV

“Children! There are not enough chairs or desks in this class.” Ms. Mutumanu paused and looked at her first-grade students. “We only have twenty-five chairs and twenty-five desks. Can you count to twenty-five? One, two, three, four, five—”

The class picked up the count and boldly steered to ten by themselves. At fifteen the chorus dwindled and at twenty only one remained. Ms. Mutumanu looked at the wafer-thin Indian girl with sable hair and big eyes with a mixture of praise and gratitude. All was not lost. Ms. Mutumanu asked for her name.

“My name is Gina Patel.”

“Thank you, Gina.” Ms. Mutumanu turned to the rest of her class. “I can see we need to work on our counting. Now, we have to decide who will get a chair and a desk.”

As one, the class made a dash for the chairs. The bigger boys pushed their way to chairs and sat upon their thrones with pride. They pointed at those without one and laughed.

“No! That is not how we are going to do it,” said Ms. Mutumanu. “Get off the chairs! Off! Thank you. We shall decide who gets them in one way.” The students looked at each other. “Tests,” she said. “Every

Friday we shall have tests. On Monday I will read out the marks. You can see the tables have numbers on them: one to twenty-five. The first student, the one with the best marks, will sit where? At chair number one. The second student will sit at chair number two. The third one will sit at chair number three, and that is how we shall do it until chair number twenty-five. What do you think happens to everyone else who does not get a chair?" Her eyes raked the silent faces and settled on the Indian girl whose sliver of hand was raised.

"They sit on the floor," Gina Patel replied.

"That is correct. Everyone who does not get a chair will sit on the floor. Because," said Ms. Mutumanu, "there are not enough chairs in life."

Ms. Mutumanu asked her charges to sit on the floor that first week before the first test was written. Séraphin found himself surrounded by boys and girls of indeterminate age. In his pre-primary, just down the street from Guillome and Therése's Parklands home, he had learned how to speak Swahili and write his letters and numbers. He struggled to fit in with the rest of the children. The teacher told Guillome and Therése, in a roundabout way, that perhaps Séraphin had been through too much recently. "You know, with the *thing* that is happening in Rwanda right now, perhaps it would be best for him to recover," she said.

Guillome shook his head. "Séraphin will study, madam. He will be fine."

Ms. Mutumanu's classroom floor was cold and hard. Séraphin found it difficult to write in his book with nothing to press on. He held pencils like someone learning how to use chopsticks for the first time. That week's test was the alphabet and writing all of the numbers from one to twenty. The following Monday, when the test marks were read out, the hierarchy of the class was established. Gina Patel was at the top of the class.

Chair number one.

Séraphin was on the floor. Things had gone badly for him at the letter *R*. What came next? Was it *T* or *V* or *S*? He could not remember. Then in another section of the test, after number 17 he wrote 81 instead of 18. On the floor, looking up at all of the students with a seat and a table, the injustice of it all made him seethe. He hid his face between his knees and arms so the rest of the class could not see him cry. If they did they would probably call him what they'd called him the week before when he'd tried to join their soccer game: mkimbizi.

One of the students in third grade had walked up to him and asked him if he was from Rwanda. When he said yes, Séraphin was told he was a refugee. No team would pick him. Everyone knew refugees were sick and dirty. At home he asked Therése what being a refugee meant and she burst out crying. He was asking questions she could not answer herself. "Is this what they are calling you?" Guillome asked. "Do not worry. Just beat them in school. Show them."

Séraphin was determined to show them all. In the third week of school he won chair number twenty-five after completing his letters, writing the school's name, naming Kenya's capital city, and writing the president's name. Gina Patel was still in chair number one.

Séraphin was quickly removed from his seat in the fifth week. Colors were a difficult test. In the seventh week, when household items were being tested, Séraphin climbed to chair number fifteen. The teacher was proud of his performance. The mkimbizi was showing them.

Gina Patel was still in chair number one. The boy in chair number two, Hasham, had tried to supplant her but was unsuccessful. Séraphin could see them at the front of the class sitting next to each other, sharing pencils, crayons, and the most precious of commodities: smiles. Séraphin decided if anyone was going to be seen smiling with Gina Patel it would be him. He had to close the gap.

On the Monday of the ninth week, he secured chair number eleven. Progress. For Friday's test, the biggest one yet, he needed to memorize colors, household items, countries, numbers, food, and simple addition.

The following Monday, seat names were called out from twenty-five down. Not hearing his name, Séraphin felt his eyes take on water. Taunting would await him if he slipped back to the floor. Boys and girls eagerly took their seats in the pecking order. The swell of tears in his eyes flooded his cheeks. "Chair number three is Hasham Mohammadi. Chair number two is Gina Patel," said Ms. Mutumanu. Shock snatched the sound from the classroom. "Chair number one is Séraphin Turihamwe!"

Séraphin wiped his tears and walked to the front of the class.

The mkimbizi had shown them all.

The rest of the class did not applaud like they usually did for the owner of chair number one. This was a most evil usurpation of power. As he eased himself into his seat, Séraphin turned to Gina Patel, ready to be welcomed into her smiling presence. Instead he was met with a sulky stare.

It was lonely at the top. Gina Patel hated him. Hasham hated him. Everyone all the way down to chair number twenty-five hated him. Chair number one was all-consuming. It demanded constant attention and fending off the twin assaults of Gina Patel and Hasham, who, as the term moved from start to end, intensified their efforts to depose him. It was all in vain. The two would come within a mark or two, only to find their prey bounding away with a flawless handwriting assignment or spelling test mark.

At least he was not called a refugee anymore.

The High Lords and Silmary were at Tara's when Séraphin told the story of his ascension from the floor to chair number one. Tara shook her head in despair. From what Séraphin could gather, she had attended one of those schools where common colds, migraines, and divorcing parents were considered suitable reasons for staying home. Already, she had mentioned two reluctant tours of Europe, from which she returned with scars of poor service for memories. She was scheduled to do another one with her family and she was not excited for it. "I wish they knew there were other countries in the world," she said. "If I see London or Paris or Barcelona again I'll die."

"Imagine," said Bianca to Séraphin, "the day when excess travel becomes the leading cause of death." Séraphin asked Tara what her father did for a living.

"Honestly," she replied, "I don't know. Something with shipping and logistics."

Séraphin's mother had told him when he asked for new basketball shoes in tenth grade that children who did not know how their parents made their money were more likely to spend it. Tara was proving her right. She complained about the London traffic and how hot it was in Mallorca. She said the *Mona Lisa* was unimpressive. "I had to see it because Daddy was dying to."

BeeEffGee: Are you hearing these first world problems?

Sans_Seraph: Hearing them and crying inside, Bee.

Tara's three-bedroom apartment in Green Point hogged the sea view, leaving little for its neighbors. The balcony where they were sitting was decorated with fairy lights and potted plants. The deck sofas were constructed of wooden pallets crowded with scatter cushions. The balcony was suffused with gentle jazz playing through the outdoor sound system. Séraphin was reluctantly impressed. He thought she might force them to listen to cheerless indie music.

The High Lords' presence in Tara's apartment had been occasioned by an accidental meeting between Tara and Silmary earlier in the evening at First Thursdays.

KimJohnUn—HiLos_Of_E: What's that?

KentTouchThis: It's this walking tour of the city center held on the first Thursday of each month. Everything's open later and there's food and live music.

BeeEffGee: So, basically, it's white people walking around Cape Town telling themselves they're cultured.

KentTouchThis: It isn't just white people.

BeeEffGee: And better blacks then. And Coloureds who're better than the better blacks.

KentTouchThis: Why must it always be about race with you?

BeeEffGee: Because 1652.

AddyWale: Hahahaha.

RichDick: Eish!

KentTouchThis: This is going nowhere. Anyway, I spoke to Silmary and she's keen.

Sans_Seraph: I'm in.

BeeEffGee: Of course you are.

KentTouchThis: Everyone else?

GodForTheWin: How much is it?

KentTouchThis: It's free.

GodForTheWin: Which means we're going to wind up spending money out of our ass cracks.

KimJohnUn: Basically.

When the High Lords descended upon the city bowl Bianca became what they called ungovernable. She invaded the first art gallery with loud whispers complaining about the absence of free drinks. Godwin agreed with her, also at barely whispered volume, that art without alcohol was not art at all. Andrew, embarrassed, marched all of them out. At the second gallery, they made courageous attempts to enjoy the framed sketches on the wall.

"I don't understand anything in this room," said Séraphin. "Which means it must be art. Or women." The statement drew a couple of chuckles from the room, Silmary included. Andrew peered harder at the canvas in front of him, trying to immerse himself in the paintbrush scratches and bruises. After a few minutes of sulking at it he was forced to follow his friends out of the gallery.

"I can't take you guys anywhere," he said.

"Come on, Drew," Séraphin said, "there was nothing in that gallery. Just a lot of white space and Helvetica."

The subversion spread. Even Silmary caught it. At a food truck that sold gourmet burgers she pulled her bun apart and asked, "Am I missing something here?"

The rosy-cheeked chef said, "It looks small but it has a lot of flavor. And it's organic."

"Fuck this organic shit," said Bianca. "I need some radioactive chips."

"Go and find them, then," Andrew snapped, "but stop being a bitch about everything."

"That's not how this thing works, Andrew. Remember when we went to watch the Ajax and Santos soccer game at the Athlone Stadium and you spent all the time bitching and whining and we didn't say anything? This is payback."

"You're bringing up shit from a year ago?" asked Andrew.

"Look, we're here," James said. "Let's just see what else is out here. If there's nothing else, we'll head home."

They resumed walking, with Andrew and Adewale at the front. Richard, Godwin, and James shadowed Bianca, more to contain her volatility than to keep her company. Séraphin and Silmary brought up the rear.

"How's the English?" he asked.

"The poetry courses suck," she said. "I don't know why I signed up for them."

"That's why I dropped poetry in my second year," Séraphin said. "I have a better chance of being Pablo Escobar than being Pablo Neruda."

"You and drug dealers." Silmary laughed. "Not a fan of poetry, then?"

"I approach poetry like other people's dogs. With great caution."

"Hmm."

Séraphin tried to decipher the nature of Silmary's "hmm." From his experience there were three types. The first one was inquiring. The second one expressed indifference. The third was amusement. He hoped there was a fourth that meant she wanted to carry on with the conversation.

"Is Bianca your ex?" Silmary asked.

"What?" Séraphin was surprised. "No."

"Okay."

"What makes you ask?"

"I couldn't figure out what you were to each other. First I thought you were dating but when I asked Andrew he said you weren't. Then I thought maybe you were former somethings."

"She would laugh if she heard you say that," he said. "Bee's a friend. Yaz and I met her in law school. She's a hottie so obviously we kept her around for our rep. She's into girls, which means all the guys are into her too."

"Weird how that happens," she said.

In Shortmarket Street it was dark. There was an open-air party where a disc jockey in a bowler hat and thick black spectacles bobbed his head while cuing up the next song. An appreciative cheer went up from the crowd, who sang along to Skee-Lo's "I Wish."

That was where they met Tara and her friends, Nikita, Jana, Jess, Cameron, Troy, Ethan, Declan, Byron, and Bjorn. Séraphin could not tell which was Byron and which was Bjorn because they wore similar red-and-black lumberjack shirts with black skinny jeans. Nikita and Jana, Séraphin decided, were pretty by the law of averages, and Jess, who might have been Chinese or Korean, was quite the looker. The others looked like what Bianca would call generic white boys and would, according to her, probably be differentiated by the number of ignorant things they said. The two groups stood apart like two armies about to confront each other on a battlefield while Tara and Silmary went forward to discuss terms of potential surrender.

"I'm so bored with this," said Tara. "We're headed to my place. You should come through. Bring your friends."

"Sure, we'll see where we wind up," said Silmary. When it became darker yet, and cooler, the First Thursday traffic ebbed. She suggested Tara's. If it was boring, they could always leave.

They had found Tara and her friends spooning salads and hummus onto plates, with glasses of red and white wine on the tables. From the moment they walked in, Bianca said there was something she did not quite like about Tara. "I swear she's going to call me 'babes' or 'love' or something," she told Séraphin, "and that'll be it for me. I think I'm done with white people for today."

"I'll get you a Wembley curry and a Gatsby on the way home to make up for this, Bee."

"You know me too well, Séra. Also, fuck you."

Bjorn and/or Byron were in advertising. The one who was most likely Bjorn was a copywriter and the other was an art director. Everything they said was a case study of a commercial they had seen or a reference to an ad they had worked on. Andrew was in deep conversation with them, interested in every one-liner they uttered. Declan and Cameron were fascinated by single-speed bicycles in the exact way James and Richard, who sat nearest to them, were not. "They're a purer ride," said Declan while Cameron nodded. "Gears clutter the experience." Adewale chatted with Jess and Jana. They were studying fashion in Stellenbosch and had their own blogs. Their conversation seemed mutually interesting because Adewale had never been so animated in all of the time Séraphin had known him.

Tara was taking a year off from her third attempt at completing a year in university. She had dropped anthropology because it was not for her. Then she had dabbled in fashion design. She left that—"It was just too competitive. Everything was so rushed. People prepared to climb over each other. It was so sad"—to try her hand at being a pastry chef.

"What's wrong with competition?" Bianca asked.

"What's the point of it all? For awards? I don't really believe in awards. Like the prize-giving ceremonies at school. Those were horrible."

"You wouldn't have made it at my primary school," said Séraphin.

And then he told them about Ms. Mutumanu and Gina Patel.

"That's so sad," said Tara.

"What is?" asked Séraphin.

"How she made all of the other children sit on the floor. It can't be healthy to have that kind of competition at such a young age."

"I think it's good. Gets you acquainted with the rules of the real world."

"There's no point in lying to children," said Godwin.

"It's better that way," said Bianca. "Then you aren't too shocked when you grow older and shit is fucked up."

"It's still sad," said Tara.

"There aren't enough chairs, like Séraphin said," said Bianca. "There just aren't. You know this, I know this, everyone knows it. Something is sad when it happens once. If it happens more than once then it's just fact and you need to deal with it."

"You're saying there's a point when something like poverty should just be accepted as a fact of life?" asked Bjorn. Or Byron.

"When you aren't doing anything about it, then, yes," Bianca replied. "You can't sit on this balcony and tell me you feel sad about children sitting on the floor in the same way you felt sad when Mufasa or Bambi's mother died. Please. You feel sad the first time, then after a while you don't feel anything. Same thing with poor people. First you feel sad, and then they just become normal."

"That's fucked up." It had to be Byron. He was the one who said his favorite commercials were the socially responsive kind.

"That's life," said Séraphin. "You can't feel sad forever. I have shit to do with my day."

"Our lives," Bianca said, looking intently at Tara and her friends, "yours and ours, just aren't the same. And I think it's better if people don't act like they are. That'll just perpetuate the lie. Or, worse, make people think everyone's on the same level so that they can say dumb shit. Especially at things like First Thursdays. Or at work."

"Especially at work," Adewale said. "If only black South Africans knew how little white South Africans think of them. My supervisor, Afrikaans guy, came into the lab the other day and spent fifteen minutes talking to me about the incompetence of the black guys he works with. Lazy, useless, idiots, imbeciles. Then he turned to me and said, 'But you're fine. That's why I like you foreigners. You work harder and complain less.' I was so stunned."

"You know why they like us, right?" said Séraphin. "Because they don't owe us an apology. But black South Africans, they owe them everything."

"Everything," said Godwin. "It's easy to live and work with someone when you don't owe them an apology. But when you apologize for the fucked-up shit you did then you need to carry the guilt and the shame." The whole balcony fell silent. "Isn't that what apologies are? Acknowledgments of guilt and shame. And the other person takes your wrongdoing and agrees to carry it and let you be human again. That's why I don't believe weak people can forgive. What're you going to do when a weak person forgives you? They can't harm you, they can't take anything from you. Forgiveness from the weak is just words. Forgiveness, real forgiveness, requires the other person to remember, not to forget. When people forget the reason they forgave the forgiven forget to earn their forgiveness. That's why white people in South Africa get to treat black people the way they do. They don't have anything to lose."

Andrew sighed. "These conversations always end up in the same place."

Bianca would have said something but Séraphin shook his head at her almost imperceptibly.

"How'd we wind up here anyway?" James asked.

"Chairs. Never enough of them," said Séraphin.

"What happened to Gina Patel?" asked Silmary.

"Which, really, is what everyone should be concerned about. I whipped her ass for the rest of the year. I left Nairobi in second grade so I'm sure she reclaimed the throne I left behind. I like to think she and Hasham married and had second- and third-place children."

"Wow, Séraphin."

"Anyway, it doesn't matter. I was chair number one." Séraphin rose from his chair and stretched. "Been on top ever since."

"See what I mean by competition?" Tara asked.

"I wouldn't say I'm competitive," Séraphin said. "I'm always willing to settle for first place."

"Sheesh."

The conversation slowly pulled away from race. Séraphin went to the kitchen to find some juice. Silmary came in when he was putting the box back in the fridge.

"So that was an interesting conversation on the balcony," she said. "I think Godwin managed to convince Tara she shouldn't invite strangers to her house."

Séraphin leaned against the counter and sipped his juice. "I'd apologize for my friends, but I'm one of them."

"I like them. They're honest and full of funny stories."

"Which reminds me, I'm owed a story. I'm Shylock about shit like that."

"Mine aren't as good as yours, though," she said.

"Then," Séraphin said, "you can tell me some until we're even."

"We might be here awhile."

"Fine with me," he said. "There's no one on the balcony I'm particularly missing right now." He had to work hard at keeping eye contact after he said it.

"Me neither," she said.

Bianca walked in on her way from the bathroom. "We're about to head out," she said to Séraphin.

"Cool." He tried to make it sound casual, as though he had not just secretly called upon the gods to smite Bianca for her intrusion. As he walked back to the balcony, Bianca poked him in the side.

"What was that?"

"Nothing, Bee, we were just talking."

"Right," Bianca said. "That's how it all starts."

XXV

Every couple of years in the shantytowns around South Africa, where zinc roofs glisten like scales in the sunshine, firewood and coal supplies, the precious fuels needed to boil water and light cooking fires, run desperately low. That is fine because nothing burns—for a shrieking instant—like a foreigner. In Cape Town, this means the Zimbabweans and Congolese who stand by busy suburban intersections selling black coils of cell phone chargers, rolls of dustbin bags, plumes of feather dusters, beaded jewelry, and wire cars with Coca-Cola and Fanta can wheels.

The regularity of the attacks and the long wait for his refugee status permit to be processed by a largely indifferent immigration bureaucracy had one effect on Maxime: he refused to support any South African sports teams. He grouped all of the country's sports teams into one entity he called "Home Affairs," in which he invested his hate. He prayed for Springbok dismemberment, for cruel petal-plucking for the Proteas, and for Bafana Bafana to be manhandled by bigger teams. When the FIFA World Cup rolled into town his muti man told him to put his money on France; they failed to make it out of the group stages and quadruple his investment. His other team, Ghana, seemed as though it would deliver on the witch doctor's predictions. He placed a hefty wager on the Black Stars of Ghana defeating the United States and walked home with his pockets fat and his spirits high, like many across the continent that night. But when Asamoah Gyan missed his penalty against Uruguay, dashing hopes of an African team progressing to the semifinals of the competition, Maxime lost all he had previously won. At least, he thought as he made his way home, Bafana Bafana had been sent packing on home soil. A sliver of spite gladdened his soul.

Later on, perhaps because of his glee at the country's national disappointment, Maxime's application for a refugee permit was denied. He had failed to sufficiently prove his life would be in danger were he to return to the Democratic Republic of Congo. He had two weeks to leave the country. This state of affairs soured him even more. He refused to leave South Africa and chose, instead, to become an illegal resident. In his current state any professional qualifications he possessed were meaningless. Only a handful of vocations were open to him: to clean, hawk, drive, or cut hair. Maxime was too proud to clean. He also would not sell curios by the roadside to sunburned tourists. Driving required a licence, which required too much paperwork. So he chose to cut hair.

With a pair of clippers and a crown in front of him he could become a kingmaker. With everything handled on a cash basis there was no need for him to present anything to the shop's owner besides his own combs, clippers, hair sprays, and oils. The shop's foot and head traffic was constant, the money was good, and the conversations he could have with his clients and the other barbers—also illegals from Cameroon, Central African Republic, and Congo—were always loud and amusing.

"So I walk into the restaurant and ask the waiter to change the channel to the Chelsea match. I tell her, my sister, if you change the channel I will sit down and eat. She says okay, she will change it. So what do I do? I sit down and order. Didier Drogba is killing everyone. It is hot match. He is dribbling like this and like that. Suddenly the channel changes to rugby. Home Affairs is playing the All Blacks. I call the waiter over and I tell her, my sister, when I came in I said I would eat here if you let me watch the game. Now I even ordered from page three, where the prices are not small-small. I tell her I should be saving this money for my family back home. But now I am spending it in your restaurant. And now, my sister, you are telling me I must watch Home Affairs play rugby." Maxime paused his cutting and looked around the barbershop. "I look at her and then I tell her get the fock ourra here!"

Le Bel Homme Barbershop, just off the Main Road in Mowbray, nearly had its doors blown off its rusty hinges from the explosion of laughter. Some of it escaped beneath the door and spilled onto the pavement strewn with cigarette butts and flyers announcing gold would be bought for cash.

Two things were promised at Le Bel Homme: a haircut and a story. Everyone who came in for a trim or a cut joined the queue on the couches unless they were elevated to Big Boss status, a jump facilitated by the size of the tip given to Maxime. As soon as he saw a Big Boss walk in, Maxime would come over and pull him into a bear hug. He would walk back to his current customer, make his clippers dance and whir, finish the job, and usher the Big Boss to his seat ahead of everyone else. "What style you want? Something new? Or you want the usual?" Maxime would ask. Maxime's haircuts were an institution, a rite of passage from boy to man, from ordinary mortal to head-turning lady killer. When he was finished Maxime would pull off the cover with a flourish, like a matador taunting a bull, and make the same joke: "I've done what I can do. From hair on you are on your own."

Séraphin, James, Adewale, Godwin, and Richard were Big Bosses. It was love at first cut since they walked into Maxime's and their loyalty to his craft was eclipsed only by their loyalty to their chosen soccer teams. They came to his shop every three weeks or so to have their hairlines lined up, their sides faded, and their tops trimmed to just the right height. Richard was a bit of a novelty. It was not every day a white boy walked into a black barbershop for a haircut. Still, there was no hair Maxime could not cut. Second only to a haircut from Maxime was sitting on the couch listening to his capers.

Maxime's tales made up for his height deficiency. He met impossibly beautiful women in improbable circumstances and they loved him beyond race, reason, and rhyme. Or as he enjoyed a glass of Guinness in a bar he found his honor insulted for wearing the wrong soccer team's jersey and before he could negotiate a truce he was embroiled in a fight—always with men larger than life and in swarming numbers. After a briefly contested scuffle he vanquished all of them, as though he were Jean-Claude Van Damme on his way to the final round of an underground kickboxing tournament. "One by one, I tell you, I beat them!"

Always, without fail, there would be a customer—from last week or two weeks ago or this week or yesterday—who had insulted him by requesting what he deemed to be an ugly haircut. "Why you come to me for the chiskop? Your lawn mower can do that for you. *Je suis un artiste!*"

Everyone laughed at his stories, not for their truth—which has never been a requirement in the telling of a good story anyway—but because everyone knew Maxime and the other barbers who floated in immigration limbo would not engage in any behavior capable of drawing the attentions of the dreaded South African Police Service. They also would not turn down money, regardless of where it came from, chiskop or not.

"So what happened next?" asked Séraphin.

"I told the waiter, my sister, you must change the channel. Drogba is better than this Home Affairs shit!" replied Maxime.

"And she changed it."

"Of course. But then the white man who had asked to change the channel came to my table to cause big-big trouble."

The barbershop burst into laughter.

"Big-big trouble" was the flourish and fanfare of Maximic hyperbole. Like the first notes of a wedding march it made everyone's ears stand up to listen to the train of bullshit about to parade down the aisle. Big-big trouble would start a narration about Maxime being swindled out of some money, or a husband coming back home to find him in bed with a straying wife. Big-big trouble always ended with Maxime threatening to recover his money with Scarfacian violence, or parlaying with an angry husband who went into the next room to load his gun, leaving Maxime just enough time to jump out of a window half-clothed.

"The man comes to my table and he says to me, comrade, the Springboks are playing. Can we watch the rugby match? The soccer is from England. And I say, I am not your comrade. And I came here first. If I want to watch English or Spanish soccer I will watch it. Even if I want to watch Zambia Super League—where the highlight of a game is a throw-in—I will watch it. I tell him, please, there are many places where you can watch Home Affairs play. Then I tell him, your home is one of them."

"Maxime, you lie," said Chris the Cameroonian barber.

"If I lie," Maxime retorted, "then let the Lord God Most High strike me down now! Eh? You see, nothing. I tell the truth. This white man looks at me and tells me this is his home. And then he says to me, but you are not from here. Is big-big trouble now, you see."

"Of course," said Godwin, dabbing at his eyes. "Big-big trouble now."

"I tell him, look, whether I am in Kinshasa or Harare or Accra, it is all my home. From north to south and east to west. And they will always change the channel so I can watch Didier Drogba, Yaya Touré, and Emmanuel Adebayor because everyone knows the English Premier League is actually African Premier League. It is called English Premier League because the Queen has not died yet. We are just waiting for her to go and then we rename everything. But you see, your Home Affairs comes only from Bloemfontein. So, please, I tell him, I am watching Chelsea right now. He was angry-oh! He could not say anything to that, because he knows I am right. But, you see, now is big-big trouble because I am the only black person in the restaurant. I can see everyone is angry at me because we are not watching Home Affairs. But I also cannot be asked to leave, you understand. You know the only thing worse for Cape Town people than to be told they are racist is to be given a chance to show it is so. So, anyway, I sit and I watch."

"Just like that?"

"Not just like that. You know this is Cape Town. When something is making people uncomfortable they give it over to someone else to deal with. What is that thing called when I send someone instead of me going myself?"

"Delegation," Richard volunteered.

"Yes, that is it. So the white man, eh, he gives over delegation to the manager and he walks to me like he is sent by the Lord God Most High, but I fear no evil for I am anointed, gifted, and blessed." Everyone in Le Bel Homme applauded. "The manager, he comes over to me. You know how polite white people get when they are about to ask for something foolish. Eh, look at your friend turning red, Séra. This manager, he asks me if I mind that they change the channel. I look at him and say I am minding very much. If you change the channel to Home Affairs I will not pay for my meal. He is in shock like he has been given a slap. Now he has a big-big problem because I have ordered food and drinks, not small-small things, you see. The manager he says, okay, enjoy the meal, sir. He leaves me alone and we all sit and we watch the match."

Le Bel Homme vibrated in mirth. Séraphin sensed the storyteller holding back the kicker. "How did Chelsea do?" he asked.

"Lost three-zero," said Maxime, paying careful attention to the hair he was cutting. "Home Affairs beat the All Blacks." The barbershop gurgled with laughter like a pot of chips with the top on. Séraphin decided to lift the lid.

"Where was this restaurant, Maxime?"

"Newlands."

Now the barbershop's business came to a standstill because the laughter was too much. The probability of Maxime—a Congolese immigrant who lied to refugee status determination officers about throwing a stone at the president's motorcade during a protest and subsequently being pursued by the military police from Kinshasa to Lubumbashi before escaping to Zambia, commuting by bus and truck to Cape Town—holding an entire rugby-mad Newlands restaurant hostage on the day the Springboks played the All Blacks was as ludicrous as one ant threatening to storm Table Mountain.

Most likely the channel was changed to the rugby just as Drogba prepared to launch the ball into the back of the net. Most likely Maxime exclaimed loudly. Most likely he asked for the channel to be changed back. Most likely it was not. Most likely Maxime ate the rest of his meal in resentful silence and paid for it in full. Even more likely, Maxime was never in any such restaurant.

Still, the story was a good one, and its principles were sound and true. Supporting or watching Home Affairs and its teams was not permitted in foreigner circles.

"What are you going to have today?" Maxime asked Séraphin, settling him in the barber's chair. Séraphin said, the usual: faded and framed at the sides, thin at the top. Maxime said, "So when will you finish? This year, no? Then where are you going?"

"Back home. Maybe."

"Rwanda?"

"No. Namibia."

"So that is home now?"

"Sort of."

"You are Namibian now, no?"

"No, still Rwandan."

"You must get your papers. Even if it is just Namibia. Otherwise Home Affairs will be after you. Visa this, permit that, certified copy of this, proof of that." He swept Séraphin's head with a brush filled with hairs of nationalities and ethnicities unknown. "So you will do law in Namibia?"

"Maybe."

"Listen to this boy." Maxime raised his voice and looked around the shop. "He thinks he has a choice about what to do after he finishes his studies. Maybe he will do law, he says. Or what instead? You will become a rapper or a soccer star? My friend, you will become a lawyer so you can help your family—and us when Home Affairs comes for us." Séraphin remained quiet. "Eh-ba! Why are you not South African yet? How long have you been here? I would have your degrees and a South African wife with papers too. Were there no girls at that fancy university of yours?"

"There were girls," Godwin piped up from the couch.

"Too many," James said.

"So what is the problem?" asked Maxime. "You should have got one of them pregnant, then married her and gotten papers." Séraphin shifted in his seat. Maxime told him to stay still so he could work on the fade. "By now," Maxime continued, "you should even have had a white one. Everyone knows fancy universities are the only places white girls will like guys like you. It is called experimenting. You should have told me, 'Maxime, today I need a style for the white girls,' and I would have delivered for you."

"I don't think that was the problem," Adewale said, chuckling. "He was in white girls like a green salad."

"Eh-ba! So what was the issue? The white women, they are good for the papers and the black women are good for the children. With Coloured women you are only renting her for a while. Always she will go back to her people. Eh-ba! Trust me, I know. Or you must be worried for when she upgrades to a white man."

"Séraphin, do you have something to add to Maxime's point?" asked Godwin. Séraphin threw him a withering look.

"I can see he knows the truth," said Maxime. "But even with white women you must also look out for your fellow black man. They take that as a sign she wants all of them. The only girl you do not want is an Indian woman. Big-big trouble, those ones." The murmurs of agreement in the room supplemented the buzzing clippers and hair-spraying. "At least a white woman will look at you and maybe be curious, and a Coloured woman will look at you and potentially love, and a black woman will look at you, compromise, and settle. But an Indian will look at you like you are here to clean and serve them."

While the rest of the barbershop agreed with Maxime, Séraphin felt a gnawing discomfort about the subject matter and was about to say something and decided against it. When masculinity waded in its own pool of ignorance like a hippopotamus enjoying its stretch of river the safest thing to do was become a limp fish and go with the flow.

As Maxime clipped the top of Séraphin's hair he said, softly, "My friend, you must get serious. Seven years and you do not know what to do next? There are people taking buses from Congo to South Africa who know what they are going to do next every day for the next thirty years. They come with nothing and then they make a life. You can do everything with your degrees. But you must make a plan."

The two made eye contact in the mirror. Séraphin nodded slightly before Maxime averted his eyes and went back to lining up the front of Séraphin's hair. He raised his voice once more: "You know, the other day I was in one of the trains coming here and I was wearing my Black Stars shirt. Some white guy asked me if I was Ghanaian because he had just visited Accra. I told him no. He asks me if everyone in Africa supports Ghana, Nigeria, and Côte d'Ivoire. I tell him they are the only teams which do anything in soccer. Then he says what about Egypt? I tell him, my friend, Africa ends at Mali. In the Olympic Games we are for Kenya and Ethiopia when the running is on. In soccer we are for Cameroon or Ghana or Nigeria or Côte d'Ivoire. Not these Arab countries who are African only when Cup of Nations is on. Everyone on the train is listening, eh. I sense that there could be big-big trouble—"

Le Bel Homme settled back into a familiar routine.

A new story and a new impossibly heroic ending for Maxime the illegal immigrant.

When all the haircuts were done they flagged a minibus taxi back to Remms.

"Where to, my boss?" asked the driver.

"That's a very good question," said a Séraphin, climbing into the taxi and sitting next to Séraphin.

"Town," said Séraphin. He fished the group's fare from his pocket.

"Not town," said the Séraphin. "Big-big trouble."

"Why?" asked Séraphin.

"It's already May."

XXVI

As soon as someone gets what they want, they find out what they need, and the words which start the romance are usually the ones that end it too.

It is winter in Cape Town. The city is besieged by cloudy skies. For days and weeks the falling rain and bone-deep chill bring out the trademark Capetonian surprise that winter could actually be cold.

At Remms, the upcoming June examinations send everyone scrambling for the warmth and huddled stress of the libraries. The High Lords are scattered as they are wont to be at this time of the year. Long lunches and late nights are put aside. Everyone keeps to themselves. It is a lonely time of hot chocolate mugs and coffeemakers worked overtime, showers forgotten, and facial hair grown in studious isolation.

This is the perfect time to be in a situationship.

For the past two weeks, Séraphin has been secretly seeing Nike. Neither has said what it is or what it is not. Things have progressed to the stage where Séraphin and Nike are comfortable without reason. This is the hallmark of a situationship, endowed with all of the features of a relationship minus the assurance of crying poetically into pillows, lamenting the loss of love when pain inevitably comes home to roost.

Some background first.

Séraphin and Nike floated around each other in law school separated by a couple of rows in lecture theatres. They passed one another with the hesitancy of people who know they should greet each other but look away because they should have been doing that since the first year. In addition, Nike was always cocooned by a circle of wooden earrings, dreadlocks, and earthy colors who made a habit of pointing out the flaws of patriarchy in family law and the absence of feminist thought in constitutional cases. Of the lot, Séraphin thought Nike to be the most attractive. She had a smooth forehead, shapely eyebrows, and eyes slanted at their ends. When she laughed at something her lips exposed a brilliant flash of white. Her hair was thickly braided, and from having accompanied his mother to a braiding session back home in Katutura he could tell she would have long, soft hair that would stand up like the rays of a black sun when the braids were undone. She and her posse of friends were older than the rest of the students in law school. In the library, when they were talking about the nuances of some case in whispers loud enough to be heard on helicopters, they would petrify anyone with the gall to shush them with venomous looks.

Since Nike and Séraphin never interacted, or had reason to, it was left to a photocopy machine in the law library to arrange their meeting at the commencement of the two-week study period.

"You have to press the yellow button to pause it, open the paper tray, and remove the stuck paper before pressing the green button to continue printing," Séraphin said. He stood behind her, listening to the sound of crunching paper and her exasperation. "Here, let me help you."

"Thank you," Nike said when her printing resumed. He glanced at the papers coming out onto the printing tray.

"Is this for administrative law?" he asked. "I have summaries of this case. If you give me your email address I'll send them to you."

Nike was surprised. She had seen Séraphin around the faculty, always in the company of the Coloured girl and boy. He sat next to the three white girls who exchanged the top position in law school among them. After four years in the law faculty she came to assume coldness was de facto between student groups that seemed organized according to high school cliques and class delineations. Still, she accepted his offer, paused her printing, and accepted his cell phone as he handed it over. "It is saved under Nike," she said when she passed it back to him.

"*Nee-keh*," he said. "I had a feeling it wasn't pronounced the way it was written. I'll send the summaries when I get home."

Later that evening, an email popped into Nike's inbox.

Hi Nike,

As promised: the summary for that pesky admin law case. Also I have attached the notes and summaries for everything else we've done so far. Remember the golden rule: if it's not highlighted or underlined, then it's not the law.

Séraphin

Nike opened the attached documents and laughed at the annotations Séraphin had pinned to relevant parts of case law or important principles. When she found the case, she saw a comment attached to its headnote: *Fuck this case and its general irrelevance. All you need to know is that white people win. As usual.* She looked at the case as well as the annotations, amused by the righteous anger in them. She completed her notes in less than half the time it would have taken her to read the case. She replied to Séraphin's message.

Hello Séraphin,

Thank you for the notes. They made me laugh. Do you mind if I send them to my friends? We're all struggling with this section and these notes are really helpful. Let me know how I can repay you for this.

Nike

The response came immediately despite the late hour.

> **Forward the notes to as many people as you wish. On the thanks side, no sane man has ever said no to food and I'm quite sane. Most of the time.**

"Not your best," said the first Séraphin. "But it'll have to do. Brain's tired from all this studying anyway."

"You could've just told her it was all good and left it at that," said the second. "You're trying to drag out this conversation."

"He is," said the third.

"Did she reply?" asked the first.

"She just did," said Séraphin.

> **Food I can do. Nigerian cooking, of course.**

The response was read once, twice, and then a third time.

"Is that what I think it is?" asked Séraphin.

"That's a dinner invitation," said the second. "You know what the next play is?"

"There's no play," said Séraphin.

"Reply to Nike," said the first Séraphin. "With a name like that you know you need to just do it."

Séraphin looked at the glowing laptop screen for a while. All-too-familiar parts of a former personality were stretching from their slumber. He had made a concerted effort not to succumb to the lures of The Sauce. He inhaled deeply and reread the email. "Let's just see what happens, okay?" he said.

"Attaboy," said the second Séraphin.

> **Your lobola may or may not be calculated according to your cooking skills and company. No pressure at all.**

"Bold," said the first.

The response was speedy.

Funny. Dinner it is then.

Midway through another grey afternoon two days later, Séraphin's phone pinged.

So . . . dinner?

Séraphin showed up at her apartment, a warm place with floating shelves holding an assortment of Buddha charms. The fireplace looked unused and above it hung monochromatic pictures of Nina Simone, Gil Scott-Heron, and Hugh Masekela. When she walked to the kitchen to check on supper he perused her bookshelf and found it burgeoning with activism. Her music collection harbored Lauryn Hill, Wyclef Jean, Lucy Pearl, and D'Angelo.

"Boney M.?" he called out to her.

"Do you know them?"

"You might as well cancel Christmas if you aren't going to play any Boney. You have Joan Armatrading? She's a gem. You have a cool music collection." Nike walked back from the kitchen and began setting the table in her dining room, an intervening space between the lounge and the kitchen, clearing away her laptop and writing pads. "I grew up with some of those CDs," Séraphin said. "My parents liked a lot of that music."

"Thanks for making me feel older," she said.

"Good music has no age. Nor do its collectors." Nike beamed at him.

Dinner was bean and plantain pottage with a zing that made Séraphin's tongue rub around his mouth looking for respite.

"Too hot?" Nike asked.

"It's fine," he replied. "Not used to spicy foods, though."

"Strange, considering this is Cape Town."

"I try to steer clear of three o'clock curries," he said. "The ones that make you sweat like a sauna." Nike giggled, a strange sound. "Shit's hotter coming out than it was going in."

"This isn't dinner conversation," Nike said.

"Small talk, law talk, dinner conversation, death. Those are the steps."

"But you're doing law," she said.

"I don't talk about it."

"You don't like it?"

"It's okay."

"What're you going to do after you finish?"

"Don't know. You?"

"Family law," she said. She chewed delicately and swallowed before continuing. "Maybe working with gender or development groups. You seem like a corporate type. Suits and ties and shiny cars."

"I'm sure that would make my parents proud," he replied. He flicked the conversation back to her. "Human rights don't put food on the table. Just more people in the ground."

"That's morbid," she said.

"Enough law talk. What d'you do when you aren't being a law student?"

"Depends on the day and how much time I have," she said. "Photography mostly. I used to do that back in the day, before law school. Tried to see as much of Africa as I could that way. I spent a lot of time in Lagos, Kampala, and Bamako. But then assignments became scarce. I needed something with more security. What do you do when you aren't swearing in your notes?"

"My story doesn't compare," Séraphin replied.

"We aren't comparing stories, just telling them. I'm sure yours is fascinating too." Her head tilted a little to the side.

"Some other time," he said. "What else have you gotten up to in your life?"

"Well," she said, "I got married and divorced."

"Why'd it end?"

"Are you sure you want to hear it all?"

"Just the highlights."

Nike put her spoon down. "Unequal ambitions, unequal drives. He became complacent, I put on more weight than makeup. He didn't like the weight, I didn't like the complacency. So it ended." She paused. "But not before I was traded in for a younger model."

"I knew there'd be some other crime," he said. "Marriage makes no sense."

"Not all marriages are bad," Nike said. "Some work."

He thought of his own parents and whether they made things work. But thinking of them made him feel sad about taking up so much of their time when he was younger—and even now that he was older. He remembered them at the bus station. The grey hairs which snuggled amongst the black, the skin which used to be ironed smooth, now wrinkled. "The new model can't have been that much younger," he said after a while.

"How old d'you think I am?"

"Thirties," he said, after making a show of scrutinizing her. "But I can't tell whether you're in the half that misses their twenties or the half that's learned to embrace the inevitability of their forties."

"Thirty-seven."

"Damn," Séraphin said. "It's your husband's loss."

"He didn't think so."

"Shame. If I put it in I wouldn't take it out," said the first Séraphin.

"What?"

"Nothing." Séraphin reached for the jug of orange juice on the table and poured himself a glass. From the way Nike smiled he knew she'd heard what he said.

"How old are you?" Nike asked.

"Twenty-four."

"I thought you'd be older."

"I will be, unfortunately."

"It's good to grow older. Especially when you're a man. What you don't want to be is a black woman. We have a very short shelf life."

"Now that's morbid," Séraphin said.

"That's the truth," she said.

The truth was followed by a clearing of the table. Nike went over to a floating shelf and pulled a CD from it. Then she walked to a silver CD player. The tray swallowed it like communion and music filled the room.

"Sade," said Séraphin. "I like this album. 'King of Sorrow' is my favorite."

"It's a good song," Nike said, joining him on the couch. "That's the life of a black woman."

"Not all black women are sad."

"How d'you know?" she asked. She leaned her elbow on the backrest so she was facing Séraphin. "Have you ever asked your mother if she was happy with her lot in life?"

"I don't think she's happy all the time," Séraphin said. "But she'd have changed her situation if she wanted."

"Really?"

"You haven't met my mom. She'd smack life in the mouth if it disrespected her."

"You speak of your mother well," she said. "But are you one of those men who speaks fondly of their mothers and unkindly about other women?"

"Guilty," said Séraphin. "You do the same. Hating us while dreaming of Prince Charming."

"Some of us dream of other things. Decent jobs and decent lives. It only so happens men stand in the way of both of those. It's easier to go with you than to go through you."

"Decent," said Séraphin, "means adequate. Why not have magnificent lives instead?"

"You're still young—I don't mean that as an insult. You haven't come to grasp your full power over yourself, or over the world." She paused and looked at him directly. "The world will always bend to your tune. Always. One day when you realize this you'll understand why decent will be enough for some of us," she said. "It's more than nothing."

For a while they sat in the stillness that follows wisdom. Then Séraphin got up and stretched. He came and stood in front of Nike. He nudged her legs closed and sat on her lap, his legs on either side of her, and put his arms around her shoulders. Feeling no resistance, he leaned down to kiss her. She tasted like supper, and the pressure of her lips was firm and responded to his rhythms. He pulled away. "So," he said.

"So," she replied softly.

"Are you going to give me the stop-well-I-don't-usually?" he asked.

"Well, I don't usually—"

"Shut up."

"Foolishness," she said. "I'd just like to say from the beginning that it's been a while for me."

"That's okay," said Séraphin. He reached around her and made the zip of her dress purr as it raced down her back. He unclasped her black bra, ran his hand over her breasts, and then sucked on one and then the other. She moaned softly and then asked if things were not moving too fast. "If they are," he replied as he pulled off his T-shirt, "then we can stop right here and I can go home. But I'm definitely taking these with me." He cupped her left breast and squeezed gently.

"Foolishness," she whispered with her eyes closed.

They were on the couch for a few more minutes, lips locked, hands rubbing and caressing soft and muscle-hardened contours, before Séraphin stood up, pulling Nike to her feet. He let her lead them to the bedroom, where their bodies pressed together in the blueish-blackness of the night. When the heat of their pleasure cooled, their skin registered the winter chill. Séraphin pulled the duvet over them.

"So," said Nike.

"So," said Séraphin.

"That was decent," said Nike.

"Foolishness."

"I was joking."

"I know."

"Sure you're that good in bed?"

"No," he said. "I know ninety percent of a man's sex life is spent rolling over and apologizing. But I also know *that* was in the remaining ten percent."

"Foolishness." They lay breathing in the smell of her room, which was fragranced by shea butter. "Okay, it was really good," she said.

"I know," he replied. He sat up. "I'm not done yet."

Nike felt her cheek kissed, then her neck, then her breasts, and then her navel. In the distraction of each fleeting kiss and some sly acrobatics, Séraphin popped up between her thighs. She scrambled to sit up, holding Séraphin's head at arm's length.

"What?" asked Séraphin.

"I don't want you down there," Nike said hesitantly.

"If it makes you feel any better, I promise not to blow on your vagina."

"Is that how it works?"

"Wait," Séraphin said, "you just asked if that's how *it* works. Am I correct in assuming nobody's ever gone down on you?"

In the dark, Nike was glad he could not see her expression. She was silent for a long while before she said, "My ex-husband was my first and my only for a very long time. He never did that."

"What is *that*?" asked Séraphin. He laughed at Nike's hesitancy.

"*That*," she said. "He said my things looked funny. That it looked dirty."

"The fuck?"

"Kind of made me insecure about it."

"No shit."

Séraphin looked at Nike sitting up in bed, with her womanly body wrapped around itself. He always imagined women like Nike to exist beyond insecurity. They were grown women. Only now for the first time did it strike him that grown women could also be afraid.

"I'm going to get a glass of water," he said. "When I get back we're going to sort this thing once and for all. Nope. No buts."

"Unless you plan on putting that in my face too," added the first Séraphin. Nike made a sound of shock. "Thought so."

Séraphin bounced off the bed and vanished into the kitchen. A running tap announced the glass of water and before she could compose herself he came back in, picked up the duvet, and crawled underneath it, pulling it over his head. Nike felt her legs stretched out and pried open.

"Relax," said Séraphin from beneath the duvet.

"I'm trying to," said Nike. She felt a warm *something* brush up against her, softly at first, and then more firmly. The sounds coming from beneath the duvet were slippery. She felt ashamed for how her body responded to the shapes and figures being painted between her thighs. "Are you—is it—okay?"

"This isn't dinner conversation," said a muffled voice down below.

She clutched the sheets as a trembling began in her legs. A short while later she broke the Third Commandment at volume.

Séraphin clambered back to the pillows and lay next to her. It took her a minute or so to work up the courage to lie in the crook of his arm, feeling his chest rise and fall with his breathing. Before they drifted into sleep he muttered, "Nothing weird down there. Only what you bring to it." He thought he heard her say, "Foolishness," but he could not be sure.

Unspoken, unnamed, unclassified, uncategorized, the conditions for situationships were present and the Nameless Thing That Was a Relationship but Not a Relationship flourished. They met up at Nike's apartment, ate whatever she prepared, and then, as best they could, put their minds to the law and its intricacies before they looked up from their notes and proceeded to chase more intricate intimacies.

On another night, with their notes spread before them, Nike said, "I have a question." Séraphin did not look up from his papers. He hummed a reply. "How many people have you slept with?" Séraphin looked up. "You don't have to answer."

"Enough," Séraphin replied.

"Does 'enough' have a number?"

"Yes," he said. "More."

"Foolishness. I've only slept with three people, you included," she said.

"You should use your body to rack up a better body count," Séraphin said, and turned back to his papers.

"Are you always so complimentary?"

"I've been known to reach for nice words when I'm trying to get laid after a study session."

"Foolishness," she said. He looked up and found she had turned back to her piles of paper. "I have another question," she said after another while. "Have most of the women you've slept with been white or black?"

"Why?"

"I just want to know."

Séraphin studied her for a while. "Hoping my reply doesn't sound like a tick on a to-do list, now I can say I've slept with a black woman."

"So I'm your first," she said. Séraphin noted the absence of surprise.

"Nobody asks questions like that just for their own sake. What's on your mind?"

"You never struck me as the kind of guy who slept with black women."

"What does a black guy who doesn't sleep with black women look like?"

"It isn't a look," she said. "More of a bearing. As soon as you speak to them you just know they're loved by white women. They're the right kind of handsome and smart, they tend to be distant around black women. Either very polite, or not polite at all, because now they date or sleep with white women."

"I've no idea what you just said," Séraphin said, "but I've always liked girls who like me."

"So no black girls have ever liked you?"

"I'm sure some have," he replied. "I don't know, when I'm trying to get in someone's guts I don't have time to provide cutting-edge research on romantic race theory."

"Guts." Nike giggled. "That's how I know I've been hanging around you too long. I've started figuring out the nonsense you say." She hesitated and then said, "I kind of like it, actually." Séraphin stayed silent. They looked at each other across the table until Nike looked away. "So it didn't feel weird when you first came around?" she asked, to move the conversation along. "You know, when we, you know?"

"When we what?"

"You know!"

"Right. Hooked up, slept together, hopped on the good foot and did the bad thing, f—"

"Foolishness!"

"No. It didn't feel weird," he said. "Look, you're attractive and smart. You could've been blue or green, you were still going to get these strokes."

She giggled. "Not strange even a little bit?"

Séraphin gave Nike a long look, his head tilted to the side as though he was seeing something in her for the first time. "Well, now you mention it," he said, "I realize there was *that* one thing." He turned his attention back to his notes hurriedly.

"What?" She sounded distressed.

"Well," he said, "when you finished coming, I didn't ask you when you were going to give the land back."

Nike laughed. A deep laugh, from her core. "Idiot," she said.

While the land was never an issue between them, it certainly was in the rest of South Africa. The land made the difference, then as it did now, as it would continue to do in the near future when the red berets formed and organized into an angry mass, jaded by patience and flagging political will. None of that mattered in Séraphin and Nike's situationship. They made their study notes and lived in the shadow of questions that demanded answers. Séraphin's wants were being adequately satisfied, in highly experimental and adventurous ways, which made Nike blush but then acquiesce out of curiosity. It even reached the stage where she was brave enough to ask Séraphin to do *that thing* on more than one occasion. With the June examinations a few days away, it seemed as though there could be nothing else to possibly want from the situation. That was when the needs made themselves known.

They were lying in bed, notes forgotten on the dining room table. Séraphin seemed far away, something that had become more frequent. Nike took it as boredom. She sat up in bed. "Where is this going?" she asked.

"Where is *what* going?"

"I guess that answers my question."

"Where would you like it to go?" he asked. "Don't say nowhere because you'll be lying."

"I have places I'd like it to go. You know this too," she said. "But I don't want to even try going there if all you're going to do is be bored with me."

"I'm not bored. I'm just— Never mind."

Nike looked at him, seeing, as though for the first time, just how young Séraphin was. "Exam stress?" she asked.

"Maybe."

Trying to be playful, she reached into the sheets and felt a defeated limpness. "What's the matter?" she asked as she kissed his neck. She cast around for some conversational spark to pull him into her again. He always responded to wit more than emotion. "Is it my stretch marks?"

"My phone had a cracked screen and I managed to stick with it for a year. Trust me, it's not your stretch marks."

"Then what is it?"

"I don't know."

But Séraphin did know. A week ago everything with Nike was nothing more than something to pass the time. But now it was taking on the shape of something real. Nike, even though she never expressly said so, expected this thing to continue into the exam season, and beyond it.

Nike sat up in bed once more. "Would you like to take a break from this?" In her face he could see a finality. All he had to do was sign on the dotted line.

"I guess so." He sat up in the bed next to her.

"Okay," she said. Her voice was distant. She inhaled, and then she exhaled. "I think I misled myself with all the fun we were having. You have a lot to figure out and I have a lot to do."

"Was I unkind?" he asked. He desperately hoped he'd done the homework.

Nike looked at him. He really was young. "No," she said, "if anything, you were too kind. You even had the grace to keep quiet when I said I was liking our time together. But take this from me, Séraphin, sometimes actions become promises."

"I'm sorry."

"I'm not." They sat in the bed for another while, and then Nike said, "Success always demands a sacrifice, and if we're to make it through exams we need to end this." Then she stood up, wrapped herself in her bathrobe, and walked to the kitchen. Séraphin remained in the bedroom.

"She's right, you know," a Séraphin said from the edge of the bed.

"I know," Séraphin replied.

"Do you now?" Their gazes locked. Séraphin looked away.

"Anyway, it's better this way. You have exams to focus on, and a future to fret about." The Séraphin watched him dress, casting around the room for his clothes. "You didn't notice, but you never even closed the door once."

Séraphin paused with his T-shirt halfway on. "Does that mean something?"

"Do you want it to mean anything?" asked the Séraphin. He was not given a reply. "Then I wouldn't ask questions I'm not brave enough to answer."

"What do we do next?" asked Séraphin.

"What're you in the mood for? Sauce or success?"

"No more Sauce," said Séraphin.

Séraphin found Nike sipping a cup of coffee in the lounge, seated on the sofa where they'd first listened to Sade. He wondered whether sofas were designed for breakups. He sat down next to her. "So," he said.

"So," she said.

"Dinner?"

XXVII

Unknown: Hi. Are you busy?

Sans_Seraph: Who's this?

Unknown: Silmary.

The reason why distractions beat focus nine times out of ten is because they let you know that you are going to win the lottery before you have even purchased a ticket. That is their beauty. But if it were easy to resist temptation, everyone would do it and the Our Father would become irrelevant. Distractions would not be the scourges of the present times—which is where we pick up our tale.

Springtime flirts with the warming air. It is all quiet on Séraphin's academic front. Cases are being summarized. Nike is a distant but occasional ache. Focus is adopted as a new god. With the end of the year in sight, most of the High Lords know where they are heading. Some are going to remain in Cape Town. Bianca, unfortunately, seems set to do another stint in the Jail City, where her parents pray every day for her sexuality to change. Yasseen is luckier. Johannesburg called. Adewale weaseled more funding from sources unknown and will remain in Cape Town next year as he completes his PhD. Godwin and Richard are determined to head home to Zimbabwe and turn their country's fortunes around. Andrew plans to travel.

Then on a Saturday saturated with sunshine, a message appears on a phone and it is from Silmary.

Silmary: I'm on the way.

There was the perfunctory debate about whether it was a good idea to abandon that morning's planned study for something so impromptu. Good, logical arguments were presented about the need to be less impulsive. The Great Council of the Séraphins listened politely and then slammed the gavel down in favor of upholding existing precedent: "Let's just see where this goes, okay?"

Sans_Seraph: What's all this then?

Silmary: We're going on an adventure.

Sans_Seraph: What kind of adventure?

Silmary: The kind that needs you to be ready in ten minutes.

A pair of jeans and a T-shirt later, he stood in the brisk air. Perhaps a jacket would be necessary, he thought, but before he could act on his prudence, an old, dark-green Citi Golf with a couple of dings and one large dent was pulling into the paved driveway.

"Meet Yoda," Silmary said.

"I know this one," he said. "Because he's old and green."

"But the Force is still strong with him," she replied. "I got him for a steal yesterday and this is his first official outing."

Either the wind or Silmary's smile made him shiver, almost imperceptibly. "You're going to need a jacket," she said.

Séraphin dashed back to his room to fetch something warmer, settling on a light grey hoodie. As he zipped it up he saw the other Séraphins. "What are you doing?" he asked nervously.

The first Séraphin finished tying his shoelaces. "Getting dressed."

The second pulled on a sweater and spritzed himself with some cologne.

"You're not coming," said Séraphin.

"He's funny. I'll give him that," said the third, joining the others as they walked out the door. Séraphin hastily locked his room and raced after them to make sure they did not arrive at the car first.

"How long d'you intend on keeping me hostage?" Séraphin asked Silmary as he climbed into the passenger seat.

"This isn't a kidnapping. You're coming along voluntarily."

"You have to say you've taken me against my will so I feel better about abandoning my books," he said, reaching for his seat belt.

"You won't get that pleasure," she said. "But you might get others."

The split second before Yoda's engine thrummed into life stretched long enough for Séraphin to turn around in his seat and look at the other three in the back. All of them had their mouths open, stunned. The Séraphin in the middle shook his head and said, "She's good."

"Foolishness," said the third. And then, "Too soon?"

Séraphin turned back in his seat as Yoda coughed himself into life. "Right," he said, rubbing his hands, "so where're we going?"

"All over," said Silmary.

All over began with Yoda croaking through the gears, leaving Remms and working his way towards the M3 highway. The traffic was light and as Silmary switched lanes to put them on the straightest route through the Southern Suburbs only the old car's humming was heard in the interior. Silmary reached for the radio, flipping through stations without finding anything she liked.

"You got an aux cable?" asked Séraphin.

"There should be one in the glove box," replied Silmary. "Simon and Garfunkel?" she asked, as the slow foot- and finger-tapping drum and tambourines started.

"Of course," said Séraphin.

"I like this song."

"Me too."

They shared a look, the kind of look that made the other Séraphins roll their eyes. Nonetheless, no one could resist the magic of "A Hazy Shade of Winter."

Silmary and Séraphin belted it out as Yoda zipped past the University of Cape Town.

"Do you have the one with the tapping beat?" Silmary asked.

Séraphin thumbed his way through his music collection and found "Cecilia." The familiar jingle made him pat the rhythm on his thigh.

"So what's our first stop?" asked Séraphin.

"Muizenberg."

The ice cream in Muizenberg was sweet and soft. The old woman behind the Majestic Café's counter had fleshy arms that wobbled when she reached for their sugar cones. She coiled the vanilla to a point and handed it to Séraphin. Silmary ordered vanilla and strawberry.

"Strawberry's a pedophile's flavor," said Séraphin.

"And bubblegum," the second Séraphin chipped in.

"Why pedophiles?" asked Silmary.

"That's the kind of shit they'd use to lure a kid to their house," said Séraphin. "Hey, kid, guess what I have at home? Bubblegum and strawberry ice cream. What do you think about that? Get in my big white van and you can have all the ice cream you want."

"You're weird," she said. "You know that, right?"

"You have no idea," he replied. "I'll get this. You did all of the driving."

The woman handled his money carefully. When he reached for the change with his free hand, she placed it on the counter instead. The coins scattered. The other Séraphins inhaled sharply. Séraphin sighed as he swept the change into his palm with the hand that held his cone.

Some of his ice cream dripped onto the counter. The woman looked at the spillage and made a disgusted noise in her throat. When they had walked out of the Majestic Café, Silmary said, "That was fucked up."

"In town people still try to be slick with their bullshit," he said, "but the further out you go, the less diplomatic they are about it."

"And you're fine with it?" she asked.

"Nobody's fine with it," he said. "But it takes stamina to be pissed off all the time. And nobody runs that prejudice marathon like racism."

"That's really sad," she said.

"You'll get used to it."

They walked along Muizenberg Beach, licking their ice creams. A handful of families were picnicking, umbrellas and windbreakers straining against the wind. Seagulls cawed and wheeled across the sky, looking for some stranded morsel on the sand below. Despite the bright sun, the wind prickled and Séraphin shook his head in disbelief at the surfers who braved the water. "That's some white-people shit," he said, pointing. Silmary *hmm*ed her agreement and they stopped for a moment, watching one of the surfers rocking unsteadily and then falling into the water.

The first time Séraphin saw the ocean it had amazed him. The great blueness stretching further than he could see, further than his ten-year-old imagination could map. The trip from Windhoek to Swakopmund was filled with Bee Gees and UB40. His mother was on cassette duty, rarely letting silence enter the car. She sang along and made her shoulders roll.

Séraphin watched his father slowly unwind and even sing the chorus when UB40's "Bring Me Your Cup" came on. His mother turned in her seat and said to Séraphin, "We liked dancing to this song when it came on the radio."

"Papa used to dance?" asked Séraphin, looking at the man behind the wheel, trying to imagine him being anything other than serious. His imagination could fathom *X-Men*, *Gargoyles*, *Darkwing Duck*, and everything Roald Dahl could stuff into his young mind. But he could not imagine his father dancing.

Then, just like now, the width of the shoreline was inviting and intimidating. His father, in black board shorts and an old grey T-shirt, took turns walking Éric, Yves, and Séraphin into the water until it splashed up to their stomachs, holding them while they shrieked and clung to him in fear. The shock of the Benguela Current made prolonged time in the water impossible and when they started shivering his father walked them back to their mother, who sat above the tide line. She looked up at her tall, smiling husband, surrounded by their sons, and she was a long way from a fear which occasionally lanced through her, making her shiver.

"Is it a nice place, where you went?" Silmary asked, pulling him from his memory.

"It's decent," he replied. He finished his ice cream. "Where to next?"

"Only thing that can chase ice cream is fish and chips, duh."

"I like her," said the first Séraphin.

"Don't we all," said the second.

Kalky's in Kalk Bay had its deep fryers gurgling with hot oil, chips and fish writhing in delicious agony. Séraphin and Silmary stood in the queue that wound outside the shack. After placing their orders they spied a family vacating a table outside and rushed over to take it. From there they could see the harbor filled with sea-weathered boats. Near the restaurant, fisherwomen with sharp knives—their rough hands scarred, their skin leathery—descaled freshly caught fish. A waitress walked outside with a loaded tray. "Jirre!" she shouted. "Who is three-thirty-three? Is it you? Julle mense moet praat! I can't sommer smell your order!"

"I like this place," said Séraphin.

"It's quaint," said Silmary.

"Such a tourist word," said Séraphin. "It's always used to describe places that are the right kind of exotic to warrant only one visit."

"What would you call this place, then?"

"Smelly," said Séraphin.

"Or dirty," offered the first Séraphin, squeezing next to him.

"I'll actually be disappointed if they bring us a ketchup bottle without the black crusty stuff on the nozzle," said the second from his other side.

"That's nasty," said Silmary. Séraphin shrugged.

"I've been meaning to ask," said the third Séraphin, sitting down next to Silmary, "about your name. Where's it from?"

"I guess now's as good a time as any," Silmary said. She reached into her handbag, pulled out a green identity book, and placed it on the table. Séraphin looked at the photograph inside. A younger Silmary looked back, frowning at the camera. Then he looked at the name.

"No fucking way," said the first Séraphin.

"You're joking," said the second.

"Nope," said Silmary.

"Silmary Lillian Joan Wallis," Séraphin read aloud. "You're named after *The Silmarillion.*"

"My father loved the book and my mother's an accepting woman."

"That's badass."

"Séraphin's pretty cool too."

"When I found out what a seraph was I thought it was cool. The nuns at my primary school thought it was some sort of sign when I started there. They soon realized I wasn't the chosen one, though."

"How come you've never been back to Rwanda?" she asked.

"I don't feel like going gorilla-trekking."

"Of course not, that's the kind of thing Darth Boyfriends tend to do."

"Yoh!" The first Séraphin clutched his heart.

"You went there," said Séraphin.

"You were being a smart-ass. You've still got family there, right?"

"I do. But it's weird being related to so many people you don't know."

"Isn't that family?"

"Good one," said the third Séraphin.

"Anyway, home is that other place now," he said.

"You can say its name without wincing, Séraphin," said Silmary.

The waitress came out again, carrying a tray. "Number two hundred and fifty-three. Two-five-three!"

Séraphin raised a hand.

They ate the greasy chips with gusto and swallowed each other's conversation just as greedily. Silmary told Séraphin that her parents traveled often, doing nebulous consultancy work for developmental agencies. The kinds of project initiatives her parents did sounded like the things any reasonable person might think of—clean water, mosquito nets, vaccines. Silmary had followed her parents around the world, first as squealing luggage when she was a child and then as sulky baggage when she became a teenager. While Séraphin considered her lucky to have moved around often, Silmary disagreed. Young loves were found and then lost whenever a ministerial project was concluded or a health center was handed over to the community. Then it was time to pack up, stamp passports, fly to a new country, and go through the motions all over again. Silmary allowed her thoughts to trail into silence. They sat watching the fisherwomen. After a while Silmary perked up. "Tell me something," she said.

"What?"

"Anything."

So Séraphin told her lots of things. He told her about kicking grandmothers. She agreed Ralph had it coming. Dale not so much. Then he told her about the time that Godwin, Richard, Adewale, and Yasseen got in a fight at a club because Godwin had danced with a Coloured girl whose boyfriend was not happy about it.

"Where was Andrew? I never hear about Andrew in these stories."

"Location, location, location," said Séraphin. "To be in a story you have to be in the place where it happens."

"How'd you guys become friends anyway?"

"Proximity, I guess," said Séraphin. "He just started hanging around us in res. Probably because of Rich. Or he liked having black friends. I don't know."

"When I met him he couldn't stop going on about you guys, and all of the cool shit you all do. He was the star of most of the adventures."

"Him?" scoffed the third Séraphin. "He's like Madagascar on a tattoo of Africa a volunteer gets when they visit and fall in love with the damn place. Sometimes it's there, sometimes it's not." Silmary snorted into her food.

"Sometimes he does some shit that makes you wonder whether he's aware of present company. He tried to get us to befriend some jock friends and wondered why we wanted to kill them when they called us the QBs—quota blacks. Sometimes he's cool. Sometimes he's just Andrew."

"Hmm."

"These *hmm*s are going to have to come with their own omniscient narrator soon," said Séraphin.

"That *hmm* was for when we nearly hooked up and Andrew said he'd never been with a half-and-half."

"That's rough," said the first Séraphin.

"But small evils are punished instantly," Silmary said with a smirk. "He couldn't get it up."

"No!" said Séraphin.

"Yep."

"So what did you do when it happened?" asked the second Séraphin.

"He made it more awkward than it really was."

"Big mistake," said Séraphin.

"It's happened to you?" she asked.

"Many times," said Séraphin. "First time, I'd been talking a whole lot of shit, promising to fundamentally restructure the laws of physics. When she gave me the chance, biology failed me. The more I thought about it, the worse it got." The Séraphins nodded along. "When that shit happens, your nerd brain needs to kick in and pull conversations about random shit out of your ass crack. When one head lets you down the other should not."

"You need to school your friend on some shit," she said.

"So you guys aren't together anymore?" Séraphin said quickly.

"We were never together."

"Cool," said Séraphin. "I mean, whatever."

They cleared their plates and decided to have words for dessert until the slant of the sun made them quiet down. "Home?" asked Silmary.

"Home," said the Séraphins.

"You live here?" Séraphin asked as Yoda crawled through a security gate onto a courtyard of white gravel. They were in Camps Bay.

"This is my parents' place," Silmary said. "They aren't here often, though."

"People who have places like this tend not to live in them."

The interior of the house looked like it had been put together from various center spreads from *House and Leisure*. Tiles were arranged in intricate mosaics on the floor. There were Persian rugs. The art on the walls had more white frame than art, and the furniture was wooden, probably purchased at extortionate prices from a boutique that had bought it for a song from some open-air carpenter. The house had the kind of neatness that came from not being lived in.

"I don't like this house much," said Silmary. She slipped off her shoes and walked through the lounge into a silver-soaked kitchen, where she poured them juice from the fridge. She suggested they sit on the balcony because the sunset view was the one thing that made the house livable. "Put on some music first. I'm sure you can figure out how to work the sound system."

"Well, no sunset has ever been complete without some jazz," said the second Séraphin.

Annette Hanshaw's "We Just Couldn't Say Goodbye" spilled from the lounge onto the balcony. When Silmary heard the first notes she said, "This is the soundtrack of that *hmm* I should tell you about sometime."

"When you're ready."

"Well, look at you not going after the dirt and the devil in the details."

"I presume it's a deep story. I can wait." They sat on the balcony on cushioned deck chairs, watching the changing of the light guard in the sky. "This is nice," said Séraphin after a while. "Today was a good day."

"I'm glad," said Silmary. She adjusted her position to face him. "You know, I've only been trying to arrange your kidnapping for the longest while."

"Why didn't you do it sooner?"

"Well, first there was Andrew. Can't be ditching someone for their friend the day you meet them, you know—"

"Totally," said the first Séraphin, leaning over the balcony. "You do that later."

"Like a civilized person," said Silmary. "Anyway, then I had to figure out if you were available—"

"Hence the Bianca question," said the second, going to stand next to the first.

"And I couldn't just ask for your number with everyone around."

"How did you get it, by the way?" the third asked. He sat at the end of Séraphin's chair.

"Andrew's phone."

"That's *not* strange at all," Séraphin said.

"Right?" she replied. "Imagine, after all of that I still had to figure out if you liked me or not."

The second Séraphin chuckled. "People your color don't have to stress about stuff like race relations. Other people, darker people do. That's the worst part, liking someone and then having to figure out whether they could like someone like you, not even you, just your kind. But black guys are AB-types—universal accepters."

"Do you think this shit up beforehand or does it come to you?"

"Both."

"What else comes to you?"

Séraphin climbed off his beach chair and straddled Silmary on hers. He leaned forward and kissed her. They carried on for a few minutes before pausing to take a breath. Then they resumed, quicker, more fiercely. She broke the contact and sat up in the chair. "We can stop. If you want," Séraphin said.

"Don't be foolish, Séraphin." Her hands reached underneath his T-shirt and circled around to his back, running across the smooth skin, gripping the muscle.

"Morgoth," the first Séraphin said suddenly.

"What?"

"The theft of the Silmarils," Séraphin replied.

"I said you're weird already, didn't I?" She laughed lightly. "But, no, you're not him. The Silmarils were possessions. I am not." She pushed him off gently and then rose from her chair. She took him by the hand and led him back into the house.

The evening breeze picked up slightly. The three Séraphins sat looking up at the night sky, the widest ocean of them all. They heard the playlist change inside. Jamiroquai's "Corner of the Earth" always brought a certain kind of tranquility with it.

"Man," said the third, "this was such a good day."

"*Is*," said the first. "It's still going."

"Godspeed!" said the third.

They remained on the balcony, trading nothing stories about nothing times, glad that distractions beat focus nine times out of ten.

Far away from the Here, past the Now, in the Not Hereness of space and time, something stirred, grand and terrible. It was the boom-boom from a past time which uproots, the bang-bang machine-gun fire which defines and also does not, the quick-quick-hurry-hurry which removes and displaces. It stirred and rustled and then shot out towards the third rock from the sun, bringing with it general and specific doom.

XXVIII

Andrew William Kent was not good at many things. In primary school he tended to wet himself when he was excited or afraid. In high school he was terrible at all the essentials needed to survive the teenage years—sports, storytelling, wooing girls. He was called Kent Get None because he was once caught masturbating in his boarding school's bathroom. The derision drove him to depression. He attempted to commit suicide by swallowing pills he found in the school's infirmary. Pity for him they turned out to be laxatives and, to be fair, as he would later say in retellings, it would have been a shitty way to go. He secured his admission to Remms via his family's legacy and even after doing so he struggled, changing his degree program three times. First business science, then law, then politics and economics. He managed to stick to his last degree long enough to graduate and enroll in the postgraduate stream. Andrew was not the lead singer of his band. At best he played the tambourine. That he managed to make it as far as skin with Silmary was beyond comprehension. That he failed to rise to the occasion seemed a return to reality. But because the universe did not care enough about him to completely screw him over, it did allow him to be good at some things. One of these things was coming up with farfetched theories of life. He had two good ones. The first attempted to explain the dichotomy of boob and ass men.

"It all comes down to when you're kicked off the nipple," he said. "If you're cut off early, you're going to be chasing boobs your entire life. If you're weaned off at the right time, you're going to love booty forever."

Andrew's other monumental work was his theory of general and specific doom.

His magnum opus came to light, as most things did with him, when he was surrounded by his friends. At yet another one of the social gatherings littered with the kind of diversity found only in Remms's prospectus and campus guides, Andrew outlined the theory. The High Lords had been invited to a braai. True to form, the roasting ran behind schedule. As both apologies and tribute, invitees waltzed in an hour or so late carrying wine, gin, whisky, and tequila bottles; crackers and dips; sachets of handmade chips; and marinated pork, lamb, and chicken. By the time everyone arrived, the kitchen counter was a showpiece of excess. Snacks were passed around. The celery and carrot sticks with their Mediterranean dip were skirted by all but the people who had brought them.

"The chlorophyll isn't for me," said Godwin. "I came for the meat." He looked around at the crowd to drive home his subtext.

By the time the food was sizzling and spitting over the fire, too much wine and beer had been consumed. The High Lords had commandeered the conversation. Their jokes were funny; their stories were ribald. The chances of amorous connection on a night like this, when everyone was feeling happy, were substantially high. Slowly but without any subtlety, everyone tried to mingle in such a way that would find them next to their fancies.

"Man," said Godwin, "this cigarette butt's the closest I've gotten to ass in a while." He flicked it towards a bin and missed.

Bianca nodded in sad agreement. "I wish there was some way to know when a drought was on the way."

A laugh as melodic as wind chimes filled the air. It was Aqeelah's. She was biracial, with hair tied in thick braids that fell to the middle of her back, light brown eyes that jumped and danced in the warm evening light, and inviting lips that had the majority of the present company hoping they had made their guest list. Bianca and Séraphin watched as one, two, three, and then four suitors stepped up to pitch their best game. Aqeelah swung for the crowd.

Back to the conversation at hand. Aqeelah said, "When it gets so bad you start debating what you could be doing with the money from canceled wax appointments, you start feeling like you should lower your admission standards."

Godwin had had one too many beers, as usual. This resulted in two things. He would talk longer and louder and he would become political.

"You just need to tell me where to apply, Aqeelah," he said. "Motivation letter, report cards, transcripts, where I see us in five years' time. Just flash me the bat signal!"

"Sorry," Aqeelah said, "mine's a home, not a homeless shelter. And we all know the bat signal is the best way to pull jokers."

"Someone's windscreen has a hole in it because, Godwin, my guy, you just got hit into the parking lot," Séraphin said.

"I see you, Aqeelah," Godwin said, "I see you."

Andrew spoke up after the hooting died down. "What you're all experiencing is what I like to call the GSD: general and specific doom. Things go well until they don't. But nobody ever really knows when the good times are going to end, do they? Look, you have to think of the universe like a poorly trained puppy, except the puppy's huge, and it can slobber and pee on whole solar systems. So, here we all were on a winning streak, killing it at school, having wonderful sex lives, or whatever. What did we do? We asked for more of the same. Big mistake. That was too specific for the puppy. It didn't understand. It only heard 'more.' So it got us so much more that in the middle of all the moreness we didn't even realize everything else was slowly unraveling.

It's just one shit sandwich after another." Andrew looked pensive for a moment. "The more general the fortune," he said, "the more specific the doom; the more specific the gift, the more general the curse."

Silence followed Andrew's karmic lecture. Then someone said, "That was some Oracle meets Architect *Matrix* kind of shit, Drew."

Andrew said there was only one way to avoid the GSD. "Just chill. Don't do anything. Especially when life isn't handing you *L*s. If you believe things are too good to be true, that's when the GSD hits."

General and specific doom is as invisible as the threads of fate, and when it arrives on Cape Town's doorstep it is noted only as a passing huff of wind, skin tingling on the undersides of arms, four sneezes in a row, an itch on the back of a neck, and a stumble over uneven pavement. It stops and sniffs the air. Spring-summer, somewhere between the two seasons. The bluest sky above, and the greenest green below in the Company's Garden. Table Mountain's wispy veil as fragile as virtue, and Kirstenbosch blooming beyond description. The colors of Bo-Kaap rioting in the sun, the rays glinting off roofs on the Cape Flats.

It can smell things that are too good to be true. It flies off.

Bianca and Yasseen receive emails from two separate law firms. Their fortunes have changed. Bianca is Johannesburg-bound, where a small law firm will take her on. It will not pay much, but it is time to get out of Cape Town. Yasseen will remain. His law firm cannot take on so many candidates, the letter says, so they had to narrow their selections to the ones best suited for the firm's needs. Poor Yasseen. He believed Jozi was too far, too high, and so it remained too high, and too far.

Godwin has a thesis to finish and despite his drinking he is on track to complete it by the end of year. Richard too. But Zimbabwe has been hammered by the GSD for a long time so it lets these two be. There is enough doom at home.

Adewale is much too comfortable with his postgraduate funding. His latest grant is beyond his wildest dreams and before he can plan his next outing to the fashion houses, the Remms Postgraduate Funding Office writes him a letter saying he has reached his financial aid cap. He knew it was too good to be true. Which is why his supervisor is going to start giving him stricter deadlines. The faculty is under political pressure to have more South African candidates on its doctoral roster.

James is passed over. His door is splattered with humility.

In Andrew, it recognizes a familiar face. This is the one who tried to kill himself with the laxatives. A couple of months ago, though, he foolishly got it into his head that he was not good enough for a certain girl. He softened at the most unlucky hour because the GSD had hardened his doubts. Shame. What a poor stroke of luck. The GSD leaves him alone.

Here is another familiar face: Séraphin.

Where on earth is he going when he is not with the High Lords?

Follow and see.

This house in Camps Bay seems familiar.

The GSD's been here before; it has actually been in this lounge and in this kitchen and in this bedroom too.

Séraphin, you are a bad, bad man, it thinks.

The comfort is not forced, the laughter is easy, the kissing not as rationed as it is when the sensation is new. But at least the sheets are crumpled like it is the first time every time. He has come a long way from that room in Windhoek West. Another unfortunate cruelty on the GSD's part. Now, then, here is the moment when they are supposed to pull apart; instead they cling to each other. They drift in the remains of desire, part asleep for fifteen minutes. Then they get up, dress, and she drives him back to campus.

"So we're doing Tara's thing tomorrow?" she asks as they near Remms.

"Yep."

"What if we're on the same team?"

"That'll be the winning team, then."

"You're really full of yourself, you know."

"You were too a few minutes ago." She laughs.

On her drive back home she smiles as she thinks of their time together. She turns on the radio to make up for Séraphin's absence. The song is one of her favorites. She turns it up and sings along. The GSD sits in the back seat and waits for the second verse of Frankie Valli's "Can't Take My Eyes Off You" to start.

Utazi nyakatsi . . .

XXIX

The United States of America is the free world where nothing is free, where facts and black men are scary. Every second and minute is bought and paid for; every milestone has a sponsor. Spring is brought to you by this brand, summer by that. Everything is for sale. "Billboards on every building, neon everywhere else, and the star-spangled banner on lawns and doorways," said Bjorn. "Advertising and American exceptionalism hold the country together."

"That sounds about right," said Byron. "I remember thinking the same thing when I was there."

The Bjorn-Byron double-team of cultural observation and confirmation grated Séraphin something terrible. According to Bjorn, India had a smell, and Byron's follow-up comment confirmed it: "As soon as you land in India you just know you'll never get the stink out of your nostrils." Cubans complained too much about everything. Mexico was generally okay, but the cuisine needed to go easy on the beans and cheese. Kuala Lumpur was too humid. Shanghai was too sprawling. Sweden and Norway were terribly expensive, and the United Kingdom was bland. Séraphin listened to their globe-trotting tales with a familiar sense of envy, stifling it with effort. He came to a conclusion:

traveling was not the great education many professed it to be. Maybe, sometimes, all the frequent-flier miles in the world just made you a well-traveled asshole.

He told Bianca so.

Sans_Seraph: These people fly around the world to feel disappointed by everything. Why do the 1% spend 99% of the time complaining?

BeeEffGee: You expect an answer from a 99-percenter?

"I think," Byron said as Séraphin looked up from his phone, "I had a better time in some of the lodges here than I had in the United States."

"Yeah?" Séraphin had had enough. "Where the kitchen and serving staff perform a song after supper to give you the whole African experience?"

"Ever notice how there's always a chubby one with a high voice?" said Godwin. "And he's always light-skinned too."

"Don't forget the two black guys in the back row who don't really want to be involved but it's part of the job," said Bianca.

"The worst is when they start with the dancing," said Godwin. "That freedom shuffle and church-choir side-to-side isn't why Sobukwe spent years in solitary confinement."

"Are those the types of lodges you're talking about?" asked Séraphin. Byron and Bjorn laughed and waved away the comments, choosing to carry on their conversation in quieter tones.

KentTouchThis—HiLos_Of_E: Congratulations, guys. You played yourselves. Again.

Sans_Seraph: Thank you. I'd like to thank my middle-class upbringing and my inability to like guys whose nicknames are BJ and Bi.

A message from Silmary.

Silmary_Lillian—Sans_Seraph: You couldn't help yourself, could you?

Sans_Seraph: They were getting on my nerves.

Silmary_Lillian: I can't take you anywhere.

Sans_Seraph: I can think of many places, actually. The closest one is a short drive away.

Silmary_Lillian: Get your mind out of the gutter, Séraphin.

In another chat group.

Sans_Seraph—HiLos_Of_E: Is it just me or is this Jess girl giving Richard the eyes?

RichDick: Really?

Sans_Seraph: She's been giving you the up-down since we walked in.

KimJohnUn: Which one's Jess?

JustSayYaz: The South Korean one. I think Jana is checking you out, Séra.

GodForTheWin: Jana looks damn good.

Sans_Seraph: She's okay.

BeeEffGee: That sounds like someone who's getting it from somewhere else.

RichDick: I think it's time you tell us what you've been getting up to. A whole damn year and not a single peep!

Sans_Seraph: Chill, guys. There isn't anyone. Nothing like the smell of naai-palm in the morning.

JustSayYaz: Naai-palm. Andrew things.

KentTouchThis: Why am I catching strays? I wasn't even a part of this conversation.

GodForTheWin: Yo @Sans_Seraph, get on that sound system. These indie tunes are not a vibe.

Sans_Seraph: On it!

The number of social gatherings which cannot be made better by Bob Marley and the Wailers ranges between zero and none. The first time Séraphin heard Bob Marley, his father was washing their Volkswagen Jetta. His father always played Bob Marley when he cleaned the car. "Buffalo Soldier" was his favorite. His father once stamped like the dreadlocked singer on a stage, under the control and instruction of the Most High Jah and the magic of reggae. *Jump, jump, jump, head bob, head bob, jump jump, jump. Stomp! Stomp! Stomp!* Séraphin's father noticed his offspring watching. He stopped and laughed, then sheepishly resumed his work. Later, Séraphin had taken the cassette from the car and played it on the black Teac radio that kept his mother company in the kitchen and listened to the man who could make his father act so unfatherlike.

When next his father washed the car, Séraphin joined him, waiting for his father to start stomping around again. But he did not. Instead he laughed when Séraphin's small voice sang along to "One Love."

In Tara's apartment, with the throaty roar of the waves within earshot, Séraphin did something rare: he played two songs from the same artist one after the other.

Silmary_Lillian—Sans_Seraph: Did I just hear you break one of your rules?

Sans_Seraph: One Bob Marley song deserves the company of another.

The mood on the balcony lightened while the night blackened. "Jammin'" has that effect. A quick backtrack to an earlier conversation.

TaraIncognita—Silmary_Lillian: Having a chill session before everyone goes into study mode for the year-end exams. You should come.

Silmary_Lillian: Sure.

TaraIncognita: You can bring your friends.

Silmary_Lillian: I'll ask them.

TaraIncognita: And tell that cocky one I've got a team that's eager to face him. The tall black one who walks like he has an "S" on his chest.

Silmary rolled over in her bed to show Séraphin the message. He looked at it with half-closed eyes. "Tell her no team formed against me shall prosper," he said.

The invitation was relayed by Silmary to Bianca, who then invited everyone else.

The night arrived. The invitees made their way to Green Point. Those who lived nearby—which seemed to be all of Tara's friends—strolled to her apartment, eliciting a smile from the guard on duty in the atrium. They were permitted to walk to the elevators without any questions. Those who arrived via the Idriss Express received frowns. "Sign hee-ya and hee-ya. Cell phone numbers hee-ya and hee-ya. Please wait while I call the madam to let her know that you are hee-ya," said the guard.

Séraphin, while writing down their names, refrained from commenting on the absence of Tara's other guests in the visitors registry.

In the elevator, he said Richard's currency was being devalued. "You've been around us so long even black people are starting to think you're black," he said. "What good are you to us, Rich?"

The apartment was already filled with personality when Tara opened the door and ushered everyone in. Andrew and Silmary had arrived before Séraphin. Handshakes, hugs, hellos, and how-are-yous. Hidden smiles. The host plied with hastily selected wine. Everyone moving around, eating, drinking, talking, laughing, then everyone sitting on the balcony, eating, drinking, talking, and laughing some more. Conversations about tiring study timetables, brutal exam schedules, possible holiday plans. Troy saying he was thinking about traveling to the United States; Byron and Bjorn adding their two cents; Séraphin, Godwin, and Bianca giving them back their change. Séraphin playing music to defuse the situation. The mood lightens; the night blackens.

A breeze blows. Something watches, unseen. The soundtrack plays, all the actors are assembled. All the world is a stage.

And then Tara says, "Right, let's play something."

Pro tip from the wise: do not decide who your friends are until you have played general-knowledge trivia games with them. There are numerous litmus tests for friendships—trust, kindness, sincerity, forced proximity, ill-suffered duration—but surviving 30 Seconds is one of the better ones. From the first roll of the dice to the last clue which sends one team across the finish line, gloating, air punching, *Ole!-Ole!-Ole!*-ing, the game was designed to test the integrity of friendships. It has ended a few of them too.

"Before reproducing one should be able to hold their own in a few rounds," said Séraphin, "because, really, how do you carry someone's children when you know they thought Freddie Mercury was a superhero?"

The watching thing shuffles.

"Let's make the teams random," Tara said. "Makes it more interesting."

Random looks like this: Jana, Tara, Bjorn, Troy, and James are the first team; Jess, Byron, Andrew, and Godwin are the second; Cameron, Declan, Nikita, Adewale, and Yasseen are the third; and, Séraphin, Silmary, Bianca, and Richard are the fourth.

Tara is the timekeeper.

BeeEffGee—HiLos_Of_E: Smart move. Because we all know she doesn't know a damn thing!

JustSayYaz: Zero chill tonight.

When it was Séraphin's turn, he reached for a card and began. "Fruit juice named after the Roman goddess of agriculture—also a valley in the Western Cape."

"Ceres," said Silmary.

"Recipient of the worst haircut in the Bible."

"Samson," said Bianca.

"Place where NASA rockets are launched in the U.S."

"Houston," said Richard.

"No. Fuck. We'll come back to this one. Next one. Singers of 'Dancing Queen.'"

"ABBA," said Silmary and Bianca.

"Right. Back to the rockets. First name of the Mother City and also has a name that sounds like the thing Brazilians do each year."

"Cape—" said Richard.

"—Canaveral," completed Silmary.

"That's five," said Séraphin. "Which ties us with Andrew's team. Just need the rest of you to fumble your way through the clues, and then Andrew to choke his way through his card."

"Fuck you, Séra," Andrew said. He waited until it was his turn to give out clues. He managed three out of five. Séraphin looked at the rest of the clues on Andrew's card.

"'Rivers of Babylon' is every black Christmas ever," Séraphin said. "And that last clue was Charlie Brown's football to you because you ain't getting *Peanuts*. How didn't you get that one?"

"You're loathsome, Séraphin," said Andrew.

"Things are getting descriptive," said Adewale.

"Very descriptive, bro," said Richard.

"Come on," said Séraphin. "It's all fun and games, innit?" He rubbed his hands together. "Time to win us this game, Sil."

The dice rolled favorably again. An opportunity for a five-point play. The other teams groaned. Silmary looked at Tara, who held the hourglass. Tara flipped it over and said, "Go."

"Chicago Bulls basketball player!"

"Michael Jordan!" Séraphin, Richard, and Bianca were leaning forward in their seats, all of their attention on Silmary.

"Jupiter's father, also the planet with the rings."

"Saturn," said Séraphin.

"Correct. I don't think we're in Kansas anymore."

"*The Wizard of Oz*," said Bianca.

"The zeppelin which blew up."

"*Hindenburg*," said Séraphin.

"Full name of the event," said Silmary.

"The *Hindenburg* disaster!" Richard said.

"Last one." Silmary looked at the card and giggled. Later on, what Silmary said could have been blamed on the head-spinning kiss of the Bombay Sapphire or the present company and its ebullient mood. The overheated competitiveness of the atmosphere made her synapses fire at high speed, mind and tongue take the shortest route available between the clue on her card and the answer which would see her team—which had the object of her affection—cross the finish line first.

Silmary looked at Séraphin and said: "What Andrew is to the High Lords, this country is to Africa."

Séraphin screamed, "Madagascar!" and jumped up from his seat, arms stretched out to either side like a certain all-conquering Highbury hero. Bianca jumped up to join him. Richard moved his team's checker to the end zone for no other reason but to see it there. Then he and Silmary were pulled into their team's jumping huddle. Everyone else sat back in their seats and looked on. Some people laughed. Declan and Troy made their way to the kitchen to refill their drinks. Tara said, "Okay, guys, calm down, it's just a game."

To this statement, Godwin said, "Yeah right."

Séraphin ran to the balcony's railing and stood on the bottom rung and shouted he was the king of the world.

Adewale said, "I hate losing to this guy."

"Me too," said Byron. Bjorn crossed his arms and sulked. Yasseen, whose team trailed everyone else's, was the only one who saw the narrowing of eyes from Andrew's quarter. When the volume of the celebrations had been dumbed down somewhat, Andrew looked at Silmary and said, "What's that supposed to mean?"

"What does what mean?" she asked.

"Madagascar."

"It's just a joke."

"Clearly. I want to know what it means."

"It doesn't mean anything."

Andrew turned his attention to Séraphin. "I said I want to know what it fucking means." His voice leapt out of him and stilled everyone on the balcony.

"Really, Drew," Séraphin said quietly. "It's a dumb joke."

"Fuck you and your dumb jokes."

"Individually or together?" asked the first Séraphin.

"I think you'll have to choose one," said the second.

"And then you'll have to pray you can get it up."

Andrew stood from his chair, face flushed. Things were being added in his head. His eyes darted from Silmary to Séraphin and back again, unsure where to direct his anger. "Fuck both of you."

"You're biting off more than you can chew, Andrew," replied the second Séraphin. "Again."

"Guys," Richard said, "chill."

"Really," said James. "You're being foolish."

"I don't know, hey," Bianca said. "I kind of like awkward. Just me? Okay. Sorry."

Richard turned to Séraphin. "Dude, let it go. Please."

Séraphin took a deep breath. He turned to Richard. "I'm cool." He turned to Andrew. "Drew, I'm sorry. That was my bad."

Andrew turned to Silmary. She tried to hold his gaze but failed. He looked down at her, silent, and said, "Really? Him?"

Something about the way Andrew asked the question, both pleading and resigned, made Bianca look from Séraphin to Silmary and back again.

"Oh," she said.

She was about to say something else but then Andrew pinched the bridge of his nose and said, not quietly enough:

"Of all the black guys."

Godwin ("Eh! Eh!"), James ("Huh?"), and Yasseen ("What?") sat up in their chairs. Adewale leaned back in his. He believed it was his manifest destiny not to be caught in the middle of a punch-up. Especially when he was dressed for everything but combat. Bianca crossed her legs. Silmary kept her eyes on Séraphin. Everyone else looked on.

"Rich," Séraphin said, "you need to get your white boy."

"I have a name," Andrew said, turning to face Séraphin once more.

"And I'll use it when you start manifesting individual personality," said Séraphin.

Andrew threw himself at Séraphin.

"Séra—"

XXX

Here is a brief treatise on men according to Bianca Fawzia Gabriels:

BeeEffGee—HiLos_Of_E: 1) For the most part what we call men can be found in two natural states: boy-man and man-boy. The boy-to-man ratio is largely dependent on various life circumstances. Any successful relationship with the male of the species is largely dependent upon the discovery of each individual's configuration. Therein lies the problem: time and all of its concomitant aches and bumps seem to be the only way to find out which is which.

2) Men need to name things. To name is to own. And to own is manhood. Naming is preferable to all of the other things they could do to prove ownership: peeing on things (all of the time), scratching on things (all of the damn time), or marking things in blood (I volunteered at an abuse counseling center so I don't want to hear any shit about this).

3) When two men are in close proximity, their average intelligence drops at an exponential rate. Imagine, then, what hap-

pens when the houses of parliament, pubs, bars, and golf clubs have full rosters. With the reduced intellect, they a) become boy-men and b) start naming things.

4) Men are trash. Someday people will know this.

5) With that said: hello, everyone.

Sans_Seraph: Well that's as good an introduction as any.

JustSayYaz: How long have you been composing that, Bee?

BeeEffGee: It's been a while.

GodForTheWin: I just read that whole thing and I'm hurting all the way down to my soul.

Sans_Seraph: Everyone, meet Bianca.

RichDick: Is this one of your concubines?

Sans_Seraph: Alas, she is a lesbian.

GodForTheWin: Full-time or part-time?

BeeEffGee: All the days of the calendar.

KentTouchThis: So she's part of the group?

Sans_Seraph: Yep. Bee is good peoples. Yaz and I are taking her in from the cold wilds of law school.

JustSayYaz: Translation: Coloured people are panda-scarce in law school right about now.

Sans_Seraph: We've only made it because of the BWGs.

BeeEffGee: BWGs?

Sans_Seraph: I'll explain later. Right now we need to talk about The Thing.

AddyWale: How're we gonna do The Thing with her around?

BeeEffGee: What thing?

Sans_Seraph: It'll all make sense later.

KentTouchThis: Is there some sort of procedure for recruiting members or do we just spring new people on each other? And do we have to change the name for her supposed ladyship?

Sans_Seraph: We'll keep the name.

BeeEffGee: What name?

AddyWale: The High Lords of Empireland.

BeeEffGee: I see. Did you read Number 2 above?

AddyWale: That's why The Thing is going to be so funny.

BeeEffGee: I'm not liking where this is going. Do we have to make a blood pact or some shit like that?

KimJohnUn: Hahaha. No. But it's one of the things you stated in your exquisite thesis.

BeeEffGee: Voetsek! I'm not fucking getting peed on!

Sans_Seraph: Hahahahahahahaha!

AddyWale: This is going to be fun.

JustSayYaz: Don't worry, Bee. We aren't some rugby jocks from a KZN school @KentTouchThis may or may not have attended. We're civilized.

KentTouchThis: I was told that it was all part of the initiation procedure!

KimJohnUn: But you never asked why nobody else went through with that part, huh?

KentTouchThis: I told you that shit in confidence, guys.

BeeEffGee: Like I said, I'm not getting peed on!

Sans_Seraph: Relax. We aren't going to pee on you.

BeeEffGee: Okay . . . then what is The Thing?

Sans_Seraph: All will be revealed in due time, Lady Bee. High Lords. Council meeting soon.

The High Lords and Lady of Empireland, listed in order of their membership and power ranking:

Séraphin Turihamwe (24)—@Sans_Seraph; Sauce level: Supremos

Bianca Fawzia Gabriels (25)—@BeeEffGee; Sauce level: Unknown (possibly comparable to Séraphin's)

Godwin Moyo (24)—@GodForTheWin; Sauce level: Master

Richard Fletcher (24)—@RichDick; Sauce level: Master

Mohammed Yasseen Ibrahim (24)—@JustSayYaz; Sauce level: Captain

Adewale Bolaji (25)—@AddyWale; Sauce level: Captain

James John Kimani (25)—@KimJohnUn; Sauce level: Rookie

Andrew William Kent (26)—@KentTouchThis; Sauce level: Rookie

The High Lords of Empireland were a motley crew of wet-eared, brash boys well on their way to being wet-eared, brash boy-men. With the exception of Bianca, they had all met at Biko House. Séraphin met Godwin and Richard first. The morning after the Séraphin Smackdown he had walked into the dining hall, collected his breakfast, and scanned the hall for a hospitable table. He spied one at the far end of the hall. Only two people sitting at it. They looked young, like him. He made his way over. They nodded at each other in greeting.

Séraphin said, “Séraphin.”

Richard said, “Rich.”

Godwin said, “You can call him Dick if you want and you can call me God.”

“Godwin or Godfrey?”

“Godwin,” Godwin said. “How d’you know?”

“I just do. Just like how I know you can’t count your blessings in a room full of Zimbabweans,” said Séraphin, spooning cereal into his mouth. “There’ll always be five as a bare minimum.”

Godwin and Richard smiled. “Our people are unfortunately named sometimes.”

“You haven’t met Rwandans,” Séraphin said.

“Kigali or diaspora?” Godwin asked.

“Diaspora. Windhoek, to be precise.” Godwin winced. “You know Windhoek, then,” said Séraphin.

“All sunburn-hot bum-fuck nowhereness of it.”

“Sunburn? That’s soccer-playing weather, bro. We only start worrying when people start dying from heatstrokes.”

“What school?” asked Richard.

“St. Luke’s.”

“I know that one. We played you in cricket once.”

“St. George’s?” asked Séraphin.

“Yeah.”

“They’re letting anyone into Remms these days, aren’t they?”

“Whoa! Easy, bro,” said Godwin.

After a few more spoonfuls of cereal, Yasseen joined their table for the same reason Séraphin had—it was the least crowded.

* * *

Together, the First Four survived that blurry party-filled first week at Remms. In the four of them Idriss knew he had found steady clients until they graduated, or dropped out. He ferried the First Four all over Cape Town. Only Séraphin the Sober—as he was then known—can remember most of what happened that week.

A geography lesson and brief history of colonialism brought Adewale, then a year ahead, into the group. The First Four became the Fast Five. He was also the one who found out about the Séraphin Smackdown.

"Man, that took some balls," said Godwin.

Then came James. He shared their table at lunch once. He had not laughed so much in a long time and decided to stay. The Swaggering Six would add one more to their number.

Andrew was the last to join their party. Senior to most of them, privileged beyond their comprehension, sometimes cool and sometimes callous. They tolerated him. But Godwin made it clear the white boy quota had been reached.

That year they lived the Remms life. They woke each other up for lectures, lifted each other out of the Sauce, survived the Angelicapocalypse, and pulled back the veneers of the city one club door rejection at a time.

After they wrote their last exams came one of those buzzing Capetonian nights when the city lights dot the blackness with their luminescence like some underwater scene. Most of Remms's residences would close soon, and only students who had taken on extra summer courses would be permitted to remain. Godwin and Richard would head home together. Andrew would cruise the Mediterranean. James would fly back to Kenya. Adewale and Séraphin would remain in Cape Town. Yasseen would return home, but see the remaining two when he could.

Before they all headed off in their separate directions, they would have a week of splendid nothingness. On their last night together they visited the Good Night, which had just opened. They hit Avec—before

Romeo became a negotiated obstacle to them—and danced from the door to the dance floor, from the dance floor to the bar, from the bar into the bathroom stalls.

Most club nights blur into each other. But not that special night. Séraphin could even reconstruct the evening's playlist from memory and whenever he played it everyone would start talking about That Night at Avec. He called the playlist *Halcyon Days for Hormones.* It was full of Ludacris, Missy Elliott, the Black Eyed Peas, T-Pain, Fergie, and David Guetta.

When the club lights came on they were still buzzed. Long Street, though, was winding down. Reluctantly, they called it a night and phoned Idriss.

"My friend," he said to Séraphin, who was riding in the passenger seat, "I thought this time you were going to sleep in the club."

"Well this isn't the end," said Andrew when Idriss dropped them outside Biko House. "We're sunrising."

"What?" Godwin was not drunk enough to start engaging in white-people shit. He told Andrew so.

"Why must you always take it there?" Andrew asked. "Anyway, we're doing this. You guys haven't done it. Just wait here. I'll be back." He ran into the residence.

"Let's go to sleep," said Richard. "It's been fun."

"Nah," said Séraphin. "Let's do it. You're all leaving in a few hours anyway. You have enough time to sleep on the bus. James, you won't miss your flight. Promise."

Andrew returned from his room clutching a Ziploc bag. "Right," he said, "let's go and see a man about a ghost."

The chill that stalks the deep purple of the night made them shiver when they arrived at Remms Memorial. Andrew rolled and licked a thick white joint. Of the group, only he and Adewale had ever smoked before. "Small puffs," said Adewale.

Séraphin took the extraterrestrial finger hesitantly and pulled. He coughed a cloud and clutched at his diaphragm as he passed it on. The buzz hit like a southpaw punch.

"What's this, Andrew?" asked Adewale as it came around again.

"They call it Muay Thai," Andrew replied.

"That is a congruous name." This made everyone laugh.

Séraphin coughed after he took another puff.

"Virgin lungs," said Andrew.

"Probably the only thing left on him that can be described so," James said.

Richard laughed. "Whoa! Shit's really kicking in if James is firing shots."

"In the cool of night and heat of day, with toil and trouble, and God's favor too, in this land I made and dreamed of empire." Godwin was reading the words on the plinth. He giggled. "This dude made all of this with my help." Again, the collective laughter without reason.

"Isn't he supposed to say something?" asked James.

"That's what the legends say," said Adewale.

Remms remained silent.

Séraphin felt his bladder wriggle. "Damn, I need to pee."

As Séraphin walked past the statue, he read the plaque and paused. "Fuck it," he said. He walked to the front of the statue and unzipped his pants. "Gonna go from legend to myth soon," he said. He trickled a stream onto the bottom of the plinth. The others, also seized by the urge to urinate, decided to do the same.

Séraphin looked up at the statue.

In this land I made and dreamed of empire.

"Fuck your dream of empire!" Like a fisherman he leaned back. "Let's see who gets the highest." They all angled back. Richard's height proved to be the deciding factor.

"Too many inches on this guy," said Godwin.

They laughed. Long and hard.

When they were done they sat back down on the benches and looked out at the sun-streaked sky. When the sun rays came out properly, breaking through the early-morning mist, it seemed to Séraphin as though Cape Town could not be more beautiful.

"Too good to be true," said Andrew.

"Look," said Séraphin. The sun was winching itself over the Hottentots Holland Mountains. The day was starting. Cape Town was waking up. "Everything that the lie touches is our kingdom," he said.

"You're saying it wrong," said Andrew.

"I'm saying it exactly as I mean it, Sir Kent."

"I like the sound of that."

"I always preferred 'lord,' personally," said Séraphin. "Lord Séraphin."

"Got a nice ring to it," said Richard. Andrew began rolling another joint.

"Lords of Cape Town," said Godwin.

"Doesn't sound right," Yasseen said. Andrew puffed and passed.

"High Lords," said Séraphin. "Like High King Peter in *The Chronicles of Narnia*. Call us the High Lords."

"Of what?" asked James.

"Empireland," said Andrew. "The High Lords of Empireland."

They called them council meetings and they would have one every year, just before everyone went home, to celebrate surviving another year in the Remms academic engine. When they showed Bianca the ritual she laughed. "I was scared you guys would do some dumb shit like ask me to get down on my knees and then knight me with your penises or something."

"Why didn't we think of that?" asked Godwin.

First they did Their Thing and then they turned around to let

Bianca do Her Thing. She would turn her back towards Remms, bend in half, and splash against the wall.

* * *

On a day, in a week, in a month, in a glorious year:

Sans_Seraph has created the group HiLos_Of_E.

Sans_Seraph has added @GodForTheWin, @RichDick, @AddyWale, @KimJohnUn, @JustSayYaz, @KentTouch-This.

Sans_Seraph: Damn character limit won't let me be great. What is life?

GodForTheWin: I weep for you. I'm on the bus with Richard right now. Fucking murder.

RichDick: We should've stayed in Cape Town.

Sans_Seraph: Don't worry. Addy, Yaz, Drew, and I will try not to have all of the fun.

KimJohnUn: Arrived in Nairobi a few hours ago. I'm still hungry. I ate everything on the plane!

KentTouchThis: Top night, gents.

Sans_Seraph: Yeah. Let's do this again next year when we're all back.

RichDick: Indeed, sir.

AddyWale: We're really going to go with High Lords of Empireland? That sounds like a children's book.

Sans_Seraph: So? Those always have the coolest names anyways.

JustSayYaz: I'm home too. It's like all the chores of the past year suddenly have to be done right now.

KentTouchThis: I'm at the beach.

Sans_Seraph: You went without us? Bitch move.

KentTouchThis: Spur of the moment thing—but it's a long holiday. The beach isn't going anywhere.

GodForTheWin: You guys enjoy on our behalf. I'm about to clock out. Still a little high.

RichDick: Laters.

AddyWale: Check you.

KimJohnUn: Laters.

KentTouchThis: Cheers.

JustSayYaz: Peace.

Sans_Seraph: High Lords out.

Part 3

THE MIGHTY SÉRAPHIN

Ibindi ubindi.

Other things, another time.

—RWANDAN PROVERB

XXXI

"—phin!"

Andrew made two mistakes when he flung himself at Séraphin. The first was thinking his high school years spent sitting in the bleachers watching the rest of his classmates play rugby showed him how to execute a decent tackle. They did not.

The second was thinking Séraphin would stand, frozen, like some unfortunate squirrel waiting to become roadkill.

He did not. As Andrew charged, Séraphin instinctively raised his elbow. It caught Andrew's nose and broke it.

Richard caught Andrew as he buckled to his knees, pulling him away from Séraphin. Andrew held on to his face, blood streaming through his fingers, feet kicking as he was dragged away. "Fug you, Sérafi! You fuggin aso. Gonna fug you up!"

James and Yasseen tried to pry his hands apart to see the extent of the damage but Andrew would not let them. Adewale and Godwin remained seated. Bianca stayed in her chair too. She clutched the armrests tightly, sitting up. Tara was in the first stages of her disaster management protocol, a complex step-by-step process which involved shrieking, "What the fuck!" Declan, Cameron, Troy, Jess, Jana, Byron, and Bjorn scrambled to the safety of the lounge. Silmary emerged from the kitchen with a roll of paper towels. "Let's see it, Andrew," she said.

"Fug off!" He pushed her away with a claret-colored hand, shook off his friends violently, and stood up. He stumbled into the apartment, head bent back. Tara followed him inside.

Richard turned to Séraphin. "What the fuck, dude?"

"He came at me," Séraphin replied.

"Why'd you have to say that to him?" Silmary asked.

The slow-boil anger cooled the slightest bit as Séraphin looked at her eyes. He considered them to be the most eloquent parts of her body. What he liked most was the way they alighted on him in a crowd, making him feel simultaneously shy and proud. He felt awkward, uncertain of what to do with himself in those moments, until she came to stand in front of him and said, "Hello, Séraphin."

Now, her eyes were articulate in anger.

Her head tilted slightly to the right. "Why'd you have to get him worked up?"

"At least something worked *up*," said a Séraphin.

Séraphin turned to him with a pleading face. Silmary's head tilted another degree.

"Really?" she said.

"Really, really," said the Séraphin. Her eyes narrowed again.

"We need to take Drew to a hospital," said Richard.

"We can take him in my car," Silmary replied, turning away from Séraphin.

Bjorn walked out onto the balcony. "Guys, Byron and I are taking Andrew to the hospital."

"We'll go with you," said Richard.

"I think it's best if you don't. He's really pissed off at you guys."

Tara came back to the balcony in the throes of the second stage of her disaster management protocol, which was:

"Right. Get the fuck out!"

"You can just ask us to leave," said Yasseen.

"I could," she replied. "But not when people like *this*"—she pointed at Séraphin—"are acting like fucking savages."

Séraphin turned to look behind him. "Is there some other imaginary black person around here you think you can talk to like that?" said one of the Séraphins.

Tara turned to Silmary. "Just get them out. I don't need this shit here."

"So we're shit now?" asked Godwin.

"Let's go, guys," Yasseen said.

Phones, wallets, and keys were scooped up from the balcony table before feet trooped out of Tara's apartment. The High Lords let Andrew and Tara's friends take the elevator while they took the stairs. Still, everyone managed to arrive in the atrium at the same time. The elevator doors opened and out came Tara and Byron, leading Andrew, his head leaning back. At the security desk, the guard looked up from his radio. "What heppened?"

"Caught a bad case of the blacks," Andrew replied thickly.

"Fuck you, Andrew William Fucking Cunt."

"Guys. Enough!" Richard's voice bounced around the atrium. "Tara, take him out of here. Yo, Drew, let us know if there's anything you need, okay?"

"Fug you guys!"

Andrew was led away. Silmary took long strides towards the door. Everyone else made to do the same.

"Can you please sign hee-ya?"

"Chief!" Séraphin shouted. "How're you gonna let all of these people walk out without signing but make us sign?"

"I'm just doing my job."

"Then do your fucking job properly and equally." The Séraphin flared its black wings in anger. "There's a fucking white person. Why don't you make them sign too?"

Silmary walked back from the door to the registry. The pen scratched a signature. She walked out. Yasseen signed everyone out, then they walked out of the building.

"I'll call Idriss." James reached for his phone.

Outside, Silmary hugged everyone politely. When she reached Séraphin she waved at his general being and said, "Bye." Then she walked towards her car.

"I feel like someone here is going to regret not apologizing to someone else," said Bianca.

"I feel like someone here needs to grow a pair and speak straight," said the Black Séraphin. "Which might be hard when you're a full-time lesbian."

Adewale said, "I feel like we should all just go home."

They stood on the pavement waiting for Idriss to arrive. When he did, he was in a jovial mood from a night of short, lucrative trips. "They insisted on paying me double," he said. "Eh, my brothers, you are quiet today, eh? What is the matter?" He looked in the rearview mirror at the taciturn company.

"Séraphin's sleeping with Silmary, who was sleeping with Andrew," said Richard. He was in the passenger seat.

"What?" Godwin turned around to face Séraphin. "Really?"

"Godwin. Really?" Yasseen looked at him incredulously.

"Thought we'd agreed we'd not make moves on her," said Richard.

"It just happened, man," Séraphin said.

"So you were an unwilling participant?" said Richard. "Things just happened and you couldn't do anything about them?"

"I was going to tell him," Séraphin said.

"After you'd been sleeping with her for a while. You don't think that would've made him work backwards and possibly come to some bad maths? Then you had to provoke him with it."

"Look, I didn't plan on it. And I won't apologize for it."

"Of course you won't," said Richard from the front seat. He turned around. "Anyone ever heard this guy apologize for anything? Lord fucking forbid the day he has to acknowledge anything's wrong or that he had a hand in it."

"What exactly would you like me to apologize for?"

"Specifically or generally?"

"Whichever one you can articulate without sounding like a little bitch."

"Séraphin," James said, "relax, man!"

"You know," Rich said, "we just need to get home."

"Which is what I keep saying," said Adewale. "This talking when you are angry, what does it help?"

Séraphin reached for his phone.

Sans_Seraph: Sorry for what I said, Bee. That was out of line.

BeeEffGee: We can talk about it later.

"I like her."

Everyone turned to Séraphin. Even Idriss flicked his eyes towards the rearview mirror.

Richard said, "You? *Like* someone? That's strong language in your world."

"Fuck's that supposed to mean?"

"At best she's going to entertain you for a month. And at worst, well, we saw what happened tonight. This'll all be some joke or story tomorrow with the Mighty Fucking Séraphin in the lead role."

Séraphin was about to start laying about him with words when a police van behind Idriss's car turned on its siren. Idriss looked in the side mirror. "*Merde!*" he said. The blue and red lights spun around the interior of the taxi. He slowed down and pulled over. "My friends, you just keep calm? Nothing to worry about. Issokay."

XXXII

Séraphin's father liked cop action flicks where justice caught injustice. "These things can only happen in the films, though," Guillome said. "There is always someone eating on either end of police sirens in Africa."

Séraphin inherited this worldview.

The lights behind Idriss's car continued their whirligig. Two police officers stepped out of the car and walked towards it.

"You say you haven't been drinking, Idriss?" The first officer, the senior, was more stomach than man. His boots and trousers were so tight they made him look like a tube of toothpaste squeezed into his torso. Séraphin decided to call him Officer Toothpaste.

"No," said Idriss. Then he added the necessary "Sah."

"What about smoking, then? You don't have anything hidden in the car?"

"No. Sah."

"What about you guys?" Toothpaste looked into the car. "Not even a stukkie for me and my partner?"

"No, sir," said Richard. He was their envoy to the law.

"You can tell me, Idriss. What are you carrying?" His left elbow leaned through the window; his other dangled a torch. His tone was jovial enough but no person between Cape Town and Cairo could fool themselves into thinking this was a conversation between friends.

In the back seat, Séraphin shuffled. He said: "It's *who*, not *what*."

The torch stopped its hangman's twitch and flicked into Toothpaste's hand. He shone the light from face to face. They all averted their eyes from the beam.

In the back of the car, Séraphin put a palm in front of his face and said: "*What* is for things, *who* is for people. As *you* can see, *we* are *people*. So you should be asking *who* he is carrying, not *what* he is carrying. Though a better way of phrasing the question would be to ask who he is driving."

Séraphin's boldness made Toothpaste turn to Idriss, who kept looking straight ahead. "What kind of foolishness are you carrying, Idriss?"

"Nothing. Sah. Just students. Remms students."

"Of course. They are much more terrible."

"More terrible, or just terrible," said the Black Séraphin.

Toothpaste turned to the other officer—Séraphin christened him Officer Younger—who had yet to put on the weight that warranted the shoot-to-kill policy of the South African Police Service. They exchanged some words in Xhosa and laughed. "Just hold on," Toothpaste said to Idriss.

Officer Younger walked around the car, kicked the tires, and noted the plate number. He spoke some jargon into his walkie-talkie. The walkie-talkie crackled and then something only he could understand came back through it. He switched to English. "Control, can you confirm?"

Toothpaste asked Idriss for his driver's license, inspected it closely, and flicked it back at him.

"Idriss," he said, "you are one of the better ones. But your lekwerekwere friend in the back seat, he is too rude. It is not okay to be rude, you understand, Idriss?"

Idriss said, "I'm sorry. Sah. We did not mean to be—"

"You're calling us lekwerekwere and then saying we're rude," Séraphin said.

"What the fuck, dude?" Godwin whispered.

"*No. That is not the vehicle.*" The voice from the other side of Younger's walkie-talkie crackled.

"I think this *is* the car we are looking for," said Toothpaste. "Your taxi, Idriss. It is overloaded."

Idriss looked around his car in panic. "I have seven passengers."

Toothpaste made a show of counting heads. He lingered over Séraphin's. "That one in the back is stupid enough for two," he said. "That would make it nine passengers."

"Do you mean I'm stupid enough for two people, which would make it eight altogether, or do you mean that I'm stupid enough for two extra people, which would make it nine?" Everyone in the car turned to Séraphin.

"Make it ten," said Toothpaste. "It's a nice round number."

"I can see why you would feel an affinity to round things."

"That one is very funny," Younger said.

"He is," said Toothpaste. "Ten passengers it is. Makes it easier to calculate the fine."

Idriss's shoulders dropped. "Sah. Please. Ten is many."

"Three thousand," said Toothpaste. "You can pay it or I can keep you here. It is up to you." Younger remained leaning on the bonnet.

Idriss was still. Then he reached under the seat and pulled a wad of rolled-up rands. He counted the money and then looked at Toothpaste. "I do not have enough. Sah."

"Idriss, you are wasting our time."

"How much do you need, Idriss?" Bianca asked.

"I need one thousand, two hundred," he said quietly. Bianca reached into her purse and pulled out a two-hundred-rand note. Richard took the note out of her hand and added his own. Four hundred—took Yasseen's—six hundred—then Godwin's one-hundred-and-fifty and Adewale's two-hundred-and-fifty. James turned to Séraphin, who shook his head.

"I got you," Séraphin replied. He pulled out his wallet and leafed through the notes. Three hundred and fifty. "There's a tip in there for the good officer—he looks like he can always use a tip."

Toothpaste took the money and stashed it in a pocket. "Idriss, you should relax, my friend. It could have been Pollsmoor Prison. You know how many of you refugees we collect each night?" He leaned on the window again. "I was happy with five hundred like usual. But your friend at the back, he is too clever but not too smart."

"That's a decent play on words, if not for all the gears turning in your head." Séraphin ignored his friends.

Toothpaste continued, "You need to choose better clients, Idriss." He motioned for Godwin to open the door. "You at the back, do you want to step out of the car?"

"Not really," the Black Séraphin said. "Since you're asking."

"Step out of the car, then."

Bianca whispered to Séraphin not to do it. Séraphin told her not to stress. "This isn't the U.S.," he said.

Outside the car, Séraphin stood with his hands in his pockets, shoulders back, chest pouting. The Black Séraphin and Toothpaste looked at each other for a while.

"What is your name?" Toothpaste asked.

"Séraph—"

The rest of the word was lost in a roundhouse swing of the arm that changes life trajectories and alters destinies forever. The slap seared the right side of Séraphin's face before it went numb. He stumbled against the car and then fell to his knees, blinking away tears.

Idriss jumped out of the car and said, "Please, please. I take them all home now. Sah."

The other High Lords made a move to get out of the car but Younger shouted at them to remain where they were. When the Black

Séraphin managed to regain his feet, he held his face, breathing loudly. He turned to Toothpaste and did a strange thing.

He laughed.

Then he said: "You can't slap like that and not talk dirty."

The second slap came at him from the right again but this time Idriss got in the way. He blocked it with his forearm. Toothpaste seemed surprised by this brazen act of rebellion. Idriss, however, stood his ground and said, "Sah. Please. Let us go."

The seconds oozed by.

Toothpaste shrugged his shoulders, pulled up his belt, and signaled Younger to follow him back to the van. Only when they'd pulled away, with their tires screeching, did sound seem to return to the street.

Séraphin opened his mouth slowly and deliberately. "Now I know how Dale felt."

Idriss looked at him, face pulled into a serious grimace. "My friend, you need to get in the car."

Idriss's taxi, overburdened by the mood it transported, hummed all the way to Remms.

"We'll repay you, Idriss," Bianca said.

"Not to worry," Idriss said. "I always lose money to those two."

"This has happened before?" Bianca asked.

"All of the time."

Nobody said anything else until they were at Remms.

"Wait here," Séraphin said to Idriss.

Séraphin went to his room and returned with a wad of cash. Idriss tried to push it back to him, saying, "Issokay. Issokay."

Séraphin insisted he take the money. "Thanks for taking us home, Driss." Then, more quietly, he said, "I don't know what happened."

"My friend, you could have wound up in serious trouble. You should know how it is here—for me, for us." A string twanged inside Séraphin.

How it is here—for me, for us.

"I know." The string refused to stop vibrating.

How it is here—for me, for us.

When Idriss drove away, the remaining High Lords stood around.

"That was fucked up," said Yasseen after some passage of time.

"Yeah, corruption is fucked up," Séraphin said.

"I wasn't talking about that," said Yasseen.

"Why didn't you just shut up?" Richard asked.

"Because," Séraphin said, "fuck that guy and his bullshit."

"Yeah, you taught him a good lesson, didn't you?"

"I'd say it was an educational night for him," Séraphin retorted. "A bit of English, bit of maths." They stood and watched him and he stared back at them. "I was just tired. Just tired."

"Tired of what? Your common sense?"

How it is here—for me, for us.

"Just tired of Cape Town and its bullshit."

"Can I ask that we all get a fucking memo when you're tired of something that could get all of us in trouble?" Bianca said.

"Of course, Bee. First thing I'll do. Send out a general warning of race fatigue."

"Would you like that with your weather report?" asked the Black Séraphin. "Mild racism with scattered xenophobic showers. Watch out for house parties, folks!"

"Don't give me that, Séra."

"Guys, let's just go to bed, okay?" James looked from Séraphin to Bianca.

"I'm with James," Adewale said. "We can talk about this tomorrow."

They all moved off towards their separate residences. As they did so, all of their phones vibrated.

KentTouchThis—HiLos_Of_E: Fuck all of you. AND I MEAN IT!

@KentTouchThis has left the group.

XXXIII

Andrew's defection from the High Lords was the start of Cape Town's unofficial fifth season, when all of the days in the city are the same. It stretched all the way through the Remms examination period to the day Séraphin's father arrived in Cape Town.

A bit happened before that day, though.

From Bianca, who found out from Silmary, who received the news from Tara, the remaining High Lords heard that Andrew's nose had been reset. But it would have a little bump in the middle, an unbecoming reminder of the last night all the High Lords were together. He severed all ties with them. Godwin contemplated calling him to see how he was doing, but abandoned the idea.

"He's a racist wanker," he said. Séraphin, Godwin, and Adewale were in Godwin's room. "Maybe it's better he left."

"Maybe you pushed too hard, Séraphin," Adewale said.

"Maybe," said Séraphin.

After a long silence, Adewale turned to Séraphin. "Are you and Silmary serious?"

"We never spoke about anything long-term."

"But you like her," Adewale asked.

"Hmm," Séraphin said.

"You should tell her," Adewale said. He looked at Séraphin pointedly. "Have you apologized yet?"

"For what?"

Godwin let out a long whistle. "Make things right."

"Seriously," Adewale said when they walked out of Godwin's room. "Just apologize."

"Sure," Séraphin said.

Yasseen also told Séraphin to apologize. So did James.

Richard wanted him to make things right with Andrew first.

"I'm perfectly fine with not speaking to him" was Séraphin's response.

There was a spell of silence between them, and then Richard asked Séraphin about Silmary. "Is it serious?" Séraphin said he did not know. "Well," said Richard, "find out."

Séraphin tried to the next day. He texted Silmary and asked her if she wanted to meet up but she said she was busy.

Bianca looked at the messages and said, "Nothing in this message says you're sorry." Séraphin gave her the kind of look which made her say, "Suit yourself."

Séraphin burrowed into his books. More than once he picked up the phone, ready to call her, only to put it back down, scared it would not be picked up, that she would not answer.

The final-year examinations crept closer.

And then:

YvesSaint: Papa says he'll be down in Cape Town in two weeks.

Sans_Seraph: Oh. Why?

YvesSaint: Your excitement could power a small city. Conference. But he'll stay until your graduation.

Sans_Seraph: Cool.

YvesSaint: What's the plan after that?

Sans_Seraph: Ha! You find me exactly where you left me. And down one or two friends.

YvesSaint: What did you do this time?

Sans_Seraph: I don't know.

YvesSaint: Which means it was big.

Sans_Seraph: Why must you be like this?

YvesSaint: I'm also going to guess you didn't apologize. Then you're going to keep quiet long enough for the thing to be forgotten or for the other person to just forgive you for their own peace of mind.

Sans_Seraph: Don't lie like this.

YvesSaint: We grew up together, man. We've survived you.

XXXIV

Fathers and sons have this thing where they see either too much of themselves in each other or nothing at all. Depending on what they find they will be proud or disappointed.

When Séraphin picked his father up from the airport they embraced like awkward pieces of a jigsaw puzzle. Séraphin glanced sideways at his father. He seemed shorter. Séraphin could not tell whether this was because he had grown or his father had shrunk.

In the taxi, Idriss looked from father to son in the rearview mirror. The father, Idriss decided, looked like a serious sort. His physique spoke of athleticism in his youth. He looked at the townships spread on either side of the highway without curiosity. Idriss tried to make conversation by saying that most people who landed in Cape Town were surprised by the poverty.

Séraphin's father said, "Poverty is poverty. It is the same everywhere."

Idriss chose to keep quiet after that.

"Séraphin says you are from Benin," Guillome said. They were approaching the city center. "How are you finding it here in Cape Town?"

"This place is not for black people."

"You are thinking of going elsewhere?" Guillome asked.

"Johannesburg. You must always have a plan to leave this place. Otherwise you will be here too long and not know that anywhere else can exist."

"My son," Guillome said, "might not want to hear that."

"He is young," Idriss said. "He will know soon."

When he dropped the two of them off at Guillome's hotel, Idriss received a generous gratuity. "*Pour les plans*," Guillome said.

"*Merci beaucoup, patron*," said Idriss.

Guillome's room overlooked the sea. Séraphin placed his father's suitcase on the bed and walked to the balcony. Inside, his father began to unpack, placing his belongings in neat stacks. He told Séraphin the training workshop and conference would only be in the mornings.

"I have to write a report and send it in, but in the afternoon you can show me around?"

"Sure," Séraphin said.

"You would have preferred that I did not come?"

"It's good that you are here." Séraphin did his best to press sincerity into his voice.

"So how did the exams go? They went well?"

Séraphin noted East African parents' tendency to frame questions in the affirmative. There was no invitation for negative answers. "Yes, they were good," he said.

"So graduation is definitely happening?"

"Papa, that was never in doubt."

"Of course," Guillome said as he stepped onto the balcony, "but everything else is."

Séraphin felt a tightening in his stomach. "What?"

"We can talk about that later." He looked at his watch. "I want to see this city that my son loves so much he feels the need not to come home in the holidays."

They started with the Company's Gardens. Guillome thought the squirrels running around were disgusting. Then Séraphin took him on a walk through the city. His father looked up at buildings and into shop windows and stopped to buy some chin-chins at a roadside stall manned by a Somali. When they resumed walking his father said, "Your mother would kill me if she saw me walking and eating."

Séraphin raised his voice an octave. "Your feet and your mouth can't move at the same time. One of them is going to do something stupid."

"That is actually how she says it," Guillome said. "She has many wisdoms."

"I'm sure of it."

"No, you do not understand," Guillome said. "To you she is wise because she is your mother. But she was smart even before she was that."

Their stroll turned to silence again. Father and son ambled down into Long Street. Then, heeding a signal from his father, Séraphin turned their walk towards his father's hotel. In his room, Guillome telephoned home.

"Yes, he is here with me. Séraphin, ni Mamma." Guillome handed his son the phone.

"Bite? Biragenda?"

"Yes," Séraphin said. He told his mother about the walk and the plans to take Guillome to some of the tourist attractions.

"He will like it," she said. "He must get out more."

"Yes, Mamma."

"You must take pictures."

When he hung up, his father came out of the bathroom, toweling his face.

"So when am I meeting your friends?"

"Soon."

* * *

In the afternoons, Séraphin would arrive with Idriss to shuttle his father around the city. They started with Cape Point. The drive was devoid of conversation besides Idriss trying to show them interesting landmarks along the way. At the southernmost tip of Africa, Guillome and Séraphin posed for a picture. When Guillome sent Therése the photographs that evening she said they ought to smile more. "You two look so miserable."

The next day, Séraphin took his father on a tour of the Iziko Museums. His father stopped to read every display's explanatory note, refusing to leave even the most obvious of plaques unread.

"Knowledge is—"

"I know, Papa."

They ascended into the Bo-Kaap after that. The rainbow-colored houses fascinated Guillome. "This is a nice neighborhood," he said. "You know, we were going to paint our house in Rwanda bright orange."

At the hotel, before they parted ways again, his mother provided commentary on that day's photographic haul. "But you are not in any of them," she said. "Honestly, the two of you do not know how to take holiday photos."

Boulders Beach was full of penguins waddling all over the place, which did little to interest Guillome, so they proceeded to tour the seaside towns. "Come, let's walk." They walked all the way to Muizenberg and even further along the beach. Despite the cheerful weather, Séraphin's mood was dampened with reminiscence and he maintained a brisk pace. His father kept up.

"Are the two of you even enjoying the trip?" Therése asked that evening.

"I am," Guillome said.

"And Séraphin?"

"He is how you know him to be."

Guillome had little interest in shopping malls or markets. He wanted to do everything outdoors. "We have malls in Windhoek," he said. "All that ever changes in malls is how fat people are. That is all."

"Then we can go up Table Mountain."

Guillome insisted they hike. "I am not so old that I cannot make it up there."

Séraphin was surprised by the pace his father maintained all the way to the top, where the whole of Cape Town was spread before them. Guillome would point at something and Séraphin would readily explain a particular detail or the cultural makeup of a suburb. "You know a lot about this place," Guillome said.

They took some photographs standing next to each other. ("At least in this one you don't look like you are going to kill each other," Therése said.) Guillome insisted on hiking down again. When they reached the bottom he turned to Séraphin and said, "Where to next?"

"Aren't you tired?"

"I've not had a holiday in a long time. So I'm not going to spend this one sitting down."

Idriss took them on a sunset drive through Green Point, Sea Point, and Camps Bay. He took a road from which Silmary's house was visible. Séraphin looked up and saw the balcony. The next day they visited Kirstenbosch and walked without talking until Guillome said, "Your mother always liked parks or gardens. She never wanted to leave them when we were in Paris."

"How was she when you were staying there?"

"She was like you," Guillome said. "She had many friends, and she was more Parisian than Parisians. She did it all. She did not want to return to Rwanda."

"What made her?" Séraphin asked.

"A good reason," Guillome said. He smiled. "A very good reason."

"What?"

"We were going to have a life that was not like anything in Rwanda. We were young. And things went well for a long, long time. Then we had to leave." Guillome sighed. "Your mother, she has never complained about anything since we left." They stopped every so often so that Guillome could take photos of the flowers. When they left, Guillome turned back for a last look and said, "I should bring your mother here."

That night, Therése said to Guillome, "The pictures are wonderful. I wish I could see everything."

"I will show you," he said.

The emotion Séraphin heard in his father's voice made him feel like he was intruding on a private moment.

"So, what are we doing tomorrow?" Guillome stepped onto the balcony.

"The exam results will be out tomorrow. So we can go out with my friends after that," Séraphin said.

"So I finally meet them."

"I'm not hiding them," Séraphin said. There was annoyance in his voice.

"I know," his father replied gently. "You will let me know how the results go?"

"Of course."

The day the final law results came out was the day Guillome met the High Lords. Séraphin, Bianca, and Yasseen walked to the faculty building together and scrolled through the exam results looking for their names. They had passed everything. They would graduate. The law atrium was filled with students hugging each other, shaking hands. Kim, Kelly, and Megan were there with their parents. Séraphin hugged them fiercely. "Thanks for everything," he said. "You guys saved my ass."

"So what's next?" Kelly asked.

"I'm gonna go where the people are." They all laughed together and then hugged each other some more before Séraphin went back to Yasseen and Bianca.

"My father wants to meet you guys," Séraphin said.

"Is he like you?"

"Not in the least," said Séraphin vehemently.

"Then we definitely want him around," Yasseen said.

Guillome congratulated Séraphin, embracing him and saying, "This is good news, Séraphin. For you. For us."

His mother, over the speakerphone, cried. "Séraphin, I hope you are happy."

"I am, Mamma," he replied.

"You are going out for supper with your father?"

"Yes, but we're meeting some of my friends."

"I hope it is fancy."

"He wants to go to the place me and my friends usually go. He says it is more genuine."

"And affordable," Guillome said from the bathroom, where he was freshening up.

"Your father," Therése said. "He does not know nice things."

"Then how do I know you?" his father called out.

"I'll just leave the two of you to your conversation ,then," Séraphin said.

"We were just having fun, Séraphin," his mother said. "You must have a nice time tonight."

The conversation at the Good Night was scrubbed clean of all innuendo. Guillome inquired courteously about everyone's future plans, giving words of encouragement at the appropriate times. When supper arrived they ate in relative silence, broken only with scattered conversation about all of their previous times at the restaurant, and about the time Andrew brought Silmary. Richard accidentally let it slip that it was probably then that Séraphin had started hitting on Silmary.

Séraphin coughed on his burger bite.

"My son had a girlfriend?" Guillome asked. There was a gleam in his eye. "A real person?"

"Yes," Richard said. "Silmary."

"What was she like? Did you look at her and ask yourself: 'Why him?'"

Bianca burst out laughing. "Your father's roasting you, Séraphin."

"What happened to her?" Guillome asked. They all turned to Séraphin.

"Leave it alone."

Guillome looked at his son for a long time and then turned back to his food. For a while there was no talk, just the clinking of knives and forks on plates. Guillome disturbed the lull by saying, "Okay, let me tell you all a secret."

"That's about to be a very loud secret," Séraphin said.

"Keep quiet, Séraphin," his father said.

"Yes, Séraphin," James said. "Keep quiet." Séraphin usually dominated their conversations; seeing him play second fiddle to his father was entertaining.

"Since you are all old now, and you are going into the world with all of your degrees," Guillome began, "this is my graduation present to you." He popped a chip into his mouth. "Do you know how to play poker?" Everyone nodded. "Well, then, let us say you have terrible cards. Maybe it is a four and a ten. Different suits. But there are cards on the table. Strong cards. The right thing to do is to fold, no? But in love"—Séraphin groaned—"things are not like that. You go all in." He looked around the table. "If you lose, then you will lose everything. But at least you played the game the way it is supposed to be played. But if you win"—Guillome paused to swallow another chip—"then you will win the whole game. Forever."

The whole table had stilled listening to Guillome. Then Bianca said, "Your dad has some serious game, Séraphin."

"That is what you call the skill of courting?" Guillome asked.

"Yes, that's game," Séraphin said, laughing.

"Games are for players. I do not play." Guillome bit into his burger. "I win."

Bianca fanned her face while Adewale flicked his fingers together. Yasseen said, "Yoh!"

Everyone relaxed after that. Séraphin noted how easily his father laughed, how widely he smiled. He did not resemble the stern father Séraphin knew growing up, always tired. He was loquacious, making jokes. When he laughed it was deep and throaty, and infectious. When the bill came he insisted on paying for it, brooking no argument.

Back at the hotel, while Guillome arranged his clothes for the next day, Séraphin stood on the balcony responding to messages.

BeeEffGee—HiLos_Of_E: Your father's cool, Séra.

AddyWale: Yeah man.

Sans_Seraph: I didn't know he could be like that.

RichDick: Parents are only parents to their children. But you know they're people, right?

Sans_Seraph: Duh. But how often has your father dropped hellfire game on you?

RichDick: Never.

KimJohnUn: Yeah, your dad is cool. I can see where you get the sense of humor from.

Sans_Seraph: That's self-made.

BeeEffGee: Keep telling yourself that.

His father came and joined him. "You have good friends, Séraphin," he said. Guillome looked at his son. "So you had a girlfriend."

Without the dilution of company their awkwardness made itself known. "She was not my girlfriend," he said stiffly, hoping it would close the discussion.

"But the two of you had something?" Guillome said.

"Yes."

"What happened?"

"It doesn't matter."

"Then you should be able to talk about it."

"He's got you there," said a Séraphin from the bedroom.

"Was it an argument or was it circumstances?"

Séraphin refused to respond, and then he said, "An argument."

"Then it is not so bad," Guillome said. "All arguments can be fixed. Circumstances, not so much."

Formerly tall father stood next to tall son.

"You have to decide whether you want to be right or whether you want to be happy. It is a simple choice."

"Those are nonsense choices," Séraphin said.

"They are real choices."

Séraphin did not say anything. He focused on the traffic below.

"You know, if something is broken it will not bring itself together again. You have to do it—if it is worth it to you."

Séraphin grunted a reply.

"I understand from Bianca she was funny," Guillome said.

Silence. Then, "Yes, she was."

"Then you should go all in. You do not find that often. Your mother, when I met her, she could make me laugh. I knew I had to go all in. But there was a time before I met your mother when I did not know how to play this game called poker. I was in university, about your age, and I had a choice to make."

"What did you choose?"

"I folded. Obviously, Séraphin."

"Guess she wasn't worth it, then."

Guillome rested his elbows on the balcony railing. Then softly, almost inaudibly, he said, "Yes, he was."

Séraphin had drifted out from the balcony, listening to the sound of the waves, thinking about a pair of eyes that searched and smiled. It was left to the other Séraphin to tap him on the shoulder gently to bring him back to the present.

"Wait," said Séraphin. "What?"

XXXV

Back, back again to the past when everyone was dancing and grooving. Guillome has a spring in his step as he walks down a Brussels street. The sunshine does not scorch. Food never runs low. And music never stops playing. The discotheque lights are purple and pumping, the drugs are white women and white lines.

There is a black man on the dance floor who does not stop moving and shuffling from the moment he enters the club to the time he leaves, most of the time with company. Company that smothers his muscular brown frame in kisses and caresses, pausing right before the moment of pleasure and saying, "Show me how black men do it." His propensity for skirt-chasing is eclipsed only by his love of books and jazz records. Later, he will meet Therése, the woman with whom he shall spend the rest of his life. But just like in a certain good book, before Guillome can find his Eve, Adam will come along first.

They met at a dinner party hosted by a mutual friend, Jacques, who liked to collect eclectic intellectuals. Guillome and Adam were the only two brown-skinned men at the party and they gravitated towards one another. Adam was a New Yorker by birth, a firebrand by upbringing. Guillome was enamored by how Adam dismissed ideas of equality in the United States without reparations, how he defended Malcolm and Martin alike. It was he who told Guillome to look up Aimé Césaire. "Brother, you need to get his work. And Senghor; those African brothers know the truth," he said.

Guillome, lost in the fictions and fantasies from France, recommended some titles to Adam, who said, "I ain't got time for white imagination, only black realities."

Adam was taller than Guillome. "When you're as tall as I am, you're bound to wind up in the Negro Basketball Association. I wasn't having none of that. That's why I came to Paris. Over here, a brother can do more than play sports, shuck and jive, or be shipped off to 'Nam." Adam was insistent that Guillome visit Paris. "There are brothers from all over Africa there. You'd feel right at home." Guillome said he would consider visiting.

Guillome had never stopped to consider men's physical frames until he met Adam. If the word "handsome" was made for anyone, then it must have been this man who leaned against a bookshelf in the dining room with his legs casually crossed. Even the cleft at the bottom of his neck seemed more manly than any Guillome had ever seen. Adam saw him staring and said, "You see something you like, brother?" Guillome turned away.

At dinner, Adam was given the task of being the white whisperer.

"You see," Adam said, "black people are only asking for equality, for justice, for all of the truths that are held dear in the United States. And if they can't get those, they just want the police and the real estate boards to stop beating them in the streets and shepherding them to the ghettos. They don't want to wake up with burning crosses in their backyard. I don't even think at this point in time they want to be a part of the American dream. They just want to wake up from the African American nightmare."

Sympathetic sentiments followed his every pronouncement.

"Feminism's going to upset a whole lotta folks when it gets itself organized," Adam said. "Only reason why all of us brothers are still on top is because we sort ourselves fast, especially when it's a dumb cause. But the whole thing makes sense. If you give people their freedoms, then you have to spend less time policing their infractions against their restrictions."

Genevieve, Jacques's friend, said it was about time they were offered a better kind of man, eying Adam.

Jacques, who had been trying to sidle closer to Genevieve, sat up in his chair and puffed out his chest. "You're not happy with the quality of men you have to choose from now?"

"Choose?" Genevieve creased her forehead. "In the future maybe there will be choices. Ones which do not involve losing yourself or everything." She looked at Adam for the expected approval, but his eyes were on Guillome. Adam asked Guillome what he thought of it all.

"Rights should come equally to everyone," Guillome said. "I do not like the way they come down a ladder. White men, white women, black men, black women."

"I agree." Adam looked at Guillome with interest.

When the dinner party ended, Adam approached Guillome and said, "You know, I'm in town for two weeks. You should show me around. I see too few brothers here and it would be nice to not be the only one sticking out."

"Sure," Guillome replied.

Together, they proceeded to burn the nightlife into day, stumbling out of clubs with company of various shades and hues. In the afternoon, once they'd recovered from their hangovers they would play soccer, dribbling and shooting until they were shiny and glistening in the sun. They attempted to emulate Arthur Ashe on the tennis court too. When they tired of sport or skirt-chasing they would sit in Guillome's apartment, listening to his records, which had increased in number and diversity from Adam's recommendations. The books on Guillome's bookshelf also changed their content and character. "Brother," Adam had said when he looked at Guillome's collection, "black people didn't die in nooses to be left off your bookshelf." The titles changed from Hugo, Balzac, and Cocteau to Ellison, Hughes, and Adam's personal favorite: James Baldwin. Adam lent Guillome his own wrinkled, scarred, and note-ridden copy of *The Fire Next Time.* The prose burned Guillome's soul. When he met Adam on the tennis court he gushed. Adam merely laughed and said, "I know, brother. I know."

In those two weeks of clubbing there came a day when Guillome and Adam were a little fuzzy from the previous night's cavorting. They were stuck indoors, Guillome lying on the couch reading another one of Adam's recommendations, Adam leafing through the record collection.

"When are you coming to Paris?" Adam kept insisting Guillome visit him there and mingle with all of the other black intellectuals in the city. "You village boys sure take small steps at a time."

"Us village boys also get ourselves from Kigali to Brussels, brother," Guillome replied.

Finally, Adam found something he liked and put it on. He leaned against the couch as the opening salvo of bass notes from Ornette Coleman's "Lonely Woman" escaped into the air, his eyes closed like he had taken a hit of heroin.

The two did not move for a long time, Guillome reading, Adam wandering the far fields of his mind. "Jazz and jezebels, Brother G, these things'll make you find new religions," he said when he found himself back in the apartment. "What d'you plan on doing after you finish here in Brussels anyway?"

"I do not know," Guillome said.

Adam looked at Guillome intently. "Don't be one of those brothers who leaves home for no other reason than not going back. You could be someone serious there." He paused. "And I could visit, see what it's like."

"It's not Paris."

"It's Paris, not Paradise. Don't get too hung up on these places. They're just placeholders. Eventually, we have to go home."

"You are going back home when you are done?"

"Home is where the hurt is, brother. Even still I will go back."

"To do what?"

"Whatever I can."

Adam let Coleman take over again for a while. "Brother G, you got any cards?"

"Yes."

"You know how to play poker?"

"No."

"I'll show you."

Guillome rode his beginner's luck for a couple of rounds. They were playing with peanuts and candy for chips. A healthy mound piled up in front of Guillome. Then his luck dwindled. The losses began to frustrate Guillome, while Adam laughed. Guillome all but gave up.

"All right," Adam said, "you got a choice, brother. You don't know what I have and you don't know what the next card is going to be. All you know is what you have. There's a chance it might be a good card, there's a chance it might be a bad card. Now, you can fold right now, but you'll lose everything on the table. What you want to do is go all in, you see. That way I also have to go all in if I want to win outright."

"But if I lose—"

"—you lose the right to play. But if you win, you win everything. That's how all of the important things in life go."

"All in."

"You bluffin' me, brother?" They looked at each other for a long moment and then Adam said, "All in."

The fifth and final card was shown. Three of a kind for Guillome; Adam had a flush.

"That's how it goes, brother," Adam said. "You win some, you lose some." Adam smiled and the cleft at the bottom of his throat seemed more pronounced. "You see something you like, brother?" Guillome shifted his gaze away quickly. "It's okay," Adam said.

"What is okay?"

"Whatever it is you need to be okay so you can not ask me what is okay, brother."

"You talk in circles, Adam."

"Because I can't talk straight around you, brother."

It took Guillome a while to do the maths. He looked at Adam and said, "You are—"

"—still a man."

"But you—"

"Yes."

"How—"

"I can answer it for you now as simply as I can: it isn't a process; it's an event. And to answer your next question: since I was small."

"So you—"

"—have always known. Terrible thing to have to leave home for."

The kitchen clock ticked and then it tocked. In one swift movement, Adam rose from his chair and leaned over the narrow table, kissing Guillome on the mouth, softly. Guillome told his body to pull away but found it unwilling to comply. He stayed still. Adam drew back a few centimeters. "Brother," he said, "you're allowed to participate."

Adam kissed Guillome again. This time Guillome found the mechanics of his mouth moving. The warmth of Adam's mouth tasted like the chocolate he had eaten as they played, and the smoky cologne he wore invaded Guillome's nostrils.

Guillome pushed Adam away gently. They looked at each other for a while and then Guillome said, "I'm sorry."

"Don't apologize," Adam said. He sat back down.

"It's just—"

"The flip of the card." Adam took the cards and stacked them and then cut them. "I think I should be off to Paris soon. You should come up."

"I agree," Guillome said.

"That's my line, brother."

* * *

Father and son have this thing where they see too much of themselves in each other and, like mirror reflections of truths too awkward to bear, look away to find points of interest in the rumbling darkness of the sea, the zooming cars below, the blowing of the breeze, the stars that fight for attention in the night sky. Any place that is not the interior of a black man. Father and son do not speak for a while.

"So what happened?"

"With what?"

"With Adam—did you ever see him again?"

"We were supposed to meet at a party in Paris, but he never showed. I met your mother instead."

"And that's it?" asked Séraphin.

"That is it."

Father and son are silent again. Far distance, dark sea, cars below, blowing breeze, night sky. Any place that is not the interior of a black man.

"Why d'you tell me this?"

"Is it not funny how we, after all this time, have this in common? I was also directionless, Séraphin." Guillome smiled. "But then I found a person and together we found a purpose. You are lucky to have found one of those things, Séraphin. However, I do not think the other one is here." They looked out into the night. "You have to come home, Séraphin. It will be good for you, I think."

"Maybe."

"Mamma would be happy to have you around more. And Yves. Even Éric. We won't be disappointed that you won't be a lawyer." Séraphin turned towards his father in fear. "We always had a feeling you did not want that, Séraphin," Guillome said without looking at his son, "and maybe we pushed too hard. You have done it and we are proud. Everything else is for you to figure out. Ibindi ubundi."

Distance, sea, cars, breeze, sky.

Any place that is not the interior of a black man.

"So you will come home, then?" Guillome asked.

"Yes."

"Anyway," his father said, "why would you stay? What is here for you, Séraphin?"

XXVI

Remms Memorial Hall was filled with parents fanning their faces with graduation programs. A minor academic tried to make a rousing speech to all of the assembled graduates dressed in their black gowns. Séraphin thought they looked like black crows seated in a row. When he told the person sitting next to him that the hall was an attempted murder, he saw his joke flutter away. It was not his best one and he knew it. His mind was elsewhere.

Séraphin and his father had completed their tour of Cape Town. His father seemed to change each day, laughing at things Séraphin thought he would not have laughed at. When Séraphin took him to Stellenbosch for some wine tasting, his father requested that his friends come along. "You must spend time with them, Séraphin. After all, you are leaving soon."

When the wines were brought out and the sniffing and swirling and drinking without swallowing commenced, Séraphin said they all tasted the same. "That is because you are not rich, Séraphin," Guillome said. "But all you need to know is this: white wine has fantasies in it, red wine has memories. Either way in vino veritas so be careful whichever one you decide to have."

Séraphin did not ask where his father had acquired such slickness. He suspected some other persona had channeled itself in the newfound freedom of a secret no longer carried alone. When their sightseeing came to an end and they began packing up Séraphin's apartment, his father said, "I can see why you like this place. It can relax you, make you remember parts of yourself."

Séraphin agreed, but since the games night and the police incident, the streets seemed dirtier, the service in restaurants slower. Mostly, though, his father's words echoed through his mind.

Why would you stay? What is here for you, Séraphin?

The day before graduation he had reached for his phone and typed a message. There had been no response. As he sat in the hall, he pulled out his phone to see if there was a reply. There was none. Séraphin contemplated sending another message and decided against it. Instead he wound up scrolling through playlists. He knew all their names and could recite the order in which songs would play. He was particular about that.

"First," he had told Silmary when she looked at them, laughing at their names, "you have to decide what you want to achieve with a playlist. What's it for? Jogging, gym, chilling, creating a vibe, studying, sexing. Then you have to give it a name."

"Where d'you get your names from?" she asked.

"The voices in my head give them to me. Then you chuck all the songs you think will be good together. But you can't just put all of the fire songs together. That's lazy. Playlists have to tell a story, take you into a mood, work the mood, and then take you out of the mood."

"That's a lot of work."

"It is when you don't know your music collection."

"So make me one," she said.

"What would you like on it?"

"Surprise me."

"The laziest words in romantic encounters."

"Clown. What'll you call my playlist?"

"I can't tell you. You'll just have to wait and see."

In the hall, Séraphin looked at the playlist and the name. He looked up from his cell phone, searching for a face. He found it. His father sat impassively with his arms crossed. He seemed as bored as Séraphin. He returned to the playlist again.

"Dude, if you win, you win the game forever," said the first Séraphin. He was seated next to him on his right.

"Yeah, but don't the words that start the romance end it too?" asked the second, to his left.

"Maybe. I don't know." The third reached across the first, took Séraphin's cell phone, and scrolled down the playlist.

"You really called it that? I wasn't serious, you know."

The fourth, who was sitting in the row in front of them, turned around and said, "When you get what you want, you find out what you need."

"So," said Séraphin, "what do we do?"

"Out of this diem carpe the shit," said the fifth.

"Where do I start?" Séraphin looked from one to the other.

"I'm no genius, but most good things start with hello," said the first.

"Failing that," said the second, "'sorry' is always a good place."

"In your case, Séraphin, you'll have to use both," said the fourth.

"Or, you can say nothing," said another. They all looked up. The Black Séraphin swung from the chandelier.

The Great Chamber fell silent.

The dean of the law faculty took the stage to begin the capping ceremony.

A disturbance in the crowd drew the hall's attention. Bianca and Yasseen turned around and saw Séraphin shuffling through his row. Guillome looked at his son as he stumbled into the middle aisle. They made eye contact.

And then Séraphin ran out of the hall.

* * *

The council meeting at Remms Memorial was a founding member short. It was also unlike any of those that had preceded it because everyone was of sober mind and comportment. As comfortable as they were around Guillome, they maintained some modicum of respect for him. He stood looking at the city below with Bianca, Yasseen, Richard, Godwin, James, and Adewale talking off to the side. Séraphin stood next to his father, who asked him about his plans when he came home.

"I don't know," Séraphin said. "Probably just lie around the house for a while, then figure something out."

"Your mother won't allow that," Guillome replied. "Nukwitegura gukora. You know how she is."

"I know," Séraphin said.

Behind him, Séraphin heard a silence. He turned around and saw Silmary. She took turns greeting everyone, working her way towards Séraphin.

When she reached him she said, "Hello, Séraphin."

"Hi."

Guillome coughed politely. Séraphin introduced his father. Guillome smiled at Silmary and shook her hand. He turned to Séraphin. "You are together?"

"Yes," Séraphin said.

Silmary said, "Turihamwe."

EPILOGUE

Nobody is there at the end of the end. That would be a terrible duty to discharge, to be the final witness, to put the last full stop at the end of the last sentence on the last page. Nobody is given that power.

So perhaps it would be apropos to start this long pause with a recent cell phone chat.

Sera-Fin: Are you serious?

Silmary_Lillian: Yes.

Sera-Fin: That's the story?

Silmary_Lillian: I never said it was a good story.

Sera-Fin: It's a kak story. That's what I was waiting for all this time?

Silmary_Lillian: It had interesting bits.

Sera-Fin: Yeah, no, it didn't. The part where your high school hockey coach hit on you was average at best.

Silmary_Lillian: Average? That was my life!

Sera-Fin: And it was boring, Sil. The dude hit on you, you reciprocated, you texted each other for a couple of weeks and you thought it was true love. Then you found out homeboy was sleeping with one of your friend's moms. Then you spent the next term or so down and out. That story was as bland as an egg without seasoning.

Silmary_Lillian: Screw you. It was deep when I went through it.

Sera-Fin: If you say so.

Silmary_Lillian: How is serving on the front line of ignorance going?

Sera-Fin: Telling all these children there's a fire sale at the punctuation store but they aren't buying. Their compositions look like a murder scene. Taking pages out of Mr. Caffrey's book. Drop a swear word here, crack a joke there. It's cool working with him.

Silmary_Lillian: How's everything else?

Sera-Fin: Yves is working, Éric is finally being serious with life, Dad's chilled, Mom's still sighing whenever she sees me come home from school. 'Tis the year of the Great Sigh. Windhoek is the same old shit. Life moves at the unfortunate speed of one hour per hour.

Silmary_Lillian: I see what you did there.

Sera-Fin: Of course you did. That's why I let you wear the Number One Headband.

Silmary_Lillian: Let me? I took that shit. With your bumbling, mumbling apology. "I am so sorry blah blah blah I know what I said was wrong blah blah blah and hello starts the romance and sorry keeps it going blah blah blah!"

Sera-Fin: Why must you be this person?

Silmary_Lillian: Don't forget your cheesy-ass playlist: "*Bae and Be Not Afraid!*" #Sauce #soulsnatched.

Sera-Fin: Please!

Silmary_Lillian: You'll never be able to say anything cocky in the group ever again! Anyway, it doesn't sound like Windhoek is worth it. Guess I'll change this plane ticket to some other place. What about Mauritius?

Sera-Fin: Who's in More-Issues? Not me, I'm here. Come through. Windhoek isn't that bad.

Silmary_Lillian: Hahaha. Okay. Soon.

Sera-Fin: Okay.

ACKNOWLEDGMENTS

To Cara Mia Dunaiski, my own eternal audience of one: thank you for your energy and grace. *So they kick, push, kick, push, kick, push, kick, push, coast . . .*

To Amelie Dukunde, Alia Khalil, Angé Mucyo, Shalom Ndiku, Peter Orner, and Mathabatha Sexwale: you deserve preferential judgment at the end of days for patiently wading through the monstrously long first draft. To have seen such horror and thunder and lived to tell the tale is quite a feat.

To Tlotlang Osiame Molefe: thank you for your kindness and introducing me to the wonderful Thabiso Mahlape, Blackbird Books' founder and publisher.

To Thabiso: taking a chance on an unknown writer from Windhoek, Namibia, took courage and an appetite for risk bordering on insanity. Thank you forever.

To Cecile Barendsma, my wonderful agent: thank you for DM-ing me after reading my short story in *American Chordata,* for knowing the good grass from the bad, and for your guidance, perseverance, good humour, and support. The Brooklyn Nets need to sign us. (And fast!)

To Dina Asabea Williams—or The Girl Who Picked Up a Manuscript and Didn't Put It Down: I can never tell the story of this book without your part in it. I do not have enough goats to sacrifice in your honour. These words of thanks will have to do for now.

To Alison Callahan, Maggie Loughran, Taylor Rondestvedt, Jessica Roth, and Bianca Salvant—the mightiest of seraphs: thank you for pushing this book from start to completion. Your patience, dedication, and generosity with the handling of this story can never be repaid. Then, also, thank you to everyone from Scout Press and Simon & Schuster who wrestled full stops, facts, page layouts, marketing, and media: thank you, thank you, thank you, and thank you.

To Leye Adenle, Bisi Adjapon, Mekondjo Angula, Sarah Badat, Melinda Burrell, Thomas Daughton, Jakobus De Klerk, Bonita De Silva, Clement, Elizabeth, Querida, Alexandra, and Hannah Dunaiski, Chiké Frankie Edozien, Kalaf Epalanga, Abubakar Adam Ibrahim, Nozizwe Cynthia Jele, Mubanga Kalimamukwento, Louis Kato Kiguundu, Josie Kustaa, Sarah Koopman, Maaza Mengiste, Terry, Amy, and Ernie Liang, Nicole Ludolph, Tshuka Luvindao, Mohale Mashigo, Reuben Mkandawire, Yara Monteiro, Zanta Nkumane, Natasha Omokhodion-Banda, Ondjaki, Troy Onyango, Oatile Phakathi, Heike Scholtz, David Smuts, Adam Smyer, Mukoma Wa Ngugi, and Zukiswa Wanner—I am flattered by your friendships. I hope this book repays you with some laughs.

This book has a longer story, a story too long for me to write alone (I've tried!). For me, it started with my parents and their unyielding determination to provide me and my siblings with love, shelter, and stability in the face of disappointment and tragedy. Because I thought I knew where it started, I arrogantly believed I had the power to stop it when I put down my pen. But a writer only chooses their first sentence; the last word always belongs to the reader. So where this story ultimately ends, dear reader, is for you to decide.

Good luck.

Ibindi ubindi.